Em →

The Trivia Queen!

[illegible]

[illegible]

[illegible]

[illegible signature]

Bloody Bill Anderson

CAPTAIN BILL ANDERSON.

Gayle A. Lunning

INFINITY PUBLISHING

ISBN 978-1-4958-0895-1

Published February 2016

INFINITY PUBLISHING
1094 New DeHaven Street, Suite 100
West Conshohocken, PA 19428-2713
Toll-free (877) BUY BOOK
Local Phone (610) 941-9999
Fax (610) 941-9959
Info@buybooksontheweb.com
www.buybooksontheweb.com

Table of Contents

Chapter One

A black man? Scanning the surrounding area, I do not see the owner of the farm we approach. No white man in sight except the riders now surrounding the black man. He is a large man, his stomach protruding slightly as he stands upright inquisitively watching us. A hoe handle is held loosely in his left hand, the head of which is implanted in the ground. I judge him to be one or two inches shorter than my six foot four inch height but my two hundred twenty pounds may be one hundred pounds less than the frame of this big man. Although very broad shouldered, he is round in the middle.

"Where's the owner of this property?" I ask.

"Dat be me suh!" he said with pride, his deep resonant voice booming across the open fields. I half expect that voice to bounce off the trees ringing the field he is clearing. Some of my men suppress a quick laugh and the squeak of leather, as horses move about, mingles with other sounds the men make. Drawing a red cloth from his back pocket, the large black man wipes sweat and dirt from his brow, bushy black hair glistens with perspiration produced from hard work. He cautiously studies the twenty Union clad men surrounding him, shielding his eyes from the bright sun.

"Whoa!" I start but do not give voice to my thought. The palms of his hands are white! Well, they are slightly darker than mine as I glance at my palms, before questioning him. "You? You're the owner?" I reply with no attempt to conceal my surprise or contempt. "How can a slave own property?" I watch this man carefully. The farm appears meticulously cared for, as does the log cabin with a small flower garden fronting it. Curtains hang in the window above the porch. On that porch, and below the window, a straight back chair and a rocking chair are strategically placed to shield the occupants from the late afternoon sun. Looks like a nice place to rest in the early evening. A lone cow chews its' cud as it stares nonchalantly from the corral fifty or so yards away. The rails of the fence are nearly straight and the ends honed to fit in the posts, a job not haphazardly done. Even the trees that form a perimeter on the eastern edge of the property are neatly trimmed with few weeds growing around them. Someone has cared for this property: this black man?

I had not seen many black people growing up in central Missouri. We Anderson's struggled to make a life for ourselves. Father told us many farmers near the river have slaves doing the work for them. As a boy, listening to my father and uncle John talk about slave owners in Kentucky, I only imagined what it may be like to own... a person? Are slave's people? This one is looking at me, cautiously glancing at Bloody Bill's Band, as Union and Southern sympathizers alike refer to my men, although not with the same degree of reverence. His protruding belly indicates this black man is eating well.

A thin woman, in stark contrast to the big man, stands a short distance behind him, her hands, lips and body trembling in fear. Leaning forward slightly, her arms are tucked tightly against her chest with hands folded timidly under her chin. A small boy of nine or ten years stands behind her clutching the fabric of her skirt, eyes wide in apprehension.

"I'se not a slave suh! I'se a free man." The large black man proudly announces dropping his hoe and, stepping forward, carefully pulls a tattered document from a leather pouch extending it toward me.

I don't bother to take it. "What's your name free man?" I ask with a grin.

"Smith suh. Homer Smith." He replies as his huge hands carefully re-fold the precious papers.

The grin melts from my face as this black man claiming to have the same name as my boy-hood friend takes me aback. "Homer Smith!" I say in shocked surprise. "Where'd you get that name?"

"Massah Ben, suh. Massah Ben gim me his last name and calls me Homer. He say I be a good man, a real Homer dat's what he say I be 'cuz I don' try run."

I pause, settling my horse a moment as I remove my hat and shield my eyes from the bright sun before continuing. "Den who be dis?" mocking his speech as I indicate the thin woman and boy huddled behind him.

"Dis mah woman Bessie an mah boy Ben." He announces swelling with pride. "I names him afta Massuh Ben!" The boys face is nearly hidden, a pair of white eyes peering over the fabric of his mothers' skirt held to his face. A small, dirty, frayed straw hat pulled down just above those eyes covers the top of his head. Bessie openly displays the fear absent in the large man.

I ease back in the saddle and replace my hat as I study them for a moment. Leather squeaks as horses move nervously, sneezing occasionally to clear the dust kicked up during our ride. I survey my band of riders, most of whom are silently watching me, before returning my attention to the former slave. "Ho mer Smith." I slowly enunciate each syllable. "Ho mer Smith. Frank! Is Homer on the list?" I call out not looking at the rider in charge of 'The List'. I smile at the black man as his gaze darts from me to the rider beginning to thumb through the pages of a dirty notebook.

"List?" The black man inquires, returning his gaze to me as he shifts his weight on the hoe handle.

"Yes Homer, the list of faithful Union men."

"Oh yassuh! We's faithful to da Union now, yo' can be sho a dat! Yassuh! Yo' can be SHO' o dat!"

He emphatically states stretching to his full height, a smile enlarging his already large round face.

In a way I admire this man, Homer Smith. He has built a nice farm here and obviously works hard to provide for his family. But he is a Union man. I study him for a moment noting his nearly white palms before I say, "Too bad." and shoot him.

His hands fly up in the air as the bullet strikes his skull above the right eye toppling him backward to the feet of his stunned wife. Watching the bullet tear into his skull and the accompanying spray of blood, I am amazed at the pinkish color under the coal black outer layer. Did I expect him to be black all the way through? Guess I hadn't thought about it much one way or the other. Hmmmm! What color is the skin of a white man under the outer layers? I'll pay closer attention next time; see what differences there may be. His blood is red, same as a white man, and is oozing rapidly out on the ground around him. He twitches violently a couple of times before lying still, exhaling sharply.

"Bill!" Archie Clement whines dejectedly. "It was my turn!"

The stunned woman stares at her dead husband, her hands shaking uncontrollably, eyes wide as she covers her mouth, trembling in shocked disbelief. I can't see her palms yet. Touching the brim of my hat, I say coolly, "Good day ma'am." and ride away as she drops to her knees screaming hysterically.

"Well... forsooth! He was on the list." Frank James laughs and exclaims as we ride toward the next farm.

The mid July sun is hot under a cloudless sky but we make it hotter for the Union supporters listed on our note pad. Barry Brown, August Chandler, Jim Nelson and Homer Smith are now ex-supporters of the Union. Our union uniforms may have lulled Homer and many others into a false sense of security, but it is unlikely a black man would have been a Confederate anyway. The honor of disposing the Union supporters is being distributed among the raiders and I just took Archie's turn. What was it about Homer Smith that made me kill him, was it that he was black? Was it because he did not show fear? His wife showed enough for both of them. I did like the farm he had built, why did I not hesitate to shoot him?

"Sorry Archie. The next one is yours, I promise." I laugh at his boyish face turned into a pout. His long blond hair sticks straight out under his hat, which gives him a comical appearance. I love this boy who, at nineteen and only five years my junior, considers me a brother or father figure and follows my lead and wishes without question.

His name is found on the list before arriving at the Hobie Liske farm. He is standing in front of a small cabin carefully eyeing the twenty-man band riding to surround him.

"Hobie Liske?" I ask as the riders stop in front of the large elderly man, approximately fifty years old. He views us suspiciously, eyes cold as they study us. We have witnessed many reactions to our band of twenty to thirty men riding in to a farm, apprehension, curiosity, and fear in most. This is the first reaction of disdain I can recall.

"Bloody Bill Anderson." he states slowly, a sneer on his lips as he deliberately wipes his brow with a red bandana pulled from his back pocket. His denim overalls are frayed and dirtied from long hours toiling in his fields.

He knows me? Have we met? "Correct you are, and am I addressing Hobie Liske?"

"Go to hell, you low down cur dog! And take your mangy mutts with you when you go!" he said turning his large back to me and starting to walk away. Laughter erupts from the riders, I had to laugh as well, cur dog, mangy mutts, ha! Homer had not shown fear, but this man... wow, he is fearless.

The click of pistol hammers cocking prompts Archie to yell frantically. "Wait! Stop!" Archie looks to me for support as the old man eyes the short stocky boy seated atop a horse seemingly too big for him. I nod to Archie and hold my hand up to stop the others from firing.

Swinging his right leg over the saddle horn, Archie drops to the ground, a cloud of dust rising under his boots as he hands his reins to a nearby rider. A sinister smile crosses his lips as he approaches the tall man who turned his back on us. The muscular blond haired boy is dwarfed by the size of the man he is circling. Archie looks into the man's face as he passes in front of him, the top of Archie's head barely reaching the chin of the old man. Although a powerfully built young man, it is readily apparent Archie does not possess the physical strength of this Union supporter. Very broad in the shoulders, Hobie Liskes' upper arms bulge from under his tattered dirty shirt. He is bronzed from countless hours in the fields being baked by the sun. Weathered, dirty hands are huge and clenched in fists as he eyes the smaller blond boy. I feel a great respect for this old man. He is not afraid. In spite of the reputation we've earned as guerrillas, a title hung on us by Jayhawkers, he shows no fear. Everyone is afraid of Quantrills Raiders and especially of Bloody Bill Anderson! Why is this man an exception? No. This old man is not afraid of us, nor is he afraid of the young man circling him at arms length.

"Lookee dere!" Archie exclaims from beside the old man, pointing toward the cloudless sky. Instinctively the old man looks in the direction Archie indicated, and as he does Archie drives the point of his knife deep into the hollow of the old man's throat below the Adam's apple.

The old man's large powerful fingers rise quickly, grasping Archie's hand and slowly pulls the knife from his throat. Hate fills the eyes of the large man as he grasps the throat of the blond boy in front of him with his free hand. Gurgling noises come from the throats of both men. Archie futilely swings his free hand against the forearm of the huge angry man squeezing his throat. Slowly the old man's eyes soften and his grip loosens freeing the startled Archie.

"Shoot 'im! Shoot 'im!" Archie coughs hoarsely backing away from the large man. Before a shot can be fired the large man drops to his knees, blood gushing from the gaping wound in his throat. He stares straight ahead for a few seconds, before toppling to the ground clutching the wound in his neck, life flowing out with copious amounts of blood. A small cloud of dust rises as the last of his air supply is expelled through the hole in his throat, signaling the end of life for Hobie Liske. "Nudder one bites the dust." Archie squeaks as he coughs and giggles to his mates.

"Archie, cut 'im up" my instruction is hurriedly obeyed.

Stopping The Wind on a rise, I pat the neck of my beloved horse and smooth his mane as I gaze upon the fields below. This area is very familiar to me. In my mind I 'see' a slender young mother, prematurely aged by the rigors of maintaining a farm on her own. The image of her fades as I peer at rows of corn growing in the fields she labored in, not far from the out buildings my father and uncle erected. The house appears new, much larger than I remembered, perhaps just added to.

Mother is 'there' again, her sallow cheeks burned by the sun and wind. Her hair, grayed before its time, hangs in her eyes as she struggles with the hoe. Her image stands, as she did so many times in my childhood, presses her hand to the middle of her back and heaves an exhausted sigh as she wipes her brow. I look toward the heavens as the memory of her floods back. I see her collapse, a young boy running to her side. Lifting her in my arms, she smiles and sighs, "Billy" as she did then, her life expended as she breathed my name.

The pain in my throat increases, as do the popping noises in my head. I dare not look at the riders next to me for fear they will see the tears welling up in my eyes. Nudging The Wind forward we purposely skirt the farm, silently continuing toward Huntsville.

My spirits are lifting as we enter town, the excitement and anticipation of the coming fray I suppose. The local men that joined our band in recent days know which businesses are pro-union and we are determined to make them wish they were not. Citizens scatter as we approach. I smile at the thought of evoking fear in them. While dispatching groups of five to ten toward pre-determined locations, a name strikes my eye, one I hoped to see. Nudging The Wind closer to the bank building, I read the name of the bank president painted on the window.

"Cyrus Scroggins… ARCHIE!" I yell, transfixed by the name from my past.

"Yeah Bill?" He replies, quizzically looking at me from his customary position close by my side.

I look at him blankly, feeling a strange tingling in my chest before I address the riders next to him. "Frank! Jesse! Come with us!" and dismount.

As I walk into the bank I pull a pistol for each hand from my belt, as do my companions. The hands of the two citizens in the bank lobby fly upward as our weapons appear. Checking them for weapons, I motion for them to relax and put their arms down. A lone teller is behind the counter that divides the large dimly lit room, two-thirds of the space being behind the counter. He too began to lower his hands. I cock my pistol and thrust it at him. He throws his hands high in the air, tightly closing his eyes, trembling in fear.

"Where's Scroggins?" I ask the shaking teller as I kick open the swinging door at the end of the counter.

Slowly he opens one eye and, seeing Archie's pistol a couple of inches from that eye, quickly closes it again. Archie cackles uproariously at the great fun he is having. "Hello in dere." Archie gleefully laughs, tapping the clerk on the head with the barrel of his pistol. "Yo' in dere?"

The teller shakes, squinting as if the tighter his eyes are closed the more likely we are to go away.

The door in the back wall opens. "What the...!" The man stepping through the door began but stops abruptly as Archie spins his pistol toward his face. Here is the small man I have hated for years.

"Mis ter Scrog gins." I began, deliberately enunciating each syllable precisely. He looks at me, no spark of recognition in his eyes, perhaps because of the beard I wear. "We... meet... again." I move toward the light of the window continuing to speak slowly, my voice just above a whisper. His brow furls momentarily as he studies my face trying to remember where we met, and if he knows me.

"Oh puh lease sir! Let me do the introductions!" I say, my voice rising sarcastically. "These two gentlemen." indicating the pair situated on either side of the door entering the bank. "This is Frank James and his brother Jesse. Say hello to Mr. Scroggins boys." Frank touches his forehead with his pistol in mock salute.

"And!" I say placing my arm on the shoulder of the short, grinning blond boy. "Please say hello to Archie Clement." The bankers eyes widen, fear growing as he stares at the young man. Archie has gained notoriety as a merciless killer and my right hand man. The banker trembles as his eyes dart toward me, now aware of who is addressing him.

"And yes!" I say emphatically, anger rising in me, fire flashing in my eyes and my voice hardening. "I... am... Bill... Anderson. The same Bill Anderson that stood in front of your desk ten years ago, at fourteen, begging you to help my family through difficult times. The same Bill Anderson you... denied! The same Bill Anderson... whose mother died... trying to avoid your foreclosure!" I am lucky this year; the river did not flood his property entirely and receded in time to plant his crop. What happens when a wet spring comes flooding the Missouri River to the point he is unable to plant his year's crops? How then does he support his family? God I miss it!

From high above the river bottom at least a mile away, I see the farmer moving about in his fields, a small barely discernible dot in motion. I wonder what he feels about his life. I wonder how I feel about mine.

It is so peaceful here. The gentle breeze at my back caresses my cheek as it passes, its presence felt not heard. The trees on the opposite bank barely move. The gentle rippling of the river is soundless from this distance, in fact, with the exception of an occasional chirp of a bird flying overhead, there is no sound.

Closing my eyes does not bring a heightened awareness of sound, only the sizzling, buzzing and popping remains. The headaches I have experienced for two or three years are getting worse; a shooting pain enters above my right eye pressing into my skull. My eyes wince as the pain digs into my head. Pressing my fingers against the temple area brings only partial and temporary relief. Sitting on the bluff high above the river bottom has a therapeutic effect on my headaches; they don't seem to be as constant, or severe, as I sit here.

Our camp is above a sharp rise a mile west of the Missouri River and five miles south of Rocheport. From this vantage point we can see a Union squad approaching from any direction and escape, or do battle, whichever suits our fancy.

Hunger pangs invade my peace. Since midday I have been seated on my perch overlooking the river and valley. If my body did not crave food I would stay here all night, I would stay here forever! Why don't I let someone else lead this band of cutthroats? Cutthroats, ha! That particular term is most appropriate for Archie. He delights in cutting the throats of his victims before scalping them. His bridle is adorned with the scalp of thirty-three men at last count, but even Archie waits for me to kill first, or for my permission to kill. Why do they do that? Why do I have to think for them? I'd rather think of better times, times like....

Chapter Three

. . . Times like – Two years ago, or more specifically, a June day in 1862. Better times? Tension and strife has been increasing daily around the Anderson home on the Neosho River near Council Grove, Kansas. A great civil war began a year ago with the firing on Fort Sumter, South Carolina. Closer to home, Missouri is torn between an elected governor that radically advocates full alliance with the Confederacy, including secession, and the moderate majority favoring a wait and see posture. Most Kansans are bitter about the Border Ruffians, transplanted Missourians and other southern sympathizers that forcibly attempted to claim Kansas as a slave state in the late 1850's.

The Kansas/Nebraska Act of 1854 caused the influx of many people intent on preserving, or eliminating the possibility of slavery in Kansas. Although clearly southern sympathizers, the Andersons came to Council Grove, Kansas, in 1855 not to save slavery, but themselves. Now the neutrality of the Anderson farm, as well as the Hodges to the south, becomes increasingly difficult to maintain. Both former 'southern' families are completely surrounded by vehemently anti-slave "Jayhawkers" suspicious of the Andersons and the Hodges.

The Anderson brothers, John and Jacob, came from Kentucky in 1837 settling on a parcel of land near Huntsville Missouri. There, after countless hours of labor in the sweltering heat of Missouri summers and bitter cold of its winters, Jacob and his new bride Ann, began what they dreamed of for some time, a happy home and family. I was the first born, christened William, on January 30, 1839. James came the 23rd of June 1841, followed by Josephine the 19th of August 1845, Virginia the 24th of July 1846 and Kathleen January 19th 1848.

Life during the 1840's in Missouri is bitterly hard as the Anderson brothers struggle to extract a meager existence from the land. Long uninterrupted days in the fields during good weather and bad are our lot in life. Dad and Uncle John are proud men, often sullen and moody. On good days they dream of a better life for us all. Their summers are spent in grueling drudgery working under a hot sun. The winters are not much better as our father insists we study our "book learnin" so we will not turn out like him.

Even with limited classroom experience Jim and I learn to read and write quite well and are expected to expand our knowledge, and that of our sisters, by reading whatever is available. Our local newspaper, the Moberly Gazette, consists of a single page of various size prints. Frequently referencing the dictionary, one of two books possessed by the Anderson family, the other a Bible, we are able to decipher the pronunciation and meaning of many words. Jim and I read aloud from this news medium, providing our uncle and parents with current affairs. After each reading, our sisters gather around as their big brothers point out the words as part of the instruction required of us.

It is during the readings after a particularly unprofitable harvest of 1848, that Jim slowly reads an account concerning the discovery of deposits of gold north and east of San Francisco, California. My father ceases his rocking and glances at his brother John. They both listen intently as Jim completes the news of the discovery, the rhythmic creaking of the chairs silenced; father rises and walks outside followed closely by his brother.

Awakening at dawn, we emerge from the house in time to see our Father and Uncle John ride west leading Jims' horse laden with whatever they could pack. Mother tries to explain, after she stops crying. "Your father is trying his best to provide for his family by going to the gold fields of California to earn our fortune in gold." I cannot comprehend 'gold'. What is the quality of gold that has attracted our father? What is it that will cause a responsible man to leave his family on a moments notice? And… what is a fortune? These are questions a boy not yet ten years old cannot comprehend. What I do understand is my father had left, and my mother is distraught.

Later that day Mrs. Smith comes from the adjoining farm to tell us how Uncle John and father enticed Hector Smith to join them in their quest. "I know it's not your fault Ann, but..."

Our mother, much the taller of the two, places her arm around the shoulders of Mrs. Smith and said. "Don't fret yourself about it Barbara. I understand only too well." The two teary eyed women hold each other tightly for several seconds before they look at us boys. We stare back hurt, confused, looking for guidance.

Mother sighs, forcing a feeble smile as she says to her neighbor. "Barbara, why don't you bring Bush and the boys for supper tonight; we must decide what to do."

Mrs. Smith nods as she wipes away tears.

Bush! Jim and I always thought it a stupid name for a girl, and frequently teased her until she ran away crying. If mother caught us we'd get the switch from her and later from our father, who tells us Bush is a member of the weaker sex and we are responsible for their protection. He doesn't comment about the name but Uncle John does, before being scolded by his sister-in-law. Quietly, when mother is not looking, he leans close to us and whispers, "Dumb name. Dumb name." then we giggle quietly.

Our families are close; dad often remarking that, next to his brother John, Hector is his best friend.

Dad comments on how perfectly Hector Smith has planned his family. "That time of year eh Hector?" he jibes his friend as they share a laugh. All the Smith children are spaced two years apart and were born in late May or early June. Hector Jr. at fourteen is the oldest followed by Herman, Homer, Hiram, and the only girl, six year old Bush.

Hector Jr. can't be bothered with us 'children' preferring to partake in the repartee with the men. Homer, Hiram, Jim and I get along well but Herman... doesn't seem to fit with the older men or the younger children. Now the Anderson's and Smith's will try to manage two farms with only the women and young boys until the men return in the spring as promised. Bush is to look after the younger Anderson girls as Josi, at three years old, is not prepared to take care of herself or her younger sisters, Ginny or the newborn Kay.

The men do not return for spring planting; or for fall harvest that year or the next. Our struggles before our father and uncle left seem insignificant compared to the hardships we now face. We are impoverished. The older Smith brothers possess a strength and knack for farming that the offspring Anderson brothers, Jim and I, lack. In spite of being so young, Jim and I, along with our `almost' brother Hiram Smith, work long and hard hours in the fields. Ann Anderson tries desperately to aid her boys by working alongside us from sun up to sun down then assisting and instructing the other 'almost' sibling, Bush Smith. That relationship and perhaps being too exhausted from work to engage in such frivolity, we no longer tease Bush. We've gained a great deal of respect for the efforts of all in the family.

The Smith's are faring better than the Anderson's, as Hector Jr. is stronger and more adept at farming. He and his brothers, Herman and Homer, also spend long hours in the fields and do occasionally come to the aid of the younger group struggling on the Anderson farm. Life is not easy for either family as the struggle to produce crops takes precedence over personal needs thus the separation from the heads of our families is endured and made palatable by the now traditional Sunday dinner at the Smith farm.

As spring planting of 1852 approaches Ann Anderson will soon be thirty-two years old, however; the rugged life she leads is taking its toll. She looks old. Bush, now almost ten, is assuming much of the household duties and Josi, Ginny, and Kay no longer need constant attention and are able, in some capacities, to assist the family. Still the burden falls to Mrs. Anderson, and it is a very heavy burden.

She is a tall woman, nearly as tall as her husband, although standing stoop shouldered she seems much shorter. She is also very beautiful, or at least she used to be. Ann Anderson no longer fusses with her hair; or dresses for the evening meal. Her thinning, greying hair, no longer in curls, hangs limply covering part of her face. No more sweet singing as she works, no infectious smile or sparkle in her eyes, she is six years younger than the stout Mrs. Smith but it is our mother that appears the older of the two. She has always been thin but her tattered dress now hangs loosely on a boney frame. She doesn't cry anymore, but neither does she laugh. A smile appears on her lips infrequently and then only briefly. Constantly tired and weary, she finds little to be happy about. We see her aging before our eyes but are powerless to prevent the ravages of time and back breaking labor.

Jim, Hiram and I insist that this spring we are big enough to handle the field work as I am now thirteen and Hiram and Jim will be twelve and eleven respectively. She ignores our pleas for her to return to the house and let us boys handle all the heavy work. Jim is nearly as tall as his mother and slightly taller than the year older Hiram. I at thirteen have grown to nearly six foot tall and the arduous labor has built muscles on our frames that belie our age.

We had been working the fields less than a week when the man from the Huntsville bank, Cyrus Scroggins, visited us again. He had been out to see us last fall at harvest time. He makes mother nervous and apprehensive. She tries to explain to us about being behind in payments for the farm that the banker is to collect. Jacob Anderson handled making the payments but had not instructed his wife, nor made arrangements with the bank about our finances. Mr. Scroggins usually visits twice a year and has been friendly toward all of us, mussing the boy's hair as he greets us with a smile. Last fall however, he was strangely subdued and this spring does not look at us boys. Mother seems to shrink even more as he speaks softly to her. She does not watch him depart, her countenance deflated as she stares at the ground. Through tear filled eyes she tries to explain that we have to meet our back payments as well as those normally due or the bank will foreclose.

"What does that mean momma?" Jim asks.

She does not respond as she watches the receding figure ride away.

"Momma?" I ask.

She looks at us intently, then states softly. "It means we will have no place to live."

The banker returns in August; for Ann Anderson's burial. Our mother literally worked herself to death. Mrs. Smith and her sons restrain me from attacking that 'banker'. I am certain he caused my mother to die and I wish to beat the life out of him, as I perceive he did to her. I manage a venomous "Get out!" as he offers to take the farm off our hands right now. We've worked hard, mother too hard, and our fields and crops look better than ever. This is to be the bountiful harvest we eagerly awaited. This is to be the year we'll catch up on our obligations. This is the year our father returned... sort of.

Chapter Four

Coming from the fields at dusk, the harvest nearing completion, Jim, Hiram and I watch a pair of riders approach from the West. Uncle John is recognized but the man on the horse next to him... who is that? That man has a haggard beaten look about him with one eye drooping and nearly closed. His nose is bent and splattered against his cheekbone. Long ugly scars mark the face partially hidden by a dirty wide brimmed hat. Stopping in front of us, this rider sits motionless in his saddle staring at a spot a few feet in front of his horse.

"Papa?" Jim asks quietly.

I look at Jim, stunned by what he said, then at the man, shock waves engulf me as I recognize our father.

"We're home Jacob." Uncle John said softly to the rider at his side.

Standing transfixed, we look upon our father for the first time in nearly four years. Uncle John dismounts, looking at me with sad soft eyes, he said, "We heard." He hung his head momentarily then turned to assist his brother into his house.

Except for the single questioning word by Jim, none of us had spoken. Hiram finally stepped forward quietly to pick up the reins of the older Anderson brothers' horses and brought them into the barn. Neither Jim nor I move from the spot where we first saw the men, finally Jim breaks the silence. "Billy? Is that... really him?"

That night as Jacob Anderson slowly rocks in his chair, his brother relates the happenings of the past few years. He tells of how they realize too late they started off the wrong time of year and how crossing the mountains in late Fall nearly cost them their lives in bitter cold and treacherous mountain passes. They reached the gold fields and found gold north of Sacramento near a camp called Paradise. John was attacked on his way there to register their claim. Nursing his own wounds, he made his way back to the camp only to find it ransacked by thieves, their friend Hector beaten to death and his brother Jacob lying near death. John, ignoring his own wounds, for several days carefully transported his nearly dead brother to the closest doctor. Jacob was so near death it was feared he would not survive the shock of his broken bones being re-broken and then set, it was decided to not straighten his limbs but allow them to knit together crookedly. For several months Jacob lay unconscious, the sound of labored breathing confirming he was alive, until finally he awoke and tried to speak.

More than two years pass before Jacob regains enough strength to attempt to walk. The strength to walk is there but the will is not. John had to encourage and cajole his brother to expend the necessary energies to facilitate his recovery, literally pulling his brother to his feet and forcing him to walk. Several months of therapy and training ensue as he also had to learn how to speak again, all the while John earned some money by doing odd jobs for the good people of Yuba City, California. By late spring of 1852 Jacob is strong enough to make the passage over the mountains and they leave for home.

Although able to speak haltingly, Jacob is incapable of holding an intelligible conversation and rarely tries. John is never sure how much his brother understands. When John told him about his friend, Jacob did not seem to comprehend but never again spoke of Hector Smith. Several of the events had been conveyed by letters written for them by the good doctor as neither John nor his brother had learned to read or write. John is startled to discover the letters had not reached either family. Barbara Smith received the news of her husband's death calmly as she and the children had given him up for lost long ago. Looking at Jacob she said softly, "I have some news for you."

Bill Anderson looked at the pitiful figure, peering into those vacant eyes and no longer hated him.

I watch my father struggle to walk up the steps of the bank, his injuries preventing him from walking normally. With great effort he swings his right leg in front of him dragging his left leg into place beside the right then repeating the process.

Moving just a few yards is an agonizingly slow process for Jacob Anderson. Uncle John ignores his brother's infirmities, merely adjusting his pace to coincide with that of Jacob, finding something to occupy his attention other than the struggles at his side. I ask my uncle if I should help father walk, but he angrily scolds me. "Don't you dare treat him as an invalid; he is a man!"

The Huntsville bank president, Mr. Cyrus Scroggins, greets us with a smile, ignoring my hate filled stare. "Welcome back Mr. Anderson." He said extending a hand to my father.

It is my uncle that takes the hand and responds. "Thank you."

Mr. Scroggins seems perplexed by the non-response he elicits from my father. It should be obvious to the banker, and all that look upon Jacob, that he has been seriously injured. His left arm bent above and below the elbow gives the appearance of having three elbows. The right arm, broken below the elbow and healed in the opposite direction as that elbow, makes his hand trail slightly behind him as the arm hangs down in a `natural' position. The broken nose is repaired but still appears smashed against his cheek, a cheek marked by a deep red gash from his ear to his chin. Both legs broken, the right healed straighter than the left. The extent of the damage to the mind of Jacob Anderson is an uncertain guarded family matter.

I often wonder about the men that did this to my father. What kind of men could beat another human being so brutally? Why hadn't they just shot him? Did they intend for him to suffer as he had? Who did this? I dream about finding the men that callously took our father from us, leaving a shell in his place. Jim has the same thoughts and we fantasize about making them suffer as he had. They will receive the same mercy they had shown him. NONE!

Taking my hand, Uncle John pulls me to the front of Mr. Scroggins desk stating simply, "This is the Mr. Anderson you will address from now on." The banker and I both stare at John Anderson for a moment.

"OK then! Mr. Anderson." He said, a wan smile briefly crossing his face as he glances at this man-boy not yet fourteen. He is a small man, this Mr. Scroggins, nearly a half-foot shorter and a much slighter build than the youth in front of him. He peers over his round glasses, eyes darting nervously about, not wanting to address me. He is so much smaller than I had thought of him before. How should I react to this? I know I hate the man. Uncle John knows I hate the man. The man knows it! How should I address him?

"Mr. Scroggins." I began, speaking tentatively. "Since my father and uncle have returned to the farm, we shall require one more year to meet our payments. This harvest has been a good one, enabling us to pay a substantial portion of our back debt. The remainder will be paid after next years harvest." Uncle John nudges me and I continue. "But until then, hold off on foreclosure and allow us to keep enough money to get through the winter and buy seed for the spring." I feel smug, satisfied with the forcefulness of my demands, each word coming with more confidence.

"I ah... I'm ah... afraid I cannot do that, sir." He stammers as he twirls a few strands of his very thin greying hair. "Your place ah... is ah... already in foreclosure and has been sold. You have until December first to vacate the property. I'm terribly sorry but it is too late. Your property has been sold." He states, his final words coming in a rush.

I look at the banker in stunned silence, a cold gnawing sensation in the pit of my stomach. December first? That is less than a month away! How can I combat this? What do I say now? What response do I give? What argument can I make? My inexperience in these matters has me confused. I turn to Uncle John for help but it is my father that speaks. "Yooooouuuuu sssson uffff ah bitchshhhaaa!" The elder Anderson slowly spat out the words weaving unsteadily in front of the banker. There is fire in his eyes. We believed he may be unaware of what is going on around him, but he knows what the banker said. Feebly lifting his finger he points in the general direction of the diminutive man. Foam and spittle appears at the side of his mouth as he struggles to say the words. "Yyoouuu baaassss turrd! Ya! Ya! Yooouu...." His eyes close as he struggles to force the words to come. Uncle John dejectedly hangs his head before gently taking his brothers' extended arm directing him toward the door. "...Bbb bbbb aaasstturd!" My departing father shot back over his shoulder. He had lost his wife, his physical being, four years of his life and nearly that life, but he had not lost his spirit. I stare after him, at once feeling sorry for and proud of my father. How difficult it must be for a proud man to be unable to fend for himself. Now I understand my uncle's scolding. My father needs to retain his dignity.

I turn to the banker. Nervously shifting his gaze and stance, he shuffles some papers on his desk and without looking up whispers, "I'm sorry."

Placing my fists on the desk, I lean forward and stare at him. He does not return my gaze, his chin stuck tightly to his chest, hands folded in front of him. Is this futile? Should I yell? Scream? Strike him? Will anything change the decision? How? My arguments fall on deaf ears. The banker feebly shakes his head and apologizes at every argument, every plea. With a sigh I stand up and follow my family. "Why didn't you stay to fight it?" I ask Uncle John as I catch up to them. "Why didn't you help me argue? We could have... God Damn! ... Maybe he would have...!"

"Would have what?" John interrupts softly but sternly, his voice straining with anger. "I've been through these battles boy! I'm tired of fighting with bankers, if I thought it would do any good

I'd shoot the son of a bitch myself, but the only way to hurt a banker is to take his precious money! No boy! I can't fight him or his kind!" He stopped suddenly and looked me in the eye. "And where'd you learn to swear like that?"

The day we vacate the only home we Anderson children had ever known, many of our neighbors came with blankets, baked goods and other items. Jacob Anderson shook his head violently until uncle John pulled his brother to his chest, gently squelching the injured brothers' refusal of charity. Quietly my uncle conveys our gratitude.

With tear stained cheeks, Mrs. Smith gives John a letter from a friend in Palmyra offering a place to stay and work in a livery stable. "They're good people John." she said. "Go."

John quietly nods.

The cold winds of late November bare down on us as we depart, the bare limbs of leafless trees offering little resistance to the wintry blast. Under bleak grey skies an occasional snowflake punctuates the cold. I open the blanket surrounding me and envelope six-year old Ginny and four year old Kay to share warmth with me. They gladly curl up on my lap. Seven-year old Josi curls up with Jim as Uncle John urges the pair of horses forward. Father, wrapped in donated blankets, defiantly stares into the air, rocking in his chair behind the driver's bench in the wagon.

It is impossible not to look back. Our 'brother and sister' Hiram and Bush, re-united with their mother and brothers, solemnly wave as the wagon lurches over lightly frozen ground. Hiram has been a brother in every sense of the word except blood relationship, we are very close. Somehow Bush seems to be more than a sister. Josi, Ginny and Kay (we long ago stopped calling them by their given names of Josephine, Virginia and Kathleen) seem like sisters, always in the way, but Bush...?

The Huisman's, who operate the local livery, greet us upon our arrival in Palmyra. John and Grace are very bubbly people who feel cursed being childless. Grace, short and plump, is hard of hearing and speaks much louder than necessary, accentuating her German brogue. The tall slim John's English is a little more advanced than his wife's. His gruff voice and raucous laughter belie his docile nature. Grace, arms open wide, immediately comes forward to embrace the children. This is unpleasant for Jim and me as we are too old for such stuff, but to her credit she fusses more over the little girls.

"Uppa! You gairls are so pretty!" She gushes, fawning over them. "Uppa! Come! You gairls must come see da r'rroom I make for you inna house!" she said excitedly. She speaks fast and loud but is a genuinely likable person. The sincerity of her love is readily apparent.

Uppa? What a strange utterance! Ignoring the men folk she directs the 'gairls' into the Huisman's small frame house. The Huisman house is slightly behind the livery near the eastern edge of town and on the "favorable" side, the west side, of the prevailing winds that bring the "bouquet" away from the corral.

Mr. Huisman smiles after his wife as she bustles along with the girls before turning to us. "John! Jacob! Boys! Come wid me. Let me show you v'ere you vill stay." He led us to the rear of the stable. There, a small lean to had been erected against the back of the stable. Four bunks stacked in pairs on each side wall of the small room, are only a couple of feet from the front wall containing the door. Light streams through the gaps between the boards of the walls and ceiling, illuminating the crude stone fireplace against the back wall that nearly touches the bunks, as it occupies the small space between them. There is no space for Jacob's rocker. This is home?

The gaps between the boards allowing light to enter, also allows cold breezes to whistle in on us. Getting out from under the blankets to re-stoke the fire is done in haste. Sealing the gaps in our 'home' became our first priority as the fireplace barely reduces the cold.

Uncle John starts earning our keep helping Mr. Huisman as a smithy, and father's gnarled fingers repair bridles and saddles. Mr. Huisman is a willing and able trainer for all of us, especially exhibiting considerable patience with father. Jim and I are given the task of caring for the horses, and soon become adept at roping and riding. We enjoy working horses and develop a special communication with the horse. This enables us to anticipate the moves of the horse, of each other, and always seem to be in the right place at the right time. Our talent for gathering, breaking, and training horses is noticed in the summer months of 1853 and horse-trading gains greater prominence at the Huisman livery.

Our family gatherings are no longer private affairs as our readings are conducted in the Huisman home and no longer an exclusive Anderson get together. We are grateful to, and come to love the pair, and although loving, giving people, they are our keepers. We are beholding to them but may never feel close to them in spite of being treated as equals. We erect a barrier between outsiders and ourselves, remaining aloof while enhancing family bonds. Our young sisters, while not reticent, are confused, they are growing up without a mother and uncertain how to relate to this loving lady, Grace Huisman.

In addition to our burgeoning reputation as horsemen Jim and I became known as loners, preferring to remain apart from the populace. We have no friends our own age and our only friend outside the family is also a loner, an outcast from the 'good' folks of Palmyra. We are intrigued by Cody, who seems unfazed by his solitude. Although not a small man, he is not especially large and muscular but the townsfolk give him wide berth, preferring to stay away rather than risk argument, or offending him. Uncle John warns us to stay away from Cody, speaking vaguely of his reputation and the town's suspicions about him.

We tend to Cody's horse with minimal conversation and he recognizes us as of the same ilk as he. He never lacks for money, although he has no apparent source of income. Rumors abound concerning his excursions to... to who knows where. Gun for hire is the most prevalent rumor. We envy Cody. He is pleasant enough, or at least not unpleasant to Jim and me. We laugh about the attention given him as he strides unassumingly into a store, the merchant dropping whatever he is doing, excusing himself from other customers to give Cody preferential treatment.

He is envied by townsfolk for his two new Colt pistols not yet available in the Palmyra gun shops. He ignores all subtle, or not so subtle, inquiries as to how he came by them.

During our spare time Cody began to show us how to handle the Colt's. Not 'handle' in the way we had on the farm but more menacingly. We are awestruck by the quickness and accuracy with which Cody discharges the pistols. A target at ten yards is rarely missed; rocks or cans leap off the log shortly after the explosion from the Colt. Perhaps it is our look of amazement that causes him to show off a bit. After re-loading, Cody quietly holsters his pistol, winks at us and turns his attention to the target. The smile melts from his lips as he eyes the two rocks on the log. In a blur the pistol appears in his hand and two rounds are fired. We flinch at the sudden move and watch wide-eyed as he returns the explosive device to its holster. A wry smile appears on his lips as he turns to look at us. Only then do we notice the stones, his targets, are no longer perched atop the log. In the blink of an eye he drew his weapon, fired twice striking his intended targets! Our mouths hang open as we stare at the log.

We are willing pupils seeking Cody every opportunity away from our labors. The gun is heavy in our young hands but with Cody's expert guidance we are soon able to hit our targets with increasing regularity. Perhaps it is my greater strength but I outdistance my twelve-year old brother as a marksman. I also feel a bond with Cody that Jim does not. During one of our practice sessions in July, I tell Cody I want to go with him on his next excursion. He eyes me silently for a moment, shakes his head and walks away, our practice over. The next day he is gone.

Cody seeks us out upon his return the end of August. Back in the ravine, Cody unwraps the package strapped to his horse. Three new Sharps rifles and four new Colt forty four caliber pistols are carefully laid out on a blanket spread upon the ground. Cody studies the weapons a moment, selects a rifle and places it in the scabbard on his horse. He nods toward the rifles and pistols. "Those are yours." he says and rides off.

CHAPTER FIVE

Cody went away the summer of 1854 and never returned.

Early fall of 1854 we read about the Kansas/ Nebraska Act offering land to those wishing to settle the new territory. Uncle John consults with his brother Jacob and plans are made to relocate the family to Kansas. Kansas seems more appealing than Nebraska as it is assumed to be settled by those of southern heritage, as ourselves, and become a slave state maintaining the balance between slave and free states. Some "Free-Staters" are rumored to be infiltrating the state and border conflicts along western Missouri are topics read in our sessions. John decides on a new community beginning along the Neosho River, Council Grove, away from border conflicts where we can live in peace. Uncle John does not like conflict.

The Huisman's stake us to some of the necessities required to start our life in Kansas and bid us a tearful farewell in February 1855. I am sixteen years old and some thought is given to remaining in Palmyra as a horse trader. Had Jim and I been a year older we would have given that decision more serious consideration as we do not relish the return to farming. It had already cost us our mother. However, we do not broach the topic with either Uncle John or Mr. Huisman. We can't leave our family and pledge our help with the spring planting if we can pursue the wild horses of the plains we read about.

We settle upon land on the east side of the Neosho River eight miles southeast of Council Grove. The Neosho meanders mostly northwest to southeast at this point. Council Grove is still new and other people are laying claims to various plots of ground. We stake out approximately a mile square piece of land slightly longer than it is wide, sighting its boundaries as best we can on the points of the compass and register with the land office. The reception we receive from others settling the Council Grove area is warm and cordial until it is established we are Kentuckians by way of Missouri. The coldness pervading the initial conversation eases slightly when the question concerning our position on slavery is answered. "We are not slave owners and have no plans to own any." This answer somewhat appeases the 'Free Stater' majority but ensures we are not an integral part of this newly established community. They view us with caution. That suits me, as I do not want to bring down the 'walls' so ably erected.

Support for "Unionism" is rampant with hatred building for southerners and especially, Missourians. The Hodges from Tennessee lay claim to the land directly south of us along the

Neosho River and make our existence more palatable. Both families are viewed with suspicion by the northerners dominating this region making neutrality and acceptance almost impossible. The Hodges and Andersons are not shunned, but neither are we made to feel welcome in the community. Our solitude suits Uncle John, as conflict is easier to avoid if we are left alone.

There are far fewer trees to clear for farmland than anticipated and are found in abundance only along the river. Selecting a spot between the many bends in the river, we fell enough trees to build a crude log house we now call home.

After several weeks of tilling and planting crops, Jim and I set off after wild horses. Several days are spent searching the plains for giant herds until one is located and eight fine horses are returned to a livery in Emporia for a tidy profit. Proudly we leave the money with our family and return to the plains. On this excursion we befriend a small village of Osage Indians who assist us in our quest for horses. During a roundup in early 1856, Wa Kennee and I develop a bond as we try to capture the same wild black stallion. Neither is able to get a rope on this beautiful animal and he becomes a topic for much discussion at campfire meetings for several weeks. Wa Kennee speaks of the beautiful black stallion with awe and admiration.

"He is a young and brash stallion who defies our attempts to capture him. He is strong, smart and runs like the wind defying us and eluding our ropes."

"You say he is smart?" I ask.

Wa Kennee looks at me as we sit by the fire and nods as his eyes study mine.

"You say he is strong and runs like the wind? You have tried to capture the wind but I will catch him."

Wa Kennee stares silently over the fire for several moments and I fear I have offended him. I am formulating my apology for challenging him when I notice a sparkle in his eyes and the wry smile spreading over his lips.

"It is as An der son says." He began, addressing all in attendance. "We have tried to catch the wind and 'The Wind' he shall be called and shall be a great prize for one strong enough, smart enough, and fast enough to capture The Wind but, my brother An der son, it is I Wa Kennee who runs and rides like the wind that shall be seated on the back of The Wind grasping his mane in my fingers." He rises to his feet facing me. "It shall be The Wind and Wa Kennee that will be the envy of all as we glide as one across the prairie. Men will bow and women will swoon as we pass. All will know The Wind as the greatest horse and Wa Kennee... as his master!"

I rise to my feet and grasp my friend by his strong shoulders. "Wa Kennee is a great Osage brave, a man among men, a warrior among warriors... and my brother." I began. "But I also run and ride like the wind and it shall be my rope that calms The Wind. It shall be my blanket that covers and warms The Wind as the winter snows blow. It shall be my lodge The Wind obediently stands before waiting for his master. I shall not hinder my brothers attempt to capture The Wind and shall be the first to congratulate him should he succeed where I fail." I look at him with great respect and admiration and say sincerely. "Good luck my brother and good hunting!"

Wa Kennee smiles as he accepts the challenge.

Our new friends prove invaluable to our business as horsemen, aiding us in locating, capturing and breaking the steeds. With their help our time away from the family is greatly reduced and the quantity and quality of horse is enhanced greatly. Our reputation spreads quickly as the quality of horses we return with is unmatched. The Anderson boys are achieving a level of success, and acceptance in the community, not previously contemplated.

John Anderson struggles with the farm, Jacob doing what he can. By early summer of 1856, most of the farm is converted into grazing land and a corral for the horses Jim and I bring from the plains. Our "farming" is relegated primarily to gardening. Jacob spends all day in the garden, determined to earn his keep in the family. John works a small field and dotes on his brother while remaining aloof from the community.

The lone exception to our "standoffishness" is the Hodges, as they too are viewed with suspicion due to their heritage. With this common bond, the two families become close. Frank and Mary Hodges, married twelve years, feel cursed as they only have five girls to show for their marriage, no sons. Diane at ten is a few months older than Ginny but by necessity pressed into service in the fields with her father. Seven-year-old Mable, Elizabeth at five, and Dorothy at two are too young to be much help to anyone. Nine-year-old Martha is retarded, needing constant care and cannot assist the family in the fields. Ginny and Kay volunteer their services for part of a day working in the fields alongside their friend Diane. The Hodges are grateful for this and the girls become close friends.

Josi appears jealous of the camaraderie between her sisters and the neighbor girls but is determined to fulfill the chores a mother would normally accomplish for her family. Less than a year older than Ginny, Josi matured emotionally much quicker than her sisters. Perhaps we are all growing up too quickly. Only Ginny and Kay have friends outside the family. With the exception of the Osage, Jim and I have no desire to make friends. Boys our age seem so young we cannot comprehend, nor understand how these 'children' can be our age.

Once a week we read the paper from Council Grove, interspersing stories of how we capture our horses. Ginny and Kay hang on every word as we relate tales of Wa Kennee, Utipo, and the rest of our Osage friends. Indians are not to be feared as we had been taught. Uncle John cautions us to be careful as he is not sure they can be trusted. Jim, who had been so cautious at our first meeting with our new friends, cast me a knowing grin at Uncle Johns' cautioning.

Chapter Six

The reunion with our sisters is eagerly anticipated. Heading west earlier we passed a group of people on the banks of the Saline River a long days ride from Council Grove. This group has grown to nearly forty people as we return. It appears they are intent on establishing a community. We are unable to find store bought dresses for the sisters but we do purchase a few bolts of cloth from which they can make their own dresses. Shoes, pins, sewing materials and other necessities are purchased. We conceal some candy surprises.

Ginny and Kay come running as soon as they see us. Josi lags behind feeling it is not proper for an adult to jump and scream as her sisters are doing. Still her joy in seeing us is evident.

"What'd you bring us?" yells Kay, excitedly jumping up and down.

"Bring you?" I say in mock surprise. "What makes you think we would bring you anything?"

"What is it? What is it?" Ginny and Kay scream and tug on my pant leg. I smile and wink at Josi as I slide off my horse. The younger two tear into my saddlebags as I hug Josi.

"How ya doin' kid?" I ask her lovingly.

"I'm OK Billy." She replies beaming radiantly.

Ginny and Kay search my saddlebags and a perplexed, disappointed look creeps across their faces. Kay looks dejected as there is no present for them.

Jim, his right leg thrown over his saddle horn observing the turmoil his sisters are in, gives a low whistle holding aloft a bag of stick candy.

"EEEAAHHHH!!!!" They scream as they charge Jim, startling his horse sending Jim sprawling on the ground. The girls wrestle him for the prize.

"Josi?" I say, gently prodding her to join her sisters. She smiles, wavering toward her exuberant sisters, but remains a witness to the scuffling. At eleven she is neither a child nor an adult.

Turning toward the house, Uncle John stands near his brother seated on the porch. Uncle John has been working hard to improve the farm, the corral has been enlarged and the garden is beautiful. Walking toward them, I pass stakes in the ground several yards from the house. Pointing toward the stakes, my question is answered.

" A barn." Uncle John states, as he steps from my father's side to greet me. "How was your trip?" he asks extending his hand.

"Good! It was good." I watch Josi pass to stand at the side of our father, resting a hand on his shoulder as she adjusts the hair on his forehead. "We came away with eleven good horses this trip."

"Yes, I see." He said nodding toward the corral where we left the string of horses.

"We'll take them to Lawrence for sale in a couple of days."

John looks away pensively for a moment, then states. "Lawrence may not be a good place to go right now. There's... ah... been... trouble in Lawrence."

"Trouble? What kind of trouble?" I ask.

"Well." John begins. "They're still trying to decide whether Kansas will be a free or slave state." He sighs and shakes his head. "It's hard to tell what is right. As I hear it, a group of pro-slavery men, bent on intimidating, or destroying the Free State party, attacked its headquarters in Lawrence. Well... as often happens, other buildings are inadvertently burned. A few days later, an anti-slavery fanatic named John Brown, led a group that attacked and murdered five pro slavery people living near Pottawatomie." Uncle John stared at the ground before continuing. "There have been many people killed on both sides of the slavery issue. I'm telling you son, this slavery business is getting out of hand!"

I watch Josi lovingly stroke her fathers' hair as I consider Uncle Johns' assessment of the conditions in eastern Kansas. "Which... ah." I began slowly. "Which side are we on?"

Uncle John watches the antics of the frolicking children, draws a breath considering his reply carefully. "Come with me son." turning toward the 'barn', we walk toward the stakes marking the boundaries for the building to be erected. Reaching a corner of the planned structure, he takes his hand from my shoulder and points to the ground and beyond. "We're trying to build something here, more than a barn, or a farm. Your grandfather sharecropped in Kentucky, living near slave-like lives. As a boy I listened to your father's dreams of becoming a planter, of being a "Lord of the Manor". If the opportunity comes, we will have a large plantation, slaves, parties and balls attended by the finest people. However, if slavery is not permitted in this territory, we will build on your fathers' dream as best we can. To be among the gentry is your father's dream. Many a night in the gold fields before... well, he described to Hector and I how Ann would look receiving her guests on the porch of her mansion." He abruptly turns looking toward his brother seated in front of the small log cabin. "God, how he misses her." Uncle John states softly looking at his brother. "How he loved her." There is a slight crack in his voice as I follow his gaze toward Josi comforting her father as he rocks.

"Well." drawing a breath, John clears his throat and turns back to the 'barn'. "Fact is. If the sons a bitches' will leave us alone, I could care less whether this territory is slave or free."

"Sometimes..." He continues haltingly, scratching in the dirt with his foot. "Sometimes I've not... I've not... well... your father is the strong one, but... I... ah..." his eyes glisten as he looks off to the horizon. "I've not always... stood up... for..." he struggles to find the words. "Hell! Sometimes I've let people take advantage of us and not fought for what is right, or what I have perceived is right. It's just that...".

"John." I interrupt, squeezing his arm. "You've done the best you could. Don't worry about it. We're fine." He is not comforted. We walk toward the cabin Jim and the younger sisters are also approaching.

Uncle John and I travel the fifteen miles to Emporia to sell our horses and purchase the lumber required to build the barn, and some weapons to trade with our Osage friends.

CHAPTER SEVEN

As preparations for our fall trip to the plains are being made I marvel at how Josi is turning into a beautiful young woman. Only a week before her fifteenth birthday this August of 1860, she blanches at my suggestion that the boys are going to be visiting frequently to try to woo her. She has grown to five foot six inches tall and cannot hide her womanly charms. Reddish-blond hair cascades down her back, glistening in the sun as a shy smile appears on thin red lips. Shyly bowing her head, sparkling blue eyes peer from behind golden tresses.

"Cut it out Billy!" she says coyly, but she enjoys the teasing. Ginny and Kay have not outgrown their gangly appearance that at fourteen and twelve, they feel afflicted with.

Jim loads the packhorses with cartons of twenty Sharps rifles for Wa Kennee and his Osage brothers to improve their buffalo hunt. These breechloaders are to supplement the few muzzle loading Kentucky rifles earlier supplied to them. Powder and shot are carefully packed and we embark on our return to our brothers' village.

Wa Kennee and Utipo became fathers two years earlier, naming their sons William and James in our honor. Wa Kennee's squaw is again with child due this fall. Gifts for the young boys and the unborn child were knitted by Josi and carefully packed, along with the rifles and powder. Jim protests that the blankets she made are too frilly for a "Man child" such as little James. This concerns Josi until she detects the sly smile on Jims' face.

"Oh you tease!" she exclaims, laughing with the rest of us.

We come close to capturing the great stallion we had named The Wind several times but finally our luck has changed as the great stallion is cornered in a small canyon along with other members of his band. Jim and ten braves funnel the horses through a narrow chute formed by canyon walls on either side, Wa Kennee and I dismount and prepare our lariats. As the horses separate running down the chute, The Wind is alone for a moment and lariats whistle through the air settling around the neck of the great stallion. The powerful black beauty rears and bucks trying to dislodge the ropes from his neck as Wa Kennee and I pull ourselves toward the prize. Jumping from opposite sides, we grasp the shiny black mane as The Wind leaps into an all out run. I am jerked along at breakneck speed alongside the charging steed. My right hand firmly entwined in the flowing mane, I bounce against the left flank of The Wind and fight to regain my balance. With my open hand I press against the withers of the steed until I face the direction of his dash. My feet only momentarily touch the ground to propel myself upward as we rush across the prairie.

"WHOOP! WHOOP!" I hear Wa Kennee's yelp, he too is grasping the mane of the stampeding stallion. His face shows the exhilaration I feel as we rush together across the prairie.

"WHOOOEEEEE! YA HAAAAA!" I scream in delight bounding ever higher. We look at each other in joy across the back of our great prize, oblivious to danger. Wind whistles by us as the pounding hooves of The Wind strike the ground tearing through tall prairie grass. What power! His smooth stride never falters as his 'passengers' bounce alongside. The moisture in my eyes dries against my cheek as the wind strikes my face. How long can I run? My hand grasping the long mane is weakening and I must soon release that grasp. Simultaneously, Wa Kennee and I release our hold on the mane. The rope burns my hand sliding across my palm as I try to slow the prize. Finally slowing, we get to our feet; dig our heels into the ground bringing the great stallion to a halt. I wind the rope around my hand and began to step toward the neck of The Wind when he suddenly leaps into action again, jerking me off my feet. I strike the ground bouncing and rolling behind that great prize, my safety secondary to maintaining a hold on The Wind.

A horse rushes past me as I bounce and twist, wondering when my arm will break and I lose consciousness, or my hold on the rope. We slow and I see Jim and braves with lariats around the neck of The Wind bringing him to a stop. Regaining my feet I watch Utipo throw a blanket over the face of the enraged stallion. The great horses' body shakes as he stands trembling before us. How magnificent, this animal! How beautiful!

"You have captured The Wind An der son." Wa Kennee gasps in exhaustion as we coil our lariats maintaining a pressure on the prize.

"But... it is your... rope that... is on him... first!" I say panting heavily, that fact apparent as we approach the animal.

My Indian brother looks at me and without hesitation says. "Wa Kennee was not able to hold The Wind and let go of his rope. It is An der son who held on. It is An der son who runs like the wind. It is An der son... who has captured The Wind."

I peer at him across the glistening back of the great horse we both covet and see the disappointment in his eyes. We stroke the back of this prize sought for so long. I have won the 'competition' we boasted of over many campfires. The horse is rightfully mine, and I want him, but feel the urge to give him as a gift to Wa Kennee, the proud Osage warrior. It is his pride that makes up my mind.

"My brothers!" I exclaim to those gathered around. "Wa Kennee and his brother Anderson have run with the wind. When you see Anderson seated atop The Wind, know he is humbled in the presence of the great Wa Kennee. That I have captured The Wind may bring me closer to the greatness of Wa Kennee in the eyes of the Osage for he remains; the greatest of the braves."

We garner a string of nine horses, in addition to The Wind, to bring home with us before the approaching winter. These nine are designated for family and shared with the Hodges. Frank Hodges insists on paying us for the horses.

With a sly grin, Jim said, "Very well Mr. Hodges. You may help us build the house our father has dreamed of."

Uncle John looks at Jim in astonishment. With a questioning look, his face lights up when I nod.

Josi squeals, throws her arms around Jim and begins to cry.

"Very good, Jim, Bill!" Frank Hodges says. "Of course I'll help."

The original cabin is too small for all of the Anderson's and the teenage girls need privacy that cannot be granted in so cramped a space. Several months ago Uncle John had taken up residence in the barn, as do Jim and I when we are home.

A site farther from the river is chosen, on a slight knoll to allow the breeze to cool the home in the evenings. Approximately fifty yards from the barn and original cabin, a good view of the river is afforded, trees surround the site on the west offering shade during the late afternoon.

The next couple of months are spent building a home Jacob Anderson will be proud of. Although not the opulent structure John described as his brothers' dream house, it is a fine home. Our first cabin did not have board flooring; the inhabitants of this house need not be concerned with the floor sticking to their feet during rainy periods.

The two-story house is on the North bank of the Neosho River facing the Southeast and the rising sun. Here, on the porch, Jacob Anderson surveys the tranquil beauty of his ever-increasing domain. He drags himself out to the porch each morning to watch the sunrise. Jim, Uncle John and I sit with the eldest Anderson many mornings before setting out for the plains.

That summer of 1860 we add two more hired hands to assist with the building of the house and the growing herd of horses. The twenty brood mares are producing a fine group of foals that need tending. J. D. Couey has been with us two years now and part of the family. A man of fifty, J.D. has no family and Uncle John, showing his compassion for the less fortunate of the world, welcomed him.

The other additions to the Anderson "ranch" also fit the profile of the less fortunate. The first, Jeptha Bowles, or "Bo" as he prefers, has but one hand. His explanation on how he lost his left hand is to simply say, "I had an accident." In his mid twenties, of medium height and build, Bo would not accept being handicapped by the loss of a hand.

His resolve and determination eliminates any skepticism concerning his abilities. Bo constantly amazes us with the strength and dexterity he displays, utilizing the end of his left arm as if it were a hand.

The second man hired that summer is more of a boy. Although at twenty or more he is a man's age, he is quite backward, or as Bo puts it, "dumb". He is very tall, six foot eight at least, and well over three hundred pounds. He is clumsy, oafish and has to be told what to do next. Johnson, the only name he knew, is incredibly strong and follows direction without question. The boy always has a silly smile on his face and his eyes are open much wider than normal making him look foolish, well, he may be a fool. J. D. shows his sense of humor, referring to the simpleton as 'Socrates'. Bo laughed heartily and our gentle giant became known as Socrates Johnson.

All three men prove invaluable to the Anderson's in tending the horses, building and mending fences, and the building of the Anderson home.

Chapter Eight

"Name?" The uniformed man at the makeshift table asks sharply.

"James. James Anderson." My brother replies.

"Last name first, first name last!" The man returns gruffly.

"Anderson, James." Jim repeats, smiling at me.

"Where ya from?" The man continues.

"Huntsville Missouri." Jim replies, winking at my surprise as the soldier records the information.

"Term of enlistment?"

"Oh. Couple weeks, I guess." Jim shrugs.

"Look!" The soldier spat impatiently. "We have three month, six month and duration enlistments in the Missouri State Guard! The longer periods pay more. So which will it be?"

Jim shrugs again indecisively and answers with a look toward me. "Three months?" I nod.

"OK! Make your mark!" The soldier says as he completes the necessary data on Jims' form and turns it toward him for signature. Setting the page aside, he put a new sheet in place and turned to me. "Name?"

"Bill Anderson. Well… Anderson, William." I correct myself.

The soldier glances at me as he looks toward Jim, I answer. "Brothers." He nods returning to his paperwork. "From?"

I pause momentarily before answering. "Huntsville Missouri."

"Term of enlistment?"

"Oh, couple of weeks I guess." I say devilishly.

"LOOK!" The soldier began, impatient anger rising in his voice.

"Three months." I say quickly, cutting him off to quell his impatient anger.

He glares at me, the index finger of his right hand pointing at me as he rests his elbow on the table. Slowly he returns to his task. "Make your mark!" He says shoving the document toward me.

"He's got no sense of humor." Jim says as we depart the recruiting table.

"Fuck 'im if he can't take a joke!" I quip, and we laugh. "Why did you say we are from Huntsville?" I ask as we seek a place among the other soldiers.

This group of soldiers is the ultimate definition of rag-tag. Non-uniformed men are scattered in every direction, small campfires burning with a handful of volunteers around each. Few hold weapons of any type and are of all ages and sizes, children not yet fourteen among those lounging around the fires. Kids? Nearly an equal number of elderly men, some who can barely walk are going to fight the Union soldiers? What are we getting ourselves into?

"This is the MISSOURI State Guard." Jim emphasizes. "Letting it be known we are from Kansas will bring too many questions. I prefer not to answer questions."

I nod my assent. Jim is thinking ahead, and it makes sense. We are here for adventure and to kill Union soldiers, which should be reason enough, but as fighting continues to rage between the Border Ruffians and Jayhawkers, we will be looked upon with suspicion if we are known as Kansan's. Besides we did live near Huntsville, and are not accepted in Kansas. Maybe we don't belong anywhere.

Our horses draw considerable attention from the men scattered about the area. The Wind is especially admired as these men afoot recognize a quality horse. Acknowledging complimentary comments and looks with a nod, we make our way toward the horse pens near the wooded area of Cowskin Prairie. Cowskin Prairie! It is not like the prairies we know in western Kansas, not at all flat and there are so many more trees. We cautiously guide our mounts around rocks that jut out of the ground. There is not this abundance of rock in western Kansas.

Approximately three thousand men camp with the Missouri State Guard that 28th day of June 1861, a number that will grow to near five thousand before we do battle with our enemy. Perhaps one-third are mounted as cavalry but a large portion of the cavalry, and foot soldiers, have no weapons.

It is inconceivable that anyone would enter a battle without a weapon. Also inconceivable, no weapons are available for the command to issue. What kind of army did we join? Jim and I both possess two Colt six shooters and a Sharps carbine given us by Cody and are the envy of all, as most that do have weapons possess muzzleloaders.

The next few weeks are spent organizing into groups and training in the nuances of war. That is a joke! Just shoot the bastards is all we need to know. Hell! We **know** that! I allow it is necessary to form some type of organization, also realizing I am just anxious to get on with it. Lectures and speeches are given about the necessity of blind obedience and the Articles of War, which is a nice way of saying we can be shot for disobedience, desertion and a number of other offenses. These men seem content to obey; I am anxious to fight so if obedience satisfies that goal, then I will obey. Some men speak of lofty, idealistic goals such as liberating Missouri while the Anderson brothers nod, feigning agreement.

The camp at Cowskin Prairie started out as a chaotic, disorganized assembly of men surrounded by curiosity seekers and well-wishers of all kinds. People ride and walk for miles to see the 'army'. None of the officers seem to care about disruptions caused by sight see-ers, quite the contrary; each man in charge seems bent on displaying his leadership role and/or skill in full view of the public. Commands are issued sharply by extra stiff officers, soldiers try to march in straighter lines and perform various maneuvers perfectly as they discreetly acknowledge the cheers of the camp followers, girlfriends, wives, parents or friends. All this showing off is exasperating, and at the same time, laughable to Jim and me. We don't have time for such stuff.

After training sessions the men are allowed to mingle with well wishers. Fathers smile proudly, standing with their sons, but mothers are frequently admonished for crying. Wives and girlfriends are at once proud of and worried for their man. Some men walk their families about the camp pointing out various items of interest while some, with only a blanket for privacy, engage in conjugal relations within view of the troops.

The novelty of training wears thin and well-wishers come less frequently, as do the welcomed home cooked meals brought by the supporters. Forage for the horses is diminishing and the smell of animal and human excrement accumulated from a months stay in one location is becoming unbearable. Fights break out and maintaining discipline is difficult, we need to get into action so we don't kill each other.

July 25, 1861 the order to move is given and we eagerly prepare to depart for Springfield. General Lyon, commander of the Union forces in Missouri, the most hated adversary of General Sterling Price, and his force of eight thousand men are about to reach Springfield and our general is determined to crush him there.

"Are those God damned officers crazy?" A nearby soldier cries out. "We're gonna take this rag-tag bunch of misfits... half armed... half trained... led by half..."

"That's enough soldier!" A junior officer sternly interrupts.

The soldier needn't finish his tirade as many of us are also wondering how we can stand up to a large force that possesses adequate weaponry. Our 'weaponry' is woefully inadequate. Even the most optimistic men proud of and confident of their fighting abilities are concerned about facing a force nearly twice our size with three times our firepower. Our force has grown to almost five thousand during the month at Cowskin Prairie but clearly one fifth of these men have no weapon except the sticks and clubs they pick up from the woods. How bright are these commanders?

"But sir...!" The soldier whines.

"ENOUGH!" The officer yells emphatically.

As the men ride and walk, furtive glances toward the wooded areas are followed by quiet arguments on both sides of the desertion issue.

A senior officer joins our squad leader and they allow their horses to move close to the troops. "Three divisions of Confederate troops will meet us at Cassville, Lieutenant. Have your men looking sharp." he loudly reports before riding away.

"Lieutenant? Did I hear the Major right? Are we to meet with Confederate troops?" One of the soldiers asks.

"That is affirmative soldier." The lieutenant replies stiffly.

"How many?" Asked another as excited whispers spread through the ranks.

"Three divisions soldier, now look sharp!" The lieutenant replies with a smug smile.

We march with renewed vigor, yet cover an agonizingly slow ten miles per day. The news of our numbers being reinforced makes the slow march palatable. Jim and I made at least fifty miles per day on our trips to western Kansas. Of course we did not walk as much, nor did we concern ourselves with fording rivers with wagons and artillery. This march requires many trees and brush to be cut near rivers to allow the passage of wagons. More frustrating is how long it takes to get an army moving in the morning, and how early we have to stop to settle in for the night.

Throwing a saddle over The Wind when marching orders come is a waste of time, as we wait an intolerable length of time before actually mounting. The Osage taught us to take care of our horses and they will take care of us thus we frequently dismount, loosen the girth on our horses, and trudge alongside. A few members of our troops follow suit and I wonder if they too were taught by the Osage. At any rate, it seems to disrupt the monotony of the slow movement.

Brigadier General McBride's First Arkansas Cavalry arrived at the rendezvous shortly before our Missouri State Guard forces. Over the course of the next two days, General McCulloch arrives with the First Arkansas Infantry and General N.B. Pierce with the First Arkansas Artillery. The combined forces number fifteen thousand and confidence abounds in spite of few munitions for the Missourians. General Price seems more infuriated with the lack of firepower for his men than having to relinquish command to General McCulloch. We assumed our General; a former Governor with the conferred rank of full General, would be field commander for the upcoming operation. But, in all probability Missouri's still undeclared allegiance to the Confederacy has less to do with the decision than McCulloch's standing as a career soldier. The other Generals confidently follow McCulloch, thus General Price acquiesced. The desire to reclaim Missouri for the Confederacy burns more fiercely in Sterling Price than his pride.

"Hyear nah...Mizzoorah." Drawls an Arkansas infantryman leaning against the muzzle of his Kentucky rifle, his accent thick as he casually addresses the unarmed Missouri infantrymen nearby. "Whar's yer guns, y'all?" He chides. "Ya gwon stare em ta death?"

His comments bring howls of laughter from the Arkansas detachments. "Naw Cy." began another. "Tham Yankee boys'll die laffin once't dey gets a look at dese boys." Boisterous laughter ensues as another joins in. "Ya reckon mebbe dey's jes gwon throw rocks at dem dere Yankee boys?"

The laughter dies quickly as rocks are fired in their direction; the Missourians having taken exception to the ribbing. Angry shouts arise and officers from both sides move quickly to quell the fighting as rifles are raised on both sides of the camp. Relations are strained at all ranks and levels of the allied forces. The comments of the Arkansas troops amuse Jim and me as after all, we are not Missourians. "Fuck em if they can't take a joke." I whisper to Jim. We rarely speak with either side and avoid arguments.

The cavalry pulled out July 31 to assess the strength of the enemy, the remainder of the forces follow the next day. To our dismay the Missourians are assigned to the rear and those without arms sent to the end of the column with the expressed battle plan of filling in with a fallen comrade's weapon. This is a macabre thought as the vision of one soldier awaiting the death of another to continue the battle pervades my senses. Disgruntled soldiers trudge slowly along the trail made dusty by the mass of men. It is hot, dry, hard labor moving wagons and artillery pieces. The Missourians move the wagons, more punishment for being unarmed we muse. The bitterness grows daily and officers speak openly of venting our anger at the Yankees.

The evening campfire is where men rehash the day's events and tell stories to break the monotony.

Jim and I prefer to take a place on the periphery of the campfire and remain unobtrusive. We silently listen to various tales, most designed to enhance the stature and stroke the ego of the teller while others are truly interesting.

"Do you know where the name Kansas came from?" A man asks of no one in particular as he slowly pokes in the fire.

"Well of course." comes a reply from a man who just completed a tale of his daring deeds against the Jayhawkers in Kansas. "The state is named for the tribe of Kansas Indians residing on the western plains."

"Naww." said the first man slowly. "That's what they want you to believe, but I am one quarter Osage Indian and learned from my grandfather, an Osage chieftain who was there what the true story is." At the mention of 'Osage', Jim and I are in attention. The first man quietly stirs the embers of the fire.

Losing his patience the second man asks. "Alright! How did Kansas get its name?"

Slowly looking at the faces of the men peering at him, the 'Indian' stretches as he gets up from the fire and sits down to face the braggart. All eyes and ears are on him; his intended effect of drawing our attention is working.

"Well." He began slowly. "It happened soon after Lewis and Clark came through. A wagon train made its' way along the north side of the Missouri river and found its' way blocked as the river turns north. The wagon master stood on the banks of the river near where Kansas City is now and wondered aloud; 'Who can show us the way across the turbulent waters?' My grandfather heard the wagon master's question and responded, 'The old Indian can'. Now the wagon master misunderstood what my grandfather said and before he could be corrected, told the rest of the train that the Old Indian 'Kan' was going to lead them across the river.

The soldiers around the fire cast quizzical glances at one another as the 'Indian' continues. "Well now, Indians think that palefaces are dumb anyway, so he didn't try to correct him and went along as the old Indian became known as 'Chief Kan'. Well old Chief 'Kan' led that party across the dangerous, raging river and upon reaching the other side, got off his horse, knelt down and kissed the ground. Soon other trains arrive and sought the assistance of Chief Kan to cross the river. After each difficult crossing the old Indian got down on his knees in gratitude and kissed the ground. Following one particularly arduous crossing Chief Kan leaned forward to kiss the ground and died at that very instant."

The 'Indian' has everyone engrossed in his story and pauses to place a couple of logs on the fire.

"Then what?" The second man asks impatiently. "Then what?"

Without looking at him, the first man kneels beside the fire stirring slowly. Finally he continues.

"The people from the wagon train left him as he died, knelt over, kissing the ground, each throwing some dirt on him as they pass to bury him. After a time another wagon train came and my grandfather stood on the hill with the wagon master who pointed to the vast wind swept plains to the west and asked, 'What is that?'. Thinking he referred to the part of the old Indian's anatomy exposed by the winds my grandfather replied. 'Why that's Kans' ass'."

The collective gasp of the soldiers surrounding the fire is followed by raucous laughter. "Why Clarence Randall! You sly dog!" One of the soldiers exclaims, lightly punching the arm of the storyteller. Clarence began to laugh as well and I marvel at how easily a blond 'Indian' had taken us in.

Chapter Nine

We made camp fifteen miles south of Springfield, still two days march away, to await further orders and prepare for battle. My plan to 'just shoot the bastards' apparently is not adequate.

'Old Pap', as the Missourians affectionately refer to General Sterling Price, is lobbying for immediate advance on his archrival General Nathaniel Lyon. General McCulloch prefers caution and orders an expeditionary party to scout the enemy. The loud arguments emanating from the Generals' tents do little to relieve the strained relations of the Missouri/Arkansas factions. Wisely the two state forces are separated at camp. Perhaps as a concession to 'Old Pap' the Missouri troops are given the prime camp location on the east side of the highest hill overlooking the creek running through the farm we camp on. The hill is more thickly wooded at the top than near the creek that meanders toward the southeast. What a beautiful, serene setting our campsite made that first sunset.

The beauty of sunsets is forgotten August 9th as marching orders came at midnight. General Lyon's troops have moved south and are but a few miles from us and will be attacked at dawn. That night the gatherings around campfires are quiet as men facing the reality of battle ponder their future. One young man had been whimpering softly for several minutes. "I don't want to die!"

"Shut up!" a man nearby growls harshly having grown tired of the whimpering, or perhaps doesn't want to ponder his own destiny.

"I want to go home!" the young man said pleadingly to the man who yelled at him.

"SHUT UP I SAID!" The man hollered, angrily standing over the boy.

The boy continues to whimper, cowering in his blankets, overcome with fear.

Die? That thought had not occurred to me. I came for an adventure, for fun, and to possibly kill Union soldiers. The possibility of being killed never entered my mind. A strange cold feeling engulfed me, is it fear? I look to see if I detect fear in Jims' eyes as he peers expressionless at the fire. I look at others around the fire and see concern... or is it fear? Others are either unconcerned or mask their feelings well.

The pickets had just been pulled in signaling the march will begin, when a gentle rain began to fall. For two weeks it had been hot and dry but now, as we are about to attack, our concern shifts to keeping the powder dry. The order is quickly given to cover the ammunition and maintain our position. The fires sizzle and die, as rain falls at an increasing rate. Jim motions for me to follow him up the hill to the west, away from the creek. Finding adjoining trees near the top of the hill we place our pistols, rifles and cartridges under the rain slickers slipped over our heads, and lean against the trees. The broad tree trunks divert rainwater, now coming down heavily, and keep us relatively dry. I turn to thank Jim for the good idea but he has his knees drawn up under the slicker, hat covering his eyes. Sleep does not come easily in spite of the soothing effect the patter of rain has on the brim of my hat. I am besieged with thoughts of lead shot tearing into my body. What does it feel like? Will I scream? How much pain is involved? Will I cry? God, I do not want the others to think of me as a crybaby. Jim looks up to me as strong, how can I let him down? I am not a coward, am I? What will Jim think if I suggest we desert? What would Diane and my father think? I can't! OH GOD! I DON'T WANT TO DIE!

The crack of a distant rifle awakens me, although I'm not sure I had slept. Faint, golden streaks of daylight push its way between clouds over the horizon as riders gallop toward our position. Before they arrive, the words, "We're being attacked!" ring in my ears. HOLY SHIT! ATTACKED! THIS IS IT!

I stand up, accidentally depositing my dry powder on the wet ground. I retrieve my rifle, fling off my slicker, push my pistols into my belt, pocketing as much ammunition as I can. Grabbing my tack and saddle I turn to run and slide down the hill followed closely by Jim. Before we reach our horses the sound of battle cries erupt from the hill we vacated. Blue clad soldiers swarm through the trees at the top of the hill, firing as they run.

Before we can reach our horses, we are cut off by an officer pointing his pistol at us as he commands. "TURN AND FIGHT! UP THE HILL! TURN AND FIGHT! YOU! YOU, YOU! UP THE HILL! TURN AND FIGHT! CHARGE THEM, DRIVE THEM BACK! UP THE HILL! FIGHT!

Dropping my saddle, I raise my Sharps and obediently fire up the hill. A man fell. Is it from my shot, had I killed my first man? Seeing others run up the hill to meet the onrushing Union soldiers I woodenly follow them. I pull a pistol from my belt and begin to fire, aimlessly at first, then with more determination. A man falls against me causing me to fall, his agonizing scream startles me. Jim? It isn't Jim. I can't see Jim!

The pounding hooves of a horse are nearly upon me and I roll out of the way looking at the rider. "CODY!" I exclaim. "CODY!" My childhood mentor that had given me the pistols I carry is seated on his horse above me. He recognizes me before a ball enters his left eye blowing an exit hole below his right ear. Toppling from his horse Cody's screams come as gurgling sounds, his nose blown off, the left eye hanging from its socket and blood pouring out. I watch in shock and amazement as he tries to stand, his arms flailing about in pain. He falls, writhing in death.

An officer orders me to get up and fight, angrily pointing his saber at me before a mini ball enters his forehead. The saber falls against me as he topples from his horse without a sound.

"AAAAYYYYEEEEEHHHH! Fear grips me as I scream and struggle to my feet. Grasping the fallen saber, I stand with the empty Sharps in my hand. At the last second I deflect a bayonet thrust with my Sharps and slash the saber across the face of the startled soldier wielding that bayonet.

I've got to get out of here! I have to run! Pointing the saber parallel to the ground I follow its direction, screaming in fear as I run. A blue-uniformed soldiers' bayonet is poised to strike his enemy on the ground when my saber is driven into his chest. The soldier drops the rifle, standing motionless with a surprised look on his face. I kick at his chest to dislodge the saber and continue my dash up the hill as he falls lifelessly behind me. My Sharps serves as a club to clear a path, as does the saber. Swinging wildly, I barely recall blue clad soldiers being struck as I run. The realization I am running **up** the hill, the direction from which the union soldiers are coming, suddenly strikes me. I hear the fall of heavy footsteps behind me, turning in time to deflect the thrust of another bayonet and bury my saber deep into the stomach of the blue clad soldier.

The sound of gunfire diminishes as I stand amidst the trees near the top of the hill. My feet move without a conscious effort, stumbling down the hill. An officer wearing a ribbon of the Missouri State Guard approaches. "Who are you?" he asks.

Without answering I walk down the hill barely reaching the bottom before battle cries come again from the top of the hill.

"FORM TWO LINES HERE!" an officer cries and we dutifully fall into place recalling our minimal training. Alternately firing volley after volley one rank reloading as the other fires, I feel the tug in my shirt and the hum of 'bees' in my hair as the superior numbers of the Union overrun us. It won't be long now I think as I await death. My saber slashes at and on the enemy as they come relentlessly. God, how can I get out of this? I wish I was anywhere but here! Again there is a tug at my shirt. To where can I run this time? A buzz in my hair feels hot.

Cheers erupt as the First Arkansas Infantry joins the fray. Inter-rivalries be damned, they are a beautiful sight! With renewed vigor we battle on, how long we fight hand to hand is a mystery. Still gripping the saber, it must be acting on its own as my arms are extremely tired. My body tells me to stop, but to stop is to die so I must go on. My Sharps becomes too heavy and I allow it to drop as I grab a Colt from my belt, a soldier is nearly on me. The impact of my bullet throws him backward. 'Bees' continue to buzz through my hair and tug at my shirt. Running away is no longer an option as bodies stacked against my legs greatly restrict movement. How soon can I die as rest, even eternal rest, seems inviting? Perhaps if I stop swinging my saber, someone will kill me and stop this. I can't, or perhaps won't, stop.

My slashing saber ceases to encounter resistance as the enemy retreats again. I watch blue uniforms disappear into the woods at the top of the hill. My aching lungs gasp for air, eyes burn as sweat, blood and grime seep into them. I sink to the ground my body shaking.

Two men grab me and drag me to the creek where another man tugs at my shirt, wipes my face, looks at me and says, "He's not hurt." then turns to another man brought to the edge of the creek. Racked with exhaustion I roll over and push my face into the stream. The cooling waters revive me and I take a deep draw from the creek before lifting my head. Wiping the water from my eyes I look at the stream. It has an odd color to it. I see bloodied bodies and limbs strewn into and around the creek. Wilson's Creek is running red with blood.

"REFORM! REFORM!" An officer screams.

Oh God! Here they come again! Again I respond dutifully to orders that came from, who knows where, from who knows who, to do who knows what. This time the enemy does not charge down the hill to engage us preferring to form lines amidst the natural cover of trees. We are sitting ducks out in the open as Arkansas and Missouri men stand shoulder to shoulder forming three firing lines. My Sharps is loaded and raised to my cheek time after time as the battle rages. Men crumble around me and are quickly replaced by another soldier who, with the dead man's weapon, continues to fight. Incredible, the unarmed Missourians are in the fight! The firing is continuous as blue smoke erupts from muzzles on both sides. Visibility fades as the roar of muskets drowns out pained screams of comrade and foe alike. Targets are obscured by smoke as we fire up the hill at our enemy.

The whistle of a cannon ball is closely followed by the splintering sound of shot tearing through the trees providing cover for the Union soldiers. Bledsoe's Battery has joined the fray! Shot after shot rains down on the enemy and their fire wilts. More men from the Arkansas divisions arrive to bolster our lines greatly increasing our firepower adding to the dense smoke. Suddenly, it is over!

The withering fire from the downside of the hill continues for several minutes until an officer, realizing none of his men had fallen for a couple of minutes, orders a cease-fire. Silence descends on the area, every man straining his ears for gunfire and his eyes to detect movement. The realization that fighting has ceased brings feeble cheers from the bottom of the hill. Others, as myself, too exhausted, merely sink to the ground for rest.

Slowly my senses detect a distant sound. "Bill!" What is that? "Bill!" Where is it coming from? "Bill!" It is getting closer and seems to be pleading. "Bill!" Jim. Where is Jim? Is it Jim? **It is Jim!**

"Jim. Jim! Jim!" I scream with my last bit of strength. **"JIIIM!**

My brother is a welcome sight as he runs to me. "Are you…? He questions as his eyes search my body for wounds.

I nod feebly. "I'm OK… you…?"

"YES!" He exclaims joyously. We fall into one another's arms in joy, relief and exhaustion.

It is surprising to see the sun high overhead as we gather weapons, cartridges and bodies from the battlefield. The fight began at sunrise and went on until midday. Six hours? Strange, how what seemed to be an eternity also seemed but a fleeting moment.

Stories around the campfires are more muted than previous evenings. Acts of bravery and heroism are related mostly about comrades who did not make it through the battle to tell their own story. Jim and I assume our customary position on the outer ring of the group. Jim is silent as he did not take part in the charges up the hill. He didn't explain why - he didn't have to, I knew.

My eyes meet those of a man standing nearby and are held momentarily before he makes his way to the fire. The ribbon on his lapel signifies that he is an officer of the Missouri State Guard. Curiously, he keeps glancing at me as he stands at the fire extending his hands as if testing its' warmth. The faces of the men slowly turn toward the officer and conversations dwindle. He is approximately five foot nine inches tall, one hundred fifty pounds with drooping eyes that appear half closed. His stance marks him as a man of distinction, a man of confidence, a genteel man.

Slowly his eyes pan the faces of the men near the campfire before he begins a deliberate stride around the fire looking at each man as he passes. The idle chatter stops and all eyes are on this officer as he begins to address them.

"Much will be said about what happened here today." He began articulately, eloquently, in a low strong voice each word enunciated carefully to ensure its fullest impact on the listener. "Much will be written about the carnage we witnessed and were a part of. What history has to say of this battle at Wilson's Creek remains to be seen. How important is this victory today? What role will it play in the liberation of our beloved Missouri? We'll soon see. Old Pap is at this very minute pleading our case with General McCulloch to pursue and overtake the enemy we defeated today and totally eliminate the Union army of Southwest Missouri. In spite of his wounds, which are minor I must add, Old Pap is delivering a powerful argument for advancing that I am sure cannot, and will not, be ignored." He pauses in his oratory, the faces turned intently toward him illuminated by the flickering fire. Did he look directly at me for a moment?

"You lost many friends and comrades." He continues as he paces. "You lost many friends, perhaps even relatives. They…" he points toward the north. "... lost more. You suffered much pain. They... suffered more. You... stood your ground unfailingly. They... retreated, returned and retreated again. They... could not deter you from your goal of liberating your home state."

He paused. "You are all heroes! You... accounted for yourselves very well and deserve to be proud and stand tall. However... I wish to tell of one that is especially brave, one that stood especially tall, that truly epitomizes the term hero." Again he pauses to enhance the impact of his words.

"This man... displayed unflinching courage in the face of the enemy's withering fire. This man... using a rifle as a club, and a saber cut down numerous Union soldiers saving the lives of many. In spite of their concentrated effort on him he fearlessly swung his saber at the enemy. He saved the life of an officer trapped by his fallen horse as he was about to be bayoneted by a Union soldier. This hero, drove his saber into the chest of that soldier before he could deliver his blow, then kicked the Union man off his blade so he could continue the fight. This hero, then cut down all in his path until he single-handedly chased the enemy up the hill."

"I remember him!" Spoke a man on the opposite side of the fire.

"I do too!" Cried another excitedly. "He inspired me to keep fighting when I wanted to..." He stopped, his voice trailing off.

The officer stopped his pacing in front of me and asked quietly. "Who are you?"

I look up in surprise, then find the words. "B… B… Bill. Bill Anderson."

Slowly the officer resumes his pacing. Stopping on the other side of the fire he peers intently at the men and speaks again. "You men took part in a battle today on Bloody Hill." He pauses and begins a slow pace around the fire. "Bloody Hill is what it was, and Bloody Hill it will be called. But this day belongs to Bloody Bill." He stops in front of me speaking directly to me. "I am that officer you saved today and I, William Clarke Quantrill am proud to fight for liberty with you… Bloody Bill Anderson." He steps to my side, places his hand on my shoulder, looked into my eyes before walking off.

There is silence for several moments until a man rises to his feet. Coming to my side he put his hand on my shoulder, looks at me saying quietly, "Bloody Bill." and returned to his place. Another approaches then another, as they come, touch my shoulder and say, "Bloody Bill." or "Bill." Some say nothing but gently touch my shoulder and return to their place.

The brim of my hat and my bowed head conceals my eyes. I cannot look at them; I do not want them to look at me. They do not know! They did not see the coward trying to run away!

"Hy'air Nah! Hy'air Nah!" An Arkansas infantryman salutes and shouts in a thick accent as he and others wave and march past the Missouri contingent standing in respectful attention. "Give 'em hell Mizzoorah!" Shouts another. "Kick d'ere arse!"

"Good luck Arkansas!" returns the Missourians amid cheers. The derisive jeers we encountered riding into Cassville have turned into respectful cheers as the Arkansas Brigades depart the battlefields and head for Little Rock. Fighting and dying beside each other healed differences, real or imagined, between the men from adjoining states. However, that does not apply to the officers. Generals Price and McCulloch argue about the tactics to employ after the victory at Wilson's Creek. Old Pap pleads to pursue the remnants of the Union forces to annihilate them before they can reorganize, General Lyon having been killed in the battle. Pursuit may enable Confederate forces to move on to Jefferson City and reinstate Claiborne Jackson to the Governors seat he had been elected to. General Ben McCulloch declines citing orders from Richmond prohibiting him from penetrating deeply into Missouri.

With McCulloch refusing to pursue, Old Pap makes hurried preparations for the Missouri State Guard to pursue on its own. An inventory of his poorly equipped troops convinces him of the folly of taking his troops within range of General John C. Fremont, Commander of the Union

Army West in St. Louis. Prudently the Missouri commander stands his troops down as he argues tactics with ranking Confederates. General Price speaks of the vast numbers of men sympathetic to the South above the Missouri River, that are prevented from joining because the Union controls the river, break that control and his numbers will swell tremendously. A push up Missouri's western border to decidedly pro-southern areas along the river such as Independence, Lexington and Boonville will give him access to a source of manpower desperately needed. General McCulloch steadfastly refuses to venture further north seeing no advantage to the Confederacy to extend his lines far from his command center in Little Rock, Arkansas. On August 11, 1861 General McCulloch heads south from Wilson's Creek and General Price moves north into Springfield.

Our stay in Springfield consists of repairing our wounded, our weapons and recruiting from the surrounding area. The union army fled in disarray and has staggered to relative safety near Rolla, Missouri. Determined to pursue his ideal of liberating the manpower above the Missouri River, Old Pap targets Lexington to open the river to the Confederates.

The men show me great respect making the tedium of preparations for the trek to Lexington palatable. Men smile and greet me by my new nickname, Bloody Bill. Jim cannot conceal his pride in his brother nor his sense of shame in his own actions during combat. I sternly order him not to speak of our actions at Wilson's Creek, not wanting to reveal my true feelings while that battle ensued. Jim complies with half my directive as he proudly relates tales of 'Bloody Bill's' exploits, deftly embellishing deeds on the western plains. Although feigning anger I enjoy the attention, the more I downplay my role the greater respect I am shown.

"Don't be so modest!" Jim admonishes me. It isn't modesty, but I enjoy the notoriety and stop denying my, ahem, heroism.

Chapter Ten

The trek to Lexington is an arduous task of dragging wagons and cannons across rivers and streams which slow travel dramatically. We head west toward flatter terrain before continuing north. Conversations around campfires center on our hatred for 'Lanes Brigade', the Union supported Kansas troops under Senator James Lane. In Kansas the local's opinions of Senator Lane were mostly complimentary, in stark contrast to the venomous hatred shown by the Missouri men. Some of the Senators men are overzealous in their fight to keep Kansas a "free" state, notably the Pottawottomie massacre five years ago. Near that small town in eastern Kansas, John Brown hacked to death five innocent farmers whose only crime was having southern sympathies. Others such as James Montgomery and "Doc" Jennison are ruthless in their military endeavors and stir hatred in the men of Missouri.

In Kansas the past seven years we heard the viewpoint of Kansans, now in Missouri a much different attitude is displayed. Kansans view their neighbors to the east as "slave mongers, secessionists, and Border Ruffians" intent on taking life and liberty from freedom loving Kansans. In Missouri, secession from the union is a minority position as most prefer to remain a part of the union with their own right to choose on the slavery issue. Since joining the Missouri State Guard, we only met one man that had taken part in the raid on Lawrence in 1856; no other "Border Ruffians" were identified. The hatred toward the Kansas Jayhawkers by residents of Missouri is every bit as extreme although we haven't found either side to be as portrayed by the other. Perhaps Jim and I are the only ones that recognize extremists on both sides of the issues are in the minority.

Under the cover of darkness September 11th, our cavalry units noisily surround the Union post at Lexington, leaving an access to the river on the north. Old Pap hopes the noise will entice the union commander to abandon his post without bloodshed. That is fine with me! Thirty five hundred troopers garrisoned at Lexington will face a growing Confederate force numbering near twenty five thousand. A formidable force, as supporters are crossing the river in droves to join us. Old Pap proudly parades his force around the union complex in a grand display of manpower designed to show the futility of the union position. The federal forces had cut down all trees within fifty yards of the fort giving an unobstructed view of soldiers slowly advancing up the inclines. Storming the fort will cost a great deal of lives on our part - a foolish move. Breastworks built by union forces are twelve feet high and as wide; seven artillery pieces provide protection for the command post in the Masonic College building. In spite of being greatly outnumbered, the Yanks are well prepared and will not be easily dislodged. James A. Mulligan, a brash Irish Colonel commanding the union fort, amuses us by asking if the General had come to surrender. We admire his courage but question his sanity as surely he must know his force cannot hold out with odds stacked so heavily against him.

Our daily parades last two hours and are a waste of time and energy. The marching and heat of mid September only tires the men and horses. After the first parade, I ride The Wind without a saddle attempting to keep him cool; still he works up a considerable lather and snorts heavily from the dust raised by marchers. Taking The Wind to a creek emptying into the Missouri river, I wash him with cool water in the comfort of a shade tree as I speak soothingly to him.

Either our officers heard our complaints or Old Pap selected a new strategy, as our march for the fifteenth is called off. We deploy around the fort with Colonel Bledsoe's Battery placed to the southheast above the fort. Our squad is deployed along the river approximately two hundred yards west of a stately mansion called the Anderson House. Jim and I take some good natured ribbing about the nice house we have. All traffic in and out of the fort is stopped.

An old man argues he isn't going into the fort but is bent on 'shootin' some Yankees'. Setting his powder and ball pouches behind a tree, he directs his daughter and six year old grandson to safety behind him, and began to lob shots into the complex with his Kentucky rifle. Minding her son and the picnic basket, the young woman watches her father leisurely load and fire as we encourage his attempts to single handedly eradicate his enemy.

"Hey old man! If you want to get closer we'll have Bill here stand in front of you to provide cover! Bullets can't strike him!" one of our men yells to him.

The old man ignores us. Sporadic return fire rips bark off trees or splatters into the ground as rounds crash about him. After an hour the old man leans his rifle against the tree and began to stroll toward his daughter. His grandson suddenly ran toward the old man who scooped up the boy and hurried to a position of safety. Once by his daughter's side he harshly scolds them both for the boy's exposure to return fire. The boy's glee turns to tears. Hugging the boy to his chest the old man talks softly as tears subside and the boy gives an understanding nod. It is a daily ritual for the old man to lob shots into the complex and enjoy a picnic lunch before walking off with family in hand. Our attempts to engage them in conversation are met with polite smiles but otherwise ignored.

Our squad is ordered to stop the gathering of water north of the fort from the natural spring bubbling out of the ground only thirty yards from the dense thicket we have made our way to. A stairway up the steep rise has been fashioned in the rocks behind the spring and a bucket brigade is passing water up the hill as we arrive. We open fire halting the gathering of water as they run for cover. Return fire from the fort crashes harmlessly about the thick tree cover, and several union men fall under our fire as they scramble up the hill. Cannon fire whistles harmlessly overhead as we are too close for their cannon. As darkness comes we move to take positions along the stairway. Although a starry night; the lack of a moon makes the darkness near complete.

After a couple of hours, four soldiers carrying buckets creep down the steps. We allow them to reach the spring before dispatching them with our knives. I grab the chin of one of the soldiers and drive my knife into his throat; only a gurgling sound accompanies his collapse. His body lay heavily against me as I ponder what happened. I killed a man at close range without a second thought. Do I feel remorse? I push the dead man away from me. After several minutes we hear a whispered call from above. "Tasker? Tasker?" Tasker cannot reply.

As the sky begins to lighten, we crawl to the safety of our thicket. The shadows are heavy on the steps as men in the fort open fire on our position.

We assume this is covering fire but cannot make out forms of men we know must be crawling down the steps, but we open fire anyway. Finally we see men burst from the shadows and concentrate our efforts on them. None survive their exposure at the spring and firing from the fort stops.

The afternoon heat is oppressive. We imagine what it must be like inside the fort without water, but no other attempt for water is made that day. Another attempt is made under the cover of darkness; we return to our thicket before dawn having dispatched of two more union soldiers.

"LOOK THERE!" We watch a woman make her way toward the spring, tentatively glancing in our direction. "They're sending their women for water!" I feel as if I know her as she gingerly steps down the hill. She looks so much like Josi.

"Well! Send a woman to do a man's job and she'll suffer a man's fate." declares a soldier raising his rifle.

The hammer of my Colt clicks into place as I press the barrel against his temple and calmly state, "If she dies, you die." a startled look comes over him.

Corporal Clark looks at both of us, my eyes and gun not wavering from the soldier. Assured of my determination the Corporal proposes a solution. "You men! Provide covering fire! Bill, go get her."

I stare at the soldier a moment before lifting my pistol and, returning the hammer to its resting place, charge into the open space. Gunfire erupts behind and above me as I run toward her, a look of fear in her eyes as she turns to retreat up the hill. The thud of shots crashing around me ceases as I near her. "Don't be afraid." I say grabbing her around the waist. She strikes and kicks at me as I throw her over my shoulder and carry her to our position. Commands to "hold your fire" are heard from the hill above, for fear they might hit the woman.

The Corporal mutters. "I'll be goddamned!" staring at me as I hand the woman to him.

"I told you he cain't be kilt!" a soldier squeals in delight. I smile at that soldier then at the Corporal.

"Corporal, another one!" The Corporal turns toward the fort as a second woman descends the slope. He looks at me. "Bill?" This time the union soldiers are prepared for me and lay down a heavy barrage of covering fire. In a short time I return with this one over my shoulder as well.

"I TOLD YOU! I TOLD YOU!" the man gleefully dances around shouting; "THEY CAIN'T TOUCH HIM! THEY CAIN'T KILL BLOODY BILL." I take off my hat and give a sweeping bow to raucous laughter and cheers.

"Jesus Bill, are you alright?" Jim asks. I turn with a little dance to show I am unscathed. I don't know how I avoided the heavy fire from the fort. There are no more attempts to retrieve water as minutes later the fighting begins in earnest.

The ammunition train having arrived, Bledsoe's Battery opens fire the morning of September 18, and our squad is ordered back to the Missouri River for an assault on the fort. We make our way under whistling sounds of cannon shot fired from, and into, the fort. I imagine a lattice of heavy balls woven above us as we crawl through trees to our assigned position. Stopping in the relative safety of a large Maple tree, I look through the branches attempting to see the flight of cannon shot. The noise is deafening as rifle and cannon fire from the fort tear into the nearby trees. Jim crawls behind me and we duck after a shot rips into a nearby tree. That's stupid; we duck **after** the shot has struck, it's too late then!

We reach the river northwest of the fort and rejoin our company assigned to bolster a group climbing the slope to attack the Anderson house. The house is designated a field hospital by Union commanders, is marked with yellow flags and by all precepts, its neutrality should be observed. Our division commander, General Harris recognizes a military value because of its proximity to the fort. He presumes snipers in the windows and on the roof of the three storied structure can inflict considerable damage to the Union position.

Union resistance to our attack is almost nonexistent and soldiers posted in the house quickly escape. Jim and I find a position at a window on the second floor overlooking the kitchen behind the house. The windows are open to reduce the dreadful heat of an abnormally hot September. Ignoring protests from the doctor and clergyman administering to a handful of Union wounded, we take positions along the back wall of the house. "GET OUT OF HERE!" the doctor bellows. "This is where I do my operating and you men are not welcome here!" He is a large man, thicker in the waist than at the chest. Stoop shouldered with his head pressed forward slightly; his drooping eyes and jowls give him a menacing look.

One of our officers appears in the doorway of the adjoining bedroom and motions for us to remain where we are. "Sir." he begins calmly. "We have no intention of interfering with your efforts to care for these injured men. The injured will be treated with utmost respect. Those that you declare able will be escorted out of harms way. They will not however, be allowed to return to their respective units in the fort." The doctor scowls at him but says nothing. The officer continues. "Your safety is assured. Continue to carry out your oath to render medical aid to all as needed. Doctor, it is my desire that it will not be necessary to render further aid to troops whether Federal or State Guard."

Reluctantly the doctor returns to his patients. The man on the bed has a shoulder wound and moaning in pain. Turning his attention to him, the doctor probes with a long device; heightening the soldier's discomfort. His moans turn to screams the doctor seems oblivious to. Pressing down on the afflicted shoulder, the doctor places his knee on the other shoulder to steady the man until the preacher comes to his aid. The preacher holds the patient steady as the doctor twists and pushes on the probe, while biting his lower lip. The soldier passes out from pain before the probe finally extracts the mini ball. The doctor examines the ball between the ends of the probe briefly before tossing it aside.

"Aren't you going to give it to the soldier?" The preacher asks.

"No time for souvenirs." is the curt reply as the doctor steps to the door wiping his hands on his apron as he surveys the adjoining room. "Him, bring him in here." The young man carried in writhes in pain, a mini ball in his knee. After a cursory examination the doctor points to the preacher and said. "Whisky." Turning to his bag he places his hand on a saw and orders loudly. "Get some men in here! Tie a stick in his mouth!" The man on the bed looks wild eyed from the doctor to the preacher as he realizes what is about to happen. "No." He moans then began to scream. "NO! NO!" as three State Guard men hold him down. He coughs as whisky is poured into his mouth. The preacher talks soothingly to the young man. "Take another drink, a big drink." the preacher offers softly. The soldier takes a long pull from the bottle, his wild eyes fixed on the doctors' back. He takes another long pull as the doctor nods to the men to take hold of the patient.

"Lean on 'im." The doctor commands and began to saw above the knee. The soldier screams through the rag and stick pressed into his mouth before he loses consciousness. The doctor continues to saw and in a matter of seconds throws the saw toward his bag. Using his scalpel he completes the amputation and tosses the severed member toward the window. The leg lands on Jim, blood oozing from it.

"God damn!" Jim exclaims kicking the severed leg away from him, angrily looking at the doctor. The doctor returns his gaze with a look of disdain. "More rags!" The doctor orders as he bandages the end of the soldier's leg. Wiping his hands on his bloody apron, he looks around the room outside as two men carry the limp form of his one-legged patient from the operating area. He points and a scared young man walks tentatively into the room, right hand over left arm to stop the bleeding.

"Let's get out of here!" Jim says leaning forward to get up, but I stop him, mesmerized by the proceedings. Suspended in mid air Jim looks at me before slumping to his seat. "Shit!" He exclaims softly.

Pools of blood are getting deeper as I gaze about the room. The doctor examines the arm of his latest patient. As he reaches for rags to apply to the wound, the soldier expels his breath in relief. This is fascinating! I am disappointed that the bandaging of that soldiers arm is the last patient the doctor will care for. "God damn Bill?" Jim exclaims quietly. He does not like being in this room.

We have an unobstructed view of the fort to the east and a straight line of breastworks one hundred yards from the house fronted by twelve young apple trees. The view to the west is spectacular! The Missouri river flows below sloping ground, its banks sparsely populated by trees. Our troops scurry near the river two hundred yards away. I estimate it is near two O'clock, we have been in the house no more than an hour and, outside of an occasional shot at the enemy, is peaceful. Sporadic return fire from the fort slams into the walls bringing sarcastic comments. "Don't them sombitches know they aint spose ta shoot at a hospital?"

The grass behind the house is a combination of golden brown and green as the excessive heat and lack of rain have taken its toll. I wonder if our farm has escaped the damaging heat and drought. The past few years have been fruitful as the weather cooperated to grow crops planted, augmenting food supplies for the horses as well as the family. Family! I haven't had time over the past few weeks to think about the sisters. As I scan the breastworks, a mental image of Josi, Ginny and Kay dances in front of me. We weren't there for Ginny's fifteenth or Josi's sixteenth birthdays this summer. Somehow we'd make it up to them. Ginny is still thin and gangly and taller than her older sister, Kay nearly two years younger than Ginny, is taller than either of them. Josephine with her quiet serene personality has always been close to me, but Ginny's gregarious nature has drawn us closer. I laugh quietly; if Ginny is gregarious then

Kay is downright devilish! Yes, the younger two Anderson sisters are much more outgoing than their older sister. They have a ready smile for their brothers, their love readily displayed.

Returning my attention to the window, I note the straight line of breastworks that fall away to the east. Although a one hundred fifty yard shot, the federals abandon that side of the breastworks. Some movement is sighted occasionally at the works in front and a shot from the windows above keeps them down. A large open area inside the breastworks is within view before the ground is lost sloping toward the Masonic College, the Union command center. That building is in sight with no activity.

The shadows indicate it is near four O'clock and we had yet to eat. I turn to Jim. "Hungry Jim?"

"Famished, let's find some food!" He replies eagerly. I suspect, more than wanting food, he wants to get out of this room and the putrid smell developing in the heat.

"Sergeant Wilson! Jim and I are going to get something to eat." The Sergeant nods as he leans against the wall near the door between the two east bedrooms.

"Hey Bill! Bring me back a thick juicy steak!" yells W. H. Mansur as he moves into our position laughing at his own joke.

"Sure Will, with all the trimmings!" I laugh also as we step out of the operating room onto the balcony overlooking the bottom floor. Steak! We have not seen steak or any decent food for quite some time. We all long for a home cooked meal.

"I wish we were this Anderson." Jim says wistfully as we make our way toward the river. It is a beautiful house.

I respond in jest, "What, and give up our mansion in Kansas?" Jim gives me a playful shove as we walk down the hill.

As we reach the rivers edge, gunfire erupts behind us at the house. Blue clad soldiers clamor over the breastworks toward the Anderson house. Smoke from guns billow out the windows of the house and from the charging force, the sound reaching our ears a moment later. My feet are rooted to the ground in utter surprise at the activity at the place we just vacated.

"FORM UP! FORM UP!" officers cry, franticly running to assemble their troops. The rush of Union soldiers toward the Anderson house has taken everyone by surprise. Our squad is in the house. Jim and I fall in with another unit as agonizingly long moments pass before an officer orders us forward. We are the third group of thirty men rushing up the hill to reinforce the twenty men in the hospital; that is, twenty minus two.

We are too late. Twelve men escape from the house before we reach the top. Union gunfire rains down on us from the west windows forcing our retreat. In a matter of minutes we had lost a strategic position near the fort. The junior officers that ordered us up the hill, and our hasty retreat, are meeting below the hill. Senior officers run to our position, restoring order from chaos. Finding the men that escaped the house, we learn they were on the lower floor. The men on the upper floors were unable to get out before the union soldiers overran the house.

"Sergeant Wilson?" I ask. No one knows the answer. He was on the upper floor.

It is apparent that now there is an officer in charge, as General Harris stands in front of the other officers kneeling before him. The General points to emphasize his orders to a particular officer, then to the area he is to bring his men. The battle plans drawn, the junior officer's return to their men to disseminate the orders. The remnants of Sergeant Wilson's squad are sought by officers to provide detail on the house.

Less than an hour after being driven from the Anderson house, we mount a counter attack, our strength having grown to a thousand men. Masses of men swarm up the hill amid heavy fire from the house. We halt our charge only to return fire. Dust from the boots of advancing troops makes it difficult for Union marksmen to see us, but soldiers frequently scream in pain as a mini ball slams into them. Approaching from many directions make it impossible for the Union troops to concentrate fire. Although inflicting heavy casualties, the Union men relinquish their hold on the house to our superior numbers and retreat to the confines of their fort.

Other than firing several rounds at the house, Jim and I do not encounter much fighting. We step over several Union bodies as we re-enter the house. The haze from musket fire hangs heavily in the hot stagnant air as moans and groans emanate from every corner of the house. We find Sergeant Wilson at the window we occupied, a mini ball in his head. I assume he had been the first casualty of the Union assault as he would have been directing fire from another location if he had warning of the onslaught.

Carl is found in the bedroom adjacent to the "operating" room, unconscious, left hand clutching his surgically removed right hand. The doctor ignores us as we enter his domain, preoccupied with wounded on both sides of the combat. An abhorrent sight confronts us as we peer about the operating area. The blood on the floor is so deep that almost no part of the wood flooring can be seen. Body parts are scattered about as the surgeon discards them with no regard to their destination. The body of a man is slumped in a corner… dead? The preacher moves about the wounded, offering a prayer for them and for the recently departed. He is pathetically thin, a small man but this is his calling. Covered with blood from assisting the doctor, his energy renewed as he steps gingerly from man to man, soothing them as best he can.

The doctor slips on the blood, nearly falling as he moves to a different angle on his current patient. "GET THIS GOD DAMNED BLOOD OUTTA

HERE!" he bellows, regaining his balance but unabated in his work. We look at the almost black ooze on the floor. How many rags will it take to absorb this? Can we find enough? A man gingerly steps into the room carrying a drill and begins to bore a hole in the floor. We watch his struggles as he turns the bit ever deeper into the wood until breaking through the ceiling below. The blood pooled nearby begins to flow toward the hole as he moves to another spot a few feet away. The doctor glances at him, silently acknowledging his efforts. Jim began to sweep blood toward the holes with his foot, holding his hand over his mouth. More holes are drilled through the floor and soon the pools of blood diminish to streaks and smaller pools that will eventually dry.

I pick up a hand cut from its arm above the shattered wrist, the skin gray, cold, and clammy to the touch. Pressing on the skin, I am bewildered at the change in color. First a bluish gray, at my touch it turns a yellowish pink color then back to bluish gray. As I hold it by the fingers, the bones began to slide out of the skin until I turn it upright, allowing the bones to slide back into the skin as if in a glove.

I hear a retching sound and see Jim vomit pointing weakly at me.

"GOD DAMN IT! DO THAT OUTSIDE!" The doctor bellows at Jim. Dropping the hand I lead Jim out of the house to the shade near the slave quarters. "How can you do that?" Jim coughs as he looks at me ashen faced.

"Do what? You mean the hand? How is that different from gutting chickens or deer?" I reply surprised by his reaction.

"It was a man!" He exclaimed.

"Naw." I laugh. "Only part of one."

"That's not funny!" He says indignantly. I suggest we try again to get something to eat. The sun is setting as we start down the hill. Jim is sickened and not engaging in conversation, I'm not sure if it's embarrassment or if he is repulsed by the bloodshed we witnessed today. "You OK Jim?" I ask as we walk along the riverbank. Jim shrugs and with a waggle of his head, ignores the question.

Hearing a sound, I strain to hear it again. There it is very faint. "Grampa!" Jim hears it too. "Grampa!" A little louder, we are getting closer. "Grampa!" A doleful cry. "Grampa!" Louder. "Grampa!" It's a child's raspy voice weakened by crying for a long time. A small boy is restrained by his mother seated behind him sobbing. Dusk is upon us but I recognize the young boy and his mother that had faithfully attended the old man seeking to "Shoot some Yankee's". The boy gazes up the hill as he leans forward supported by his mothers grasp on his trousers. No form is visible as darkness is closing in.

"Grampa!" The melancholy hoarse voice rasps again.

What can be said to this pitiable pair? I hope his grandfather will turn up. "Grampa!" The woman does not look up. "Let's go Jim." I say softly. He stares at the boy. I hesitate a moment before backing away. Jim does not follow but moves to sit near the girl. My heart is heavy as I walk toward the river.

"Grampa!"

"Grampa!" His voice cracks straining to make himself heard, unwilling to accept the fate of the old man.

"Grampa!"

His voice fades as I walk away.

Chapter Eleven

I find Jim the next morning firing at the fort from where the old man had been. "He didn't come back?" I ask. No response. "What happened to the boy and his mother?" Ignoring me, he jams another cartridge into his Sharps and squeezes off another round. I watch for a couple of shots, quietly caution him to be careful, and leave him to sort out his emotions.

It doesn't take a military genius to determine our advantage in numbers can overrun the fort, although at a great price. The steep river bluffs will keep us out of sight until reaching the top where sparse tree growth offers minimal protection. The open area between the trees and the fort poses a difficult problem. Tree limbs sharpened at one end are positioned as large spears not only to inflict harm but to slow the State Guard's advance affording an easier target for troops within the fort. Trip wires and logs are positioned for this same purpose and our force of twenty five thousand will suffer severe casualties in a frontal assault. Time is becoming a factor in favor of the Union troops. General Fremont commands one hundred thousand men in St. Louis and can bring that force to bear against our Missouri State Guard within days, and may be coming now. General Price hopes that a successful campaign at Lexington will bring General McCulloch back to Missouri, defeat Fremont and claim the entire state for the Confederacy. Messengers are dispatched to keep McCulloch apprised of the circumstances.

Jim returns to the river by mid afternoon. "How'd you do?" I ask.

Jim looks at me expressionless for a moment before replying softly. "Couldn't tell, too far away." At least, he is talking again. We find a spot near bales at the Hemp factory to relax in spite of a constant barrage of cannon fire. We contemplate the charge across terrain strewn with obstacles and the probability of death for a large number of our troops. Jim suggests we desert and go home, an option I will not consider. Why do I not want to leave when I was in the process of running at Wilson's Creek? I don't know, but I feel a... sense of... excitement? I don't fear personal harm although I'm not sure I believe the claim I am invulnerable to gunfire. No, I will stay. Jim dejectedly sighs and sinks into a heap against the hemp bale.

We sit quietly for several minutes before Jim stands up and peers at the fort from behind the bale. He looks at me with a sly grin and studies the hemp bale we are using for shade. Each bale is almost chest high and more than twice that in length. Taking a pull from his canteen Jim bumps against the bale causing it to rock slightly. He leans against the bale bidding me to do the same. Together we roll it over without a great deal of effort. "What?" I ask as he smiles at me. Jim kneels behind the bale, points his finger at the fort squeezing off an imaginary round.

"What's going on?" The officer startles us as he stands, hands on hips behind us. Jim explains his idea to the officer who quickly heads toward the tent of General Harris. By dusk hundreds of hemp bales are rolled near the top of the bluff. Under the cover of darkness the bales are soaked with water to prevent hot shot from igniting them. The bales now are very heavy.

Before daybreak, September twentieth, we move forward behind hemp barricades. Excited cries arise from within the earthen walls of the fort as the first rays of daylight exposes our position. Each bale affords protection for four soldiers rolling it forward and another four crawling closely behind. Frequent jolts tell us our bale is taking shots from within the fort. Bales are lifted and pushed over the pointed stakes opening the way to the fort, the stakes then cleared for following troopers. We leave the safety of our hemp bales and rush the fort, comrades behind assume our positions momentarily before they too rush the Union fort. Members of the Missouri Home Guard run to meet us with shouts and screams of their own, two opposing Missouri forces engaging in combat. No time to reload, Missourians fall on each other in hand-to-hand combat. Muskets, once fired serve as clubs, the dull thud of wood stock crashing against cheeks, chins, head or body coming from all quarters.

Jim takes a blow to the back an instant before my rifle butt crushes the skull of his attacker. Raising my rifle, I stop a descending blow above me, sharply strike the union man, smashing his nose with the end of my Sharps. The butt of my rifle finds the face of another federal soldier running to engage me. The sound of breaking bone in his face is at once intriguing and sickening. No time to dwell on which is the stronger sensation, exhilaration or repulsion. Grasping the barrel of my rifle, I swing it first from the left side then the right at the onrushing enemy. A body falls against me from behind and I see the unconscious man that was about to strike me, his head split open by Jim's rifle butt. Our eyes meet briefly before returning to the fray.

Did they run first, or did we? It doesn't matter as both sides separate, returning to the relative safety of our hemp bales and their breastworks. Jim and I fall in a heap behind a bale and I grasp his hand in exhilaration. It is exhilarating! Jim sits against the bales breathing heavily, his eyes wide as he peers at his bloodied hands. He appears surprised at partaking in the battle only hours earlier he considered deserting to avoid. He doesn't seem pleased. Scared? Appalled?

The ground between forces is littered with soldiers from both sides. Men groan in pain while others lie limp, either temporarily or permanently unable to move.

"THEY ARE SURRENDERING!" comes an excited shout as a white flag appears near the Union breastworks. Word spreads that the enemy surrendered and sporadic fire ceases on both sides. Cautiously a Union soldier steps over the protection of the walls waving a handkerchief attached to a stick. Others appear, edging their way onto the battlefield to pick up fallen comrades.

"Shit!" I exclaim. "They're only tending their wounded! They haven't surrendered!"

"Why do you say that?" Jim inquires

"Because, no one is approaching with a message for our officers. They only want to remove their dead and wounded."

"Shit!" replies my brother in disgust, slumping back against the bale.

State Guardsmen also emerge from behind bales to retrieve our dead and wounded. It is strange to see men a few feet apart who minutes earlier were intent on bashing each other's heads in, peaceably removing fallen comrades. The eyes of our foe reveal what they are thinking. They are losing heart as none hold my gaze for long.

"It won't be long now." I whisper.

"I know. I see it too." Jim replies.

Silence falls over the battlefield as we tend to the wounded, remove the dead and rest.

The order to move our bales forward is followed by the commencement of firing from the fort. Confidence runs high moving toward the outer breastwork of the opposition. Leaving our hemp bale protection behind, we rush the earthen walls and scale them in time to see the Home Guard assume the inner line of defense around the Masonic College. Jim is about to jump to the ground inside the wall but freezes in horror as a concentrated volley from within cuts down our men above us. Pulling back behind their breastworks, we return fire.

"Throw the bales over!" an officer commands; but the water soaked bales are too heavy to lift over the wall. "Build steps!" he yells, and we position bales in the form of steps over the wall. Men take positions behind the bales advancing toward the Masonic College. Cannon balls rock the bales but cannot penetrate the tightly packed water soaked bale. More bales and men roll over the walls as the line moves inward. The roar of rifle and cannon fire with no delay between the red flash from the muzzle and the blast that accompanies it is deafening. Cease fire orders are issued as a white flag appears again from within the compound. Leaning against our bale, I look at Jim and say. "Now it's over."

Exhaustion from the conflict turns to exasperation over the next few days. We won a great victory with little bloodshed; at least in the eyes of the officers it is little bloodshed. The burial details dispose of nearly two hundred bodies from both sides, only about fifty who are State Guardsmen. To those buried and others screaming as limbs are severed, it was a bloody conflict. The families of the dead and wounded will not agree with our officers either. However, considering that nearly thirty thousand men took part in the battle for Lexington, perhaps two hundred dead and a like number of seriously wounded is an acceptable price to pay for victory. Is it a worthwhile price? After capturing the fort and the soldiers that occupy it, Governor Claiborne Jackson addresses the vanquished, assuring them the will of the Missouri people has been fulfilled. General Price releases all the men and officers except for Colonel Mulligan. We win and they go free? What sense does that make? They promise to lay down their arms and not take them up against any Confederate force, but who believes that promise? Officers are dumb!

Eventually we understand why the release is necessary as our provisions barely accommodate the State Guard much less three thousand or so Home Guard prisoners. We watch them returning to their homes. We win and they go home! They lose and we suffer in the heat with inadequate food or supplies. War! What sense does it make? Jim and I bear our frustrations as our enlistments are up in a few days but the fighting has excited me. I feel a powerful thrill engaging an adversary in hand-to-hand combat.

A torrential downpour two days after the fighting finally breaks the irrepressible heat. The hemp bales serve as shelters from rain as they sheltered us from the "rain" of Union bullets. Two bales four feet apart and two on top with the ends resting on the bottom bales form a roof under which Jim and I crouch. Another bale closes up one end as protection from water running off the hills. It isn't until we dig a shallow trench around our "house" that we control the runoff, diverting it around the bales. My slicker on top of the bales, covering the seam between bales, improves our waterproofing. We sit on Jim's slicker above the wet ground. Relatively dry, we stare toward the river at the downpour and occasional flashes of lightning followed at various intervals by thunder. Counting the seconds between flashes of lightning and the thunderclap, I think of the red flame erupting from cannons seconds before the boom is heard and felt. Fascinating!

"They're probably home dry and comfortable." Jim said after a time.

"Who?" I ask.

"The losers." Jim replies staring into the rain.

After a pause I state. "You've been wet before."

Adjusting his position against the bale he uncoils his legs and sarcastically replies with a snort. "Yep! Sho have."

Frustrations and concern heightens daily as the anticipated arrival of Confederate forces from Arkansas to "liberate" Missouri is not coming to fruition. Messengers from McCulloch indicate the Confederacy will not authorize an assault this far into enemy territory. Enemy territory, have we not been told that Missouri is primarily pro-southern, pro-slavery, pro-secession? How can this be enemy territory? A lot of questions abound about our cause.

The smell of fear pervades the camp September 27th as rumors of General Fremont attacking from St. Louis abound. His forces outnumber ours by four to one; although it is unlikely he will bring the entire force and leave St. Louis undefended. Still we anticipate a well-equipped force at least twice our size. The odds against us increase rapidly as men desert rather than face Fremont. Some slip away in the cover of darkness but a great many leave in broad daylight. The officer holding our enlistment papers tries to convince us to stay.

"I've had enough of killing." Jim states calmly.

The officer stares at him a moment before leaning back saying with a hint of derision. "Haven't the stomach for it do you?"

Jim returns the stare without replying. Finally the officer reluctantly signs our discharge papers.

Chapter Twelve

A saddle had not been on The Wind for two weeks and, although I tended him each day, he is excited to see me. Tossing his long black mane in the air, he flares his nostrils snorting a greeting to me.

"How ya doin' boy!" I say patting his glistening neck. The saddle alerts him that today will be different from inactive days. He is eager to run. With wild eyes and body twitching, his excitement evident, I run my hand over his trembling body speaking softly to relax him. His prancing subsides as I speak and throw the blanket and saddle on him.

"We're going home boy!" I say settling on the back of The Wind. Home! Josi! Ginny and Kay! The mental picture gives me a warm feeling. I imagine Josi shyly peering at me from behind her glistening golden hair. She is by nature gentle and loving, it is impossible not to love her. I cannot recall her uttering a cross word in spite of being tested by her gregarious sisters, Ginny and Kay.

The two younger sisters are referred to in the same breath, Ginny and Kay. Although less than a year younger than Josi, Ginny is closer to her sister Kay, who is eighteen months younger.

Both are outgoing although Ginny is slightly less gregarious than her younger sister. Kay can be downright devilish at times, for that matter, so can Ginny.

"What?" Jim asks arousing me from my thoughts. We had ridden for a couple hours before I laughed out loud recalling the nature of our sisters.

"Sorry. I was thinking of some of the pranks Ginny and Kay used to pull." I answer adjusting in my saddle to face my brother. Cocking his head slightly to the side, Jim assumes a far-away look as I continue. "Do you remember the time Kay put that frog in Josi's bed?"

"Kay? That was Ginny!" Jim said in surprise.

"No it wasn't! It was Kay?" I insist.

"But... but... Kay was only... that had to be Ginny." Jim stammers.

I shake my head and simply state. "Nope."

Jim laughs softly, his saddle creaking as he adjusts his position to face me. "Then... was that Ginny or Kay that stuffed eggs in Uncle Johns' boots?"

I laugh uproariously. "Yeah! Ha! Ha! Yes, that was Ginny! Do you remember the look on his face as the eggs broke on his toes?"

"Whoooeee! Do I ever!" Jim laughs. "He didn't think it was funny! He had to clean up the mess! Do you remember the gleam in Daddy's eye as the girls were laughing? He really enjoyed it."

Jim's mention of our father has a dampening effect and our laughter subsides. Our father suffered so much it is difficult not to feel sorry for him. To see him laugh... well, I do not recall him laughing since returning from "Paradise". A glint in his eye and the hint of a smile are rare. His left eye is blind and will not close because of the blow it received. The flattened nose and scars on his face contribute to our pity. It is not fair! He is a gentle man. Not as gentle and reserved as Uncle John, but the pride in his heritage is not overbearing. No man should endure the beating and suffering he did. I began to think of retribution.

Perhaps it is not right to exclude Jacob Anderson, or set him apart from the family, but we do. People outside the family shun him because of his ugly injuries and disabilities. How does that make him feel? What does he think? He cannot express himself properly and we become accustomed to answering for him when he is addressed, speaking of him in the third person. How he must feel, unable to put his emotions into words. Is he lonely? Can one truly be lonely in the presence of others? He is so withdrawn that hardly anyone attempts to speak to him.

I vow to talk 'to' my father when we get home.

The trip to Council Grove takes ten days as we deem it necessary to stay off the main trails and avoid a confrontation with marauding Jayhawkers. We learn during a brief stay in Independence that Jayhawkers led by James Lane, James Montgomery and Doc Jennison roam the border burning and looting homes of supporters of the 'rebellion'. Jennison attacked and burned the town of Osceola, Missouri, a berg friendly to the State Guard cause. Talk of revenge rages among pro-southern men of Independence. Their urge to 'do something' is the topic of a meeting led by George Todd. Todd states he just came from the battle at Lexington, leaving the State Guard when General Price made the decision to leave Missouri. Attempts by supporters to recruit Jim and me for an unspecified fighting group are rebuffed, as we insist on returning to our family.

From Independence we ride south for a day to avoid the pro-Union town of Kansas City. The lawless reputation of that town brought undesirable elements of Union soldiers occupying the saloons springing up in the free town; free of slavery and free of the restrictions of law.

We also stay well south of the Jayhawker headquarters of Lawrence Kansas. It is rumored that between two and five hundred Jayhawkers are quartered there and outfitted for more raids against the pro-Southern people of Western Missouri.

Luck is with us, or perhaps it is our route that keeps us away from trouble, as we do not encounter opposition. We enjoy the hint of changing colors of leaves on trees, this early in October the change just beginning, the deep reddish and yellowish hues are not yet in evidence.

We reach the Neosho River south of the Hodges place near dusk October 6th and follow it north to our place. Light is visible in the house and barn as we approach. Silently we tether our horses near the back of the barn and enter it.

J.D. sees us first and recognizes the silence sign we make with fingers to our lips. Socrates nearly knocks us down as he grabs us. J.D. and Bo restrain and silence the young giants' enthusiasm by holding a hand over his mouth as the man/boy jumps up and down; lips squeezed tightly together trying not to scream out in joy. A short greeting is shared before we look toward the house.

"They're up there." J.D. states quietly. "The girls speak of you every day"

Only a hint of daylight remains in the western sky as Jim eases the door of the barn open and we squeeze through. Toward the house a dark figure is silhouetted in the window. As we approach the figure rises silently staring at us. A few steps from the porch I peer into the eyes of my father standing bent and crippled at the top of the steps. I slowly ascend the steps keeping my eyes on his until we face one another. Without a word I close the gap, take him into my arms and hug him warmly. His tension releases as he relaxes in my arms, I feel him shake, weeping softly.

Jim touches my shoulder as he passes, silently greeting his father. Pausing at the door he looks from me to our father then pushes the door open.

"HEY YOU!" He yells into the house.

A startled scream is followed by shrieks of joy as our sister's leap upon Jim. Sounds of laughter abound as Jim proceeds into the living area. I am vaguely aware of Uncle John standing in the doorway as my father slowly drags his left leg behind him making his way back to his chair. The gentle creak of his rocker joins the raucous laughter from within. Uncle John places his hand on my shoulder as we watch Jacob Anderson contentedly rock. After a moment Uncle John pats my shoulder and quietly says. "Your sisters."

Another shriek is emitted when I appear in the doorway. Ginny reaches me first, a step ahead of Kay, and throws her arms around my neck forcing me backward toward the porch. Kay's added impetus is enough to send us sprawling on the porch in a laughing, howling, crying heap. I feel the lump in my throat enlarge as I laugh and tears began to flow in the joy of seeing my sisters and father again.

Before entering the house I see Uncle John gently rubbing his brothers' shoulders as my father leans forward in the rocker, head in his gnarled hands.

Josi stands serenely in the center of the room arms extended toward me. God she is beautiful! She's as tall as I remember our mother and as beautiful. Her reddish-blond hair glistens like gold and is pulled back in a pony tail with ringlets of hair cascading down her cheeks in front of her ears. Her eyes sparkle and a tear trickles down her beautiful cheeks.

"Oh Billy." she murmurs softly as her arms squeeze my neck gently. "Welcome home. I love you."

Chapter Thirteen

The winter of 1861 is spent expanding the fences around grazing land to retain our growing stock of horses. The best of the brood mares are segregated from the remainder of the stock for breeding with The Wind.

The Hodges have joined their land to ours, entering into a partnership with us to raise horses. Having no sons, only five daughters, Frank Hodges is unable to till much of his land and, as we need more pasture land for our horses, an agreement is readily struck. We now manage an area more than two miles square and over one thousand acres with land on both sides of the Neosho River.

The Hodges home is a mile to the southeast within sight of our place. They are proficient at gardening and reward us with fresh vegetables. Frank keeps a small herd of cows providing milk and meat for both families. They also have something else that intrigues me more and more each day.

Diane Hodges is close friends with Ginny and somewhat devilish, as are Ginny and Kay. Diane smiles warmly at me whenever she visits, which is nearly every day. In her presence, I am nervous and unable to speak properly. A strange dryness in my throat and a ringing in my ears becomes dryer and louder the closer she comes.

She is pretty although not like Josi, but then Josi is an exceptional beauty. Diane is pretty with sandy colored hair cut above the shoulder thus framing her face. Her cute little turned up nose has the slightest hint of freckles, and eyes that sparkle and when she smiles, which is often, thin lips part to reveal two rows of even white teeth. She appears a little wide although her arms are quite thin. Maybe it is the style of her dress. The Hodges struggle, as we do, to eek out a living on land homesteaded six years earlier. All the Hodges children wear clothes hand sewn by their mother, the dresses hanging straight from the shoulder reveal little curvature of the body it covers. I shouldn't think about that.

Each of the Anderson sisters have two store bought dresses provided by their brothers and share them with the Hodges girls. Josi has developed a talent for stitching and although not as fancy as store bought dresses, the every day wear of the Anderson girls are not as plain as that of their friends. Diane and her four sisters therefore have a similar plain look about them.

Plain or typical, the feelings that come over me in her presence are not typical. At times I find myself studying her as she speaks with Ginny. Can she feel my eyes on her? Sometimes her smile will widen and suddenly cast a glance toward me. I cannot hold her gaze and look away quickly.

Sneaking a glance at her again I'd see her smiling demurely.

The winter days not bitterly cold are spent felling trees and shaping them for fences around the perimeter of the two farms. Bo is the team driver pulling the logs into place as Socrates and I wield one bucksaw, Jim and Frank the other. J.D. and Uncle John trim and prepare the logs for transport. Tree after tree is felled, trimmed and pulled into place around the border of the adjoining farms.

Splitting logs is an arduous task and only Socrates is able to keep pounding wedge into tree hour after hour. As not all the areas are fenced, it is necessary to guard the horses as they graze on open ground. I sit astride The Wind watching the repeated blows Socrates delivers to the wedge, marveling at his tenacity. Rarely does he stop to rest and when he does stop it is usually to locate, or relocate a wedge, as he works his way down the log. In spite of the cool days of early March his trousers are stained with sweat as he labors, his shirt is laid aside and massive arms glisten in the sun. How can a man, even as large and strong as Socrates, keep up the pounding for hours without stopping?

I study the movements of this giant as he raises the mall above his head, swinging down with his legs, hips, shoulders, and arms. Amazing, this young giant that is so clumsy he can barely walk into a house without knocking over a chair or table, is so deft at splitting logs. His left hand grips the end of the mall handle as his right hand slides up the handle to raise the heavy metal head over his right shoulder. With knees flexed he begins the downward thrust by pushing upward with his legs and backward with his hips. A huge right hand pushes the head of the mall upward and slides into position in front of the left hand, shoulders rotate pulling the mall head into the wedge. This fluid motion is repeated as many as four times before he bends down to locate a second wedge further down the widening gap until the eventual "pop" as the log splits.

Ginny and Kay, usually with Diane driving the wagon, bring us lunch each day while we tend the horses or build fence. The timing of their visits is predictable and I wield wedge and mall alongside Socrates trying to best him in a splitting contest. I know it is showing off, but for a short time I can compete with Socrates as, at six foot four inches and two hundred twenty pounds, I possess considerable strength as well.

"OOH! Look at those muscles!" Ginny chides one mid-April day to the delight of Jim on his horse nearby. "You can stop showing off Billy, she didn't come with us today." She laughs.

Glancing at her I notice Diane is not in the wagon.

"Leave me alone! I'm trying to work!" I shout. She has seen through my charade. My face flushed in embarrassment, I continue as if showing off were not my intent. Socrates keeps up a steady pace, ignoring the laughter directed at me.

"She got you there didn't she Billy!" Jim laughs heartily. "OOOOHHH Billy! Your' soooo handsome!" He began mockingly in a falsetto voice. He is on his horse, right ankle resting on left leg in front of the pommel of his saddle and unable to get untangled before I throw my body into his. We crash to the ground and I hear the wind gush from his lungs as I fall on him. He gasps for air.

"Geez Bill!" Jim exclaims as his breathing returns to normal. "Can't you take a joke?"

"Well...!" I offer feebly, embarrassed at being caught and by the ferocity of my attack.

"Come on boys, come get your lunch." Ginny says anxiously looking from one brother to the next. Socrates has stopped his work watching us with a perplexed look.

"Sorry Jim." I offer quietly as I brush some grass from his back.

Jim looks at me, anger in his eyes subsiding as he brushes himself off. "That's OK." He begins, then with a sly grin adds, "But you are kinda cute." and runs toward the wagon with me in hot pursuit, enjoying the camaraderie of brothers.

Diane Hodges drove their wagon into our yard one morning in early June. Soon Ginny ran to me saying Diane wants me to go to town with her.

I pause in my work looking toward Diane, a strange cold feeling engulfing me as I do. She affects me in a strange way. "OK." I manage.

The ride into town is quiet with Diane managing some small talk, I'm not much for conversation therefore she does most of the talking. That is not a problem as she likes talking to people. Today she seems quiet and reserved. I am always at a loss for words in her presence and today, being alone with her, words are more difficult to come by.

In Council Grove the townsfolk eye us suspiciously, as they normally do, and give us wide berth. None seem anxious to pass the time of day, but we are used to that treatment and go about our business. She selects a few items and we began our return trip home.

The return ride is quieter; Diane seems nervous and strangely silent. I try to think of a way to start a conversation but, as usual, am unable to speak. Turning to my inner thoughts as we make our way along the river, past farms near town, I marvel at the trees that only a short time earlier had no leaves on them and now are a beautiful shade of green. The birds flit about in the air darting to and fro before alighting momentarily in the branches of the trees. The day is beautiful with large billowy clouds dotting the bright blue sky. It is a warm day and I had long ago shed my coat, placing it in the wagon.

A mile from our farm, Diane stops the wagon and stares at me strangely. Her eyes are wide and her lips slightly parted as she breathes heavily.

"Billy?" She began softly not taking her eyes from mine. I go cold. "Will you help me down Billy?"

I can hardly move. She wants to get down, here? I almost fall off my horse as I step to the ground, my legs are weak. We're out of sight of the farms, why stop here? Our eyes lock on each other, my feet heavy as I stumble toward her, arms hanging limply at my side.

I reach for her to assist her from the wagon. She places her hands on my shoulders and as I lower her, her lips find mine in a passionate kiss.

Chapter Fourteen

The fencing complete, Bo, J.D., Socrates, Jim and I sit on the rails enjoying the sight of horses frolicking in the freedom of the added space. The Wind tosses his head high, rears back trumpeting his dominion over the herd and began a furious gallop around the periphery of the pasture.

"Now he's showing off." I think, exhilarated by the magnificence of The Wind. Many of the mares stop their grazing and watch him run; I wonder what kind of thoughts they have about him. Do they have thoughts? Can a horse think? Of course they can, can't they? The Wind seems to know what I think; therefore he has to be thinking along with me. One mare seems more intent on The Wind than the others, turning her body to face him as he runs. I vow to remember that one; she's for The Wind, just as Diane is for me. I smile warmly as my thoughts return to the activities of yesterday and to Diane.

"A joust!" Jim shouts excitedly, interrupting the mental image of Diane in the prairie grass.

"What?" Bo asks.

"A joust." Jim repeats jumping from his perch on the rails.

"What are you talking about?" I ask as J.D., Bo and Socrates look at Jim bewildered.

"You know. Like in the medieval days we've read about." Getting no response he continues. "The Knight on his horse tries to topple the rider from another horse."

Bo looks at me dumbfounded as I look at the horses frolicking in the pasture.

"Not those horses dummy!" Jim laughs slapping my arm. "Socrates! Come here!" He yells motioning to the gentle giant a few yards away. Socrates approaches cautiously looking at Jim for guidance. Grasping him gently by the arm Jim positions himself behind Socrates and said. "Bend over a little." As the big man bends over, Jim leaps on his back exclaiming. "I have my horse. Bo! Jump on Bill!"

Bo and I look at one another realizing his intent. A smile spreads on my lips as I motion to Bo. "I think we're going to have to kick this whippersnappers' arse! Whadda ya say?"

"YEE HAH!" Bo screams leaping on my back as we charge the other knight. Socrates' immense strength withstands our initial charge and the riders lock hands as the 'horses' pull against each other attempting to dislodge the rider. Trying to pull the large man over is folly and we cannot make headway against Socrates' considerable strength. Jim has another advantage as Bo does not have a left hand and can only push with that side. His right hand is more developed than Jim's and, with an equal mount; would easily vanquish his foe. The difference is Socrates. In a contest of strength Jim chose the right mount. The combined weight of Jim and Socrates exceeds ours by nearly fifty pounds and we are losing the battle, being pushed and pulled at will from our positions. Defeat is something I will not accept, therefore if we must lose, we will inflict as much damage as possible before going down. Changing direction, I charge our foe. The force with which they were pulling coupled with our sudden change of direction causes Socrates to lose balance and all four jousters topple over one another in a laughing heap.

"We win!" I declare. "We are on top, we won! We won!"

"No! No! No!" Jim protests, laughing heartily.

"Boys." J.D. says calmly from his position on the fence rail.

"You didn't win!" Jim protests. "We won!"

"Did not!" I said playfully punching Jim on the arm.

"BOYS!" J.D. says sharply. "We've got company."

Four riders crossed the fence line nearly a mile to the south and east of us waiting for a fifth to replace the rail. They are headed for our farmhouse.

J.D.'s horse is nearby and I jump on him with J.D. leaping on behind.

Uncle John and my father are in front of the house as we arrive, the riders a short distance behind us. Hurriedly retrieving my pistols from the barn, I thrust them into my belt and assume a position alongside my father. J.D. takes a position alongside the corral, his Sharps rifle comfortably held in the crook of his arm.

The riders slow to a walk as they near the complex. Dressed alike, although not in a recognizable uniform; each clad in a long gray or black slicker nearly covering the back of their horse. A large black hat pulled low over their forehead conceals much of their eyes. Red leather leggings cling tightly to their shins; these five are a sinister looking group.

"Don't ever be without your horse again." I admonish myself as I wish Jim, Bo and Socrates were here to even out the numbers. Why do I feel threatened? These men could be friendly. No, a pair of riders may not be threatening, five riders mean trouble.

They are an imposing group. The first man, presumably the leader is of average height but quite round, heavy or stout perhaps a more appropriate term. His red cheeks puff up against his neck, the week long growth of beard not covering them completely. Close set eyes peer over the round cheeks under bushy red eyebrows. A dirty black hat nearly covers his eyes peering out from under the brim, his gaze not deviating from the trio of Andersons standing before him. Short stubby fingers grasp the reins in his left hand, his right hand hovering close to a holstered revolver inside the edge of his slicker. The other riders are of similar ilk, near the same height but varying in weight. All have not shaved for several days. The next to last rider fixes his gaze on J.D., ignoring the others, intent on the man in the corral.

The leader pulls his horse near us positioning his mount to look at us over his left shoulder; his right hand flips the slicker over the back of his horse as he smiles at us. I cannot see if he has drawn his weapon. "Howdy." He began, his smile revealing yellowish teeth. "You the Anderson's?"

I study the group behind their leader; none smiling, apparently ready to draw their weapons at a moments notice. The rider intent on J.D. does not look our way. Mentally calculating our odds of survival if we engage these men, I surmise that five against two are not good odds. My father and Uncle are unarmed and not fighting men.

"We are." I answer.

"Well then. How are you gentlemen this fine day?" He asks in an attempt at small talk. Perhaps he is innocently trying to befriend us but a look at his companions quickly dispels that notion.

"We're doing quite well thank you. And you?" I respond.

"Oh. Pretty good. Pretty good." He said nodding in time with his response, his shoulders rising and falling with his head. "Looks like a good start to the year. I see you've got your garden in and what is that, tomatoes coming up?"

I look past the house at the garden. "Yes they are."

"Looks like a fine stand you have there. Probably, what, four weeks before they are ripe?"

He didn't come here with four men to talk about tomatoes but I answer. "Something like that."

"What else you got in there."

Uncle John responds with pride. "Corn, beans, peppers, carrots, potatoes, the usual stuff to feed a family."

"Must be a big family." the man on the horse commented. Ah hah! He's assessing our strength!

"Oh we've got…" John began before I cut him off.

"Just the four of us." I interrupt. Is it better to say less than or more than actual. I opted for less. Perhaps he would feel more at ease if he thinks we are a small unit. Or, maybe they think they can overcome us more readily if we are a small group. Maybe I should have said we are twenty. It is done now.

"What about the dresses on the line?" He said pointing toward the house with his left hand. His right hand remains out of view.

Josi had hung out the wash and unless one of us will claim to wear a dress I had to acknowledge the presence of females. "That would be my sister's dresses." I admit.

Adjusting himself in the saddle he looked around before continuing. "And just how many sisters would that be sir?" He is no longer smiling. Soon he will reveal his true purpose.

"That would be three sir." I reply not intentionally mocking him.

"And the men with you in the pasture?" he asked leaning toward me.

"Neighbors." I answer without wavering from his gaze.

He stares unmoving for a few seconds then sits up in his saddle still looking at me. "Neighbors." He said slowly and paused again. "Then what of your brother sir?"

His probing questions are starting to annoy me. "Your purpose here?" I ask.

Ignoring my question he offers one of his own. "Would it be William, or James I am addressing?"

Obviously he knows about us and whatever his purpose, it will do no good to attempt deceit.

"I am Bill."

"And James?"

"Not here." I state curtly. "I asked your purpose here."

He smiles as he looks around before leaning forward, placing his right arm on his saddle horn. He has not drawn his weapon. "We are part of the Seventh Kansas Cavalry here to recruit for Colonel Jennison and the preservation of the Union." He states calmly, staring into my eyes. "The Union needs boys like you to fight the Missouri and Confederate menace nearby."

He knows our names and probably knows we are from Missouri, and may know we fought for the Missouri State Guard, if so is there a reason why he would seek our support? The community is well aware we do not support the Jayhawkers or any other Union group. There's something else.

"Not interested." I reply.

"You Kansas boys or not?" he asks sharply leaning back in his saddle, dropping his right hand to his side.

"Jennisons' Jayhawkers. Red legs." Uncle John exclaims softly.

The man on his horse acknowledges Uncle John with a quick glance. Doc Jennison is credited with burning Osceola, Missouri a year ago. His raids into Missouri are infamous among Missourians and his band of about two hundred men are both hated and feared.

Jennison's man looks at me again and says as if a command. "We also need horses and you have a substantial herd out there. Kansas is engaged in a war with the Confederacy, and as an officer of a duly constituted military force you realize I am authorized to use whatever methods necessary to obtain those horses." The intent of the visit is now clear.

"That wouldn't be wise!" yells Jim from the loft of the barn, clicking back the hammer of his carbine. Three other loud clicks follow. Bo and Socrates? Frank Hodges must have joined in.

The smile melts from the face of the Jayhawker and slowly he turns his head toward the barn. As he does, I slip a Colt forty four from my trousers. He caught my movement and returns his gaze toward my pistol.

"Obviously we may consider, Mr. Anderson, that if you are not for us, then you are against us?

To oppose Colonel Jennison will not be wise son." He said his eyes fixed on mine.

"GGGEETT OWOOT!" My father began, stepping haltingly forward raising his finger to point at the officer. "OWOOT! OWOOT! GETTT!" He staggers forward, shouting and waving his finger at the Jayhawkers.

The officer looks at my father with disdain. "Is that your answer Anderson?"

"You heard my father. He has answered for all of us." I say holding my voice on an even keel.

The Jayhawker looks toward the barn, at J.D. then motions to his mates nudging his horse in the direction from which they had come. The rider menacingly staring at J.D. is slow to move, the last to follow.

"I have a feeling we haven't seen the last of them." Bo said as he, Jim, Frank and Socrates join us in watching the Jayhawkers ride off.

"You think they will be back?" Uncle John asks, his voice cracking slightly.

"They want our horses, but now it is also a matter of pride. Yes! They'll be back." Jim states quietly.

He is right of course. We turned them away because we caught them off guard. Is this a reconnaissance party or is Doc Jennisons' main group nearby? If they are, they'll be back today or tomorrow and take by force what we would not give, our horses.

Our intention was to sell much of our stock to the Confederacy or State Guard but there is no time to contact them. We have heard the Union army in Leavenworth is offering a fair price and we are soon on the trail to deliver as many head as we can handle. Selling our stock to the Union was not our intent but at least they will not be taken by Jennisons' Red Legs. Is that the lesser of two evils? Diane, Ginny and Kay join the five able bodied men to deliver eighty two horses to Leavenworth. Uncle John and Josi are left behind with Jacob Anderson and J.D. Couey to look after our place. Thirty three young colts and a few brood mares are left behind with which to begin a new herd.

The "fair" price we negotiate for our horses turns out to be fair for the Union not the Andersons. Bo mutters as we begin our return trip home. "Damn Yankees!"

"Yankees!" I say with a laugh. "You realize that as we live in Kansas we can be considered Yankees?"

"Not the same thing!" Bo argues. "We don't side with Yankee principles and don't have to be Yankees! Why do we have to be on any side?"

"It's called an oath of allegiance." Frank Hodges interjects. "You're either for the Union or you are against it. Neutrality is not allowed, Jennisons' man said it, and it's true."

"But that's for the people of Missouri! They are required to take an oath of allegiance not us." Bo replies angrily.

"Not necessarily true." Frank continues, contemplating the political strife between the neighboring States. "Kansans have not been required to take an oath as have those of Missouri, but what side do you suppose the Jayhawkers consider us to be on?" We know the answer. Frank states softly, speaking to no one and everyone. "If you're not for us... you are against us."

Smoke is visible in the distance as we approach our home. Jim looks at me, a strained look in his eyes. Bo whips his horse into a gallop followed closely by Socrates.

I hold The Wind in check as I watch the riders put distance between us. I am puzzled as I see them cross the fence line a quarter mile ahead without stopping. Why are there no rails? Jim points at the forms of horses lying in the pasture.

"What is it Billy?" Ginny asks. I shake my head as I urge The Wind slowly forward. "Jim? What's going on?" Ginny pleads with her brother who also starts forward, eyes fixed on the wooded area around our house where the smoke is rising.

"Josi." I say softly as I push The Wind into a run. "JOSI!" I scream and furiously whip The Wind into a hard gallop. "JOSI!"

Smoke comes from the remains of our house and barn. Reining in The Wind while a hundred yards away, I examine the scene in near shock. Jim rides past but reins in as he too spots the two figures swinging at the end of ropes attached to the header of our corral gate. Socrates has reached one of the figures and is struggling to cut it down. Bo spreads a blanket on the ground between the corral and burned out house. Ginny and Kay pull up alongside and we walk our horses into the yard.

Ginny moans. "Oh Daddy!"

Socrates finally cut through the rope attached to the neck of Uncle John, drops him to the ground and turns toward the swaying body of my father.

"Socrates." I say softly, stopping him where he is on the header. I want my father lowered gently and nudge The Wind alongside him. His neck had not snapped as he was hung and he suffered greatly choking to death. His face is a dark reddish blue color, eyes bulging and red from the blood backing up in his head. His blackened tongue protrudes with dried yellowish spittle on his chin. I touch his face, it is cold. There is a foul odor as he lost control of his bodily functions before dying.

The giant man hands me the knife and I began to saw through the rope. As the final strands separate I ease my father into Jims' arms to gently lay beside his brother.

I hear crying. Ginny and Kay hold tightly to the pommel of their saddle as they weep.

"Josi." I say softly before turning and scream. "JOSI! WHERE IS JOSI?"

"Bill!" Whirling toward the sound I see Mrs. Hodges galloping toward us from the river. "She's OK Bill! She's alright! She's at our house! She's safe but..." She is at my side avoiding my eyes.

"But what?" I ask loudly. "BUT WHAT?"

Mrs. Hodges looks into my eyes then, turning toward her house, says softly. "Come with me."

Frank Hodges meets us as we approach. He and Diane had turned toward their own place as we rode toward our burning buildings. He said nothing as we dismount. I search his eyes until he looks away.

"Take the girls Frank." Mary Hodges directs her husband who dutifully holds the arms of Ginny and Kay. Mary leads me into the house with Jim close behind. It is dark inside, the curtains are drawn and my eyes not yet adjusted from the bright sunshine. My eyes strain toward a whimpering sound.

The whimpering stops. "Billy?" Josi murmurs pleadingly, her voice muffled and slurred.

She is curled up on the Hodges' bed, her face nearly covered by her reddish-golden tresses. Diane steps aside as I kneel beside the bed and gently brush the hair from Josi's face with my fingers. My heart stops. Her lips are puffed and cracked, dried blood evident from her nose. Lifting her hand I see her left eye is nearly swollen shut from the blows that struck her.

"Mrs. Hodges? Did they...?" My voice wavers in anger.

Mary Hodges does not reply and I whirl toward her. She nods her head slowly not wanting to speak the answer. They had.

Josi began to cry as I lift her in my arms and hold her tightly. She sobs uncontrollably as I hold her close.

After Josi drifts off to a troubled sleep, Mary Hodges relates the events of the morning. Hearing gunfire from the direction of our house, she saw several riders in the area of our barn before flames engulf the buildings. After seeing to the safety of her own children she rode to our place seeing first the sight of two men hanging from the corral header. Jacob was kicking at the air, choking to death, hands tied behind him. John Anderson, already dead, swayed gently back and forth.

Thirty to forty riders were milling about as she approached. Two men pull another man from a rumpled form on the ground she did not immediately recognize as Josi. Mary rushed toward the kicking Jacob but was restrained by the riders until Jacob stopped kicking and began to sway unmoving from the end of his rope.

"Stay out of this!" A Red Leg hissed at her as they rode off.

Mary ran to the swaying Jacob and tried to lift hopeful of getting air into him. Jacob's knees buckle and she could not lift him to loosen the grip of the rope around his neck. Desperately she struggled until the futility of her efforts became apparent. It was then she heard moaning behind her. Reluctantly she released Jacob and turned toward the sound of crying.

Josi had risen to a sitting position and was pulling her dress over uncovered legs. She managed a muffled scream as she looked at her father and uncle swaying from the ropes. Mary rushed to her side.

We found J.D. later with a bullet in his back. We surmised he was on his way to warn the others when the Jayhawkers shot him off his horse. He probably did not live to see the carnage.

The colts had been shot for spite and the mares taken or scattered. J.D.s' horse was not found.

As the last shovel of dirt was patted on the three graves, I turn to leave. Mr. Hodges called after me. "Don't you want to say something over their graves, to pray for their souls?"

I stop. Carefully choosing my words I say. "You pray for their souls Frank." Turning halfway I add, shaking with anger, revenge in my heart. "While you are at it, you may pray for the souls of Jayhawkers as well, as I will not stop until every Jayhawker is dead! Or I am."

Chapter Fifteen

We see the smoke from their campfire before dusk and reach a point a quarter mile from their camp an hour later. Jim and Socrates remain with the horses as Bo and I carefully make our way to thirty yards from the campfire. Five men, in addition to their prisoner, surround the campfire unaware of our presence. We do not encounter a sentry as we approach, surely they would not be so careless as to not post sentries?

"Dere boy! Get used ta dat noose 'round yo neck 'cause when we gits to Eudora, we's gwon hang ya, ya hoss thievin' murderin' som bitch!" The soldier in Union blue says to his prisoner, a short stout blond boy no more than fourteen or fifteen. He is tied to a small tree about two or three inches in diameter cut off seven feet above the ground. A hangman's noose is around his neck and the small tree trunk, pulled taut to keep the boy upright against the tree. A branch from the upper portion of the tree had been trimmed to place in the crook of his arms and behind the trunk and his feet are also tied behind that trunk. His hands are tied in front and he must pull against the bar and tree trunk to keep the noose from choking him. As long as the boy is able to maintain an upright stance he will not choke.

I whisper to Bo. "You circle to the left, I'll go this way. If you see a sentry, don't let him make a sound. If he does cry out, shoot 'im and high tail it for the horses. I'll meet you there." Quietly we circle the fire until we meet on the opposite side. No sentries, what foolish soldiers. They must feel secure in Jayhawker country, halfway between Ottawa and Eudora, Kansas. Secure enough that four of the five had bed down to sleep. The fifth soldier is seated on a log slowly poking at the fire. Presumably assigned the task of guard duty, he is not very attentive.

Carefully we had circled the camp and I am but a few feet away when the soldier stands and places a couple of limbs on the fire. I lie still, certain he will see me when he returns. Unbelievably, he does not look my way as he sits down, with his back to me. The sentry has his right hand in his pocket as I rise and quietly close the gap between us.

The boy attached to the tree draws in a sharp breath as I stand. The sentry looks at him quizzically before my left hand covers his mouth and my right hand drives the point of my knife into his Adam's apple. Pulling the blade deep into his throat, I hear and feel cracking sounds as muscles and blood vessels are severed. I pull the knife blade toward me until it strikes something hard, probably his spine. Supporting his body against mine, my hand over his mouth, his arms flail harmlessly against the air. A warm liquid oozes over my hand. Jerking the blade sideways and twisting, there is a snapping sound as I enlarge the hole in his neck. He falls limply against me as I raise a bloodied finger to my lips to shush the boy and gently lower the dead soldier to the ground.

The blond boy is grinning with glee and again I press a finger to my lips to quiet him. Too Late! Either he made a noise or we are unlucky as one of the soldiers suddenly sits upright and yells. "Hey!" They are the ones that are unlucky. Bo shoots him before I can get my pistol out of my trousers. A second man sits upright and looks at me just before my first shot enters his left eye, snapping his head backward. I try to get a second shot into his right eye before his head falls forward. Damn, not fast enough! The second shot enters his brain above the right eye. A third soldier is felled by Bo, the fourth throws up his hands to surrender. I motion for him to stand and he obliges in time to catch three rounds in his chest. Walking to where he lay, I place the palm of my hand over the holes to measure the spread. Cody would be proud.

The boy tied to the tree is wide eyed and gleefully cackling almost choking himself on the rope around his neck as he bounces up and down. I say to him. "They aint gonna hang ya boy. You may hang some day, but they aint gonna do it!" I laugh.

"Damn! You done 'em in good!" He exclaims after I remove the rope from around his neck.

"They is daid, daid, daid!" The ebullient smile fades as he looks at me. "You gwon kill me?"

I look at the boy whose blond hair cut short on top cascades down to his shoulders in back. Black sideburns seem out of place with blond, almost white hair. Blue eyes sparkle above a near perpetual smile flashing dimples easily with each grin. A closer look reveals a man of five foot six inches, not stout but with bulging muscles and a barrel chest. A man? His facial features appear to be those of a boy. Man or boy, he did something against the Union or the soldiers would not have him in custody.

"What were they gonna hang ya for?" I ask.

"Nuttin much." He grins sheepishly. "Stole one of their horses." Free of his bonds, he rubs his wrists and neck where the ropes had been. I wait. "And… some food." He continues, looking away while smiling, as if embarrassed.

"Is that all?"

"Well... no... I kinda kilt da guy watchin' da horses." He said with a gleam in his eye.

"And just for that they want to hang you." Bo remarks sarcastically. "What is this world coming to? Can't anybody take a joke?"

"What's yer name?" I ask, ignoring Bo's sarcasm.

"Archie. Archie Clement." He replies shyly.

"How old are you Archie Clement?" I continue.

"Nineteen." He states but looks away.

"How old?" I know he is lying.

"Nineteen."

"Bull shit! How old are you?" I ask sternly.

He looks at me. "Aw shucks, I'll be seventeen next month." He admits. He doesn't look that old, but he does have a muscular build.

"Seventeen huh."

"Yessir." He says quietly, his eyes on the ground. "You gwon make me go?"

"Go? Do you want to go?"

"You gwon kill more Yankee's?" The smile growing as he looks into my face.

"Jayhawkers." I correct.

He nods and with an evil smile, says, "I wants ta stay wid you den."

Sincerity is in his eyes as I study him for a moment. "Want to kill some Jayhawkers do you?"

"Yas suh, I do." He nods vigorously.

"How can I be sure you have the stomach to kill a man?"

His face goes blank for a moment before the impish smile reappears and his eyes sparkle as he asks for my knife. I hesitate before withdrawing the knife, flip it a half turn, and extend it to him handle first. Still smiling he peers into my eyes as he takes the knife from my hand. Flipping it with his right hand he turns toward the bodies beside the dying fire, grabbing a handful of hair, he lifts a soldier into a sitting position. Still grinning, he quickly slices around the top of the man's head until a large portion of the man's hair comes off. He raises the scalp triumphantly in the air, lets out a whoop and smears the bloodied scalp over his face.

Bo nods and states quietly. "He's got the stomach for it."

"Someone is coming!" We raise our guns in the direction of rustling leaves.

"Bill!" Jim yells before bursting into sight.

"Here!" I reply angrily. "Damn it Jim! What if we'd been killed and you come runnin' up on the Jayhawkers like that? They'd a killed you for sure! You gotta approach every situation as if your life depends on it, because it does. Now damn it, get over here!"

Jim starts to apologize but stops when he sees Archie's bloodied face. "Who is that?"

I ponder the answer as I retrieve my knife from Archies' hand. The boys' smile has faded slightly as he studies my face. Finally I answer. "This is Archie Clement... the newest member of our gang."

A huge smile spreads across Archies' face as he grabs my hand, pumping it vigorously. "Thank you! Thank you suh! You ant gwon regret dis! You ant gwon regret dis a 'tall!"

Jim notices the scalp in the newcomers hand and exclaims. "Oh my God!" recognizing its' relationship to the blood on the boys' face.

"What?" I ask in a manner that implies. 'What is the matter with you? He has done no wrong! I am not repulsed by his act, why should you be?'

"What?" Jim responds implying that I should be repulsed. "I thought you wanted to kill Jayhawkers?" He says angrily.

"So these guys got in the way!" I reply, exasperated with his questions. "So what? You said you want to avenge our fathers' death, and especially revenge for Josi's... for the way they... treated our sister! Are they not worse than Archie? What kind of beast could have done what was done to her? And why? To beat a woman! To… to… do you think that is a civilized man? Yes, I am anxious to reduce the population of Jayhawkers, and Archie will help us do that!"

There are five of us now preying on small parties of Jayhawkers that come to and from Lawrence, Kansas. Little Arch Clement is proving to be an adept killer using a knife to dispatch his victims and excitedly anticipates each encounter with our avowed enemy. Jim is losing his vigor for revenge and his disdain for lil' Archie grows.

"He's an animal Bill! He's not like us, all he wants to do is kill. It doesn't matter whether it is Jayhawker, Yankee or innocent bystander, he enjoys it! Bill? You gotta get rid of him!" Jim argues.

That gives me pause. How is that different from me? I want to kill every Jayhawker, and I am not an animal. "Do you or do you not wish to avenge our family?" I seek to determine if my brother is turning against the cause.

Jim considers his answer carefully as he studies my eyes. There is softness in his eyes and I wonder if he can be trusted when trouble comes. Will he run as he did at Wilsons' Creek? Shoot, I was scared then, but I didn't run! No one can call me a coward!

"Yes." Jim sighs. "I wish for the people that killed and... and... injured our family to pay dearly for their offenses." His voice rising, he argues. "But these people, did they hang our father and uncle? Did they... rape and beat our sister? If they are the guilty parties, we have been avenged. Are all Jayhawkers killers and rapists?"

"Yes! They are!" I exclaim. "They are the ones pillaging the Missouri countryside. It is the Jayhawkers that entered our home destroying the tranquility we built!"

"But which ones?" He interrupts.

I look at him in exasperation. "I don't know which ones! I don't care which ones! Do you want me to ask them first? Oh excuse me sir but we need to know if you are the son-of-a-bitch that raped our sister so's we'll know whether or not to kill you!" I sarcastically yell at him. "They are all sons o' bitches and deserve to die!" I calm down a little and continue. "If they want to live, let 'em stop being Jayhawkers."

Jim looks at me in amazement a few moments then turns away shaking his head.

"Jim?"

"What?" He yells angrily at me as he continues to walk away.

"Are you with me...or against me?" My question stops him in his tracks. His shoulders slump and he sighs. Drawing a deep breath he looks up, and walks toward me. Stopping a few inches in front of me he speaks softly through clenched teeth. "Is that the choice you are giving me? Is that what this has come down to? To fight with you... or against you?"

We stare at each other, neither speaking.

Finally his eyes soften and he backs away. "You are my brother. I will not fight against you. If attacked I will defend myself, my comrades… and you. But do not ask me to side with that beast Archie Clement. He's not right in the head Bill! Because of him we will be hunted as wild dogs..."

"Jim!" I interrupt. "He is useful to us. I can control him."

"Control him!" Jim shouts in exasperation. "Control him!"

I had not given much thought to that aspect. Archie has been by my side ever since his rescue, literally hanging on every word I speak. He makes me feel good, does everything I ask without hesitation, without question. I know it is hero worship but so what? I like the attention!

"Control him?" Jim exclaims again. "You mean he is doing what you want him to do?"

"He will do what I say! Leave him alone!" I shout back.

Chapter Sixteen

Bo serves as our eyes and ears, going into Jayhawker camps to learn their intentions and bring us news. With but one good arm he is considered handicapped, thus mostly ignored and able to roam freely about Lawrence as a beggar. Aiding this harmless image is Socrates; people feel sorry for, yet anxious to be away from, this overgrown retarded boy. The one armed Bo and the simpleton are tolerated as beggars and able to garner information others are powerless to get.

Bo and Socrates report the Jayhawkers are preparing a massive sweep to eradicate a thorn in their side that has recently destroyed three scouting parties.

Archie squeals with delight. "They's talkin' 'bout us! They's talkin' 'bout us!"

"A thorn eh!" I smile. "We'll just see how 'prickly' we can be."

"You're not staying here to fight them are you?" Jim asks. "Bo said they are coming after us with twenty men! We can't fight that many!"

"Jim." I began in a patronizing manner. "We have the element of surprise on our side. We will pick the spot to attack from and in a few minutes their twenty men will be none." I smile. "Archie will take fifteen and we'll take care of the rest."

Archie is smiling at Jim who fails to appreciate the humor.

"Suppose you are right Bill, and we dispatch of twenty men. Will they send forty the next time, or a hundred, two hundred? What then, how many will Archie take care of then?" Jim argues. "If we wish to keep the element of surprise, we must move now and attack from a different place. Bo says they have an idea where we are, so how much of a surprise will it be?"

Bo nods. "That makes sense Bill. They do think they know where we are."

"Aw he's jest chicken." Archie chides at Jim, receiving a hate filled stare in return.

Bo laughs uneasily before slapping Jim on the shoulder. "Naw. It's called prudence aint it Jim?" Turning to me he continues. "I think Jim is right Bill. Let those twenty search these hills whilst we go north, or south, or somewhere else to pick them off one at a time."

Bo is not cowardly and a voice of reason speaking for Socrates as well. Socrates always follows Bo.

I look at the giant and ask. "What say you big fella?"

He shrugs his shoulders as he looks at Bo. "I 'on't know!"

Bo interrupts. "Bill, we heard a lot of talk about Quantrill and what he's doing in Missouri."

"Like what?" I ask turning my attention to Bo. Accounts of an attack on Aubry, Kansas in March mentioned a Bushwhacker named Quantrill that viciously attacked, burning and looting the town. The name strikes a familiar chord and the vision of a droopy eyed officer at Wilsons' Creek came to mind. Could this be the same man?

I ask Jim. "Is that...?" I pause and study my brother.

"Why don't we find out." He says.

Several days later Bo returned from Blue Springs, Missouri with a guide to lead us to Quantrill and his band. The people of Missouri have a different outlook on the guerrilla leader than those of Kansas. A hero to the Missourians, not the savage Kansans regard him as. Our guide cautiously agrees to lead us to the Bushwhacker camp. This term, 'Bushwhacker', does not carry a negative connotation in Missouri where Jayhawker is a vile, hated term.

Several times as we approach farmers in their fields, our guide rises in his saddle to wave his kerchief over his head, explaining it is a signal. The farmers return the signal with a wave of their own. Finally we enter a densely wooded area, our guide identifies as Lake Lotawanna, and the ground slopes sharply away from us.

At water's edge, we are left to mingle with another group of men intent on joining the ranks of Quantrill's Raiders. We discover most are farmers from surrounding counties set upon by

Jayhawkers at one time or another. Others are Southern sympathizers or just spoiling for a fight, a category I place us in.

It is late afternoon when four riders approach the men by the lake and dismount. One is a smallish man of five foot nine inches and one hundred fifty pounds with a commanding bearing about him. His drooping eyelids make him recognizable, William Clarke Quantrill.

"Gentlemen." He began in the familiar low commanding voice heard more than a year ago. "You have come to join the fight for the liberation of Missouri. You have come to....!" He stops abruptly as his gaze falls on me.

"Bloody Bill Anderson!" He exclaims striding to my side, extending his hand. "I wondered if I would ever see you again!" Turning to the other men, he continues. "Gentlemen, we have in our midst one of the bravest... no, make that **the** bravest man I have ever had the privilege of meeting. His exploits at Wilson's Creek are the stuff legends are made of." He motions to the three men accompanying him. "Come here! I want you to meet the man I spoke of so many times! George Todd, William Gregg, Perry Hoy. This... is Bloody Bill Anderson!" He said beaming at me.

"So this is the greatest warrior since Alexander the Great." Perry Hoy smiles, extending his hand toward me, he addresses his leader. "He's a big 'un Bill."

"So, I finally get to meet the legend!" William Gregg says pumping my hand.

George Todd grabs my hand and with a big smile says half to me and half to Quantrill. "Shall we call 'im Bloody for short? We've got too many Bill's around here already."

I nod to each greeting, unsure of how to react to the attention. Archie moves closer, looking into my face. The other men watch curiously as Quantrill and his men fawn over me. Bo smiles and withdraws with Socrates while Jim moves quietly aside, trying to ignore us.

"Come on Todd, Perry, William, let's get on with it." Quantrill finally said. "The oath gentlemen. You men assembled here, I ask for your allegiance, and for your name to be linked with mine. Will you follow orders, be true to your fellows, and kill those who serve and support the Union?"

After hearing the expected affirmative replies he turns to me. "I'll see you later." And, along with the three that came with him, rode away.

Perry Hoy returned an hour later to bring me to Quantrill. Archie mounted as I did.

"Where you going?" Perry said looking at Archie.

Looking at Archie I say softly to Perry, "He goes where I go."

After a pause, Perry motions us to follow.

William Clarke Quantrill sits with several men near a fire; I recognize Todd and Gregg from our earlier meeting. Quantrill rises to greet us. "Bill."

he said quietly, suspiciously eyeing Archie. He continues, "Come over here Bill. I want you to meet some of our men." He places a hand on my shoulder and proudly began to speak; "Bill, these men command the forces assembled here. Our commanding officer, Colonel Upton Hays." A man in his late twenties nods at me. "Colonel Hays commands the Second Arkansas Cavalry, a squadron of which he has brought to join us. Our forces are under his command for the upcoming campaign." He sweeps his hand about indicating the other men assembled. "Some of the men that follow me, George Todd you've met, John Little, James Little." Each man nods as he is introduced. "William Haller, Joseph Gilchrist and James Hendricks. William Gregg you've met, Joseph Vaughn, David Pool, Perry Hoy of course, John Koger and John McCorkle."

Quantrill drops his hand from my shoulder and steps away from me slightly, looking into my eyes. "I want you to take charge of the men down by the lake, get them on a roster, you recall the routine from Wilson's Creek. Choose a couple of Corporals to assist you." Looking at Archie. "Make sure they are loyal men with leadership abilities you trust. Your group will be assigned to George Todds' division."

"Colonel, I'll turn it over to you for your direction." Quantrill said turning to the young Confederate officer.

Although having been identified as an officer of the Confederacy, a tall young man clothed in civilian garb rises to his feet. Long dark hair slightly curled at the ends is pulled behind his ears and cascades over his shoulders. He has the carriage of an officer, a confident swagger as he looks at his men. His mustache rises at the ends as he smiles, exhibiting a row of white teeth.

Colonel Upton Hays nods at me before turning his attention to the group. "Our mission gentlemen, is to attack Colonel Buehl and his Seventh Missouri Cavalry at Independence. More details will be disseminated to company commanders the day before the attack, which will be announced at the appropriate time. For security reasons the particulars are to remain within this group. No one is to leave camp for any reason. Should one of your men wish to leave, you must detain him in any fashion you wish. Up to and including shooting him to prevent news of our intentions from reaching Colonel Buehl."

It suddenly occurs to me that I am attending my first officer's call.

The Colonel continues. "I leave to meet Colonel Hughes and Captain Shelby to plan strategies. Captain Quantrill will direct you at the appropriate time. Gentlemen." He touched his hat in salute as he strode to his waiting horse.

"Independence!" George Todd exclaims as soon as the Colonel is out of range. "You'd better hope you have better luck than the last time Gregg." He pokes at William Gregg and laughs.

"Oh no! I hope I have the same kind of luck!" Gregg exclaims to howls of laughter from his comrades.

William Haller, while laughing, points to me. "Tell Bloody Bill about Independence Will!"

"Aw shucks! You tell 'im, you like tellin' it anyway." William Gregg smiles in mock anger.

"Yeah I do!" William Haller laughs. "It was last February, Bill." he starts, resting his hand lightly on my shoulder, the remainder of the men eagerly await the re-telling of a familiar story. "We rode into Independence with Bill, what was there, eight of us? Yeah, well, anyways we was just goin' to town to do some drinkin', not looking for or expecting trouble, when we run smack dab into a column of Union soldiers outnumbering us at least two to one." His arms excitedly gesticulating as he clearly enjoys telling the story. "Well Todd here, the crazy sombitch, pulls his pistols and with a holler charges right inta them sons-o-bitches! Well! We all musta been crazy that day 'cause we was all chargin and shootin' and hollerin as we went. Shoot! They didn't know what was happenin', didn't know whether to run or to fight. Some did run! Anyways, we was all shootin' and fightin's hard's we could and pretty soon, here comes ol' Gregg here ridin' hell bent for leather trying to get away from this here soldier who's tryin' to chop off po' Gregg's head!" The assembled laugh heartily, recalling the events and enjoying a good natured poke at Gregg.

After pausing to let the laughter subside, William Haller continues. "This soldier was swingin' his saber at po' Gregg's' head an' ol' Gregg was a-ducking and weavin' trying to spur his horse on to greater speeds as the soldier swung again and again. Finally the soldier swung so hard he fell off his horse right on to his head!" He joins in the raucous laughter, mussing William Gregg's' hair who enjoys the repartee' as much as anyone.

"What happened to him?" I ask also enjoying a laugh.

Haller pauses and wipes his hand across his mouth. Looking at me then at Gregg, he burst into laughter again and exclaimed. "Why that son-of-a-bitch cut poor old Gregg's' head clean off, can't you see!" That brought howls of laughter from the men.

I feel myself blushing but laugh and hold my hand up shaking my head. "No! No! I mean what happened to the soldier?"

Gregg answered for Haller. "Hell! That poor som-bitch hadn't hardly got to his feet before Todd put a slug in his face. Dropped him dead in his tracks! Shit! I wanted to get that saber but was too busy high-tailin' it outa there myself!"

"Yeah, that was fun!" George Todd said as he mused over that day.

"And none of you got hurt?" I ask.

The men suddenly grow quiet as heads bow.

William Haller responds after a few seconds. "Naw. Well... we... ah... lost Gabe George and Hop Wood that day."

No one spoke for a while remembering their comrades, until George Todd broke the silence by pointing to Quantrill. "Bill took a bullet in the leg." Then adding with pride. "But he still attended Gabes' funeral right in the midst of them Yankee's! Just stood there payin' his respects as big as you please, leanin' on his cane!"

The looks the men cast at Quantrill tell me how he is revered by them. An uneasy nervousness is felt by many, including myself.

I glance at Archie before asking. "How many of you are there here?"

Quantrill looked up momentarily before responding calmly. "With the new recruits we have perhaps... two hundred or so."

I look around in surprise as I estimated there were less than fifty men in the area. Where are they all?

He notes my surprise and smiles. "You have to find out if your men can handle mules."

"Mules?" I ask.

Quantrill smiles. "Have you ever walked behind a mule pulling a plow?"

"Not behind a mule, a horse." I reply. Looking at the knowing smiles from the other men, I am the only one not in on the joke.

Quantrill explains. "This area of Jackson County as well as Cass, Bates and Vernon counties to the south, is friendly territory for us. We blend in by plowing fields, chopping wood, herding cattle, slopping hogs or doing what any normal farmer would be doing as soldiers pass by. When the call goes out, the farmers answer and fight their enemy, and ours, then return innocently to their farms. We live practically undetected in the midst of our enemy and disappear without a trace much to the chagrin of that enemy."

"Chagrin." John McCorkle snorts. "There you go again Bill, showin' off your book larnin'." He says with an air of sarcasm.

"Don't mind McCorkle. He has a considerable amount of... book larnin'... hisself." Quantrill replies with his own brand of sarcasm.

"Ah yes perfesser, but ah'se ain't never been no teacher now ya hear!" McCorkle says mockingly, speaking as poorly as he can.

Everyone enjoys the camaraderie and I am anxious to be a part of it.

Quantrill turns to me. "Perhaps you should return to your men to take care of sundry administrative and logistical tasks." He says winking at McCorkle. "Did you like those John? Sundry? Logistical? You like that?"

The group howls with laughter as John McCorkle sweeps his hat from his head bowing low to Quantrill. "Sundry? Logistical? OOOOHHH! I yield to your eminent command of the King's English!" He declares rising from an exaggerated bow.

"Come on Archie." I say. "Before we get caught up in this linguistic repartee."

Quantrill and McCorkle draw a sharp breath and look at each other stunned, before McCorkle burst out laughing and pokes at Quantrill. "OOOOHHH!!! Another quarter heard from! How 'bout that un Bill?" The group laughs heartily as Archie and I depart.

Archie cast questioning glances at me as we wind through the trees, ducking branches as we ride to the lakeside area we left a few minutes earlier. "Wha'd ya say?" He finally asks.

Smiling at my little friend I answer. "It was just a good natured discussion."

"Is dat what dose words means?"

"Something like that." I respond dismounting near the men huddled by a small fire built as darkness fell.

Jim approaches. "What's going on?"

"I have been put in charge of this group of men. I need your help and support, Corporal. Do you have any paper?" He looks surprised as I continue. "I need two trusted Corporals and am designating you and Bo to fulfill that role, how 'bout taking down some information on the men for me?"

Archie pouts as he mutters. "Why caint I be a corpal?"

Stepping to a central position among the men, I hold up my arms. "Gentlemen! I have been selected to lead this squad as we fight on the side of William Clarke Quantrill. My name is William

Anderson and I have selected Jeptha Bowles and James Anderson as Corporals. Jim will take your name and age for the roster. Last name first, first name last... right Jim?" I smile at my brother. "Line up in front of Jim and state your name and age."

"Archie Clement." Archie declares quickly scrambling to the head of the line.

"Geez... you dumb... last name first." Jim snapped.

The smile disappears as Archie corrects himself, restating his name and age.

"Bowles, Jeptha. Age 26."

"Socrates Johnson."

Without looking up Jim quietly corrects the giant. "Johnson, Socrates... 20."

"George, Hicks. 19."

"George, Hiram. 19."

"Brothers?" Jim asks the departing man.

"Yassir! Twins!" He proudly replies.

"Cunningham, Albert. 21"

"Swisby, Oscar. 26."

"Skaggs, Larkin. 23."

"Emery, Jeff. 22."

"James, Frank. 19."

"Bell, Thomas. 19."

"Freeman, Will. 17."

"Wade, Sam. 17."

"Baker, Valentine. 18."

"Lisle, Marston. 31."

"Hamet, Jesse. 28."

"Guess, Hiram. 23"

"Guess." Jim looks up abruptly as the man quickly continues. "No! No! That's my name, Hiram Guess... or... I mean, Guess, Hiram. 23."

"Very well!" Jim smiles. "Guess, Hiram. 23. Next!"

"Maxwell, Thomas. 22."

"Robinson, Gooly. 20."

"Fulton, Thomas. 17."

"Burton, Peter. 16."

Jim notices there is no longer a line in front of him. "Is that it?"

"That was the last one. How many?" I ask.

Jim began to count the names on the list. "... nineteen... twenty...twenty one! No! Wait! Twenty three. I don't have our names on the list yet!" Then adds our names.

Anderson, William, 23

Anderson, James, 21

CHAPTER SEVENTEEN

My stomach churns in anticipation of what is coming when we attack Independence. Unlike Lexington, and especially Wilson's Creek, I feel relatively calm in spite of the churning stomach. Could it be I am looking forward to the conflict? We move slowly on the muddied trails as we head for a point nine miles south of Independence.

Union forces at Independence are commanded by Lieutenant Colonel James T. Buehl, of the Seventh Missouri Cavalry. The combined forces of the Seventh, the Second Missouri Cavalry and the Sixth Missouri Infantry are bivouacked a half mile to the West while Colonel Buehl made his quarters in the sumptuous furnishings of the Southern Bank building on Lexington Street. This large stone building, recently erected, rivals in size the courthouse building a block to the Northeast. The foresighted bank president built a combination office/day quarters above the bank and Colonel Buehl commandeered these quarters for, ahem, 'military purposes'.

Scouting parties report the Colonels' personal guard of sixteen men is quartered in a building across the street from the bank. The Provost Marshall and his guard are at the county jail across the street from the courthouse on Main Street a block north of Colonel Buehl. Guard posts of four to six men are posted at Spring Street to the south, Walnut Street to the southeast and Lexington to the east. No more than fifty men are located in the immediate vicinity of the commanding officer of the Union forces at Independence.

"Todd!" Quantrill excitedly addresses his friend. "Marshall Carson has been jailed on a murder charge!"

Todds' mouth drops for a moment before he swallows and asks. "At the Independence jail?" I hear hatred in Todds' voice as he stares at Quantrill who nods.

Leaning toward Perry Hoy I whisper. "What is it about this Marshall?"

Perry glances at Todd before answering. "The Marshall caught Todd drunk one night a couple years ago and, well, George probably was somewhat disorderly, maybe even obstinate. At any rate, the Marshall pistol whipped him real bad that night. That's where George got the scars above his left ear. Even as the Marshall was beating him, as George was lying on the ground barely able to move, he was promising the Marshall he was going to kill him. I have no doubt that is one promise George will keep!"

The southern forces gathered at the summit southeast of Independence the afternoon of August

10, 1862 number near five hundred. Confederate Colonels John T. Hughes, Gideon W. Thompson and Upton Hays are commanding with Colonel Hughes the senior officer.

Shortly before dusk Bill Quantrill returned from officer's call with diagrams detailing our role in the upcoming conflict. "We got it! We got the assignment of dispatching Colonel Buehl!" He gushed as he gathers his officers about him. "Todd! You get your wish as well. Take yours' and Jacksons' squad, take out the guard post on Lexington and proceed to take the jail. Kill the Provost and anyone else that resists." Adding with a smile. "If you wish to visit your old friend in jail... we understand."

Smoothing off a large area of dirt on the ground, Quantrill draws a crude map of Independence. Lines paralleling and intersecting each other are drawn in the dirt. "Spring Street." he said indicating a north/south Street. "The guard post is here... approximately two hundred yards from Buehls' headquarters which are... here!" He draws a box in the dirt. "Lexington is this east/west street fronting Buehls' location. The guard post is here Todd. Normally no more than six men are in the post behind a fallen log. There is little other cover so it should be no problem for you, but they are close to the central area, about one hundred or so yards out. Kill them quickly and proceed to... here." Quantrill points to the map. "This is the courthouse, the jail is across Main Street... but of course you know that don't you Todd."

George Todd does not smile nor acknowledge Quantrills' humor. He is intent on the drawings and his own thoughts. Fire grows in Todds' eyes.

Quantrill returns to the dirt map and indicates. "I will lead the remainder of our force up... here... Spring Street, overrun this guard post... here, and proceed directly to Buehls' quarters. It is imperative that our attack starts first... Todd? The primary focus is to kill Buehl and personal feuds must be secondary to that objective! Understood? You wait until I start the attack?" Todd nods his head slowly.

"Perry. Take eight men to this outpost, um, right here on Walnut Street. It is the weakest post, only four men. Rejoin us at the bank when you're done. The main force under Colonel Hughes will attack the tent city to the west. Buehl does not believe we will attack and his lack of concern will cost him dearly. He reportedly did fortify the bank building by moving in munitions and arms yesterday therefore it is imperative we move rapidly while we still have the element of surprise. Buehls' personal guards are across the street, if they get into the bank building it will be difficult to dislodge them. We only have a few seconds after taking out this post on Spring Street to prevent the soldiers from reaching the bank."

William Clarke Quantrill stood solemnly looking at his charges. "Gentlemen, we have nine miles to cover in darkness. We attack at first light. Prepare yourselves."

The trek takes nearly six hours; many of the men take the reins of their horses and walk alongside. In the dark we stumble over fallen limbs or rocks jutting out of the ground in this valley meandering north toward Independence. Socrates falls as his horse steps off the bank into the water of the Little Blue River. The resulting splash and laughter would have given us away had we not been three miles from our objective.

We reach that objective before first light and quiet ourselves and our horses. The sky is beginning to lighten when there is gunfire to the northeast. The soldiers in the guard post jump to their feet and turn toward the sound. A few seconds later the lead riders of Quantrill's group overwhelm these Union soldiers at their post before they get off more than a couple shots.

The breaking daylight is bright enough for us to see forms scurrying toward the bank as we descend upon them. Bright flashes and smoke from erupting pistols and carbines fill the air. The rider next to me falls from his saddle. He had not taken a shot, had not been in battle more than a couple minutes, but Will Freeman is dead at the age of seventeen.

The flash is visible before I hear the report of the carbine. I see the smoke and startled expression of the soldier behind the carbine who had me in his sights and is surprised he missed. The charge from my Colt tears off part of the right side of his head. He needn't worry about his marksmanship any longer.

We feared what may happen if we are unable to prevent Buehl's guards from reaching the bank. This stone fortress is practically impenetrable. Three soldiers lay dead outside the bank which means as many as thirteen made it safely inside. We ride by firing at the bank but the volleys from within are more damaging to us. Quantrill orders us to take cover.

Sounds of gunfire near the jail soon diminish. Mere minutes have passed since the attack began and shadows are clearly defined by the first rays of dawn. I marvel at the sight of shadows formed on and by the stone blocks atop the bank building, and watch as shadows slowly move with the emerging dawn.

Archie and I make our way into the building across from the bank. The upstairs of this general store, until moments ago, had been the resting place of Colonel Buehl's elite guard. Blankets, saddle gear, clothing and some ammunition is scattered about in disarray, a testimony to the companies hasty departure. Two windows face the bank and I set up at the one on the left leaving the window on the right to Archie.

The four windows facing us in the bank building are above us preventing us from firing down on them. Conversely they are able to fire down on us, making our position more tenuous. It isn't much of a disadvantage but we curse our bad luck. The western most window of the bank is directly across from my window, the others being further to my left. The sun rising in the east will be in our eyes as we face south, inhibiting our effectiveness even more.

"See anybody Bill?" Archie calls out between shots.

"Nope. You?"

"Nope." He replies peering carefully out his window as he squeezes off another round.

"Then whatcha shootin' at?" I laugh relaxing against the wall. My gun dangles nonchalantly at the floor as my forearm rests on my knee.

Archie looks at me in surprise before he too laughs and leans against the wall in a similar fashion. Our laughter is cut short as William Quantrill, William Haller, William Gregg and John McCorkle climb the steps into the room.

John smiles as he looks at me. "What's this, a meeting of the Bills?" Then turning to my companion; "What are we doin' here Archie?"

"I'se jest tryin' to shoot somebody in da bank." Archie says not recognizing the joke.

Gregg snorts a laugh as he casts a glance toward Archie and smiles knowingly at McCorkle. Quantrill ignores them, peers carefully out the window at the bank and glances about the room quickly. "We'll set up in here." He said.

Occasional cannon fire is heard from the west and I wonder how the battle at the Union encampment is going. We outnumber the Union forces and, with the element of surprise, there is no reason to expect anything but a favorable outcome. Sporadic gunfire pops from rooftops and windows as we keep the soldiers heads down inside the bank building. We have them surrounded, they cannot escape, but only a fool would attempt to rush that formidable structure.

George Todd and David Pool stride triumphantly into the room and stop instantly when Quantrill bellows. "Todd! You were to wait until I started the charge! Because you wouldn't wait, the soldiers made it into the bank and we'll play hell getting at Buehl now! Why didn't you wait?"

Todd stares open mouthed at Quantrill, trying to respond to the ferocity of his friends attack. Finally he whirls and without a word, leaves the room. David Pool is surprised and about to follow Todd when Quantrill intones a quiet question. "How'd you do with the Provost?" Pool shrugs, holding his palms upward in a gesture of futility. "He got away, or he wasn't there! His guards ran as we rode up so we freed the prisoners in the jail... well... all but one that is." A smile reappears on his face briefly. "George won't have any more trouble from that Marshall that's for sure!"

Three hours pass and we are no closer to getting Buehl out of the bank than when we started. William Haller walked to the window I sit near and, keeping out of the line of fire, yells. "Hey Buehl! Come on outta there!" The obscenity laced response brings light laughter as he is told what he could do to himself. Quantrill notes the response and takes Hallers' place near the window.

"Buehl! Colonel Buehl! This is Captain Quantrill! Come out, give yourself up! You will be given every chance to come out peacefully. Surrender now and you will not be harmed!" Quantrill waits several seconds for the answer. He draws another breath as if to yell again when the answer is heard. "Go to hell Quantrill!"

Captain Quantrill exhales and smiles. This is the answer he anticipated. "Colonel, there are frame buildings attached to the bank on both sides. I have given orders for them to be burned if you do not surrender. Think about it Colonel, you have to come out sooner or later. If you don't come out soon we will carry your roasted body out from under the charred rubble along with those of your men!"

This time the answer was more emphatic. "Kiss my ass you traitorous raving lunatic!"

Quantrill leaned out the window and shouts. "Burn the buildings! Burn 'em out!" barely pulling back in time to avoid gunfire from the banks' windows. We return fire and continue covering fire as men on the streets touch torches to the buildings adjacent to the bank.

"What's going on here Captain?" Colonel Thompson questions from the doorway.

"Colonel Thompson!" The Captain whirls in surprise, then hurriedly describes the situation. "I've given instructions for the bank to be burned sir!"

"Countermand that order Captain." The Colonel said sharply walking toward the windows.

"Sir? Colonel Hughes?"

"Dead, Captain! I am in command now and you will not burn anyone out... Damn!" The Colonel exclaims as he sees the enlarging fires across the street. "Colonel Buehl! Colonel Buehl, this is Colonel Gideon W. Thompson, Commander of the Confederate forces gathered here. We have taken your camp along with two hundred or so killed, wounded and captured Union soldiers. Your forces are no longer resisting. It is futile for you to barricade yourself in a building that will soon burn down around you. As an officer of the opposing forces you will be accorded the respect due you. Colonel you and your men will not be harmed! I implore you, save yourself and them!"

The voice, more subdued than earlier, answers. "Colonel Thompson? Did you order the bank to be burned?"

"I did not. I arrived too late to countermand that order."

After a pause, Colonel Buehl replies. "Do I have your assurance that my men will be paroled unharmed and not turned over to that renegade Quantrill?"

Colonel Thompson looks sharply at Captain Quantrill before responding. "You will be the prisoner of, and under the care of, Colonel Gideon W. Thompson, Commander of the Second Missouri Infantry of the Confederate States of America. Captain Quantrill is under my command and will obey my orders sir. As my prisoner you will be treated with the respect and courtesy reserved for competent adversaries." The Colonel stands erect and stared at the Captain for emphasis. Apparently this officer does not hold our Captain in as high esteem as we do.

The building to the west of the bank is totally engaged in fire and we do not have to wait long for a response. "Colonel Thompson! We will surrender to you sir! My men are coming out; I will follow and offer my sword in surrender." Colonel Buehl calls out in a disconsolate voice.

"Captain, shall we accept the Colonels' peaceful surrender?" Colonel Thompson asks in a manner more of a command than a question.

Captain Quantrill smiles uneasily and sweeps his hand toward the doorway. "After you Colonel."

Archie and I are alone at the windows. Union soldiers tentatively step from the bank. I wonder about the relationship between Colonel Thompson and our Captain. The Confederate Colonel seems to have the same opinion of Quantrill that the Union Colonel does. What does he mean by "traitorous"? I understand the raving lunatic part, but traitorous? What is that about?

I hear a pistol cock and say sternly. "Archie!" My companion is sighting down his pistol barrel to dispatch one of the emerging Union soldiers. "No Archie! They have given up, we can't shoot em, they've surrendered!"

Archie looks dejected. "Aw Bill! But they's jest standin' dere!"

"C'mon. Let's join the party." and rise to my feet, reluctantly followed by Archie.

A disheveled Union Colonel emerges from the bank as we take a position behind Quantrill. Colonel Buehl looks cautiously around before fixing his gaze on Colonel Thompson. Adjusting his coat with a tug, he stretches to his full six foot height and strides smartly to front the Confederate Colonel.

"Colonel Thompson." The Union Commander began with a crisp salute. "You offered parole to my men..."

"And to you sir." Colonel Thompson interrupts stepping toward his counterpart with hand extended. "Walk with me Colonel." The opposing officers walk together down the center of Lexington Street.

Quantrill shakes his head, turning to William Haller he voices a question that had been on his mind for a couple hours. "Where's Perry?" his eyes search the groups around us.

The question is answered two hours later. The guard post on Walnut that Perry was to take with his eight man troop held six men, not the expected four. Alerted by the early charge of Todd's group, they killed four of our men, drove three away and captured Perry only suffering a loss of two of their own.

The news of Perry's capture hit Captain Quantrill hard. It is widely accepted that the two men closest to William Clarke Quantrill are George Todd and Perry Hoy. Now due to the blunder of one close friend, the other friend has been captured.

"Todd! Take a detachment toward Lexington, overtake Perry's captors and bring him back." Quantrill calmly directs Todd.

"OK Bill!" Todd offered eagerly, then questions. "What about Leavenworth?"

The Captain ponders the question for a moment. "Lexington is closer. No! They've headed for Lexington. Meet us at Morgan's place when you've got Perry."

Chapter Eighteen

Morgan Walker's friendship with William Clarke Quantrill began when a group of five Abolitionists bent on liberating Walkers' slaves are led into a trap engineered by Bill. I wonder if this is what Buehl meant by traitorous. Our Captain revels in the adulation he receives from Morgan and friends who vow their support.

Colonel Thompson took his troops into Blue Springs the evening of August 11, as Quantrill and one hundred fifty of his "Partisans", as he likes to call our band, stop at the Walker farm. This is cause for celebration, the return of a local hero and the defeat of Colonel Buehl at Independence. Friends and neighbors gather and Morgan's slaves began preparations for a feast.

Kids are playing, running, chasing one another as laughter and friendly chatter fill the air. This is a sight we had not seen for several months as we eluded Jayhawker or Union forces before joining with Quantrill and his partisans. I thought of Diane's sisters, Dorothy and Elizabeth, who are the same age as many of the children here. A warm feeling comes over me as I picture Dorothy and Elizabeth playing with the other children and having their pig-tails pulled by the boys. My thoughts drift to Diane and the image of her lithe body running naked through the prairie grass. Her laughter fills my imagination as she tries to escape my reach with a half hearted effort. She gleefully laughs as I grasp her arms; pull her against me encircling her soft form as I lean forward to kiss her.

"Bill!" Bo interrupts my trance. "There's something over here you need to see." He backs away slowly as I rise.

The moonless night provides little light and after peering at the flickering flames of the fire, Bo has to lead me until my eyes become acclimated to the dark. We approach a form silhouetted in the darkness and I recognize Frank Hodges.

"Frank! What are you doing here?" I exclaim. "You're a long way from Council Grove!"

Frank Hodges shrugs and fixes his eyes on the ground as he twirls the hat in his hands, saying softly. "They burned me out too, shortly after you left."

"My sisters? Diane and the girls?"

"They're alright! Your sisters are with us; no one was hurt this time. We... hid by the river... Josi was near hysterics with fear and there were too many of them!" He speaks rapidly as if trying to defend his actions.

"Frank, I understand. You did the right thing. I'm glad you did not subject Josi and her sisters to any more... danger!" I reassure him he could not have stood against the Jayhawkers superior forces.

We should have expected the Red Legs to attack the Hodges, close friends of the Anderson's. That both families are from slave states is enough for most Kansans to hate us and after the killing of John and Jacob Anderson, we should have anticipated the Hodges would be next. Frank said Josi's fear was so great her screams had to be stifled with a hand over her mouth to keep from revealing their hiding place. Fortunately none of the marauders came near the river and the family watched the enemy ransack their home before setting fire to it.

"We had to leave Kansas, Bill; if we stayed they would have come back. I want to join your fight against the Jayhawks." Frank said with conviction. "I want my revenge for what they did to us." I nod my assent.

As we walk together, I ask. "Our families?"

"A family in Blue Springs took us in, all of us. We live in their bunk house, work their fields, cook, clean and do whatever possible to earn our keep." Frank suddenly stopped and looked at me. "Mr. Sanders." Frank shakes his head and looks to the ground. "I can't join you Bill. Mr. Sanders lost his farm hands to Union or Quantrill's forces. I am the only hand he has; if I leave... can he manage… will he allow our families to stay? The girls help in the fields but...!" Frank looks at me. "Mr. Sanders took in ten extra people to feed... who else would have done that, Bill?"

"Stay Frank. It is more important to know my sisters are cared for than add another gun. I would like to meet this Mr. Sanders." I also want to see my sisters and... Diane.

As Frank and I are talking, Bo finds Jim and the joyful reunion is repeated. Socrates nearly crushes the smaller Mr. Hodges in his joy. We make our intentions known to John McCorkle and leave the Walker farm. Trying to be nonchalant, I am aware of a churning in my stomach and a restriction of my speech. Stumbling over words that normally come easy, I decide it is better to remain silent.

A dim light flickers in a window of the small frame house as we approach. A man in his late forties appears at the door, a rifle over his arm.

"Mr. Sanders!" Frank calls out to the relief of the man on the porch.

"Thank God. Frank! Come in here; get the horses out of sight!" He said in a loud whisper casting quick glances side to side. "You never know who is watching. Come! Come!" Ron Sanders is nervous but relaxes as Frank makes introductions. I take the hand of our families' benefactor to thank him for what he is doing, Ron acknowledges my appreciation with a smile and turns to Mr. Hodges. "Go ahead Frank, if someone hears us... to hell with them!"

"MARY!" Frank calls out as he walks into the darkness. "MARY!"

The churning in my stomach intensifies as I hear excited voices and running feet coming toward us.

"Where is he?" I hear the unmistakable voice of Ginny and the shout of Kay. "Bill!" From the darkness emerge the shapes of three females running toward me. One stops ten yards away while the others continue a headlong rush into my arms.

"Ginny! Kay!" I exclaim gathering them into my arms and swinging them around as they shower kisses on me. Laughing, crying, we whirl about until they spot Jim.

"Jim!" They scream jumping from my arms to his. Still laughing I watch the sisters, now sixteen and fourteen years old, knock Jim to the ground in their fervor. Slowly I look toward the one that had been first. She is only a form on the edge of the darkness as three other forms appear behind her. I recognize Frank, and the woman at his side is Mary. Slightly behind Mrs. Hodges is the taller Josi, timidly hiding. Then it is... it has to be... Diane? It is Diane I walk toward. It is Diane running and leaping into my arms.

Hunger pangs bring me back from reliving my days with Diane. Seated on rocks high above the Missouri River is comforting but I disdain my return to present day reality. Life on the plains with our Osage friends was so much more pleasant than the killing I find it necessary to do.

The shadows lengthen on the river valley below. I am aware of a lone rider making his way along the West bank of the river. His horse walks slowly northward stopping frequently at rivers edge. Shadows from the hills behind me reach out to engulf him as darkness edges ever closer to the rider a mile from my location. Smoke from our campfire drifts lazily toward the river. He knows we are here, soon after dark, he will be here as well.

Hunger! I remember the feast at the Sanders', seated next to the object that made the feast much more pleasant. Her soft, sparkling and warm eyes; are alive as she looks at me. I could not hold my gaze on hers more than a moment or two although she openly stared at me.

Mrs. Hodges beams as she watches her daughter across the table; Frank is perplexed by the looks his daughter is giving a man six years older than she. I wonder if he will object to our being married. HMMMM! Why should he object? I feel uneasy. What would he think if he knew she and I had... ah... we had done... we had been... well... close? Would that anger him?

I lean toward Diane, brushing her hair with my chin. She looks at me, smiles and leans her head against my shoulder as her father quickly looks at his plate.

The next day Bo arrived with a message that Quantrill wants us at the Walker farm. Saying goodbye brings tears to the eyes of our sisters and a lump in my throat. Josi remains aloof during our stay, never as gregarious as her sisters, now even more reserved. Diane tells me Josi feels she has been dirtied, that no man will want 'damaged goods'. Does Diane feel she has been damaged, concerned I will not marry her? Somehow I cannot bring myself to broach the subject with Diane. I assume marriage is in our future but have not discussed it with her. After this... conflict, or war, is over there will be time for that.

Marston Lisle met us upon our return to the Walker place. "We've had an election for officers of the first Confederate Partisan Ranger Company. William Hailer was elected first Lieutenant, George Todd Second Lieutenant and William Gregg as Third Lieutenant." He said.

"What about Quantrill?" I ask, surprised he had not been elected a leader of what is considered 'his' Partisan band. My surprise is dispelled as Marston smiles. "You mean Captain Quantrill? He was elected Captain and commissioned into the Confederate Army by Colonel Thompson himself!"

I wonder about the looks Colonel Thompson gave Quantrill in Independence and the near insubordination of our Captain. Is this a commission of choice or convenience?

Being part of the Confederate army gives a measure of comfort to the Partisans considered renegades and outlaws. A "no quarter" policy has been advocated by Union military leaders toward Quantrill's partisans. Rumors of men executed mercilessly are rampant. Cries of an eye for an eye, and a determination to fight to the death, pervade the Partisan camps. Recognition as a Confederate force engaged in a declared war ought to ensure the safety of any unfortunates captured.

The First Confederate Partisan Ranger Company has grown to two hundred fifty men in the four days since our victory at Independence and men are added daily to this count. General Order nineteen ordering all in Missouri to take an oath of allegiance is the motivating force for many men to take sides. Neutrality is not an option, rather than being forced to serve the Union, many opt to follow their hearts and support the 'genteel South'.

The Captain, as William Clarke Quantrill prefers to be addressed, sent a third of his partisans to camp at Lake Lotawanna under First Lieutenant Haller. The remaining one hundred seventy men return to Independence for whatever weaponry and booty that can be gathered. I and my squad are assigned under Todd.

Unsuccessful in his mission to rescue Perry Hoy, George Todd returned to the Walker farm after three days of the search. No word as to Perry's fate.

We approach Independence anticipating Union forces from Kansas City or Leavenworth to have moved in after we left four days prior. The city is quiet and Jeptha Bowles and Socrates Johnson are called upon to scout the town unnoticed. Bo and Socrates return to report the nearest Union forces are miles from Independence in Kansas City. Warning pickets are dispatched toward Kansas

City and Lexington to watch for approaching forces.

The bodies of the dead had been removed from Buehl's tent city west of downtown Independence and buried by the locals. Munitions are lying around and eight wagons are commandeered, one owner threatened with bodily harm to release his wagon. Independence has been friendly toward the Captain and I thought it odd he would commandeer wagons from friends, although the wagons are necessary to carry munitions to fight our mutual enemies. It is for the good of all.

We camp at the Union tent city that evening, prior to returning to Lake Lotawanna. Finishing our reconnaissance of Independence, we began the short ride to our main camp pleased we had not encountered Union forces.

Arriving late that afternoon, the Captain appears bewildered looking about the deserted camp. "Gregg, take a detachment and scout the area." He orders. Before Lieutenant Gregg could designate his detachment, riders began rapidly streaming in from the east, First Lieutenant Haller at their head.

"You missed it Bill!" Haller exclaims excitedly, reining in his horse in front of the Captain. "We had one hell of a fight in Lone Jack!"

"Lone Jack? How the hell did you get to Lone Jack?" Captain Quantrill asked.

"Colonel Thompson sent a messenger last night telling us a company of Union soldiers arrived at Lone Jack and for us to join him in battle. And what a battle it was! God! You should have been there! You should have seen Cole!" Turning in his saddle, he yells. "Cole! Cole Younger!" Not detecting movement from the group of men behind him he continues. "Five men fired down on Cole from close range, the smoke almost engulfing him, but with a six gun in each hand ol' Cole kilt every one of them sons-o'-bitches! Then he reaches down, picks up a rifle and swings it like a club knocking down a sixth man trying to bayonet him! Wow! It was something!"

I feel a tinge of jealousy, until now, I had been the hero since being recognized by Captain Quantrill. My exploits at Wilson's Creek were a motivating factor for our band and I had been looked upon with reverence by the same men now craning their necks to get a glimpse of Cole Younger. I too wonder what he looks like. Had I met him? Oh well!

Colonel Upton Hays joined us the next day accompanied by a Union officer, Lieutenant Coleman, captured at Lone Jack. From interrogating the Union officer, Colonel learns of the plan to eliminate the Confederate forces from western Missouri. Major Emery S. Foster led a cavalry division of eight hundred men, in which Lieutenant Coleman commanded a company, south from Lexington on the fourteenth. He was to be joined in Lone Jack on the sixteenth by the First Iowa Cavalry out of Clinton, Missouri, commanded by General Fitz Henry Warren. That same day Brigadier General James G. Blunt commanding the Department of Kansas out of Fort Scott was to arrive and assume overall command. These combined forces are to drive the rebels toward the Missouri river and the Fourth Kansas Cavalry under Colonel John T. Burns. With over six thousand men against them, the partisans will be forever eliminated.

"But!" Colonel Hays exclaims with a grin. "Major Foster made the mistake of being on time while none of the others were. Too bad!" Only the captured Lieutenant does not laugh at the 'misfortune' of the Union.

With approaching forces numerically three times his own, Colonel Thompson opts for prudence and avoid confrontation. Colonel Hays is to utilize the Partisans in harassing Union forces allowing the Confederates to escape to Arkansas. The Partisans, masters at the hit and hide method of warfare, will be on their own once the main body of Thompson's forces is safely across the Arkansas border.

"Colonel!" Captain Quantrill calls to his superior officer. "Do you believe the information this Lieutenant Coleman has given you?"

Colonel Hays looks at the captive Union officer a moment. "It doesn't matter, Captain, whether I believe him or not. Colonel Thompson does and has issued my orders."

"Sir! Would you or any of your officers so readily reveal your battle plans? He's either trying to lure us into a trap or is a cowardly officer." The Captain states.

"Your point is noted Captain Quantrill. You have your orders and I expect you to carry them out." With that Colonel Hays looked at the Union prisoner and walked away.

The Colonel prepares us for a possible suicide mission. Seriously outnumbered, a frontal encounter with any one of the reputed forces approaching will be suicide. We are instructed to taunt but not engage the enemy in prolonged battle. My heart races as I contemplate the thought of our two hundred fifty men engaged with six thousand highly trained Union soldiers in a field of battle. We will hit and run, always leaving ourselves an avenue of escape, still there is great concern as we contemplate the overwhelming odds.

"You're right." I state nonchalantly to the men riding near me. "The odds are unfavorable. Maybe we should divide our force in half." after a momentary pause. "Give 'em a chance." The ensuing laughter lightens the mood and some of the men announce to others. "You shoulda heard what Bloody Bill said!"

Our Partisan troop is approaching Kingsville, Missouri when Archie excitedly exclaims. "Dat's mah home! I live o'er dere!" bouncing in his saddle as he points.

"Where? I don't see you?" Jim chides the boy.

"Right dere! O'er dem hills!" Archie continues not aware he is being made fun of. There is no time to explain as a column of Union soldiers appears over 'them hills'. An advance column of

General Fitz Henry Warren's First Iowa Cavalry is approaching Lone Jack from the south just as Lieutenant Coleman said.

The skirmish with Warren's force is brief. We entice the Iowans to pursue to the west, drawing them away from Thompson's southeasterly retreat toward Arkansas. With the verification of General Warren's position as revealed by our captive, we no longer doubt Brigadier General James T. Blunt is approaching from the south, probably near Harrisonville. The question is; how far west is Colonel Burns as he comes from the north? If Burns joins Blunt to the south and west we will be surrounded on three sides and forced northward toward the Missouri river.

Riding west past Pleasant Hill, we disperse in groups of two to five dissolving into the countryside. An assembly point near the headwaters of the Little Blue River had been predetermined for a week later, presumably when the Union troops have given up the search for us. Jim, Bo, Socrates, Archie and I light out for Blue Springs and the Sanders farm.

Diane wants to have a picture taken at a photography shop in Blue Springs. Diane and Ginny explain what a photograph is as I had not heard of such a thing. With my curiosity aroused, Jim, Archie, Diane and I accompany the sisters as we enter the 'picture' store.

The tinkling of a bell on the door signals our entrance to the parlor. It is a stark room, two chairs and a wooden counter fronting a wall across the back, with what I assume are 'pictures' on the wall. A doorway with a black curtain for a door is just to the right of the counter. "Well, who do we have here?" A man in his late twenties asks emerging from behind a curtain.

"We've got Bill and Jim Anderson of the Confederate Partisan Rangers!" Ginny proudly states before I can stop her. Reflexively my hand had started up to stop her but, as it is too late, let it drop to my side. I should have warned her not to reveal our identity as we cannot be sure of the loyalties of people we encounter. As I study the eyes of the man standing before us, he does not blink nor waver as he looks from me to Jim.

"The Anderson's." he smiles. Extending a hand to me, he asks. "Jim?"

His hand is not trembling and does not display nervousness. I take his hand and respond suspiciously: "Bill."

"Ah! Bill! Then you must be Jim." extending a hand toward Jim. "And what can we do for the Anderson's today?" His eyes flit between Jim and me, nervous now. Does he recognize us or is he just naturally nervous in front of people.

I began. "My sisters tell me you can put my face on a piece of metal?"

"Yes sir, on tin type, well... your image that is. It's called photography a new science, more accurately, a daguerreotype process, care to try it?"

"How much?"

"Two bits per picture."

"Whew! That's expensive!" My sisters and Diane are pooling their money as I turn toward them. Jim said, "Let's do it Bill! I've got some money."

We have not used money for several months. Food is foraged from the land and people friendly to our cause. Since leaving our farm in Council Grove, I doubt I'd spent a dollar total. Now for each picture the cost is a significant portion of a dollar!

"How many do we want?" I ask Diane. Ginny and Kay squeal with delight as the proprietor smiles, directing us to the back room behind the curtain.

Chapter Nineteen

Charlie Cowert, another friend of the Captain's, operates a large farm near the head waters of the Little Blue River where we join Quantrill on August 21. We are a couple days early but not the first to re-assemble as half the Partisans are in camp when the five of us arrive. Finding a spot by the small stream, we build cover to avoid detection.

The Union troops have yet to give up the search and are combing the countryside for Quantrill and his raiders. We are within a few miles of the search parties at all times - hide and seek for real. We limit our movement, build no fires, keep quiet and take advantage of the dense tree cover by the river.

The next day is hot as I walk The Wind into the stream to wash and cool him, a task I do frequently as he likes it. Wading into knee deep water, The Wind sips on the cool water as I gently wash his body. His coat glistens anew as dirt and sweat is washed away.

I enjoy it as much as The Wind does. As I lean over to re-soak a rag in the water, he nudges me with his nose sending me headlong into the water. Scrambling to my feet I wipe water from my eyes and hear Archie laughing heartily and, is it my imagination or is The Wind smiling at me?

"Why you!" I say in mock anger as I slap him on the rump. He raises his hind leg and kicks out, but playfully kicks short. The Wind neighs and jumps in the water splashing me.

"Now I know you are laughing at me you ugly beast!" I laugh and kick water back at him. He moves deeper into the stream, shakes his mane and points his rear end at me, turning as if to say. "Come down here into the deep water."

"Oh no! You're not getting me down there! I'm going up here." I kick water at him moving toward the bank as Archie laughs.

"S'matter Bill? 'Fraid he'll drown ya?" Archie laughs.

As I lie on the bank propped up on my elbow, The Wind looks at me. When I make no move at him, he turns downstream slowly as the deeper water laps at his underbelly.

I move to lean against a tree, press my hat down over my eyes, peer out from under the brim, and wait. The Wind looks at me, cautiously easing his way toward me, stopping frequently, perking up his ears at sounds from other Partisans. He walks slowly past me, one step at a time, watching to see if my head turns with him. Carefully he steps closer as Archie quietly watches. My eyes focus on his feet, hat covering my eyes, and note his position as he steps from the river near my bare feet. He stretches his head forward to nip at me just as I move my knee slightly, he flinches jerking his head back. When I make no other move he tentatively moves closer, baring his teeth. I jump from my position and strike him playfully on the nose.

"Gotcha!" I laugh as he leaps back into the water. He runs a few steps downstream and turns to look at me again. Taking a sip of water he looks at me and waits. When I make no move, he slowly walks out of the water and begins to nibble on grass at the waters edge.

"'Spose he's done playin' Bill?" A disappointed Archie asks.

"Looks like it!" I unroll my wet pant legs, lie on my shirt and cover my eyes with my hat to nap. This is the life.

Dawn, signaling the start of our day, has barely broken when riders scurry in from Cowert's farm. "Soldiers!" they holler. The fourth Kansas Cavalry under Colonel Burns is entering the wooded area to the east.

"Make a break for it!" is a redundant command given as Partisans hastily mount and ride in every direction but east.

Having wandered about a hundred yards away from The Wind, I began the sprint in his direction. The sound of gunfire and horses crashing through the thickets spur me on. Is it the Partisans escaping or the Fourth Cavalry entering? Branches and bushes tear at my face and clothing as I leap over and under fallen logs, furiously running toward The Wind to escape.

"Bill!" Archie yells pulling the cinch tight on The Wind as I emerge from the thickets near the clearing. A rider in Union blue burst from the opposite thicket, and I quickly shoot him off his horse. Archie downs the next rider as I leap upon The Wind. Archie clamors aboard his mount as we spur them on to the West.

"THERE THEY ARE!" comes a cry to the north. "WHERE?" that questioner is to the east, we are heading west. Barely breaking stride, The Wind splashes through the Little Blue as the sound of gunfire and bullets push us into a headlong dash for safety.

"Come on Wind! Run!" I scream as Archie whips his horse to its' maximum speed, both of us ducking under branches and guiding our mounts over potholes and fallen logs sprinting as we enter the clearing seeking to gain valuable distance from the pursuing gunfire.

Union soldiers break into the clearing one hundred yards behind us as we angle south pressing on as fast as our mounts will carry us. Dashing over the plains, up and down small hills in this heat takes its' toll on the horses and they lather heavily with sweat. Looking over my shoulder, the cavalry is nearly a quarter mile behind us.

"Archie!" I leap from The Wind's back and bounce along beside him, grasping his mane and the saddle horn. "Get off!"

Archie complies and we bounce alongside our slowed mounts giving them a breather as the cavalry begins to close the gap. I wait until the cavalry is nearly one hundred yards away and bullets begin crashing about us before mounting and resuming maximum speed. Again we put distance between us and our pursuers but in a few minutes lather is coming off The Wind in copious amounts. Having opened a sizable lead, we leap from the saddle. The Wind slows, but barely breaks stride, as he pulls me alongside. Once more the cavalry gains on us before we remount and run away from them.

Our headlong dash has covered ten miles and we are approaching the banks of the South Grand River when we overtake other Partisans. In the last mile we passed two dead horses abandoned by riders presumably picked up by comrades. The cavalry is not in sight, their horses probably having given out in this great heat. I slow The Wind to a slow gallop then a trot to warm him down until his breathing returns to normal. At the river, I must not let him drink much as he dips his nose into the cool water. Dismounting, I allow him three long pulls from the river before I forcefully lead him away from the water. He reluctantly follows as we walk from the wooded area, my eyes searching the direction from which we came. The cavalry is not in sight. The Wind is still breathing heavily and tries to pull me toward the water. I run him again in a slow trot, twice stopping for a small amount of water. Archie follows my every move quietly caring for his horse as I do mine.

Finally The Wind is walking normally again and I give him another short drink and tether him to a tree out of reach of the water as I wipe him down with a wet rag. Once cooled, Archie and I walk our mounts along the river keeping a wary eye for the Union cavalry. We come upon Bo and Socrates washing their horses in the river.

"Jim headed west to look for you. We are to meet him at the Round Mound tonight." Bo said as we dismount.

Other Partisans are gathered at the Round Mound, the highest point in the area, as we arrive. This vantage point will give us ample warning if Union forces approach. There are twenty one Partisans on the Mound when Jim returns from his search. He is relieved to see us. Colonel Bums had come close but not close enough.

Our return to Lake Lotawanna takes several days as we travel mostly at night and along streams avoiding open areas. Less than fifty men assemble at the camp by August 27th. The majority of our men accompanied Colonel Hays into Arkansas while some others 'melted' into the surrounding countryside.

The Union Lieutenant is being grilled heavily about the whereabouts of Perry Hoy. It is likely the Union officer would not know of Perry's fate even if he had been brought to Lexington. At any rate the Captain finally left the Union soldier alone.

"Perry's been executed!" one of the later arrivals brandishes a newspaper from Leavenworth giving an account of Perry's execution on August 21, 1862. We know how close the Captain is to Perry and wonder what his reaction will be.

Quantrill reads the account and quietly retires to his tent without comment. The camp is strangely quiet, devoid of the normal revelry.

Two tense hours pass before the Captain emerges from his tent regaled in a Confederate uniform we had not seen him wear before. He stiffly and solemnly stands in front of his tent looking at the group of Partisans. His eyes fall on mine.

"Bill Anderson!" He commands

"Yes sir?"

"Bring Lieutenant Coleman to me."

The Union Lieutenant has been guarded by no less than two men, and not allowed away from the central positions in camp where additional guards are constantly available. As I walk the few yards to where the captive is held the men look from me to the Union man wondering what is happening next. William Clarke Quantrill has exhibited a propensity to parole captives with no particular pomp rather than provide food for them thus seeing our Captain in full military regalia is confusing.

I motion for the Lieutenant to rise. He calmly looks at me, takes a sip of his coffee and discards the last remnant. Carefully setting the cup down, he rises, brushes himself off and straightens his uniform. Placing his hat squarely on his head he nods and follows me to the Captain.

The Lieutenant stands smartly before the Captain, each eyeing the other quietly. For a few moments neither speaks until the Captain leans toward me without taking his eyes from the Union soldier. "Kill him." he orders quietly.

Did I hear him correctly? The startled expression on the Lieutenant's face confirms Quantrill had said, 'kill him'. The Captain's command was spoken quietly with no emotion. I mentally repeat the Captain's command and hear it as if from inside a barrel, a hollow distant quality about the sound.

Time stopped; no sound exists except the ringing in my ears. My hand grasps the forty four caliber Colt and moves slowly upward, the Lieutenant's eyes widen and mouth opens as the weapon moves toward him. How can all this happen so slowly? I see men speaking, their mouths move with no sound emitted, they slowly, but with the appearance of haste, disperse from the immediate area. The Lieutenant's chin drops, his mouth forming the word "No!" but I do not hear it. His hands move slowly from his side reaching outward and upward to protect his face. His right leg begins to reach backward as if to run.

I feel the recoil of the pistol and see the smoke. I imagine, or do I actually see, the bullet enter his left cheek. His eye winces as the projectile travels under the eyeball into his brain, exploding out the top of his head. Patches of hair and scalp splay out into the air, momentarily frozen against the backdrop of the surrounding trees and hills. All is quiet, no sound or motion except the object in front of me. The Union Lieutenant reacts in extreme slow motion to the impact of my bullet. His head snaps back, then forward and back again. His hands rise slowly over his head as he falls backward twisting slightly to his right, falling so slowly I am sure I could catch him before he hit the ground. The dead captive bounces twice before sound and motion returns to normal. The sound of my weapon reverberates as it echo's against the trees.

The lifeless form of the Union officer comes to rest on the ground, blood spilling out the top of his head. A new sensation is felt, is it revulsion? No, I don't think so. I have killed men before but this was an execution. This man was unarmed standing a scant few feet in front of me, looking at me. No! It isn't revulsion. I quickly acted upon Captain Quantrill's order to kill, without question, and am not sickened by it. Am I excited? Yes! Pleased? Well... yes!

Archie is laughing, cackling with glee. "Yo' done it! Yo' done it Bill! Yo' kilt da sombitch!" The Partisans in the immediate vicinity stare at the dead soldier. Some look at me in shock and horror at the sudden turn of events. I peer into the eyes of my comrades then turn to Archie, smile and say. "Fuck 'im if he can't take a joke."

William Clarke Quantrill moved slowly toward the body of Lieutenant Coleman. Without lifting his eyes from the prone figure he motions for Partisans to move closer to him. Quietly his men comply, carefully surrounding the dead Union officer.

Speaking in a subdued manner he began. "Perry Hoy..." the Captain sighed, lifting his head as he sought the eye of each man surrounding him. "I loved Perry Hoy. As your commander I care for each of you. I do care for you. But Perry Hoy..." his head bowed as he looked upon the dead form. "Perry... Perry was like... a brother to me. Many of you loved Perry as well. He had a devilish way about him that made him likable but most of all he sincerely liked people. Everyone was his friend. At least that's the way Perry saw it. He loved me. He loved you."

The Captain gently tapped the Union man's boot with his toe. Drawing a deep breath he raised his head. "I've often wondered if the Union knew of this place, if anyone had spoken of our haven here, if anyone had betrayed the safety of his brothers. I wonder if the Union questioned Perry about us. Do you suppose they tortured him, to try to find this sanctuary?"

Quantrill's face reddens, his voice rising, each word spat out in anger. "How much pain did Perry endure for us? Did he cry for mercy? How long did he suffer torture at the hands of his captors before they finally killed him because he would not betray you?"

His eyes and voice soften. "I wonder what Perry was thinking as he faced the firing squad? Perry loved life, he lived it with exuberance. He had so much to live for. Did he not tell us about his girl in Liberty?"

The Captain looked at the men hanging on every word, the mental picture of a smiling, impish Perry Hoy, indelibly etched in our minds. "Consider his last thoughts. She... his girl... was in his thoughts. He quietly said good-bye to her, told her how much he loved her. YOU were in his last thoughts. He told you how much he cared for you and for you to carry on. He told you... not to let him die in vain, to dedicate yourselves to avenging his needless death until the oppressive threat of the Union is vanquished, and men like Perry, and like you, may live in peace and tranquility!"

Quantrill's voice rose and cracked as he again kicked the boot of the dead soldier. "And avenge him we will! Today! This is a start! For the death of Perry Hoy, a brave loving man who is better than any ten Union men, ten Union men will die!" Shouts rise in unison as the men vent the anger aroused in them. "Mount up!" Quantrill ordered.

The excitement is great as we yell and dedicate ourselves to avenging Perry Hoy. The men leap to their horses eager to embrace the cause that ended our beloved Perry's life. I guess I loved Perry too... although I really hadn't known him very well... but he did seem likable.

The eager band had to exercise restraint to follow the Captain. Men eagerly pass Quantrill only to rein in as we head west toward the Kansas border, an ominous band of fifty riders stopping at places of men known to be sympathetic to the Union cause.

"James Henry?" William Clarke Quantrill calls to a tall blond man working his field, his wife and two small boys a few yards behind him. A questioning look appears on the man's face as he looks at the large contingent of men before him.

"Yes?"

"You are said to be a member of the establishment, to be favorable to the Union cause."

"Yes but..." at least twenty bullets rip into the man amidst screams of terror from his wife. The force of the volley lifts James Henry, propelling him backward as his chest explodes from the multitude of bullets striking him nearly simultaneously. His wife's screams subside as she looks in shock at her husband, her hand covering her mouth in horror and disbelief. The two young boys do not move as they look at their father lying dead a few feet from them. Without a word we turn and ride to other known sympathizers where similar scenes are repeated.

Jim remained near the back of the pack and had not drawn his weapon. Archie and I, as do several others, maneuver our way to the front of the pack eager to carry out the next execution. Jim did not seem to relish the avenging of our beloved Perry, maybe he didn't like Perry.

"Jim! What's wrong?" I ask after the sixth Union sympathizer had been disposed of.

"Bill? What is wrong? This... is wrong... barbaric!" Jim replied angrily in restrained tones.

"Wrong? What do you mean, wrong?"

"What you're doing... what we are doing, is killing innocent people." he said in exasperation. "These men had nothing to do with the death of Perry Hoy. These men are entitled to their beliefs as are you and I. My god Bill, the Lieutenant! Do you realize how wrong that was? How could you do that?"

I shake my head. "Quantrill ordered it. Besides it was Union men that killed Perry. It was Union men that killed our father and raped our sister! And it is Union men who are paying for it!" I reply forcefully.

"These aren't soldiers? These are farmers! Why should farmers pay for the senseless actions of soldiers?"

"This is war!" I say surprised at his softness.

Jim looks at me for several moments waiting for me to change my position. Finally he shakes his head and pulls his horse away from mine.

He's just weak, doesn't understand.

CHAPTER TWENTY

Palmyra, MO. October 8, 1862
Joseph C. Porter

Sir:

Andrew Allsman, an aged citizen of Palmyra, and a non combatant, having been carried from his home by a band of persons unlawfully arrayed against the peace and good order of the State of Missouri, and which band was under your control; this is to notify you that unless said Andrew Allsman is returned unharmed to his family within ten days from date, ten men who have belonged to your band and unlawfully sworn by you to carry arms against the Government of the United States, and who are now in custody will be shot as a meet reward for their crimes, among which is the illegally restraining of said Allsman and of his liberty, and if not returned, presumably aiding in his murder.

Your prompt attention to this will save much suffering.

Yours etc.
W.R. Strachan
Provost Marshall General
District N.E. Missouri
Per order of Brigadier General
Commanding McNeills'
Column

"Pretty well written if I must say so myself, Sergeant Parman." Colonel Strachan said as he places the Palmyra Gazette on his smallish desk. He obviously is pleased with the letter he had me deliver to the newspaper. Leaning back in his chair he pulls a cigar from the box on the corner of his desk eyeing me smugly as I hurry to light his cigar.

"What do you think Sergeant?" he said, his steely dark eyes peering at me over the billowing smoke from his cigar. He casually rests his left ankle on his knee.

"Excellent article sir." I say, trying to muster enthusiasm for something written by a man I detest. "Very smoothly written, concise and to the point. The Confederate Colonel should have no problem understanding your meaning, but sir?" I pause as he waits for me to continue. "Didn't you say you were sure Mr. Allsman is already dead?" The Colonel nods as he puffed on his cigar, slowly blowing smoke through the small opening he made in his mouth. He does not take his eyes off me waiting for me to continue as if the answer is obvious. "And if he is dead, why publicly plead for his safe return? Sir?" I almost forgot the address demanded of all his subordinates.

He chuckles softly and pulls the large cigar from his mouth rolling it slowly between his thumb and forefinger. Shaking his head slightly he says. "You've got a lot to learn about war son. This is a business of killing."

Son! I hate it when he calls me son. I'm almost as old as that son-of-a-bitch, almost as big as he is too. At six foot tall he is only two inches taller than I and probably near the same weight, a solid one hundred eighty pounds. At twenty eight I have served eleven years in the Union army, one year less than he, and he calls ME son! The braggart tells everyone how he'd made Colonel in only nine years of service without the benefit of field promotions. That is quite an accomplishment I'll admit, but I am tired of hearing about it.

"If I could meet Colonel Porter in the field I'd show that guerrilla leader what a real military man can do. I'd wipe out his command and be rid of him once and for all. But... I am not in the field Sergeant Parman." he continues whimsically. "And I must take public opinion into account." He leaned back in his chair and took a deep draw on his cigar, a reddish glow brightening.

"Public opinion sir?" What does that mean?

He looks at me with a wry smile. "How would you propose to get rid of the rebels we have incarcerated?"

The smart son-of-a-bitch loves to use big words! Jailed you bastard! Just say jailed! I wish to yell it at him but I am no dummy. "Well sir, I'm just the Sergeant of the guard sir. My job is to make sure they don't escape from jail, ah incarceration, not what to do with them."

"I know what your job is son! Don't forget that I am the one who gave it to you." he said with apparent exasperation and the hint of a veiled threat. "That's why you're not officer material son. You've got to be able to think and see into the future with your actions."

You arrogant egotistical son-of-a-bitch! I earned my job by being a proficient soldier and I hate having to kiss up to officers like you. See into the future? You couldn't see your ass if it was held up in front of your face! Of course no one can tell them apart, your ass or your face that is!

One of these days I am going to say that out loud.

Actually he is quite good looking... for a man, coal black hair trimmed neatly above the collar. A thin black mustache gives him a debonair, yet sinister look, and at six feet tall and a trim muscular one hundred eighty pounds, he does cut quite a dashing figure. He considers himself God's gift to women as well as to the military.

"Yes sir." I reply politely, I'm no fool! "But what do you mean sir, about... seeing into the future?"

I had him now, buttering him up real good. If he could read minds I would be in deep trouble.

"Good for you son, you're still trying to learn." He loves it when he can talk down to somebody. I hate it but learned to manipulate him by appealing to his ego, small price to pay for good duty.

He rises from his chair switching the cigar to his left hand and walks the few feet to my side. Draping his right arm over my shoulder, he assumes his 'fatherly' tone. "If we were to kill the incarcerated rebels, which is what they deserve, without sufficient reason then public opinion would label them as martyrs and greatly increase the number of men joining their cause. But!" the embers of his cigar glow brightly as he takes a deep draught exhaling the smoke in front of my face. He shakes his head. "No son. We must be smart. We must make it appear as though the rebels are at fault and deserve the severity of their sentence. By making Andrew Allsman the martyr, people will clamor for retribution and we can dispose of these guerrillas without adverse comment." He steps away taking another draught from his cigar. "Now Sergeant, I wired the commanding officer in Hannibal to send five men from his jail to be executed at noon October eighteenth and five will be selected from our list of inmates here. These ten men will serve as an example to the populace of what happens to those who engage in combat against the Union."

"This is General McNeill's orders sir?" I ask and suddenly wish I hadn't.

The Colonel eyes me suspiciously as cigar smoke curls about him. "The General, Sergeant, follows the recommendations I give him." After satisfying himself that I am not questioning his authority, (I mask my true feelings well) he continues. "Now Sergeant! Assemble the prisoners in the courtyard at noon today and I will read the names of those selected."

Selected! He makes it sound as if it is an honor to be chosen to die. Geez! To die! That very real possibility of killing or being killed had occurred to me when I joined the army from my home in Warsaw, Illinois that November day of 1851, but I hadn't shot at anyone as yet. As long as I continue to appeal to the ego of my mentor, Colonel Warren R Strachan, I figure to remain out of the line of fire. Not that I am afraid of fighting, well... maybe I am, but if I can avoid dying... sheeeesh! It'd be dumb not to!

"You men as soldiers of an unrecognized government are involved in an illegal insurrection against the government of the United States of America." Colonel Strachan began addressing the twenty three prisoners assembled in the courtyard at noon. They are disinterested in the Colonels speech. Some shuffle their feet while others scratch their chin, watch the passing clouds, yawn or other actions indicating they are bored with the Colonel and would rather be sitting in their community cell, out of the sun, than listening to his drivel.

"You have wreaked havoc upon the countryside in support of the guerrilla tactics employed by Colonel Porter." That brought wry smiles and prideful snorts from the men pretending to ignore Warren. (He'd 'shoot' me if he ever heard me refer to him as Warren.) "Innocent people suffered greatly at your hands. Considerable property damage has occurred as you indiscriminately destroyed the homes, buildings and crops of the good people of Missouri. Your punishment should fit the crime. Your property should be confiscated and distributed amongst your victims, a fit retribution for having destroyed theirs. For each animal you destroy one of yours should be destroyed... or... perhaps more! As these were innocent people upon whom you perpetrated your crimes, perhaps they deserve a greater payment, say... ten for each? For each horse you kill ten of yours will die!" Some of the prisoners snicker and whisper to one another and are making the Colonel angry, he enjoys being the center of attention and these men are ignoring him.

"Therefore... for each innocent man that dies... ten of you will die! An innocent citizen of this town, Andrew Allsman, has been taken by you, your band of guerrillas and unless he is returned unharmed by the eighteenth of this month... ten of you will die for his presumed demise!" The Colonel said emphatically. He has their attention, all the shuffling, whispering and scratching stopped. The prisoners turn their faces toward the Colonel staring at him in disbelief. Had they really heard him say... ten of them would... die? Ten of twenty three?

The tension and anger subsides from the Colonel's face. He paces back and forth in front of the now attentive group, maintaining ten foot spacing between himself and the prisoners. The twenty guards on duty ready themselves for a possible riot.

"I have here." the Colonel states, walking a few feet to a box on the ground, stooping to pick it up. "Sergeant!" he calls extending the box toward me with one hand. Moving to his side, I hold the box as he turns toward the prisoners. "In this box I have placed a slip of paper with the name of each of you. From this box... I will draw the names of five that will suffer the penalty of death at noon October eighteenth, unless Mr. Allsman is returned unharmed. Five more are being selected from Colonel Porters' men currently jailed in Hannibal. They will be transported here to suffer their just retribution along with the men about to be named."

No one moves or scarcely draws a breath, all eyes fixed upon the Colonel, all ears intently listening to his every word.

The Colonel ceremoniously lifts the lid off the box I hold high and withdraws a neatly folded slip of paper. Slowly Colonel Strachan unfolds the paper gazing at the name written on it as the suspense builds in the men. Looking dramatically at the men he announces in a firm voice:

"Eleazer Lake!"

The prisoners glance about briefly as I try to determine which one is Eleazer Lake. Hard stares return to the face of the Colonel as he reaches into the box again.

"John M. Wade!"

None of the faces turn from the Colonel. I cannot tell from their expressions which of the prisoners is Eleazer Lake or John Wade, as silent blank faces stare at the Colonel. Another name is drawn from the box.

"William T. Humphrey."

Still no response. I wonder if the Colonel expected them to break down and scream for mercy. If he had, they are disappointing him.

"Morgan Bixler!"

The tension is etched into the faces of the men before me and I wonder what they must be thinking now. There is one name yet to be pulled from the box. Are they praying it will not be theirs?

The Colonel took the box from me and held the lid tightly closed as he shook the contents, prolonging the anxiety of the moment. Holding the box against his tunic he opened it and withdrew a slip of paper. Pacing, he held the slip in front of him as he looked at the men staring at the paper. The son-of-a-bitch is intentionally making them sweat. Unfurling the paper, he continues to pace as he studies the name on it. Glancing at the men he slowly returns to his position and stops in front of the prisoners.

"William J. Baker." he finally announces.

A collective sigh and murmurs escape from some of the more fortunate which obviously pleases the Colonel. Silence is quickly restored as the prisoners return their attention to the Provost Marshall that read the sentence of death for five of their companions.

"Sergeant. Return the prisoners to their cells." He said calmly.

I hate him now even more than before.

The prisoners return quietly to their cells. I wonder if I would have tried to escape if I had been in their place. Probably not, as an attempted escape by any of them would have meant immediate death at the hand of the armed guards, I am sure of that. Surely I am dreaming, this must be a nightmare, soon we will awaken and discover they hadn't really been selected to… to die?

Subdued murmurs replace the normal raucous behavior in the jails. No one laughs any more. The five men from Hannibal arrive October eleventh; Captain Thomas A. Sidenor, the only officer among the condemned, tries to maintain high spirits among the ten as well as the others. The other four from the prison in Hannibal are; Thomas Humston, Herbert Hudson, John Y. McPheeters and Francis Lear. All are young men, younger than I and I am a young man.

Realization of what is to happen to them comes around the thirteenth. One man requests paper and pen with which to leave instructions on how his family should carry on after... well, after! One man, William T. Humphrey, looked despondent as I hand him paper and pen. "I... can't..." He began haltingly.

"Sure you can." I somberly assure him. "Just tell your family or friends you love them or anything else you wish to convey."

He hung his head. "I mean... I can't... write. I would like to tell my wife the things you said, and more, but... I... can't."

It is not uncommon for men to not be able to read or write and I curse myself for embarrassing him.

A short young man had been standing nearby and moved to the side of his comrade. "I'll write it for you William." He said softly. William Humphrey looked at Hiram Smith and nods in appreciation. They withdraw to a quiet position where Hiram began to scratch William's words onto the paper I provided them.

It is a sad sight, the other prisoners solemnly comforting the condemned. They are fed the best portions, the fortunate sharing with the unfortunate. I try to add comfort by providing writing material and posting their messages for them.

The afternoon of October sixteenth a private enters the jail and states, "Sergeant Parman. Colonel Strachan wants you in his office immediately."

Now what could that S.O.B. want with me I thought, making my way to his office a few yards south of the jail. Since the wretched assembly a week ago I hadn't been stroking the Colonel's ego as had been my practice. I'd like to tell him why but prudence prevails, to borrow a favorite phrase of the Colonel's. Maybe he wants me to assemble the firing squad. Those assignments haven't been made known. Whoa! Talk about tough duty! I'll have to give considerable thought to the type of person that can perform that task. The thought of actually shooting someone that is unarmed, standing a few feet or yards in front of you, looking at you… or will they be blindfolded? We've never had to assemble a firing squad. Surely they will be blindfolded. Boy, am I glad I'll just be giving the command! Or wait, maybe that is the Colonel's job and I won't have to do anything! Yeah, that'll be better!

"The Colonel wishes to see me sir?"

"Yes Sergeant Parman." He said slouched in his chair in the familiar pose of left ankle on right knee, facing to his right. His left elbow rests on the desk, fingers spread wide the tips of which press against the digits of his opposite hand, chin resting lightly on those fingertips. This is his contemplative pose when he wishes to give the impression he is deep in thought. "I've been getting some disturbing reports Sergeant."

"Disturbing reports sir?" What had I done? My mind races over the past week or so and cannot recall a regulation I violated. I try to be a model soldier doing whatever it takes to stay out of trouble what had I done? "What kind of reports sir?"

"I understand you have been consorting with the enemy." He said calmly without averting his gaze from mine.

"What!" I shake my head incredulously.

"Yes Sergeant. Consorting, I understand you have become quite friendly with the prisoners, actually running errands for them."

"Sir?" I am stunned, can't believe my ears.

"Have you been providing writing materials and delivering their letters to the post?" He turned in his chair to face me.

"Why... ah... yes... yes sir? They are trying to notify their families as to their fate and... and... and make last minute decisions, their last will and testament sort of thing and... and...."

"And what, Sergeant?" He interrupts.

"Surely sir there is nothing wrong with helping them put their house in order, to..."

"To help them notify the rebel forces about military matters?"

"NO SIR!" That is treason and I feel the cold chill of fear. "I am not a traitor sir! I read each of those letters sir! None of them contained anything military, or anything else that could betray us! They were all personal!" This is serious!

"Are you aware of the codes they can use to notify comrades? Do you have the last decision in military matters? Why didn't you submit those letters to this office Sergeant?" His face darkens as his anger grows.

A strikingly beautiful young woman interrupts as she flings the door open and stands in the doorway. She is tall with coal black hair cascading over her shoulders. She is wearing a new dress that accentuates her figure, and oh my, what a figure! Can any dress hide that figure? Green is definitely her color, but then I suspect one as beautiful as she can wear any color. My mouth is hanging open.

"Colonel Strachan?" She asks timidly.

"Why… ahem… yes Ma'am" the Colonel answers after catching his breath. He is taken by her beauty as well. "What can I do for you miss…?" He said pulling himself together and putting on his authoritarian air.

"My husband… has… is… you have…." Her voice cracks as she struggles to speak. She draws a deep breath lifting her chin, making the Colonel's eyes widen as her chest rises. "My husband is William T. Humphrey and I am told he is to be executed for something he didn't do!" She blurts out the words as quickly as possible. Expelling her breath she looks at the floor, breathing heavily as if the effort of speaking has taken her breath away. No one spoke, no one moved, the only sound the labored breathing of this beautiful woman.

The Colonel eyes her, carefully inspecting her. She feels his inspecting eyes, dips her chin and folds her arms across her chest unable to conceal the object of the Colonel's stare.

"Your husband Ma'am..." His eyes dart back and forth as he searches for the words. "Has been sentenced... and the uh... sentence... must uh... be carried out." Not his normal suave self; she is making him stammer and squirm, as he makes others squirm for a different reason. Get 'im lady!

Colonel Strachan leans back and smiles, regaining his demeanor. "Colonel Porter has recruited a group of guerrilla fighters that causes consternation to the good people of Missouri. That cannot and will not go unpunished or insurrection and chaos will reign supreme. Your husband willingly participated in acts against the people of Missouri, the most dastardly of which was perpetrated on Palmyra's citizen, Andrew Allsman, and we must enforce discipline."

Oh shit! He's into his big word speech making mode, about to pontificate, I thought, coming up with a big word of my own. Must we listen to this pompous asshole?

"Mr. Humphrey was selected at random to pay for crimes committed by he, or others of his and Colonel Porters band. This retribution is necessary to maintain discipline and order in these unsettled times." The Colonel rose from his chair moving toward the young woman. "I cannot free him from his fate... without consideration."

"Consideration?" The young woman asks through her tears, not comprehending what he is about to demand, the lecherous bastard!

"Sir...?" I start.

The Colonel whirls, having forgotten I was present. "Sergeant?" pulling himself erect he quickly orders. "That will be all Sergeant. Return to your post."

Leaving his office I admonish myself for opening my mouth. Well so what, I could not change what he is about to do. I hope she slaps his face and reports him to the General. Maybe I should report his conduct to General McNeill. "No, you fool!" I say aloud. "Don't volunteer... out of sight... out of trouble!" Several idioms pop into my head all of which tell me to mind my own business and not get involved.

I turn in time to see an angry Mrs. Humphrey slam Colonel Strachan's door and stomp away from his combination office and sleeping quarters.

"HA! HA! HA!" I laugh aloud at lover boy being unceremoniously rejected. "WAY TO GO MA'AM" I shout. Oh shit! I should have kept my big mouth shut! The Colonel's standing in his doorway glaring at me.

Chapter Twenty One

The afternoon of October seventeenth is sunny but cool as I sit in front of the jail. The sun warms me as I doze in my chair trying to forget the events scheduled for tomorrow. I maintain a hope that Allsman will be returned even if the Colonel said he is already dead. Any hope the prisoners have of his return is waning.

"William." came a mournful cry. "William?" It comes from my left, around the side of the jail. "William?" It is the beautiful Mrs. Humphrey that came to plead for her husbands' release. I feel sorry for her, and for him, she apparently came to say her last goodbyes. I don't blame her for not wanting to watch her husband shot. Strachan could release him! What difference will it make if only nine men die for Allsman?

"Anna? Anna! Anna!" The excited voice came from within the jail as 'Anna' stands outside the barrier preventing contact with the prisoners. "You came." He says joyfully.

She stands with head bowed and began to cry.

"I know. I know sweetheart. You have to be strong. You'll have to...." He could not complete the sentence.

She looks longingly at him, tears streaming down, her beautiful face contorted by the pain in her heart. I feel hatred for the situation, for the war and especially for Strachan.

"William?" She looks at him questioningly.

"Yes Anna. Go home now Anna. Go home." William answers through the window of the jail. "I don't want you to stay, go home please."

She stares at him for several moments before saying. "I love you." Quietly she looks at her hands, standing slump shouldered in front of him. "I love you William."

"I love you too Anna." William responds softly. "Now go home Anna."

She stares at her husband. "I love you William. I love YOU!" She began, moving to her left, keeping her eyes on her husband. "I love YOU William! I will always only love YOU!" She turns and walks slowly away.

"I love you Anna! I love you! ANNA! ANNA! I LOVE YOU ANNA!"

She does not look back as she strides slowly and resolutely toward the Colonel's office.

Oh jeez! I watch her open the door. No. No, please don't! She steps inside.

The Colonel hasn't spoken to me since yesterday but I know he is not going to let me off without some sort of retribution for laughing at him. I stood kitchen duty as a private but a sergeant surely would not be subjected to so demeaning a task. He will be creative of that I am sure.

I am still confused about 'consorting' with the enemy. How can that heartless bastard think that giving writing materials to the prisoners is aiding the enemy? How can he punish me for being humane to the prisoners? The General won't let him do that! Oh yes, he will punish me for laughing at him, that's what he'll do. I'll surely lose my soft job but he can't make a case for consorting with the enemy. My mind wanders while I try to guess what punishment the Colonel has in store for me.

She's been in there a long time as my thoughts return to Mrs. Humphrey. She truly loves her man if she will subject herself to... well... to him. Surely now he will release William T. Humphrey after she had... It will not surprise me if he betrays her and shoots her man any way. The bastard!

We are ordered to be in dress uniform at eleven O'clock for the ceremonies. What a way to refer to what is about to happen, ceremonies. Detail? Nah, that term is not much better.

I hadn't been directed to select the firing squad. Has the Colonel appointed some one else? It's OK with me but as Sergeant of the Guard it is part of my responsibilities. Am I being relieved of my position? Is that my punishment? My squad is directed to be in dress uniforms and at the jail by eleven, does that mean we are the firing squad?

Yeah, that's gotta be it! My twenty man squad will be on the firing line. There is strength in numbers. My men will rest easier if their bullet is one of many to end a life.

My mouth drops as the Colonel and Mrs. Humphrey emerge from his quarters. That S.O.B. kept her all night! Still dressed in her pretty green dress, her hair is not neatly in place as it was yesterday having lost some curl, her hair hangs lifelessly on her shoulders. Colonel Strachan is very chipper, proudly displaying his prize as he guides Mrs. Humphrey, by her elbow.

Her head is down as he guides her crisply toward the jail. Pity wells within me as I recognize the sacrifice she made. I hope it is worth it. Surely...

"William T. Humphrey!" The Colonel commands loudly as he and Mrs. Humphrey enter the jail. The prisoner had been preparing for death and rose slowly to his feet, a perplexed look on his face as he looks from the Colonel to his wife standing beside his antagonist. I read the question on his face as he glances from his wife to the officer. "Your wife has made a convincing argument for your release William, a very convincing argument." Colonel Strachan declares smiling at the prisoner.

His meaning is so evident that the prisoner at Humphrey's side exclaims softly. "You son-of-a-bitch!" A sentiment shared by all including this Sergeant of the Guard.

The smug grin disappears from the Colonel's face as he glares at the prisoner that spoke up. "Sergeant Parman! This prisoner's name?" He demands.

"Hiram Smith." The prisoner firmly replies, his voice even, no hint of fear. The two men stare at one another.

"Anna?" William Humphrey softly questions his wife. She covers her face with her hands and sobs. "Anna." He repeats, dragging out her name not wanting to believe what he knows to be true. He turns away, staring at the floor.

"William Humphrey." The Colonel said; a sinister smile replacing the anger in his face as he stares at Hiram Smith. "Today is your lucky day Mr. Humphrey. Not only has your wife... ahem... argued successfully for your release but Mr. Smith just volunteered to take your place in front of the firing squad."

All eyes in the jail turn to Hiram Smith as he and the Colonel stare at each other, neither blinking nor turning away. Finally Hiram turns his back on the Colonel, strides slowly to the water bucket, picks up the ladle and calmly takes a drink. Returning to face the Colonel, Hiram Smith looks him in the eye, raising the ladle toward the Colonel. "I will die as freely as I took that drink of water."

Colonel Strachan looks startled for a moment as if not knowing how to respond. With his eyes still on Hiram Smith, the Colonel finally says. "Sergeant, release Mr. Humphrey." and stomps out of the jail.

"Hiram?" William Humphrey said to his friend, then yells after the Colonel. "Take me! Take me you bastard! TAKE ME! YOU SON-OF-A-BITCH!

TAKE ME! TAKE ME!" He painfully screams after the Colonel who does not look back.

"WILLIAM!" The woman screams and sobs as I open the cell door.

"Take me. Take me." William whimpers softly as he sinks to the floor. "Take me."

I direct two men to remove him from the cell. "You are free." I say softly as he nears me. "Take your wife and go home."

He looks toward the no longer visible Colonel Strachan, his eyes revealing the rage within. He rushes the door but I throw my arms around his legs, pulling him to the floor inside the compound. "William!" His wife screams flinging her body on his to prevent him from rushing the Colonel.

"Get away from me!" He rages, throwing her aside.

"Listen you!" I snarl, angrily grasping the front of his shirt as he lay on the board flooring. "You are free! You... are alive! That's all she cares about! You! You're alive!"

"I don't care!" He screams struggling against me.

"Tie him up!" I instruct four guards nearby. After he is subdued I whisper in his ear. "For your own good you will be thrown on her wagon and she will take you home. HOME... your home... yours and hers!" Turning toward the woman I say. "Mrs. Humphrey, take him home, everything will be alright, he will understand... eventually."

She sobs into her hands. I want to comfort her but the last thing her husband needs to see is his wife in the arms of yet another strange man.

The Humphrey's are barely out of sight when the Colonel steps from his quarters and marches to the jail. "Ready the prisoners Sergeant." My disdain must be clearly evident as he looks at me. "Is there a problem Sergeant?"

"You...!" I began venomously.

"Careful Sergeant. Mustn't say something we will be sorry for now shall we. No, that wouldn't be prudent now would it?" The Colonel growls at me.

I can only stare at him as disrespect or disobedience to an officer is a serious offense. No. I cannot tell him what I want to.

"You will follow your orders as I give them to you Sergeant... without question." He said emphatically.

The march is over too quickly. It is only a half mile to the point Colonel Strachan leads us to outside Palmyra, a distance covered too rapidly. If it seems to pass quickly for me I wonder what it must feel like to the condemned.

They have no opportunity to escape. The forty man firing squad, another squad has joined mine, marches several yards ahead with columns of ten men riding ahead, behind and on each side of the ten unfortunate prisoners. Troops are assembled to witness the execution and townsfolk quietly gather to watch the condemned march, as five hundred troops and townsfolk stand in somber respect.

Colonel Strachan is mounted on his horse facing the procession as we enter the encircled area. General McNeill is here as well. Has he sanctioned this butchery? Will he allow this barbaric act to be completed? Surely he will announce a reprieve at the last minute.

I halt the column ten yards in front of the General who watches the prisoners take their assigned position, then nods to Colonel Strachan.

The Colonel unfurls an official looking document and reads. "For the crime of murder against Andrew Allsman, Citizen of Palmyra, the following men have been sentenced to die for said crime. The sentence is to be carried out at noon, October 18, in the year of our Lord eighteen hundred sixty two. Baker, William. - Bixler, Morgan. - Hudson, Herbert. - Humston, Thomas. - Lake, Eleazer. - Lear, Francis. - McPheeters, John Y. - Sidenor, Captain Thomas A. - Wade, John M." The Colonel pauses for effect, smiling at a particular prisoner. "And... Smith, Hiram."

As the names are read, the crowd of townsfolk murmur and an occasional muffled scream escapes as the name of a loved one is read. A woman faints.

The Colonel calls out in a loud voice. "Captain Thomas A. Sidenor."

The prisoners glance at one another as the Captain hesitates a moment before smartly marching to the assigned position in front of the Colonel.

The Colonel states. "As leader of your men, you will lead them into death." The Colonel turned, took two large steps before holding up the document and announced. "Baker, William."

Baker quietly walks to the indicated spot. After each name is read the designated man stepped to his appointed position. The Colonel takes great delight in positioning Hiram Smith.

"Sergeant Peters!" The Colonel commands and the sergeant directs his men to give each prisoner a shovel.

Captain Sidenor looks at the shovel in his hand for a moment then stands erect and tosses it aside. The other condemned men follow suit.

"Pick up the shovel, Captain." The Colonel ordered.

The Captain stood quietly, a smirk on his face.

"Captain! Pick up your shovel!" The Colonel orders sternly.

"If I don't, what are you going to do, shoot me?" The Captain intoned sarcastically.

Colonel Strachan stares at him silently before turning to Sergeant Peters. "Sergeant." The Sergeant's men begin to dig shallow graves behind each prisoner. Ordered to bind the hands and feet of the condemned, I avoid their eyes as I do. A few stand calmly while most are shaking and breathing heavily in fear, some have small puddles forming in the dirt below them. My stomach churns at the thought of what is coming. The mundane tasks complete, Sergeant Peters and his men return to their positions. The Colonel lifts the document again. "By order of Brigadier General John McNeill, the sentence will be carried out." Carefully rolling up the document the Colonel turns to me. "Carry out the execution order Sergeant."

The words hit me like a fist, I expected it, still, my knees weaken and my voice cracks as I command. "Squad... atten... tion!" The familiar snap of rifles pressed in unison to the side of the soldiers legs is my cue for the next command. "Right shoulder - arms!" They respond to the squeaky voice and again the familiar snap-snap-snap as the rifles are smartly placed on the shoulders.

What next? Oh yeah. "Right face... hut!" My voice has returned but the knees are wobbly as I direct the men into two ranks of twenty in front of the poor souls. "Front rank... kneel!" The men dutifully turn and kneel, rifles still pressed to their shoulders. Oh shit. "Port arms." I hastily order and the men obey, even from their kneeling position. I am losing it, can't think straight. Are all eyes on me? I don't want to do this!

"Get it right Sergeant!" The Colonel says without the anger anticipated for my foul up. He even sounds somewhat pleased... because I am giving him more reason to replace me?

I am cold, numb, ears ringing, my mouth dry and breathing heavily. "Nooo." I moan.

"Carry it out Sergeant!" This is an unmistakable command given quietly but forcefully. I look into the Colonel's hate filled eyes. Hate for me, I have to carry out the orders.

"Squad... ready!" Oh God! I should not have looked at the prisoners. They stare at me with fear and disdain. I'm sorry! Oh God, I'm sorry! Should I say it out loud? Should I tell them it's not my fault; that I don't want to do this? Should I...

"Sergeant!" Barks the Colonel.

"Aim?" How can I get out of this? I turn to the Colonel, lifting my palms in desperation.

"Carry out your orders." The Colonel says sternly, losing his patience with me.

"Oh God! Please forgive me!" I mumble as I turn toward the prisoners slowly raising my hand.

"Sergeant!"

"FIRE!" I close my eyes as the roar of the muskets explodes in my ears.

"Sergeant." The Colonel calls out in disgust.

I open my eyes. Oh no! One man remains standing. Hiram Smith is untouched by the fusillade. Apparently none of the men wanted to kill the brave man taking the place of Mrs. Humphrey's husband. Does this mean he gets to go free? The Colonel stares at me as he gestures with his saber at the prisoner. Oh God! The Sergeant of the Guard is supposed to finish off any prisoner left alive by the firing squad! THIS is my punishment for laughing at him. Again I appeal to Colonel Strachan. He is enjoying this, his hate for me evident in his eyes. I have to carry out my orders.

My hand falls heavily to my side, slowly dragging my feet I stumble toward the prisoner stopping but a few feet from him. I do not wish to look at him but I have to know where to place the shot. My hand wavers as I raise the heavy pistol toward his heart. Hiram Smith looks at me expressionless, defiantly accepting his fate. I dare not look into his eyes as my hand shakes uncontrollably.

"Sergeant, carry out your orders! Do your duty Sergeant!" The Colonel hovers over me yelling for me to shoot the prisoner. My arm weakens as I try to push my hand upward as the world darkens and sound fades away. Remnants of the breakfast taken hours earlier come out as I sink to the ground vomiting violently.

"Sergeant! SERGEANT!" The Colonel won't leave me alone. "Shoot him Sergeant!" He continues to yell as he extends the pistol toward me that I dropped. I try to reach for the gun but cannot support myself. My gaze shifts upward to Hiram Smith whose eyes are saying. "I forgive you." He forgives me? He forgives me! In slow motion the Colonel raises the pistol toward Hiram's head. From a great distance the scream comes from my lips. "NOOOOO!" I watch Hiram Smith's head jerk backward and his body fall limply into his grave.

The sound of the last shot reverberates in the stunned silence of the assembly.

Chapter Twenty Two

After eight months the eyes of Hiram Smith still haunt me. Every inactive moment is filled by the recollections of 'That Day'. My sleep is interrupted by the piercing eyes and slight smile on his face as he forgave me, or perhaps it is a smirk and disdain for my weakness. Is it weakness to be unable to kill defenseless men? In the field of battle I could kill. Hell, I joined the army not for the express purpose of killing, but I knew it was a possibility. Of course the prospect of killing seemed fairly remote the fall of 1851 as I left my father's farm near Warsaw, Illinois.

Warsaw! I miss home. While at Palmyra I occasionally rode home for visits. Dad is getting up in years, almost sixty and, thanks to my three older brothers, no longer struggles in the fields. Damn I hate Kansas City! As places go, I suppose Kansas City is OK, it's just too far from home. A visit to Warsaw is a week's hard ride now instead of the one day from Palmyra.

Hard ride indeed! With the Partisans in control of the countryside any Union soldier traveling alone is in extreme danger. An encounter with William Clarke Quantrill and his guerrilla band is akin to suicide. Fortunately I have not had the misfortune of such an encounter but scuttlebutt around camp convinces me my good fortune should be appreciated.

Good fortune? My transfer from Palmyra was good fortune. I could not look my comrades in the eye after 'That Day' and they didn't speak to me either. Perhaps they didn't know how to console me, or considered me weak for not following orders. Either way, I hate them. Worst of all - they know!

Their knowing eyes were always on me, staring. Was it pity? Disdain? What was it they felt for me? I could not hide from them.

I am grateful for Colonel Richard William "Dick" Clark for my transfer. He is a friend from Warsaw that replaced that bastard Strachan. Excuse me, let me use the term he is now known as, 'Beast Strachan' a well deserved title that should be shared with General McNeill. Rumor has it the Confederate President, Jefferson Davis, demanded General McNeill be tried for war crimes and if not, the first ten Union officers captured would be executed in retribution. No loss.

There is little doubt General McNeill condoned the actions of his subordinate on 'That Day'. He could have stopped it at any time. The furor raised by that barbaric act took the General by surprise and he successfully deflected blame onto 'The Beast'. Before 'That Day' I hadn't had a great deal of respect for officers but those two destroyed any respect that remained. Watching the General maneuver blame onto the Colonel is laughable as the image of General McNeill calmly dismissing the troops 'That Day' left little doubt he supported the actions that took place. He ordered the execution and others as well. Reliable sources say he secretly ordered over thirty of Colonel Porters followers executed after capturing them at Kirksville the September before 'That Day'.

That Day! That Day! That Day! God, I can't get it out of my mind! I have not mentioned my service at Palmyra to my new companions, preferring that no one knows. Colonel Clark sent a letter to the commanding officer at the Kansas City garrison, requesting he keep my background from becoming common knowledge. Colonel Clark is an understanding officer. What a misnomer! Understanding and officer just do not fit together. If he wasn't from Warsaw... if he hadn't known me before... well, Dick probably would not have helped me as he has.

At least the weather will be warmer now that June is here. When I arrived in December I thought I would freeze. Our barracks in Palmyra cut off most of the wind and cold but these tents, shared by four men, never seem to get warm in the winter. The temperature some days is well below zero and no amount of clothing will keep me warm. It is said that Quantrill moved south for the winter to escape the cold. Now that is a bright officer! Geez! Well I suppose we have to stay here.

Shit! I need to change my attitude, I hardly talk to anyone. Even in the tent I share with three other Sergeants, I am a loner. If they ask about my background... shit, if someone comes along that knows of 'That Day'... well, somehow I must learn to face it. Damn! Oops! I also need to stop swearing so much.

My second six year term of enlistment is up in November and I'll return to civilian life, I've had enough of this killing bullshit! My brothers will take me in but until then, I must make the best of the situation at hand.

The tent camp isn't too bad as we are below the hill that Kansas City is on, at least where the rich folks of Kansas City are located. From our position near the Missouri river east of the confluence with the Kaw River, we see new homes being built on the hill to the south. Snob Hill is what the soldiers call it. Some of the older buildings are in terrible shape even though they are only about twenty years old. Kansas City is hard on buildings because of its terrain, which is... hilly! The hills slope steeply up or away from the buildings on winding streets. Spring thaw and rains erode portions of the dirt from the foundations making the older buildings very unstable.

"J.V.!" Sergeant McClain yells at me. "Wanna hit some saloons?" Sergeant Gary McClain tries to engage me in conversation and is the only one of my tent mates that hasn't given up on me. Maybe I should try to be one of the boys, couldn't hurt.

"Yeah Gary, sounds like fun." I respond and a smile quickly replaces his look of surprise.

"Aw' right! Big Jim here we come!" Gary excitedly slaps my shoulder.

Big Jim is just that... big! A huge man well over six feet in height and three hundred plus non fat pounds with a mean streak as big as he is, made Big Jim Pendergast feared by all. His is the largest establishment on the West Bottoms, as the flat area by the rivers below Snob Hill is called. Here the undesirable elements of Kansas City meet for fun, where the riff raff frequents and where fights, bloodied noses and busted heads are a common sight. No one starts a fight in Big Jim's however, as damage to his place may have to be paid with the life of the participants, according to rumor. Tangling with the oversized fists of Big Jim Pendergast makes even the bravest of men fainthearted; consequently Big Jim's is the safest place to celebrate.

"What are we celebrating Gary?" I ask my companion.

As we walk, he touches his chin with his finger, rolls his eyes as if pondering the question. "How about, the arrival of a new commanding officer, Brigadier General Thomas Ewing."

"Right! Now there is something to celebrate." I reply sarcastically. It feels good to laugh and have a friend. Maybe there is hope for me.

General Ewing is intent on removing the Partisan's families, believing the raiders will follow and we'd no longer have to deal with them. That will suit me, just let me slide by until November and I am out of this chicken shit army! I have not encountered Quantrill, or his band, but know we can expect no quarter in battle as we have been ordered to give no quarter; thus a fight to the death is expected. We know the banishment order has not been given, but the General is lobbying for that through his mentor, Senator James A. Lane from Kansas.

Our command is the Border District of Missouri and the General is bringing in companies from Kansas. Gary and I feel having Kansas soldiers in charge of affairs in Missouri is dangerous, given the natural tensions between residents of the neighboring states. Tensions are heightened when General Ewing orders the women of the Partisans picked up and jailed for various crimes such as, making food and clothing for them. Huh? What else are wives, mothers, sisters and relatives supposed to do? To arrest these women for their actions of making food etc… makes no sense. It's ludicrous! Officers! There I go again, none of your business J.V., just do as you are told. The official charge is aiding and abetting the enemy.

Summoned to Lieutenant Day's tent, I part the canvas slit and step inside. "You wanted to see me sir?"

Lieutenant Ken Day, a soft spoken officer commented on a change in my attitude, expressing appreciation that I decided to 'rejoin' the army.

As I stammer a response to his kindness he smiles saying, "I know Sergeant. I know." I know? Does that mean he knows about Palmyra, or that he knows I welcome his kindness? Whatever the meaning, I feel more at ease around this officer than any officer other than Colonel Clark.

"Sergeant Parman, this is Arden Carlson, a photographer in Blue Springs." The Lieutenant said indicating a man standing beside the small table serving as a desk for Lieutenant Day. I nod at the guest with a nervous smile as he extends his right hand toward me. "Mr. Carlson has information about a Partisan's family in the Blue Springs area. Form your squad Sergeant and go with Mr. Carlson to arrest the sisters of the Partisan's, Bill and Jim Anderson. Sergeant McClain's squad will accompany you."

"I have pictures." Mr. Carlson began. Fumbling in his pocket, he produces five pictures of various people. I've not seen anything like this before. I carefully inspect them, mesmerized by the images displayed on the thin metal plates.

My wrinkled brow gave me away as the Lieutenant smiles saying. "I don't think the Sergeant has seen photographs before Mr. Carlson." Turning to me, he continues. "The people in the photographs are the ones you are to arrest."

One picture is of three pretty girls, the older seated surrounded by the younger. Another shows a man seated with a young girl standing behind him. Two other pictures are of two and three men posing for the camera.

"This is Bill and Jim Anderson, and this one is the two brothers joined by Arch Clement. This one is Bill Anderson alone."

"Bill Anderson is a Lieutenant in Quantrill's Partisan Rangers." Lieutenant Day interjects. "He is said to be devoted to his sisters, these three in this picture... and to his fiancé in this picture with him. It is these four young ladies you are to pick up. I caution you, Mr. Carlson believes this is not a routine pickup of four females. The Anderson's are frequently near their sisters and an encounter with them could be disastrous. They are cold blooded killers, you must exercise caution in your assignment."

"His eyes!" Arden Carlson stammers. "His eyes are cold, scary!"

I look at Bill Anderson and see a bearded young man staring into the distance. His eyes?

Mr. Carlson nods as I look at him. "He scared me when I looked into those eyes. There is... nothing behind them, he made me shiver. I was so glad when he left my studio that day." The man is blurting the words out as if relieved to say them.

Leaving the Lieutenants tent, I study the pictures closely. The girls are quite pretty and young, probably in their late teens.

"Whatcha lookin' at?" Gary teased as we meet outside the tent.

"Our assignment." I say smiling as I hand him the pictures.

"OOOOH!!! These are a lot prettier than the fat old ladies I picked up earlier!" He said with a laugh.

I look at him curiously. "You've been on these excursions before? Why did the Lieutenant put me in charge when it is my first?"

Gary smiled. "He recognizes a natural born leader?"

"Yeah, right! You probably had something to do with my selection." the appreciation apparent as I speak.

"Me?" He says innocently holding his palms upward unable to hide the impish smile on his lips. I lightly punch his arm and we return to our tent laughing together.

We left camp that morning having been cautioned to reconnoiter the area prior to confronting the Sanders for the Anderson sisters. Should the brothers be there without their guerrilla band we are to capture them as well.

We travel slowly in the heat of July 27, meandering over hills, around trees and through gullies, thus the thirty mile journey lasts until well after dark. It is an eerie feeling camping north of Blue Springs, an area known to be friendly with Quantrill's raiders and especially Bloody Bill Anderson. Our two squads of thirty one men travel quietly enough to keep from alerting the locals. Knowing the guerrillas travel in bands of fifty to two hundred men makes for a long uneasy night, the slightest sound interrupting our sleep, expecting the rebels to come charging out of the woods. Pre-dawn finds the men preparing their mounts for the descent on the Sanders farm a mile away. We are anxious to finish this assignment and return to the safety of our camp in Kansas City.

At the first sign of light, the men are positioned around the farm awaiting my signal to close in. Edging closer to the farm house I try to remain out of sight of those inside, yet in view of the half circle of riders closing in, when a young girl emerges from the barn carrying a basket to spread grain for the chickens. The chickens stand still and quiet, with necks stretched to their fullest, staring at me in the woods. She looks in our direction and I pray that at fifty yards we are far enough away that she cannot see us. No such luck! She drops her basket and runs toward the barn as I give the signal to move in. Quickly surrounding the house, I order the inhabitants out.

I nervously sit atop my horse, my saddle squeaking as my mount moves beneath me, in front of the house. If they shoot I'll be one of the first to go. Prudence dummy, you are not being prudent!

The front door opens slowly. "I'm coming out! Don't shoot, don't shoot, I'm coming out!" Cautiously a stout man appears easing his way to the front porch, hands raised shoulder high. Suspenders support his not completely buttoned trousers and I am relieved we had found the family asleep.

"Mr. Sanders?" I ask. He nods. "Please gather your family and all the inhabitants beside you sir." I say as pleasantly as I can yet with authority. I hope a pleasant demeanor will prevent a nasty confrontation.

"Patty!" He calls inside. A woman, I take to be his wife, emerges from the house. He quickly confirms the relationship. "Dear, would you go to the..." He turns and looks at me. "She'll have to go to the barn..." I nod and he continues addressing his wife. "Get Frank, Mary and the girls please."

Patty returns with a man and woman of the Sanders' age and eight girls that look to be ten to twenty years old. I recognize the Anderson sisters from the photographs, also the girl friend of Bill. I call Mr. Carlson to come forward to confirm identifications as I open the official document and read. "By proclamation of Brigadier General Thomas Ewing, Commanding officer, Missouri Border Region, the following are to be placed in the custody of the United States Army at Kansas City: Josephine Anderson, Virginia Anderson, Kathleen Anderson, Diane Hodges.

The younger women exchange glances as I read the names. "On what charge?" Frank asks as he holds the girls back.

That question takes me aback as I hadn't been told of a charge. "Sir, I have my orders to pick up the young ladies and I assure you they will be treated with utmost respect."

Frank looks at the soldiers with guns at the ready and sighs. "So many men, to capture so few innocent little girls."

It does look ridiculous, thirty one armed men confronting two old men and ten females, mostly children. It may be embarrassing but we load the four young ladies into the wagon and hurry toward Kansas City. We leave them at the Union Hotel, which has been transformed into a prison, crowded with wives, mothers, sisters and girl friends of the Partisan's. Now there are four more.

Part of the return journey I spend trying to engage the older of the Anderson sisters, Josephine, in light conversation but she ignores my feeble attempts. She is beautiful. Gary encourages me to try again, and one of her sisters encourages her to speak with me, so I keep up my efforts. I detect a slight smile but her head is bowed, shyly staring at her hands clasped in her lap. Long reddish blond hair glistens in the sunlight and I am smitten by her beauty. A demure nature enhances that beauty and I find myself drawn to her in spite of being ignored. She gave me neither a glance nor a word until I help her from the wagon in front of the Union Hotel. Hesitating momentarily at the edge of the wagon she peers into my eyes before acknowledging my assistance with a quiet, polite, "Thank you." as she is safely placed on the ground.

Gary takes great pleasure in his teasing refrain. "J.V.'s in love! J.V.'s in love!" My face flushes with embarrassment and I try to quiet him with a scowl. He keeps up his banter in a whisper so that only I could hear. "J.V.'s in love!"

"Shush!" I smile. Perhaps I am in love although I don't know what that is; I only know what I think of Josephine Anderson... alot!

"Hey J.V.!" Gary calls, after the girls are led upstairs in the Hotel. "Why not ask Bloody Bill for his sister's hand in marriage, surely he wouldn't object! Just get down on one knee and say; 'Mr. Anderson, may I have the privilege of marrying your favorite sister'? Would you mind if it was a Union wedding?" Gary's ribbing brings howls of laughter from the men in our squads. They are not ridiculing me and I revel in their good natured teasing. I am part of something again.

A few days later, as Gary and I sit in Big Jim's tavern. "Gary, look at that one!" as I set my mug down and indicate the giant of a man entering Big Jim's. "We thought Big Jim is big! This guy must be a half foot taller and every bit as wide as Big Jim! Wow, look at him!" I watch the giant clumsily follow a much smaller man into the saloon. The smaller man leads the giant as they make their way to the back of the saloon and sit at a table.

"Did you see that Gary?" I grab my companions arm.

"Shee what?" Gary asks thickly.

"The little guy only has one hand."

"Whish liddle guy?" Gary asks bumping against me.

"You're drunk!" I overstate the obvious, although I am not far behind.

Gary turns toward me with eyes half closed and expels air from his mouth, lips flapping together to make a funny noise. "Sho?" He unsteadily lifts his mug to his lips.

I laugh at my mate and almost fall off my stool. As I regain my position I look once more toward the large and small men noticing they have been joined by two others, one of which passes a slip of paper to the one armed man. The man passing the paper looks anxiously about as the one handed man quickly slips the paper into his pocket and rises to leave.

"They didn't even get a drink." I laugh raising my mug toward Gary. I've got some catching up to do.

Our squads are relegated to guard duty as are other Missouri squads. Forces from Kansas and Colorado patrol the surrounding countryside and we wonder if the General is concerned the Missouri troops may not be loyal and will aid the guerrilla's. Aid the enemy? Sounds familiar.

Lieutenant Day tries to maintain morale by insisting we are doing necessary duty. Necessary, ha, first we make war on women by capturing and imprisoning them now we guard them as if they are dangerous criminals.

My squad is assigned to relocate prisoners to a three story building in McGee's addition on Grand Avenue between fourteenth and fifteenth Streets. This westward facing structure typifies the poor planning that had gone into the building program in early Kansas City as the water runoff toward adjacent ravines has caused considerable erosion. When originally built it was probably a formidable structure of rock piled upon rock with smaller rocks filling the gaps. The walls are three foot thick in this forty by forty foot square structure, timber girders supporting the second and third stories are designed to protrude through the outer walls several inches. On the south side the walls are separating toward the ravine making that protrusion non existent and a gap of several inches has developed between the wall and floor. Cracks wide enough to see through are in the walls. Large long poles propped against the juncture of the first and second floor stave off what appears to be inevitable.

"Surely they are not going to keep anyone in this building?" I ask of no one in particular. "This definitely does not look safe!" I am dismayed to see the Anderson sisters among the women being led to their new jail.

As the women trudge the nine blocks from the Union Hotel to their newly assigned prison, spectators line the streets to gape at the women of the Partisan's. Some jeering as the women pass but most offer no comment or perhaps sympathize with the women. I am surprised to see the giant man that had been at Big Jim's a couple days earlier. It is impossible not to notice this man six foot eight inches tall and over three hundred pounds towering above every one around him. He has a slight paunch with massive shoulders, heavy set muscular arms and a strange, silly look on his face as if he... that's it! He's a simpleton! Next to him is the one armed man leading the giant around. What a combination, a dummy and a cripple.

I make eye contact with Josephine and may have detected a slight smile as she glances toward me. Is it a coincidence she walks only a few feet from my side as I march with my musket at the ready, should any of these 'dangerous' criminals attempt an attack?

"Are you... ah... are you being treated alright?" I whisper. She turns her head slightly, nods almost imperceptibly, and returns her gaze to the street in front of her. She acknowledged me; perhaps I am making some headway.

Trudging up the stairs to the third floor where the women are to be kept, I feel the building sway slightly. "Did you feel that?" I ask Josephine who stops, looking at me quizzically. I wait, and listen, but cannot detect movement again. Did I imagine it? "Did you feel the floor move?" I ask her. She shakes her head.

The third floor was living quarters for the first inhabitants of this building but unoccupied for a few years. The rough board flooring gives way slightly under my feet providing a bounce to my step. Ticking is thrown on the floor, a sleeping place for the girls. Girls! That is what they are, none much older than twenty. Yeah, real dangerous!

Leaving the building, I sought out Lieutenant Day. "Is there no safer place to hold these women?"

The lieutenant shrugs his shoulders as he peers into my eyes. "I share your concern Sergeant, but they won't be here long. The General is in St. Louis petitioning General Scofleld, and I am seeking other facilities. I will attempt to secure his permission to relocate them upon his return."

General Ewing returned August thirteenth amidst rumors he is not happy with the result of his meeting with General Scofleld. Apparently the Commander of the Department of Missouri does not see things as his commander of the Border Region does. Perhaps banishing the Partisan's families will not rid us of the Partisan's. This is just another difference of opinion between officers.

I look forward to guarding the Bingham building owned by the famous artist, George Caleb Bingham, who built a new home in Independence a few years earlier. During guard duty I contact Josephine trying to break through her shy exterior and get to know the inner person. We don't speak of anything important just small talk to get acquainted and I enjoy it immensely.

Arriving at the Bingham house to relieve the guard on the fourteenth, the proprietor of the shop on the first floor is hurriedly loading a wagon with boxes of bottles, blankets and other goods from his store. He is moving out of the dilapidated Bingham building and I can't blame him. Breathing heavily he runs in and out of the building aided by a stout woman I know to be his wife. Both are sweating profusely and, although obviously tired, do not stop to rest.

Something seems amiss this evening, something different about the building. As I ponder what, there is a creaking noise. The shop owner hears it and pauses to look at the building; stare and hold his breath. Small rocks tumble out of place among the larger rocks in the walls on the ravine side of the building supported by... OH MY GOD! THE TIMBERS ARE GONE! THE SUPPORTING POLES ARE GONE!

The building creaks again, louder this time. The man throws his box in the wagon yelling at his wife to leap aboard. Another creak, more like a loud groan, comes as the wife drops her box in terror, running as rocks tumble from the wall toward her.

Am I imagining it or are the walls moving? They are moving, I am not imagining it! OH GOD! THE WALLS ARE COMING DOWN! "JOSEPHINE!" Screams from the inhabitants on the third floor are drowned out by crashing rocks and timbers as the building crumbles toward the ravine.

I stand transfixed by an unbelievable sight. The three story building nearly forty feet to the top, collapses inwardly at first, gently swaying, then in a cloud of dust, the walls twist and crash loudly toward the ravine. A state of shock grips the witnesses. Not until the rocks stop tumbling and moans and screams are heard from the rubble do the nearby men, who had run to avoid the collapsing building, rush to remove rubble from possible survivors. Pain filled screams muffled by rocks and timbers fill the air as a cloud of dust rolls toward the ravine.

Darkness begins to envelope us as we climb onto the rubble and roll the larger rocks aside. The large pile has just stopped shifting as men frantically search for survivors... or victims. I uncover an arm and try to pull the person free from the debris but only pull a painful scream from the woman attached. There is bone sticking through the upper arm. She no longer screams, fainted I hope. Frantically I dig into the pile around the exposed arm until I reveal the entire person. She is blood soaked about the face, her nose broken and... and... and is not Josephine! At once relieved and apprehensive, I yell for someone to get her and dig in another area where I hear moaning. I do not try to extricate the woman until she can be carefully lifted from the rubble. It is not Josephine.

I stumble over rocks to see a woman being lifted by a pair of men a few feet away - not her! I uncover another and recognize Virginia Anderson, eyes wide in pain her mouth trying to form words. No sound comes as she tries to draw breath but cannot.

Her eyes widen in horror, hands reaching for me, for someone, for anyone, her fingers clutching as she stretches out her arms. Her eyes soften and she falls limply against the pile of rocks. Damn, did she die? Suddenly the giant man is there and lifts Virginia Anderson free from the jagged board that had pierced her between the shoulders.

Oh God, Josephine where are you? I struggle to move rocks, pausing only to check as another form is revealed. Suddenly I see the bloodied, lifeless form of Josephine. Furious activity continues around me as I stare at the beauty crushed by boulders. I feel empty, unable to move. Slowly I back away, oblivious to the pain in my bleeding hands. Blinking back tears, I pause to look at the carnage, at men struggling to find others in the rubble. A young girl screams as the giant man carries her from the flattened building, is it Kathleen Anderson?

What happened here? The building was obviously unsafe, everyone knew that! Why did it happen? The timbers! Why had the timbers supporting the walls been removed? Why? So many questions, so few answers.

Chapter Twenty Three

As usual, Bo and Socrates report what they learn in Kansas City to Captain Quantrill. We learn Diane and our sisters have been taken to Kansas City and where they are being held. The Captain vehemently opposes my suggestion to storm the Union Hotel. The city is heavily fortified and even the element of surprise cannot succeed, or so he says. Perhaps it is foolhardy, but I feel I can do it alone, however; it is possible the women might get hurt in such a daring rescue attempt.

Quantrill emerges from his tent and walks briskly toward John McCorkle. John steps back, apparently stunned with his news. The Captain places his arm around the slumping shoulders of John McCorkle.

The Captain's eyes meet mine as he starts toward me, his eyes soft and apologetic. Jim sees it and says. "Something's wrong." Bo and Socrates stand at the Captains tent, Bo solemnly looking at us. The Captain is standing in front of me.

"Bill. Jim." He begins slowly. "The Bingham house has collapsed."

Over the Captains' shoulder, John McCorkle meets my gaze with a pained expression.

"WHAT?" I yell as if asking John to explain why he is looking at me. My ears start to ring loudly. Something bad has happened. "WHAT?" I yell again as the Captain grabs my arm, John turns away.

"Among the dead... are... John's sister, Christie McCorkle Kerr... and... Ginny... and... Josi... and Diane Hodges." He says quietly.

My ears are ringing and a strange buzzing sound nearly drowns out what the Captain is saying. "Kay is badly hurt. Socrates carried her to the Sander's, who are taking care of her... Bill? Bill? Do you hear me Bill?"

Hear you? Of course I hear you, even though you are moving farther away from me, getting smaller. How are you able to shake me, you are too far away, but you are shaking me? How...? It's getting dark! It's too early for darkness! Where is everybody going? Where's ev'..iy....

Jim is sitting on a log near my feet looking at me with red ringed eyes as I stir awake.

"What's the matter?" I ask, the buzzing in my head at a lower level.

"You fainted."

"I did not! Fainting is what women do! I did not faint!" I insist.

"Crying is for women too." He said softly.

"I DID NOT CRY!"

Jim starts to say something but shakes his head gazing at his hands, folding and unfolding them in his lap.

The buzzing intensifies as I sit up. "What...? Did...? Did the Captain... say?" Jim nods and watches me struggle to speak.

"They are... dead?"

He looks away and the buzzing is louder, much more intense. "Who... saw... them?" I ask, squinting against the painful headache.

"Bo and Socrates." Jim answers softly. "Socrates carried Kay all the way to Blue Springs. The Sanders have her. She's pretty bad off Bill."

"What about Ginny?" I ask. Jim shakes his head. "Josi?"

Jim looks at his hands.

"But... Diane... Diane is not with them... was she?"

Jim says nothing, looking at me before returning his eyes to his hands. The buzzing intensifies as does the headache.

"Where's that coming from?" I ask.

"What?" Jim looks at me. "Where's what coming from?"

"That buzzing sound."

Jim looks around. "What buzzing sound?"

"THAT buzzing sound!" I say, waving my arms in a circular motion. "Can't you hear it?" It is much too loud for him not to hear it. "Where is that buzzing coming from?"

He looks at me quizzically without answering. Why won't he tell me where that buzzing is coming from? "Are you OK Bill?" He asks.

"Am I OK? Am I OK?" I am stunned by his question. "Why shouldn't I be OK? What kind of question is that? Am I OK? Are you OK? You're the son-of-a-bitch that can't hear! Are YOU OK?" I have to leave him; he must be going crazy, asking if I am OK!

Archie went wild when hearing the news about Josi, Ginny, Kay and Diane. He hardly knows them but he knows how much they mean to me and it is his typical response if something affects or offends me. He's a good friend. He mounts his horse screaming for revenge, wanting to attack Kansas City, to extract a measure of revenge against the Union boys that inflicted pain on his friend. Some mount to join him but others restrain them, trying to convince Archie of the folly of his proposed reaction. Is it folly? We are two hundred men, if we ride in shooting they could not get the almost one thousand troopers organized before we kill nearly all of them. We can do it!

"Bill? Where ya goin?" William Gregg asks as Archie and I mount our horses. There is concern in his voice and other faces turn toward us with puzzled looks. If I declare for Kansas City, how many will follow?

I look at Gregg from the back of The Wind as he nervously pulls against the bit. "The Sanders. We're going to the Sanders' to see Kay." The buzzing is barely audible and, whatever type of insect, it must have moved away.

For an hour he had been watching me carefully as we rode, finally I whirl at Jim angrily. "What are you looking at?"

"Ah... mmmm... nothing Bill, nothing." He offers apologetically, responding as a child caught in the act. He is really starting to annoy me.

Mrs. Sanders is sweeping the porch as we arrive and stops to face us.

"Can we see Kay?" I ask.

"She's not here Bill, Jim." She says in a low tone as she peers at her broom. "The Mr. took her to Jefferson City. Doc Hansen said she needs a better doctor than he is. Bill, she's hurt real bad." Patty Sanders stifled a cry, waggling her broom with no purpose. "Frank and Mary went with the Mr." she could not hold back her tears and cries into Jim's shoulder as he wraps his arms around her.

"How bad is she?" Jim asks leading Mrs. Sanders to a chair.

Her eyes sparkling from tears, Patty sniffles into her handkerchief, draws a deep breath. "Doc says her left hip is crushed, she may never walk again, and... and... her left arm is broken, but Doc fixed that. Her ribs are crushed... Oh Jim! The poor dear can hardly breathe. Doc went with them to Jefferson City but... he's not sure she will make it to the hospital."

I walk to the edge of the porch, Patty Sanders weeps openly into Jim's shoulder as he tries to console her. Diane's sisters solemnly go about their chores, feeding the chickens, tending the cattle and pigs. Martha stands by the barn looking at me. A year younger than Diane, the retarded Martha has been cared for by her older sister.

"Where's Diane?" I ask Mrs. Sanders without looking at her. Her crying stops abruptly and after a pause I turn to look at her. She and Jim are staring at me, a startled look on their faces.

"What has happened to her body?" I continue to their relief.

Mrs. Sanders drops her chin and turns slightly toward me. "She... ah... they... I don't know! Bo said they were dead... and we were so concerned about Kay, we... we didn't think about bodies." She stammers.

Martha is still staring at me as her sisters continue their tasks. The grain soundlessly strikes the ground from the hands of Elizabeth, drowned out by the incessant buzzing. "Archie, shall we retrieve the bodies?" It is more of an; 'I'm going, do you want to came along', statement than a question.

"You can't Bill!" Jim offers immediately.

I look at him with disdain, wondering about his courage.

He takes a couple steps toward me and continues. "If you, or anyone goes to claim the bodies, they will be arrested as Partisan's! No one can go! They hope you will do just that, ride into a trap to claim the bodies."

The buzzing intensifies and I look for the origin. Surely they are close as the buzzing is so loud and it's a clear day, why can I not see them? I point into the air. "Do you hear it... the buzzing? Do you hear it?"

Jim looks at me with a blank stare.

"What?" I ask angrily as he buries his head in his hands. "Alright! I'll just go into Kansas City to see where they died, you have any objection to that?"

"Jim is right Bill." Mrs. Sanders quietly spoke. "They have photographs of you and will arrest you if you go to town."

"Photographs?"

"Yes, the ones you took last year with the girls. They have those photographs and know what you look like; you will not be able to go to Kansas City without a terrible risk of being recognized."

I wave my hands in front of my face to chase away the buzzing sound. "Photographs?" If I ignore them maybe the critters will go away. "Then we'll go to Blue Springs and shoot that bastard that gave the photographs to the Union." Those pests are a persistent lot.

"Bill. That photographer knows what we look like and who we are. At first sight he'll have soldiers coming down on us immediately. There will come a time for him, but now is not that time." Jim's voice of reason is starting to piss me off.

We return to the Lake Lotawanna camp August 17th and thoughts of travel to Jefferson City are set aside as it may be too late already. Kay has

Doc Hansen with her, and Frank and Mary, there is nothing I can do.

Looking for Bo and Socrates as we reach camp, they are nowhere to be seen. Asking for their where-a-bouts, I am told the Captain has gone to Perdee's farm on Blackwater Creek and wishes to see us there.

"You wish to see us Captain?" I ask as I press open the canvas slit in his tent.

"Bill! Jim! Yes, come in! Come in!" He said rising from behind a table pausing until we are inside, Archie as well. He looks at Archie for a moment; no one seems to like Archie but me! "I have sent messengers to gather the partisans in Western Missouri for a campaign that will make the Union wish they had never caused the collapse of the Bingham building and the death of your sisters." the Captain began.

"Caused?" I interrupt.

He draws a breath studying my eyes. "Yes... caused." he sighs softly but with feeling, "Reliable information has it the walls of the building were weakened, stones removed, to make the building collapse." His voice begins to fade as the buzzing sound grows in intensity. "We have information that General Ewing was warned the day before that the building was dangerous and the prisoners must be moved. A warning the General reportedly laughed at."

"Then we will be attacking Kansas City." My voice rings hollow in my head. The Captain smiles. "Better! Who is the most hated man in Missouri?"

"General Ewing." I respond without hesitation.

"By ALL Missourians." the Captain said shaking his head at my response. "You have ample reason to say General Ewing, but what one man is more hated than even the General?"

"Jennison." Jim said quietly.

"Ah yes, Jennison, the leader of the Red Legs. But still better, Jennison's boss; the number one Jayhawker himself!" Quantrill said smiling.

William Clarke Quantrill smugly pulls himself to his full height nodding proudly. "Bo and Socrates are on their way to Lawrence to ascertain the precise location of Senator Lane and scout the town. We intend to slip quietly into town at night, capture the Senator and make him pay with his life, for the lives lost in Kansas City."

The sound of a horse approaching interrupts us. The rider dismounts and delivers a message for the Captain. After reading the dispatch, the Captain lowers it slowly and makes no comment. Finally he looks at us, attempting to restrain his anger. "General Scofield will allow banishment." Lifting the dispatch he read. "The state of affairs in Missouri may dictate drastic measures from time to time. The measure of removing families from homes they worked years to develop is not one to be taken lightly. Eradication of the Partisan's is, and must be, of uppermost importance. This extreme measure will be authorized, providing utmost care is taken to identify and remove only the families of known Partisan's."

He quietly folds the paper placing it in his breast pocket. "They are declaring war on our families, on innocent women and children, those that have absolutely nothing to do with the conflict!" Drawing a deep breath, his eyes flash as he proclaims. "If they want that type of war, they shall have it!" Brushing past us, Captain Quantrill exited his tent.

Gathering the men together, the Captain reads the dispatch in its entirety. Stunned silence greets him as he completes the reading. "Gentlemen." I recognize his speech making tone. "The Union has declared war on our women. The decision to attack Lawrence and capture the hated Jayhawker has already been announced as retribution for the deaths caused in Kansas City four days ago. James Lane symbolizes the Jayhawker cause. He is THE Jayhawker. Will his execution... be ample retribution... for the death of four innocent females? Is James Lane that important a man? Perhaps John McCorkle... is prepared to accept the life of James Lane... for the life of his sister... Christie... McCorkle... Kerr... but!" He said waving a finger in the air. "Is he important enough to appease the Anderson's? Bill and Jim, who lost two of their beloved sisters, Josephine and Virginia; and Bill who also lost his fiancé?" placing his hand on my shoulder he spoke for the benefit of the entire group. "Should Bill be satisfied if that one man alone dies? Should we be satisfied..." he begins to move among the men. "...with one life to pay for the wrongs perpetrated on our families and friends? Can this one man satisfy the rage that builds within each of us?"

The men grumble, nodding as they murmur, before returning their faces to William Clarke Quantrill. I admire how he incites men, how he pauses to heighten the effect of his words. They are mesmerized, as am I, at how he manipulates our feelings toward his own. Hell, I am getting excited! I am mad! I have been mad and getting madder! The buzzing grows louder and I still cannot see them cussed varmints!

"So, shall we hang the hated Jayhawker... James.... Lane?" The Captain continues. "...or, shall we stand him in front of our guns and collectively blow him apart? Then each of us may be appeased for the tragedies initiated by his hatred and narrow mindedness some eight years ago? Would the sacrifice of that one man be sufficient? I think not! I think our families... your families... your friends... that at this very minute are being thrown out of their homes... would not feel appeased. I believe any society... any army... any people... that willfully wars against women and children... should be dealt with in like manner. I think you should be allowed to wipe out James Lane and HIS home, Lawrence Kansas!"

"YEAH!" comes a resounding roar from the men now whipped into a frenzy.

"Tomorrow... we embark toward Lawrence." Quantrill continues as he walks among the men, who slowly part to allow his passage and turn to follow his every move. He looks intently into the eyes of the Partisans as he approaches, speaking to each directly. "...and I propose... we inflict such damage... that the WORLD will know... the Union erred... gravely... in pursuing war against our families... but WE will NOT war against women and children. OH NO! Chivalry shall remain a paragon of the South. The men of that city... shall any be spared?"

"NO!" The men thoroughly fired up, roar in unison, eager to do whatever the Captain decrees.

Lawrence Kansas is nearly one hundred miles from the Perdee farm on Blackwater Creek northwest of Knob Noster, Missouri. Determination and anger are apparent on the faces of the Partisans as we set about our menial tasks awaiting the departure date. A messenger is sent to the Confederate camp of Colonel John D. Holt, requesting they intercept us at the middle fork of the Grand River. "Burn Lawrence" is the rallying theme.

The morning of August nineteenth, the normal revelry is noticeably absent as we are serious about the upcoming task. Burn Lawrence! Kill James Lane! Slowly we begin our trek forming a military column of four, never exceeding an easy trot. The Captain wishes this column to proceed in an organized military fashion and we keep in close ranks, frequently hearing his reminder. "Stay focused, your enemy awaits you."

The Wind presses against his bit dissatisfied with the slow pace of the column. Gentle words have a calming effect on him yet I feel the tension twitching in his body through my legs. He is anxious to run, to get away from the dust and the close quarters we share. He loves to run and so do I. Seated on the back of The Wind, at a gallop, the wind pulls my hair from my face whipping it on the back of my neck. God it is great! Many times after a hard run as The Wind is breathing heavily, I wind his mane through the fingers of my right hand, his signal to slow a bit, and leap from his back to run or bounce along at his side. He is such a beautiful horse; never does his gait exceed my ability to keep pace with him. Smart horse!

Even at a slow trot the dust is nearly unbearable, The Wind snorting and sneezing frequently, as do other horses. Looking back I am glad we are near the front as the dust and riding conditions are much worse at the rear of this group of three hundred Partisan's. In columns of four the end of our force is concealed in dust.

At noon of the twentieth, Colonel Holt and more than one hundred Confederate cavalrymen meet us at the appointed location and quietly settle in to the march.

We hadn't ridden far into Kansas, almost to Aubry, when the column stops. A line of one hundred Union cavalry soldiers sits atop a knoll to the west. Captain Quantrill issues the order for us to form battle lines four deep. Colonel Holt glances frequently at the Captain as masses of riders form on each side of the officers. It is apparent the Colonel has relinquished command to the junior officer, Quantrill.

Nearly three quarters of a mile separate us from the Union forces we outnumber four to one. Before the columns finish forming up the Union cavalry breaks ranks and rides for Aubry. We can cut them off before they reach town, but the Captain makes no move as he quietly watches them run. He then issues a new order to march again in columns of four.

Slowly we ride past the Union encampment in Aubry, at one hundred yards well within range of their muskets, but no shot is fired. We are prepared to turn and over-run the small town should they fire, but the Union soldiers wisely watch us pass. Cowards!

Bo and Socrates rejoin us as we stop for an hour near Spring Hill to rest, feed our horses and ourselves. It is almost dusk when we stop and Bo spends most of the hour with the two officers describing in detail his diagram of Lawrence. Using water from my canteen, I wipe the dust from the eyes and nose of The Wind as he calmly stands, appreciative of my attention. His coat glistens in the bright moonlight of this cloudless night as I remount with the rest of the Partisans to continue our quest.

The moon disappears as we reach Gardner, Kansas and it becomes almost impossible to see. The going is slow and we come to a halt as four men are dispatched to a farm house to bring a guide. After a wait of several minutes the column slowly makes its way again toward Lawrence. We hadn't ridden more than an hour when a shot rings out from the front of the column and once again we stop.

"Wha' happen Bill?" Archie asks from beside me.

"I don't know but... be ready!" I reply tensing for the worst. It was a single shot! If the Jayhawkers had discovered us there surely would have been more gunfire than a single shot?

What's going on? Word finally filters back to us. "The Captain shot the farmer he used as a guide."

Four riders are again dispatched to find a guide and after a wait, we again proceed slowly through the dark toward our objective.

Another shot rngs out. "OOOOHHH!!! DAT"S TWO!" Archie cooed joyfully. We ease our way toward the front of the columns. Four guides are likewise dispatched before we stop at a farm house near Lawrence. This time we walk our horses quietly toward the cabin door.

"What's going on?" I ask the rider in front of me.

"This is the farm of Joseph Stone the man that caused George Todd to be jailed in Independence a while back." He whispers.

I squeeze The Wind between two horses in the front row assuming a position a few yards from the front door as George Todd emerges dragging a man clad in a night shirt. A woman is beating on Todd's back and we laugh as two Partisans pull her away from George.

"Joseph Stone, you son-of-a-bitch! Do you remember me?" Todd yells at the man flung to the ground. "Stand Up!" He commands pulling his pistol from his belt.

"Todd!" The Captain yells. "Quietly, we're too close to Lawrence."

Todd looks at the Captain, at Joseph Stone, and then slowly walks to the ring of horsemen, handing his pistol to me. "Let me have your rifle." He said extending his hand without taking his eyes from his adversary. I slide my Sharps from its' scabbard handing it to him butt first. He holds it in his hands still looking at Mr. Stone. Slowly Todd walks the few steps necessary to face the older man. George Todd and Joseph Stone are the same height and for several moments stand inches apart staring into one another's eyes. Joseph Stone exhibits no fear in spite of being surrounded by unkempt menacing men. He stares at Todd with disdain. These two know, and dislike each other.

Without a word Todd steps back slightly and slams the butt of my Sharps into the face of his antagonist. Mr. Stone's head jerks back and his hands fly to his face. George redirects the butt of the rifle into the farmers' groin. A groan comes from Mr. Stone and a scream from Mrs. Stone. Her scream is quickly stifled by the hand of a nearby Partisan clamping down over her lips. Mr. Stone sinks to his knees in agony, his hands grasping his groin area as he topples face forward. George swings the rifle with all his might into the face of his enemy, reversing the direction of his fall. The sound of breaking bone as the wood and metal of the rifle meet his face is unmistakable, I have heard it before. Mr. Stone falls backward, blood oozing from his smashed face as his wife struggles against her captor.

"NNYYAAH! EEEEEEE! OOOOAAAHHH!" Archie squeals with delight. He's enjoying this too!

George Todd stands over the twitching form of Joseph Stone.

"He's getting up George." One of the Partisans comments as the man struggles to sit.

He doesn't get far before George strikes him again with a vicious blow causing him to fall on his back, blood gushing from gaping wounds in his face. Raising the rifle over his head like an axe, George 'chops' down on his victim, repeating the chopping action until the man no longer moves. Twice more Todd chops into his foe.

"Todd!" Colonel Holt finally yells in a commanding voice and, turning to Captain

Quantrill, said. "Enough! How dead do you want him?"

"Mount up George." The Captain said quietly.

George drops my Sharps from his hand. Just as well, the bastard broke it! Todd, breathing heavily, looks at his victim for a moment before turning his attention to the group surrounding him as if searching for something. I hold up his pistol. He nods and retrieves it.

As Mrs. Stone is released she falls to the ground sobbing, slowly crawling toward the lifeless body of her husband. She reaches an unsteady hand out to nudge him. "Joseph?" She pleads softly.

I notice the form of a young boy in the doorway staring at his mother crawling toward his dead father.

"Now maybe you will understand what it is like to watch your father die." I murmur softly. Small retribution for Josi having to watch our father die before she was... before she was....

Chapter Twenty Four

The eastern sky is turning light blue and pink signaling the start of another day as we halt the column on the outskirts of Lawrence Kansas, August 21, 1863. These people will long remember this day; we will make sure of that!

The Captain holds Bo's diagram as he outlines instructions, giving out lists of men to be executed and pointing out homes to be burned. Does he know all these people? Aw, who cares! In addition to the lists he instructs us to, "Kill every male big enough to carry a gun."

My squad is assigned to ride with Quantrill to the Senator's house and take him alive. The public execution of James Lane in Missouri will delight the citizens there. After the capture we are to join the burning and looting of the Jayhawker's camp in Lawrence, killing all men encountered. All the men? The population of Lawrence is estimated at two thousand and if half the population is men... WOW! A whole lot of killing is about to take place! Archie is grinning excitedly in anticipation of drawing more Jayhawk scalps.

The columns of Partisans break into a hard ride as we reach the corner of Delaware and Adam's streets from the southeast. Splitting on Quincy and Rhode Island streets, the town is quickly overrun by yelling, screaming Partisans. Perhaps we should have been less enthusiastic in our ride into Lawrence as, with our zealous rebel yells piercing the air, the Senator escaped. His bed is still warm as we reach his house but a thorough search of the area proves futile.

The Captain storms through the house smashing the furnishings of the hated Jayhawker. A chest is kicked over, its' contents spilling onto the floor revealing a gold plated sword. Seizing the General's flag, symbolizing his command of the Seventh Kansas Cavalry, the Captain uses it to wrap the golden sword and orders the house and its' contents burned. Archie delightedly grabs a coal oil lantern smashing it against an interior wall igniting its' fuel. Flames burst quickly along the wall and floor in shades of blue, green and orange, curtains ignite and smoke begins to thicken in the house.

"Let's go Archie!" I yell running from the building. Pausing outside to admire our handiwork, we note other buildings with flames shooting from them. The early morning light forms a perfect backdrop for crackling flames and screaming citizens running panic stricken into the streets, the men being shot almost as soon as they appear. One man's upper body is forced backward, feet flying into the air as Archie places a round in his face. The man is unarmed, but that doesn't matter as most of the men coming out from their nights sleep are unarmed, he is a Jayhawker or at least lives in the Jayhawker haven. Any man in Lawrence this day is condemned to die.

Finding our mounts, we accompany Captain Quantrill to Massachusetts Street shooting every male that appears until we reach the Eldridge Hotel. A white flag waves frantically from a second story window of the Hotel. The Captain looks at the towel attached to a broom handle and holds up his hand to order a cease fire.

"Come down from there!" He bellows.

"Sir, do you guarantee my safety should I surrender?" A voice asks.

Quantrill smiles, as he looks at the men eagerly awaiting his order. "Guarantee your safety? Now why should I do that? I can shoot you as you come out or, perhaps I'll just burn down the hotel and you can decide whether to be shot or burned to death, your choice." The Captain toys with the man for our benefit amidst howls of laughter.

"Sir?" The voice from within is much more subdued. "We, the guests of this hotel, display our flag of surrender assuming it is a military commander facing us and that military commander, according to common decency, would guarantee our safety. We are defenseless and at your mercy. The house is surrendered but we demand protection for its inmates."

"Common decency? Boy did you guess wrong!" Quantrill yells back at the man. "...and who are you to make demands?"

"I sir, am a newspaper reporter from the Chicago Sun." The voice replies.

Quantrill eases back in his saddle. "What is a newspaper man from Chicago doing here in Lawrence Kansas?"

After a pause the voice responds. "I am here for a story... why are you here?"

The Captain laughs at the reporter's brashness, commenting under his breath. "Story!" We all laugh as Quantrill smiles before returning his attention to the hotel window. "Plunder, reporter! We are here for plunder and sport!" Pausing to dismount, Quantrill smiles at us again and looks up at the window. "You shall have your guarantee, reporter." Looking at Archie and me, he directs. "Bill, Lawrence, Kansas is yours. Do with it as you will."

I look down Massachusetts Street toward the sound of gunfire. The sound is nearly drowned out by the buzzing in my head, a buzzing that has been increasing in strength since we rode into town; I turn The Wind in that direction.

"Bill!" Jim yells. "Enough!"

I look at him in disbelief for a moment before spurring The Wind into action.

"Whoooeeeee ha ha!" Archie yells, spurring his horse to a full gallop as he flings himself onto a man running across the street. Pulling him upright by the hair, Archie tilts the portly man's head back, thrusting a knife into his pink neck. The startled look on the portly man's face causes Archie to squeal with delight. The woman who was running with that man leaps on Archie's back, flailing at him with her fists until Archie gains the upper hand. He grasps her long hair and pulls her head back.

"Archie!" I yell before he can thrust his blade. "Remember, no woman is to be hurt in any fashion! Let her go!"

He looks at me for a moment, then smiles at the woman as he runs to his horse.

"YEE HAH!" I yell goading The Wind into a run with the reins loosely tied to the pommel of my saddle. Holding a Colt in each hand, I fire at men as my mount gallops furiously down the street. Archie follows, alternately shooting from one side to the other, yelling and laughing uproariously. Men topple over as they are hit. This is fun!

We gallop back the way we came, finding some we had shot are still alive. Archie uses his knife to finish his victims, but not me. I stand them up so I can look them in the eyes. I enjoy watching the expression of pain and fear as I raise my gun to their face. I barely hear the sound of the gun going off, but feel the recoil in my hand and watch each man's head jerk backward as my bullet enters his face. Pieces of flesh and blood explode in a circular pattern as if dropping a stone into a pond. I like shooting them in the head as there is a greater reaction than those shot in the chest or stomach. Head shots die quicker as well. Some of the men shot in the stomach take a long time to die while in great pain. Archie's method of poking them in the Adam's apple with his knife is not as slow. His men open their eyes wide and gasp for air or yell, unable to do either. Most of them struggle and kick a couple minutes before they die.

I pull The Wind to a halt cornering a young boy. "How old are you boy?" I growl.

"Eleven sir." he says about to cry. His voice is shaking with fear.

"Can you carry a gun?"

"A gun? Yes sir." His lips curl upward as he starts to cry.

"Then, you're big enough." I declare before I put a bullet in his chest. The force of the shot carries him several feet backward. I am amazed at how far, but then again, he didn't weigh very much.

"BILL!" Jim screams as he leaps from his horse, knocking me off mine. "He is just a kid, you bastard! HE WAS JUST A KID!" he screams as his fists flail against me. "WHAT IS WRONG WITH YOU?"

I struggle to my feet and strike back, knocking him to the ground. Righting himself, he lunges at me and we roll and punch each other in the dusty streets for several minutes. Finally, as is always the case when we brothers fight, I get the upper hand and sit on his chest, my knees pinning his upper arms.

Grasping his hair above the ears, I scream at him above the buzzing. "What is wrong with YOU! He was big enough to carry a gun! He could have shot us!"

It is nearly an hour before Archie and I return to the Eldridge Hotel and find a table near a window so we can watch flames devour much of the city.

"How many'd ya get Bill? I kilt nine!" Archie declares proudly.

"Eleven." I reply, setting my drink on the table.

"Ten and a half!" yells Jim angrily from a corner table. "You can't count that boy as a whole man. Ten and a half, you heartless son-of-a-bitch!"

"Go to hell!" I snarl, raising my whiskey glass again.

His glass and its' contents come flying as he rushes me once more. His first punch sends me reeling, and before I can retaliate, he is on me with a fury never before displayed. My lip and eye began to swell from the force of his blows when they suddenly stop. I look up just in time to stop Archie from thrusting his blade into the throat of my brother.

"ARCHIE!" I yell.

His eyes are ablaze with hatred as he stares at Jim.

"Let him go."

Jim looks at me with hatred as I get to my feet. He does not acknowledge the presence of Archie Clement. Jim's arms fall to his side. I strike him in the face with all the strength I can muster, knocking him over a table occupied by other Partisans. Jim does not try to get up. Shaking his head clear, he wipes at his bleeding nose, looking at me in an unfamiliar manner. Again, he wipes at the blood trickling from his nose as he slowly stands. Bracing myself for the expected rush, he picks up his hat and speaks instead.

"You have really earned your name now, you bastard! Bloody... Bill... Anderson. You're an animal." His voice is cold. Words hatefully spat out, he trudges out into the street.

The buzzing in the room returns to normal as the Partisan's divert their attention from the scuffle and raise their glasses in celebration. The buzzing in my head has also returned. Is it in my head? It follows me around! The buzzing as if from large bugs I have been unable to locate. If it is in my head, what is causing it? A low pain accompanies the buzzing, not a vicious biting pain, just a pain in my temple area. How long has the pain been there? Was it present before the buzzing started, or is it a result of the buzzing?

"Mr. Anderson?" A man in a tweed suit interrupts my thoughts.

A tall slender man with sleeves too short for his gangly arms invades my private thoughts. A derby hat sits atop thick curly sandy colored hair. The collar of his shirt is unbuttoned and he is unshaven, a days growth of beard on his narrow face. He seems harmless.

"Mr. Anderson, may I sit here?" he meekly asks touching an empty chair at the table Bo, Socrates, Archie and I occupy. I give a slight nod and he pulls the chair back tentatively before seating himself. He glances at the occupants of the table and turns his attention to me. "I heard the other... ah, gentleman ... you... are called... Bloody Bill Anderson?"

I snort a short laugh, raise my glass to my lips and take a drink while looking into his eyes. What is he up to? What is he after? "Who wants to know?" I ask.

"I am Kenneth Meyers, a reporter from the Chicago Sun. I'd like to do a story on you if I may." He responds.

"You came here… to do a story on me?" I ask, surprised that a Chicago reporter knows of me.

"Well... um... no sir. I came here to do a story on the Jayhawker's but I think my readers will be interested in your exploits." he said pulling a note pad from his coat pocket. His voice is stronger as he gains confidence.

"Exploits?" What can I tell him about me? I've done nothing of interest.

Archie interrupts the pause, excitedly saying. "Lemme tell ya 'bout Bloody Bill Anderson!" The reporter looks at Archie, back to me and listens attentively as Archie began to relate my 'exploits'. I rise to leave. Exploits! Harrumph!

The flames that destroyed the buildings across the street are dying down and other buildings are in various stages of burning. Bricks crumble and fall to the ground as supporting beams are consumed. It is a good thing Massachusetts Street was built so wide, must be at least thirty yards. The heat from the fire is intense, burning away the cool of early morning.

Early morning! It is not yet nine O'clock and the town of the hated Jayhawkers is in ruin. This town of some two thousand inhabitants paid dearly for the wrongs perpetrated on the Anderson's and the citizens of Missouri. Maybe this will deter them from attacking us again. Well, at least two hundred of them won't be attacking again, I laugh. That is the approximate number of men that died this morning. Men! We made the men pay for the attacks into Missouri. The MEN paid for the senseless deaths of my father in Council Grove and my sisters in Kansas City. Not a single female in Lawrence was harmed in any fashion, unless losing a father, brother or husband is considered harm. Chivalry was displayed here today. They raped my sister, and killed my father and uncle. THEY killed Josi and Ginny who innocently sat in an old decrepit building. And Diane! Kay was... is she alive? At any rate, that reporter will write about how we did not harm the innocents, he will tell of our restraint, how only the men paid for the vicious nature of the Jayhawker's.

HMMMM. I hadn't given it much thought, but if the population of Lawrence is about two thousand and we killed two hundred men, what happened to the rest? If half the population is men, then eight hundred or so escaped. Are they hiding in the cornfields around town, or down by the river? The cowards! They should come back to town so they can be killed, I laugh. I'll sic Archie on 'em.

Had all our men participated in the killing as instructed, we would have killed a lot more. Hell! Colonel Holt's group of sissy confederates hardly came into town. They stayed on the outskirts and did not do any killing as I recall.

"That's alright! Archie and I made up for them!" I laugh. Some of the men at an adjacent table stop their conversations and look at me quizzically as I had unintentionally voiced my thoughts.

The repercussions from our attack on Lawrence are surprising. The people of western Missouri seem cold toward us as we return. Maybe it is my imagination but they seem more distant, not openly glad to see us as they were in the past.

Newspaper accounts are not favorable toward us. "Senseless killing of 150 men and boys" a story read. Nearly as many articles are devoted to Bloody Bill Anderson as to Captain Quantrill. I had not seen my name in print before. "Led by William Clarke Quantrill and the barbarous Bloody Bill Anderson..." one story read. Hell! I wasn't a leader at Lawrence, and I am certainly not barbarous! What did Archie tell that reporter? Of course newspapers controlled by Union forces are not expected to be sympathetic toward us, but not one newspaper presented the fact that it is the Jayhawkers that are barbaric, not the Partisan's.

From newspaper accounts we learn that Larkin Skaggs was found drunk in the streets and viciously ripped apart by the citizens of Lawrence. Ripped apart! They tied ropes to his arms and legs, mounted horses and pulled him apart! And they call us barbaric?

We don't have much time to dwell on attitudes of our friends as our enemies' attitude is more determined than ever. Relentlessly pursued by troops of the Frontier and Border districts of Missouri and eastern Kansas, Quantrill orders us to disband and scatter for safety. Homes of known Partisan supporters are searched and, in many cases, burned to the ground in retaliation for the massacre, as it is being called. We cannot go to Lake Lotawanna, as it was discovered by Union soldiers. A site along the Missouri River five miles east of Sibley is selected for us to reconvene September 1.

Bo, Socrates, Jim, Archie and I make our way to the Sanders'. Jim, resolutely silent, refuses to respond to my overtures toward him. Mrs. Sanders tries to illicit an explanation from him but he ignores her, preferring to sit in solitude. Let him!

Frank and Mary had not returned from Jefferson City, but Mr. Sanders has returned with the good news that Kay is still alive.

Our rest at the Sanders' is frequently interrupted, as we hide in the woods at the approach of Union patrols. On August twenty eighth a patrol came to the Sanders' door and read General Order Number eleven, issued from the venomous pen of General Thomas Ewing. The Sanders and all other residents of the Missouri counties of Jackson, Cass, Bates and the northern half of Vernon, living more than a mile from a Union post are ordered to evacuate their homes and leave the state within fifteen days.

Leave the state? To where? The people of Jackson, Cass and Bates Counties are especially friendly to us, but all the people have to leave the state?

Ron Sanders turns to me after the patrol leaves, desperation in his voice. "What have we done?"

"You're a friend of Bloody Bill Anderson." Jim says sarcastically as he angrily strides from the house.

"Lemme kill 'im Bill!" Archie said angrily.

Ron looks at Archie in surprise as I shake my head. "Not ye... He's my brother Archie, leave him alone." I state calmly. Turning to Mr. Sanders, "Ron, it's not a matter of what you have done, this General has long advocated removal of the friends and families of the Partisans, and now he is doing it." I start slowly, "...and not because you know me." I glance toward the door where Jim had gone. "Your association with the Partisan's is well known, as is that of many of your neighbors and, you know who the Union sympathizers are as well."

"Can you defend our home Bill?" Ron asks quietly his eyes pleading.

"Defend your home?" my mind races.

"Yes! With you and Quantrill's forces facing them, the Union soldiers would not dare remove us." He said in a determined voice.

The thought of assembling the four hundred plus Partisan's that attacked Lawrence did seem like a deterrent to a Union attack. We could prevent it, but for how long? What then? Would Quantrill risk his forces for one farm? No, even if it were up to me to make that decision, the risk is too great. To make a stand against numerically superior forces could mean the end of the Partisan force. We do our best fighting in the hit and run fashion. How do I tell my friend he will lose his place with no help from me? What help can I give him?

"Ron." I began, wringing my hands and squirming in my chair, not able to look at him.

"Don't give me that 'I can do nothing for you talk', this is my HOME!" He interrupts shouting angrily. "We've given you shelter and comfort when you needed it! We took your family in when they had no place to go! We were there in your time of need... now we have a need, and you... are going to turn your back on us?"

"Ron. I can't do anything for..."

"You heartless bastard! GET OUT OF MY HOUSE!" He interrupts angrily knocking aside my outstretched hand. His chair clatters to the floor as he abruptly stands.

My hand still reaches toward him, unable to respond. "Ron..."

"GET OUT OF MY HOUSE!" Fire shoots from his eyes as he yells at me.

Cautiously I edge my way toward the door. "Where will you go?" I ask quietly.

"WHAT DO YOU CARE?" he yells, staring intently at me.

I return his gaze, but not in kind.

As his glare softens, he looks away. "I don't know." Hanging his head, he put his hands over his eyes, chokes back tears, and continues. "We have nowhere to go. This has been our home for twenty five years, what can we do?"

Patty opens his arms, wrapping hers around his waist, she nestles her head against his chest. "It's not Bill's fault." She says soothingly.

Ron sighs, raises his eyes to the ceiling, blinking them rapidly, and holds her tightly as I leave the house.

Chapter Twenty Five

More and more I wonder why I joined this god-damned army! I can't believe the brutality we are committing under the protection of the U.S. Government. Even before 'Beast' Strachan killed the prisoners in Palmyra, I was becoming aware that our side, the U.S. Army, is blatantly committing what would be considered atrocities if the Confederates did it. Looting and burning homes of suspected southern sympathizers is commonplace. Just the mere suspicion of sympathizing with the Confederates or Partisan's, causes an extremely heavy fine to be levied upon much of the citizenry.

Gary tries to reassure me by saying. "J.V. Parman, you cannot go against your orders. It is not your doing, but you have to follow orders!"

I know in my heart that innocent people suffer greatly at the hands of my superiors and... mine. Perhaps I'm not hard enough to be a soldier after all. I couldn't handle the looks, whether real or imagined, after the Palmyra incident, and had fortunately been transferred to Kansas City. Unfortunately, I witnessed another tragedy here. The collapse of the Bingham house was senseless, and some believe those innocent girls were intentionally killed. I cannot bring myself to believe she was purposely killed, although the removal of the supporting beams and many of the rocks is hard to rationalize.

She... there were others that died in the collapse, but one is of special importance to me. I didn't get to know her although I tried to overcome my shyness and talk to her. Gary urged me on and what little conversation we did have was due to his urging. Why do I feel so uncomfortable in the presence of females?

War! Tragedy after tragedy seems to follow me around and now I am forced to partake in yet another tragedy. General Order Number Eleven can only be considered a tragedy. A month ago when General Ewing wished to banish all Partisan families and supporters from the state, it seemed like a plan that could weaken the strength of the Partisan's. The reality of it, now that we are doing it, is deplorable.

My second visit to the Sanders is even less pleasant than the first, when we arrested the girls. This time I lead a detachment not to arrest them for real or imagined crimes, but to banish them from their homes possibly forever! The Sanders are not the only ones affected by the banishment order as all people, not just those guilty of sympathies to the Partisan's, are required to give up property some had fought years to attain. Many of the citizens argue vehemently that they did not support the

Partisans and as loyal Union citizens should be exempt from the banishment decree. Exemptions are made and I find it disheartening that those with greater wealth are more likely to be exempt than those without. Is this another example of greed and graft on the part of the Union officer's? I am sure of it.

The Sanders arrived at their farm in 1837, a newlywed couple from Allentown, Pennsylvania. The land they claimed is four miles north of Blue Springs at the bottom of a hill where the land flattens out over what may have been a river bed in ages past. The small creek winding its' way below the house is certainly not large enough to have created this fertile valley a mile wide, and who knows how long. Their house on the hill above the other out buildings overlooks the choicest farm land in the region. Facing the Sun the greater portion of the day provides warmth in the winter and the leaves of the large trees surrounding the house provides cooling shade in the summer. It is an idyllic setting, one I dream of having some day.

I watch the Sanders slowly load their wagons. Solemn expressions reveal pain, but their true agony is evident in their posture. Bent and broken, they trudge in and out of the house sometimes carrying only a small article. I remember them as proud people from the first occasion, the arrest of the girls, standing tall and erect that day. Today the sparkle in their eyes comes from moisture as they choke back tears. No anger is displayed, or perhaps they are too beaten to display anger. Arms hang limply at their sides as they return empty handed into the house to retrieve another valuable.

They have been successful in their farming, accumulating many personal items that are now agonized over as limited space in the wagon means a decision of what to keep has to be made. Tearfully, each item is inspected and a niche in the wagon sought. Mrs. Sanders ponders over a small table used as a flower stand. Mr. Sanders made this treasure for her on their twentieth wedding anniversary, but her wagon is nearly full. Caressing it lovingly she carries it to the wagon being loaded by Mr. Hodges, and hands it to him with little conversation.

The Hodges wagon has very little in it, in spite of carrying the belongings of the Hodges and their four girls. He hangs his head as Mrs. Sanders began to load some of her possessions in his wagon. Hugging him silently, she then trudges back into the house. Ron Sanders nods to Frank as he sets another item in Franks' wagon.

I remember one of the girls arrested five weeks ago was one of Mr. Hodges daughters and, although I remember a Mrs. Hodges, I do not see her.

Some of my men are too young and immature to recognize the significance of this event, they laugh at the hapless victims of General Order Number Eleven. Cavorting around the farm house, as its former inhabitants are loading their possessions into wagons, these young boys make derisive remarks toward the Sanders and Mr. Hodges. Some make improper advances toward the Hodges girls and to their credit the girls try to ignore the lewd talk and leers of the boys. Rebuffed by the girls, the boys turn to harassing Mrs. Sanders. Her trunk is accidentally dropped in the loading process, spilling its contents. Two of the boys grab pieces of undergarments and 'model' them, chiding the older woman as she tries to retrieve the dainty things. Mr. Sanders grabs one of the boys who quickly shed the older man, angrily pushing him to the ground.

"Hey! Hey! Knock it off! That's enough!" I direct angrily, getting between the boy and the innocent farmer. I let this frivolity continue too long, and it has gotten out of hand. These people have a right to their dignity. Boys! How callous and uncaring can they be? I snort as I think they probably can be as callous and uncaring as their leaders are.

The Sanders show their appreciation for stopping the insensitive playfulness of these boys, but the look they give me is not a thank you, more of an 'about time'. I am an object of their hatred for what is being perpetrated on them. Carefully they re-pack the trunk and the two men lash it to the back of the Sanders' wagon. This is the last item loaded. Husband and wife share a look for a moment before turning their gaze to the house that has been home for twenty six years.

"Shall I torch it Sarge?" One of the young soldiers asks.

"NO!" came the immediate and emphatic reply from the Sanders.

"No soldier, no building here is to be destroyed." I command loud enough for all my men to hear.

The look the Sanders give me is softer, a thank you in their eyes. Mr. Sanders turns to the other man. "Frank, where will you go?"

"We... um" He pauses looking at me momentarily. "We... after making a stop will return to Kentucky. We have family there we haven't seen for twenty years or so. We'll go there. How 'bout you Ron, what are you and Patty going to do? Will you go back to Pennsylvania?"

Mr. Sanders silently ponders the question, looking about his home before answering. "No, we've.., thought about... Texas. I guess we'll probably head for Texas. All our... we have noth..." He states haltingly.

"I know Ron" Mr. Hodges said, mercifully preventing his friend from admitting to being destitute. "We'll be praying for you." He grasps the other man in a lengthy hug.

Goodbye friend and fare thee wells are exchanged and with a last glance at the home, the wagons began to move. The moment the Sanders wagon begins to pull out, a neighbor emerges from a thicket to lay claim to the property. "I claim this land as abandoned and lay claim as legal owner." He yells as officially as he can. He had been waiting out of sight until the farm is officially vacated. The vulture! I hate this man, although profiting on the Sanders misfortune is not illegal, it is hateful. "You are my witness Sergeant! They have abandoned the property and I am the first to lay claim! You're my witness, this is now my land!"

"Sergeant?" Mr. Sanders addresses me as he watches his former friend and neighbor run into the abandoned house. The hatred he must feel for this man. Our eyes meet for a moment before Mr. Sanders turns to his wife. She looks at the man who has returned outside, and now is inspecting the roof. Mrs. Sanders touches her husband's arm and nods.

Ron Sanders looks at me with intensity in his eyes. "Burn it!"

It is so ordered.

Repercussions from the Kansas City debacle and Lawrence massacre happen quickly in mid September. My unit is transferred to Lexington, relieving us of the sight of the barren lands left by the banishment decree. Our task is to pursue and capture Quantrill and his guerrillas. They are no longer referred to as Partisan's, but guerrillas, a much more negative connotation than Partisan.

Doc Jennison's Red Legs swarm into western Missouri to assist in the removal of its citizens. He and his men use the Lawrence massacre and General Order Number Eleven as an excuse to commit their acts of atrocities. Looting and burning was their forte' earlier in the war, and they return to seek vengeance on the innocents required to leave.

Frequently I consider deserting my post and joining the guerrillas, as what we are doing to the citizens and families of the former Partisan's is terribly wrong. How can we justify, in the name of right and wrong, the displacement of these people? I hate this; I hate myself for being a part of it.

It is heart wrenching to see the results of the Jayhawker 'assistance'. Some of the homes are burned before the owners can load their wagons, prized possessions forever lost to them. Many of the people escape with only the clothes on their backs. Worse yet, some do not escape at all. Some that resist, or even dally a little, are shot!

The transfer to Lexington is a welcome change. My mind still pictures the exodus of families, most of who go south for a safe haven. Who is the enemy, the Guerrillas of Quantrill or the Jayhawkers of Jennison, who are supposedly allied with the North? Them or us; who is the enemy? Surely it must be confusing for the locals.

The Guerrillas fight a running battle against the Jayhawkers and our soldiers; striking out of the bush they hit our patrols, shooting, killing and disappearing. Seldom do we hear of a guerrilla band larger than ten to fifteen although their total strength is reputed to be in excess of five hundred. How can that many men remain undetected? Even in bands of ten to fifteen we should run into them occasionally.

It is rumored the Guerrillas have uniforms of the Union army, which could explain why we haven't been able to detect them. Our patrol often meets other patrols and who knows whether they are Union men, or Guerrillas dressed in Union blue? Each patrol met is scrutinized carefully, can we afford not to?

Perhaps the banishment is having a calming effect on the area as we are certainly more popular than before the banishment. Of course those that remain are avowed Union supporters and even if they are not, they are not foolish enough to let the army know, especially Jennison's army.

Bloody Bill Anderson... surely this is the same Bill Anderson that was, or is, the brother of Josephine Anderson. What would the proper term be? She is dead so does that mean she is or was his sister, present tense or past tense? Oh well, why dwell on silly questions, they are brother and sister. Or is it were, damn.

He is developing quite a reputation this Bloody Bill. Not all talk centers on William Clarke Quantrill, a new savage beast is upon the frontier. As I recall his photograph, he had not impressed me as a savage. The photographer expressed a fear of him from their first meeting. I see a handsome man perhaps five years younger than myself.

Younger than myself, I am twenty nine years old, no wife and no prospects of a wife. What are you going to do with yourself J.V. Parman? This November my enlistment is up and I think of not re-enlisting, of settling down somewhere with a family. I think of Josephine, could we have developed a relationship, become a family? She seemed to be warming to me, who knows. Oh God! I didn't know her, but I miss her!

Chapter Twenty Six

Before we left Missouri, Quantrill announced he was assuming the rank of Colonel and called for elections to be held for other officer positions. I was elected Captain over a company of one hundred men. Also elected Captains were George Todd, William Gregg and David Pool.

Our first act after the October 1 election is to lead more than four hundred men out of Missouri for winter quartering. Although too early to be thinking of winter, the Union is making it hot for us so we departed early. Many of our band spent last winter outside, and did not relish the thought of doing so again, thus the decision to head to Texas is welcomed by all.

The southward trek in western Missouri is disheartening. Land once occupied by fine farms and homes of partisan supporters had been laid to waste by the torches of Jayhawkers and Union soldiers enforcing the banishment order with zealous diligence. Only a few hundred of the ten thousand inhabitants of Cass County remain. Bates County is almost devoid of people; perhaps only a hundred had not been dispossessed.

Our depression is eased near Baxter Springs as we learn of a wagon train approaching Fort Baxter carrying General James G. Blunt, Union Commander of the District of the Frontier. Todd's' company and mine are tapped by Colonel Quantrill to meet the Generals' wagon train as Gregg and Pool engage the Fort.

Ten wagons and one hundred mounted Union troopers approach from across the prairie and are visible from three miles, as we are to them. Quantrill orders the men dressed in Union uniforms to the front as we await the wagon train.

The subterfuge is working as the approaching troops scurry about to assemble in orderly lines. A four piece band in one of the wagons begins to play as they continue at a leisurely pace toward us. They must think we are a Union detachment sent to escort them to the Fort.

We hold our weapons out of sight of the approaching Union troopers. Within fifty yards, Quantrill opens fire into the neatly formed ranks of the soldiers. A tremendous volley ensues from the partisans; whooping and screaming, we fall upon the unsuspecting troops, causing a great deal of confusion. Most of the troops break ranks and ride for cover with two or three Partisans chasing each. A woman and her driver leap from their buggy onto horses, riding hard to escape. We laugh at the sight of a woman sitting astride her horse, her dress billowing up into her face as she whips the horse into a run. They are ignored, as we will not fire upon a female.

The band members hold up their arms as they stand in the wagon; easy targets. I manage to get two of them and Archie only one. I laugh at him.

The flurry lasts but a few minutes and now seventy nine Union clad bodies lie on the prairie. Bodies are stripped of uniforms, pistols, rifles and ammunition, as we rummage through pockets seeking the Generals' body. A whoop goes up when the son of Major General Samuel Curtis is identified among the dead. A man in civilian garb with papers bearing the signature of General Blunt, and possessing the General's sword, triggers an impromptu celebration. The Commanding General of the District of the Frontier has been killed. What a glorious victory for the Confederacy and more specifically, the Partisans as we only leave behind three dead Partisans. The ten wagons laden with supplies bound for Fort Baxter, are given a new destination; Texas.

Approaching the Confederate camp near Bonham, Texas, a cocky euphoria is felt by the Partisans as the feared General Blunt has been vanquished. The mixed reception we receive by officers and men alike is confusing; some treat us as conquering heroes, while others distance themselves from us as if we are a pariah.

Colonel Quantrill wrote General Sterling Price, commanding the District of Arkansas, of the victory over Blunt at Baxter Springs. The General returned a congratulatory letter in support of the actions of the Partisans. General Price's superior officer, Lieutenant General Kirby Smith, Commander Trans Mississippi Department, does not share the views of the former Missouri Governor. Of our guerrilla activities he wrote. "...war in Missouri is only entailing new persecution and misery for our friends there without advancing the Confederate cause in the slightest." Major General J. Bankhead Magruder, Commanding the District of Texas, differed with General Smith by issuing a general order congratulating Colonel Quantrill for the defeat of General Blunt. However, the commander of the sub district to which we were assigned, General Henry McCulloch, wrote of Quantrill. "...I do not know what his military status is... we cannot, as Christian people, sanction such savage, inhumane warfare..."

This General obviously does not understand the savage persecution we endured at the hands of the opposition. Does he not consider it inhumane to war against females as they had? Is it not inhumane to banish innocent people from homes they labored years to develop, as the Union had? Yet our own Confederate General considers us inhumane.

General McCulloch assigned Colonel Quantrill and his Raiders to rounding up deserters from the northern Sub District of Texas, an assignment the Colonel declined, angering the General greatly.

McCulloch ordered Quantrill to report to General Kirby Smith in Shreveport Louisiana.

In the Colonels absence, Todd is placed in command of the Raiders, the term Raider seems to fit as well as any other. Have we been officially assigned to any particular unit? I recall no such order.

While we await the return of our commander, we read that General Blunt escaped us by riding away with Mrs. Chester Thomas who. "...set aside her dignity and rode astride a horse..."

To those of us revered by the southern troops as the conquerors of General Blunt, his escape is a bitter pill. Not having conquered the General pushed a portion of our supporters toward the detractors. As Quantrill defied his orders, so do we openly flaunt our defiance of unfriendly officers. Not answering to the Confederate command does have its advantages.

Confederate soldiers clear a path when a raider enters a saloon and, when he speaks, the regulars listen. No regular Confederate soldier challenges a raider to a conflict, as bodies of those challengers have mysteriously shown up. Confident in ourselves, we develop a disdain for the regular Confederate soldier as a lesser fighter, a lesser man, an inferior soldier. We push them aside at will, daring them to oppose us.

Colonel Quantrill returned mid-November with a hatred for the commander of the Trans Mississippi Department. General Kirby Smith wrote General

McCulloch that 'Captain' Quantrill was to rejoin his command and perform his assigned duties, rounding up deserters.

'Captain' Quantrill, upon his return, enters into a diatribe against the Generals, Smith and McCulloch. It angers Quantrill that he is not afforded the status of Colonel, as are others of the Confederacy commanding similar forces. The Colonel, or Captain, directs his four Captains to take our forces into winter camps separate from each other and seek out deserters, if it meets with our purposes.

"If it meets with our purposes, what the hell does that mean?" Todd is not the only one to voice that concern.

Todd and Quantrill, opt to remain near Bonham while Gregg moved his men to a position near Paris, Texas. David Pool took his men west to Gainesville, while I position my troops near the Red River at Mineral Creek. In this tranquil setting I determine our purpose to be one of relaxation and honing our skills as guerrilla fighters. We will wait here to see if any deserters show up.

Visiting Sherman fifteen miles to the southeast is a welcome diversion for our troops and from twenty to fifty of 'Bloody Bills Raiders' can be found in town at all times.

Men speak to me with respect and the ladies, ah yes... the ladies openly flirt with me. The personal attention I receive makes me appreciate the bustle of town over the solitude of our camp near the river. Archie at first follows along as I stroll along the streets of Sherman. He is uncomfortable in the company of ladies and my proclivity toward entering into conversation with them causes him discomfort. After a time he opts to remain in the Mineral Spring camp.

Jim prefers to be anywhere Archie is not; and took up residence in Sherman soon after our arrival. Bo and Socrates also avoid the public as Socrates, having endured much ridicule in Missouri and Kansas, is never far from Bo's side. Bo returns this loyalty by remaining with Socrates in a place the large man will not be subjected to ridicule, our camp.

Texas is a tranquil place as Christmas of 1863 approaches. How can it possibly get better!

Chapter Twenty Seven

This is better! Last winter in Arkansas was colder than it has been so far in Texas. Of course it is still early December, the worst of winter is yet to come.

Walking the streets of Sherman, Texas, I am becoming accustomed to ladies smiling at me as I meet them. They giggle and blush as we meet, usually walking in pairs but sometimes as many as four young ladies walking together. Their flirtatious eyes make me feel good. Some say I cut a dashing figure, although I've never given it much thought. At six foot four inches and two hundred twenty pounds, I suppose I do possess some good looks but, I've never thought about a man as having good looks. Now the ladies, that is a different matter entirely. There is no such thing as an ugly woman; just some are better looking than others.

"Ladies." I tip my hat to a pair of beauties that hasten their step past me as they giggle and whisper to each other. Bill Anderson you devil you! Making them poor girls swoon like that! Shame on me! What would they look like totally naked? I laugh aloud as I continue down the street, a bit more of a swagger in my step.

Ah, this is terrific! No fighting and killing for a while, Missouri is but a recent memory. I think about Josi and Ginny quite often and wonder how Kay is doing. I have not heard about her since we left Missouri in October.

"Girls." I say tipping my hat to a pair of gray haired ladies. I like to call the older ones girls, most appreciate it while others act shocked that a strange man would speak to them. Ha! No thoughts about them undressed. These two shake their head, frown and hurry on their way as I return my hat with a smile.

I think of Diane, especially at night when my thoughts run wild. Mostly I remember her cavorting through the prairie grasses naked, skin soft to my touch, her hair as I push it away from her face before kissing her. I think of her often. Nearly every young lady that approaches, I imagine what she might look like with her clothes off, how she compares with Diane. Like this one walking alone on the boardwalk toward me, she is very pretty. A small gray hat is perched forward on her head, the brim covering most of her forehead. Long brown curls touch her shoulders and fall behind her. Carrying a small basket in front cannot hide the narrow waist, nor can the tightly fitting gray dress buttoned to the neck hide the gentle full curvature of her body. The full skirt nearly touches the walk, sweeping gracefully from her hips. One quick examination of her delectable form and I return my gaze to her face. Her dark eyebrows arch gracefully above large dark eyes that are... looking intently at me! This one starts to smile, slows her walk and seems to be openly studying me. Unlike the others that smile flirtatiously this one is not flirting, but staring.

"Miss." I say doffing my hat. She stops as I pass, looking at me as if surprised. Bill, you charmer you, I think smugly. You're stopping them in their tracks now, next they will be throwing themselves at your feet.

"Bill?"

Did she call after me?

"Billy?" She says again as if knowing me. Recalling the image of her face, I turn toward her. Do I know her? She's a decent girl isn't she; I mean she's not one of the whores I've been to that I wouldn't recognize with clothes on?

Her body is turned at a ninety degree angle to the direction she had been walking, turned to face me peering over her shoulder. Oh what a body! Standing erect, her back slightly arched in perfect posture, the side view of her form is better than the frontal view I enjoyed while meeting her.

She smiles at me. I am perplexed.

"Miss?" I say taking tentative steps toward her while removing my hat. Who is this gorgeous creature? If she is a whore, I have not been with her. None of the whores have this 'clean' look about them. No, this one is not a whore!

She smiles as I stand transfixed by her beauty and perplexed at her apparent knowledge of me. "You don't recognize me do you Billy." She says softly, her bright smile revealing an even row of sparkling white teeth.

In shock I stammer. "I... ah... think..." I try to think of who she is and where I have seen her before. She knows my name, why can't I recall who she is? "No... I ah… I'm sorry, I... I don't." is all I can manage. "Have we met before?"

Flashing an impish smile she says demurely. "Yes we have." and turns to go.

"Wait!" I call after her. "Where... when... how..." I stammer.

She stares deeply into my eyes. "A long time ago Billy." and walks away.

A long time ago? Rooted in my tracks, my mind races over the past few years to the females I had met outside the brothels. Except for the whores there weren't that many, who could she be? Social functions were not a staple for us, neither in Missouri nor earlier in Kansas. Who could she be? Where could I have met her? Surely I would remember one as strikingly beautiful as she is!

I look in the direction she was headed. She is gone! I walk briskly down the walk attempting to overtake her, to get another glimpse or perhaps question her as to where we met. Where is she, who is she? I look into every shop along the way, not there! How did she disappear so quickly? How will I find her again?

The next day I wait on the walk near the spot where my 'dream' girl appeared. My patience is rewarded as she suddenly appears, walking toward me on the boardwalk. I bolt upright from the wall while she is still two blocks away. She is wearing a light brown dress today but I recognize the walk I'd visualized in my mind a thousand times since I first saw it. She said I knew her, God do I want to know her well! My mouth is dry and my stomach churning in a fashion I had not experienced since my first battle. This is fear but a different kind of fear! What will I say to her?

She smiles brightly as she approaches. "I knew you'd be here today Billy." She said softly as she came within a few steps of me. She approaches at a steady pace, neither fast nor slow. Is she walking with a little swagger? She walks past me, smiling demurely as she does.

Falling in beside her, I match my stride with hers. "You knew I'd be here?" I feel like a childish fool.

Her smiling eyes sparkle as she looks straight ahead. "Have you figured out how you know me?" She tips her head toward me when I do not respond immediately. Her smile telling me she is enjoying my discomfort. She has me at her mercy and is not going to let me off easily.

"No... I haven't, and it's driving me crazy!" I do not want to mention any of the saloons or brothels in Kansas, Missouri or Texas where I must have met her. She's too clean, or else the cleanest whore ever; I do not want to offend her. "Where did we meet?"

"Think about it." She smiles, strolling on.

"Think about it! I have done nothing but think about it since yesterday!" I say lightly touching her arm. She stops, looking down at my fingers resting on her forearm. "I have thought of nothing else since our meeting yesterday." I repeat more softly, removing my hand.

Her eyes sparkle as she speaks. "You used to tease me about my name." I stare dumbfounded, my mind racing.

She gave me another clue. "You were closer to my brothers."

"Your brothers?"

"Yes, especially Hiram." She resumed her stroll.

Hiram? "Hiram?" I whisper, watching her walk away as images of my youth began to flash by. "HIRAM SMITH!" I yell as recognition strikes. "You! You are... Bush... Bush Smith?" I say bounding after her.

As she turns toward me, I sweep her up in my arms. "Yes!" She laughs. "It's Bush. Now put me down you big oaf."

"Bush Smith. My God! Its' been... its' been..."

"Eleven years." She said completing my sentence as she straightened her dress.

Visions of a ten year old girl close friends with Josi, Ginny and Kay, looking at me in a strange fashion return. Her eyes gave me a strangely uncomfortable feeling as a youth of thirteen. Not old enough to recognize what those feelings were; Bush had been all but forgotten in the years to come. My last recollection of her is that of a young girl staring sadly at me as I sat in our wagon riding toward Palmyra and an unknown future. Now...?

"Are you still Bush... Smith?" I ask.

"Not the same Bush Smith you remember but... yes, I am Bush Smith." She replies.

"You've not been... married?" I ask tentatively.

She glances away quickly and draws a breath as she contemplates my question. "I had been promised to someone, but..." She said softly, staring at her hands.

"But you wanted to wait for me." I said interrupting her, and instantly sorry I had. You vain S.O.B. how do I apologize for that remark?

She smiles, peering into my eyes before shyly looking away. "He would have been good for me, he was a good man." She said softly, her hands wringing a handkerchief. Her voice drops to a barely perceptible whisper. "But he was not you."

Had I heard her say... he was not me?

She moves silently down the boardwalk. My boot heels make a loud click as each step descends heavily on the boards. Her step is light, hardly making a sound as dainty feet alight on the walk. I listen to the clicking of my boot heels as we walk in silence. I try to re-open a conversation but each topic is quickly discarded.

"He's... you... didn't marry him?" I finally manage glancing toward her. She is silent, a tear slowly sliding down her cheek.

She shakes her head. "I guess I would have."

After a pause I ask quietly. "Would have?"

She nods, softly saying. "He died in Palmyra with Hiram."

"Who did! Wha..." I stammer meaning to ask about, 'died with Hiram'.

"Morgan Bixler, my betrothed. We were to be married last spring but..."

Still uncertain as to what she said I ask. "You said he died... with... Hiram. Hiram is dead?"

She nods. "In Palmyra."

I stop. After a couple of steps she stops as I ask. "Hiram... was one of the Palmyra ten?"

"As was Morgan." She replies sadly.

Recollections of my boyhood friend return and I began to feel angry. I also hear the buzzing that has been absent for almost two months since our arrival in Texas. I look around for the origin of the buzzing. Bush follows my gaze. "Do you hear it?" I ask.

"Hear what?" She asks with a puzzled look.

I shake my head. "Nothing. Tell me about Hiram."

"Mother is expecting you for supper tonight, the boys and I will tell you all about it then." She said with a wan smile.

The boys, Hector Jr., Herman, Homer and... well, I guess Hiram won't be there. I wonder if Herman will try to pick on me now. I used to be afraid of him, and his being three years older frequently put me on the bottom during our scuffles. Let's see him pick on me now, HA! NO ONE picks on me now. My reputation causes men to step aside, Herman will respect me.

Jim and I ride silently to the Smith ranch, as he still does not speak to me. I gave up trying to engage in conversation with him and my only contact is in breaking up verbal arguments between he and Archie, of which Archie is at a distinct disadvantage. Mediating their fights, the hatred they feel for one another is clearly evident to me, neither making an effort to hide it. Perhaps Jim doesn't realize it, but Archie will kill him in an instant if I would allow it. Mentally Jim has the advantage but cannot match Archie's physical powers or his aptitude for killing. Archie is willing to kill any man I want him to; merely a nod or a pointed finger will send Archie relentlessly after a target, much like a dog after a bird on the hunt.

"Shall we at least pretend to be brothers tonight?" I offer.

Jim remains silent, staring straight ahead.

I marvel at the size of the Smith ranch. They have done quite well for themselves as we have ridden nearly four miles since passing under a sign proclaiming, "HBBH" ranch. I surmise they left out some of the H's but that is their business.

Bush meets us as we dismount, grasping Jim by the hand, pulling him forward slightly to plant a kiss on his cheek. I feel a tinge of jealousy. Smiling, she takes my arm as we walk into the house. Jim is stunned at the sight of Bush, but then she is a stunning beauty.

The ranch house looks large from the outside but inside, the size of this mansion is impressive indeed. We step into a large foyer off which sweep two spiral staircases, one on each side of the entry, ascending to the second floor. A large chandelier hangs from the ceiling in the foyer, lit candles casting a soft yellowish glow to the room. From between and under the staircases, through a double doorway, came two men and an older woman.

"You remember Hector." Bush said as a broad grizzled man appearing to be more than five years older than I, extends his hand. With a broad grin he greets us. "Bill! Jim!"

"And Homer." Bush said of a man of much the same physical stature as the eldest Smith son but apparently not having weathered the hardships his brother had. This man appears much younger than the four years that separate the brothers.

"And of course, our mother." Bush introduces the woman I easily recognize in spite of the added pounds and aging that has taken place the past eleven years. Barbara Smith is bent and tired looking, her hair gray, almost white, perhaps not unusual for a woman near fifty.

"Mrs. Smith." I say as pleasantly as possible. "You haven't changed a bit." I lie.

"Mrs. Smith; as beautiful as ever." Jim says giving her a hug.

"You boys!" She exclaims with embarrassment. "I don't remember you being such liars!"

"So!" I began with a laugh looking around. "I suppose Herman is waiting for me to pass by a doorway so he can jump out at me. Where is..." I stop as I see the faces of our hosts. Hector and Homer look at each other, then nervously toward the floor.

Hector speaks quietly. "Herman was one of Porters' boys killed in Kirksville."

I feel stupid, how I can get out of this embarrassing moment. "I'm... ahm... I'm sorry, I didn't know." It seems so inadequate but is the only thing I could say.

Hector looks around the silent room, then smiles at me. "Of course not Bill, how could you have known? Let's sit down to supper and I'll fill you in on Herman and Hiram. Mom, Bush, why don't you sit on the ends. Bill and I will sit on this side while Jim and Homer take that side. Dolores! Rita!" He calls toward the kitchen. "Our guests are ready to be served." Hector is used to giving orders.

Two young Mexican girls scurry to the dining table, each with a tray of food. An elderly Mexican man appears at the doorway holding a bottle. "Ah Patricio! Come everyone, Patricio will pour our wine."

Before I know it, I am seated at Mrs. Smith's right hand while Jim is next to Bush across from Hector. For several minutes the Mexican girls bring the food and we enjoy a sumptuous meal. I am envious of Jim seated next to Bush, they seem to be having an enjoyable conversation.

Jim ignores Homer to his right and Hector across the table. Jim hasn't smiled this much in months. Bush frequently catches me looking at her and smiles sweetly before returning to her conversation with Jim.

From across the table Homer began. "Bill, we understand you are a Captain in Colonel Quantrill's Partisan Rangers?"

I nod.

"How many men do you have in your command? Tell us about some of the battles. What about Lawrence?" Homer excitedly leans forward to listen, obviously enthralled by tales of war.

Jim leans forward, suddenly interested, listening intently as I speak of the campaign against the Jayhawker headquarters. He does not comment.

Near the end of the meal, Hector relates how Herman and Hiram died. My head begins to ache as I think about the unnecessary end Hiram came to. Herman was killed fighting in Kirksville along with nearly fifty other men of Joe Porters' band of guerrillas, but Hiram died with his hands and feet tied together. The buzzing grows louder.

Lightly touching Bush's hand, Hector explains that Morgan Bixler willed his considerable property holdings in Missouri to his betrothed. The sale of his property, and theirs, enabled them to purchase this land in Texas.

Homer and Hector were in the crowd at Palmyra when Hiram and Morgan were executed. Mrs. Smith shrank from the table as Hector related the story in detail. Finishing the story, he pauses to sip his coffee.

Mrs. Smith leaned forward and with a forced smile, put her hand on my arm. "Enough of tragedy, tell us of your father, Bill. How is the dear man?"

The buzzing intensifies.

Listening to Hector nearly made me forget what happened to us, now faced with answering the question; I am unable to find the words. My headache is worse and the ringing in my ears competes with the buzzing to drown out most sounds. Jim speaks as if from a distance. "Uncle John and our father were killed about a year and a half ago. They... were... ahm... hung by the Jayhawkers. Our sisters..."

My chair scrapes across the wood floor loudly as I shove away from the table. Boot heels clatter on the hardwood floor as I stride briskly outside.

Jim continues the story in my absence.

After a few minutes Bush joins me on the verandah. "I'm so... Bill" she is crying softly. "We have mourned the loss of Herman and Hiram, I didn't know that you suffered so much." She leans against my arm, her perfume wafting sweetly up to my nostrils. I feel the hairs on the back of my neck tingling, as well as a tingling in my loins. She squeezes my arm against her bosom gently.

We stand in silence for a few minutes until she asks meekly, not lifting her head from my arm. "Jim told us about... Diane. He said... you were... close? Did you...?"

The buzzing that started to go away returns with a greater crescendo. I can't think straight with all this noise! I have to get away! Without a word I walk away, mount The Wind and return to Sherman.

Homer sought me out the next morning. "Bill! The family would like you and Jim to stay at the ranch. We have plenty of room, and we could use your help with the Vaquero's." Jims' expression tells me his preference.

"My company?" I protest.

Homer looks away briefly before continuing. "We don't have room for a hundred soldiers. We do sell our beef to the Confederate command in Sherman but that many soldiers will be disruptive to our operation. Jim tells me you have some able lieutenants that can oversee the wintering of your troops. Leave the troops in their care."

Able lieutenants? Marston Lisle is able enough but I cannot imagine Jim calling Archie able! Still all we are trying to do is feed the men until spring when we resume the war in Missouri. I suppose Archie and Marston can keep them together, besides, Bush is at the ranch.

"I suppose we can manage that." I say with a smile.

"Good!" Homer replies excitedly. "We'll see you for supper tonight!"

"Tomorrow night Homer, let me tie some things together in our camp."

Chapter Twenty Eight

"You were able to buy all this with the sale of two Missouri farms?" I ask Hector Jr. as he and Homer take Jim and me for a tour of the ranch.

Hector looks over the vast expanse of grasses turned to a brownish green by the coming winter. The grasses are lush where the property borders the Red River to the north. Panning the horizon, he contemplates his answer. "This land was paid for by blood and sweat." He began solemnly. "From the time we were kids we labored long and hard in the fields to provide for mother and Bush... you know that... none of this has come easy."

"I know Hector, I remember those years. Mother died trying to provide for us, to keep the farm, big... so much land.... how much property did Morgan Bixler have?" I ask. "...and during these troubled times, how were you able to sell the land for a decent price?"

These questions make Hector squirm but he faces me saying. "Mother and Bush do not know this, and must not know, but Herman and Hiram gave us money from their activities with Colonel Porter."

"Looted money?" That possibility had not occurred to me.

"Homer and I refer to it as spoils of war. Perhaps it could be called loot, but it was taken during and after skirmishes with Union soldiers or citizens, it was earned in battle. Our brothers paid for it with their lives." Hector, obviously saddened by the loss of his brothers appears uneasy about the way the ranch was purchased. "Also!" He continues; a smile lighting up his face. "We had incredibly good timing and luck. Patricio Calderon, this was his place, came from Mexico as a small boy before the siege of the Alamo. In a few years, Americans bought or claimed surrounding properties, and began to make life difficult for the Calderon's. There is more bitterness about the Alamo than the Calderon's anticipated. We happened along last winter at the time Patricio decided he could no longer battle to keep the property. The adjoining rancher, Duval, has been after the land for several years trying to coerce the Calderon's to sell. The underhanded tactics employed by Don Duval strengthened Patricio's resolve not to let him have the land. When we came along and offered a fair amount, even though less than Duval, Patricio willingly sold his land to us. He and his family agreed to stay on to help us get the ranch off to a good start, but... they really didn't have anywhere to go. Patricio was raised here, as were his children and if things work out, as far as we are concerned, they may stay here forever." Hector paused watching the cattle grazing below us. There must be a couple thousand cattle spread out for miles as we sit on a ridge overlooking the river valley to the north.

"Most of the Vaqueros stayed and it has worked out well for all of us so far. Patricio, his wife Maria and his daughters Delores and Rita, act as servants for us, but they are friends. Ha! Just ask Homer how friendly we are with the Calderon's." Hector said smiling at Homer.

Homer laughs nervously and shrugs his shoulders.

"Anyway..." Hector continues. "We could not have managed the land without the Calderon's and their Vaqueros. They have been loyal to us, unfortunately..." He pauses, a pensive look on his face. "We are not popular with our neighbors. Keeping the Mexes met with considerable disfavor from the locals. I did not understand the hatred and prejudice the Calderon's faced, and that we now face."

"Especially from Duval!" Homer adds with a tone of bitterness.

Hector snorts. "Yeah! He was mad as hell when we bought the land he wanted. He's visited a few times, made offers for the land."

"Also some threats as to what might happen if we don't sell." Homer interjects.

I look at Hector questioningly.

"Threats? Why Homer, whatever do you mean?" Hector smiles at his sarcastic reply. "When a man tells you your cattle may wander too close to poisoned water, or that your house might mysteriously catch fire some night, if we don't sell to him, surely you wouldn't call that a threat?" Hector's laugh is not one of humor.

"Would he do that?" I ask.

Hector shrugs.

"Patricio thinks it was Duvals' men that killed his father the summer before we came." Homer said answering for his brother. "Someone should kill Him." He adds softly.

"Yeah! That would solve everything." Hector laughs.

Jim had not left the ranch since our arrival eight days before Christmas. I made one trip back to the camp at Mineral Creek soon after my tour of the HBBH ranch with Hector and Homer, to deliver special instructions for Archie. The men are enjoying the peaceful surroundings, although some want more action. Neither Jim nor I have visited Sherman since taking residence at the ranch.

The tranquility of Christmas day at the HBBH ranch is interrupted by the Sheriff from Sherman. Approaching the verandah in the back of the house, the young lawman and four of his deputies present imposing figures as they dismount; something is wrong. The Sheriff smiles as he approaches but the expressions on the deputies are not pleasant.

"Hector. Homer. Mrs. Smith." The sheriff doffs his hat with a smile toward Mrs. Smith and Mrs. Calderon as Hector and Homer rise to greet him.

"Sheriff Orwick. To what do we owe the pleasure?" Hector says extending his hand.

The Sheriff takes that hand and quickly forces Hectors arm behind his back. In the same motion a pistol appears in his other hand, the barrel pressed under the chin of Hector Smith.

I leap to my feet, but the sound of rifles cocking stop me, the mounted deputies have carbines leveled at us. "Just stay where you are!" the lawman commands pointing his pistol at me, then at Homer and Jim in succession. Satisfied we are not posing an immediate threat he returns the muzzle to the chin of Hector. "Hector and Homer Smith, you are under arrest for the murder of Don Duval."

"What!" Homer says incredulously. "Dick! You can't be serious! Murder? When...? How....? Duval is... dead?"

"Nice try Homer but you two are coming with me!" The Sheriff states as he began to back up pulling Hector with him.

Sighing loudly, I calmly state. "No they're not Sheriff."

Jim and Homer stare at me. Astonished at what he heard, the sheriff turns his pistol on me and said curtly. "What did you say?"

Strangely calm and supremely confident facing the muzzle of a Colt pistol similar to mine, I smile at the lawman and repeat calmly. "I said; they are not coming to town with you."

Homer and Hector still look at me, mouths agape.

"Who the hell do you think you are?" Sheriff Orwick says his face red with anger as he spat out the words. "Who is this guy?" He yells angrily.

Homer opens his mouth, but Jim answers for him. "This is Bloody… Bill Anderson from Missouri."

The red subsides from the sheriff's face as his eyes widen. Those eyes tell me everything.

"Bill... Anderson?" He says softly. "Are you...?"

I nod.

His eyes dart back and forth as he ponders his next move. "I... ah... still have to bring them in for... questioning." He stammers.

I sigh heavily and take a sip from my glass as I approach the lawman. The deputies raise their rifles unsure of whether or not to shoot. "Sheriff… Orwick is it? Must I repeat myself? Homer and Hector had nothing to do with any crime last night. I can vouch for that. My brother Jim can vouch for that and if necessary I will bring my troop of one hundred men into Sherman to... ah… vouch for it?" My threat is palpable. God I love this power! The Sheriff squirms as he wonders how to save face and get out of this jam. "Now, Mr. Orwick." I state calmly taking the gun from his hand. "Why don't you put this away, sit down and have some tea with us." Without taking my eyes from those of the Sheriff, I address Barbara Smith. "Would that be alright Mrs. Smith? Can the Sheriff join us in a glass of tea?"

Mrs. Calderon darts into the house, as Mrs. Smith sits in stunned, wide eyed silence.

Bush comes out to the verandah. "Hello Dick!" Bush bubbles, her smile fading as she sees the arm of her brother loosely pinned behind his back. Stopping abruptly she asks. "What's going on?"

The Sheriff exhales and releases Hectors' arm.

"Homer, why don't you get the good Sheriff a chair. Sheriff, would you tell your men to put their guns away and leave us alone? They can return to town." I say in a fashion that is not a request. He directs his men to put their guns away and sits in the chair offered by Homer, as the deputies ride away.

"Now Dick, why don't you tell us what this is all about?" Hector asks, looking at me as we take our seats.

"Don Duval was killed last night as he stood on his verandah. This knife was thrust into his throat right here." The lawman said, pointing to the hollow below the Adam's apple and above the collar bone. "Do you recognize this knife?" He extends a large Bowie knife toward us.

"No Sheriff, I don't. Homer?" Hector said turning toward his brother who shakes his head.

I recognize it; Jim does too as he shoots an angry glance my way.

"It's just that..." The Sheriff stammers. "Well... everyone knows you and Duval don't get along so... we thought..."

I stand. "Aren't you glad you cleared this up Sheriff? Now if you don't mind." Indicating it is time for him to leave.

Mrs. Calderon arrives with the tea dutifully setting it on the table as she glances from the Sheriff to me.

The Sheriff rises from his chair, nervously twirling his hat, and says. "Mr. Anderson? There is one thing. Your boys? Well... last night they... ah... created quite a ruckus in town."

"I'll tell them to behave Sheriff, I assure you they will do whatever I say." my meaning quite clear as I place my hand on his shoulder.

"Well sir." He is unsure of how to proceed.

I prod him. "What is it Sheriff'?"

"They did quite a bit of damage to Ben Christians Hotel last night."

"Tell Ben I'll stand for the damages." Hector offers immediately.

"They did a lot more damage too!" The Sheriff returned.

"We'll take care of it Dick." Homer added his support to his brothers' position.

"Naw!" I say. "I'm sure the good people of Sherman will be happy to contribute this small sum to the Confederate cause, won't they Sheriff. Now run along."

Sheriff Orwick nervously twirls his hat in his hand and opens his mouth to speak, then thinking the better of it, slowly steps off the verandah and mounts his horse. We watch in silence as the Sheriff departs, the uneasy silence broken as Jim asks me quietly. "Did you know about this?"

Bush came to my side. "What was that Jim?"

I look at Jim and say for all to hear. "Jim reminds me we need to return to camp for a couple of days to restore order. Let's go Jim."

Chapter Twenty Nine

Perhaps it is a little too cool for a picnic, after all what could be expected for the last day of 1863. There will be no picnics today in Missouri; it is much too cold for a picnic. Bush wants to take a basket down by the river and I cannot refuse that request.

After the blanket is spread, I watch the slowly meandering river recalling a much smaller river in Kansas. The banks of the Neosho are not as steep or thickly wooded as the Red River, and not nearly as wide. I hadn't paid much attention to the Neosho, as my mind was preoccupied that day. I smile, recalling the object of preoccupation, Diane.

"What are you thinking of?" Bush asks.

"Wha... oh! I... um..." She caught me off guard. "I... ah... I was just... listening to the water... thinking about how contented I am right now." That is true, Bush makes me comfortable and at the same time nervous. I want to reach out and tear the clothing from her to reveal the body I only imagine. Something about her causes me to exercise restraint.

Our blanket is spread on a sand bar about twenty yards from the river. Bush talks, although

I am barely aware of what she is saying. I study her as she sits properly on the blanket. She is seated, legs bent under her, leaning on her right arm, occasionally rubbing it with her left hand indicating she is chilled. She continues to chatter, a sparkle in her eyes, excitement in her voice. God! Her dress accentuates the curvature of her breast line. Diane's dresses concealed her delectable body, hanging loosely from her shoulders. The bodice of Bush's dress is filled to overflowing and is driving me wild.

I am propped up on my left elbow facing her, my hands twisting a stalk of grass picked up as we walked near the water. My mouth is dry, breathing coming in short breaths, desire bubbling toward the surface. The ringing in my ears nearly drowns out the words Bush speaks. I allow the fingers of my hand to touch the fabric of her dress at the knee a few inches from my chest. She stops speaking, her eyes shifting to the hem of her dress and my hand.

My fingers nonchalantly return to their task of twisting the stalk, my eyes on the grass. She begins to speak again at a slower, less excited pace. I do not know what she is saying; my thoughts on other things. I touch her knee, she stops speaking. I look at her, take her hand, pull her toward me and kiss her lightly.

She smiles briefly and takes her hand away. Her eyes look into her lap then turns her face away from me. I reach out to caress her breast through the fabric of her dress. She pulls away, rising to walk up river.

Frustrated, I exhale loudly and leap to my feet to follow her. Catching her, I turn her toward me, she looks away.

"Please don't Bill." She whimpers.

Now I am frustrated. Why did we come on this picnic?

"I've never been with a man." She says shyly staring at the sand beneath our feet.

"I'll be gentle." I offer quietly.

"No Bill!" She cries softly, shaking her head as she pulls away from me. "I can't."

"Why?" I catch her again.

"Please. It's not right."

"Not right?" I say perplexed as she nods, a tear trickling down her cheek. What can't be right about this; I am totally enamored with her and want her. Had I read her wrong? I thought she cared for me as well. "What do you mean, it's not right?" I ask anger creeping into my voice.

Her shoulders shake as she cries. "For... two... people who are not... who are not... married... to..." She sobs as I lift her chin to face me.

Her eyes are closed as she cries softly. Even with tears streaming down her cheeks, she is beautiful. "Then let's get married." I say with a grin.

She draws a sharp breath as her eyes pop open. "What?" She says as if she did not hear me.

"I said, then let's get.... wait a minute let me do this right." I kneel down on one knee, her sparkling eyes follow me questioningly. "Miss Bush Smith, will you marry me?"

Tears flow from her eyes as she laughs and cries at the same time. "Oh yes! Yes! Oh Bill, yes!" She exclaims thrusting her arms around my head pushing me over backwards. We roll in the sand as she kisses me passionately. I feel my loins heating up until she says. "I'll make you so happy that we waited until our wedding night!" She said leaping to her feet, grabbing the basket and running toward the buckboard.

Happy? What? Wedding night? Wait? What? Happy to wait? God damn it! I dare not break the spell of this moment as she is obviously very happy and I am... aw shit! I painfully follow.

Barbara Smith and her daughter practically ignore me as we return from our picnic, our basket unopened, the two females excitedly buzzing as they move from the verandah to the house. Mrs. Smith suddenly stops in the doorway. Bush also stops her chatter as she looks at her mother. Barbara Smith walks to me, gives me a peck on the cheek. "Son." and returns to the excited preparations for the wedding.

Hector and Homer pound me on the back welcoming me to the family. Jim looks at me dejectedly, unable to hide his jealousy. He is in love with Bush, I have known that for some time.

"Jim!" I say with enthusiasm. "Will you be my best man?"

Jim looks at me solemnly for what seems minutes. Why is he hesitating? Leaning against the rock wall surrounding the verandah he smiles briefly. "No." and walks away.

Homer and Hector shuffle their feet uneasily not knowing what to say after I am rebuffed by my brother. I look in Jims' direction, my blood boiling with anger. My vision blurs as the ringing in my ears and buzzing sound drown out anything the Smith brothers may have said. The headache accompanying the ringing is much worse than ever, the pain biting into the back of my eyes.

The wedding is planned for Sunday, February 18, 1864 and haled as the social event of the New Year. Word spreads rapidly and enthusiastic responses to invitations are returned from people the Smith family barely knew. Many people around Sherman still believe the Smiths' are involved in the death of Don Duval and assemble out of morbid curiosity.

Jim and I no longer speak, any hope he had of winning Bush now dashed by his older brother. He has been cold to me for several months and I return his disdain in kind. Archie is overjoyed at being best man, walking as if ten feet off the ground as he tells everyone. "I'm gwon be Bill's bes' man!"

Colonel, or Captain, Quantrill arrives Saturday the seventeenth as does Todd, Greg and Pool with part of their troops. Over two hundred Partisan Rangers pitch camp on the HBBH spread in preparation for the following day's festivities. The afternoon is spent in updates on the war and our relationship with local Confederate troops.

Todd is vocal in his disdain for the manner in which the official Confederate hierarchy treats Quantrill. No one knows what to do with the guerrilla leader and his men. Officially we have been declared separate from the Confederacy, acting on our own, seeming to anger and at the same time satisfy Quantrill. His ego is more evident than ever now that he commands an entire army, displaying arrogance not previously evident. He insists upon being called Colonel Quantrill, the rank still denied him by Confederate leaders.

Guests began arriving early Sunday in groups of two to ten, many pitching tents and making camp for a few days while the celebration continues. Sheriff Dick Orwick stays close by Jim and Tom Duval, Don's younger brothers, to avert trouble. He needn't worry; starting a fuss against the Smith's would be suicide with a couple hundred Raiders in attendance.

A hundred or more of the townsfolk and surrounding ranchers are in attendance making the total well over three hundred people. The Vaqueros kill five prime steers and began preparing them over spits early morning. What a day! It is almost cloudless and a very mild temperature, nearly perfect.

The verandah is beautifully decorated with greenery from the ranch. Early blooming flowers are used to provide color to the ornate decorations. The Calderon's have done themselves proud.

At the designated hour of two PM, Archie and I wait on the verandah alongside the preacher as four Vaqueros provide music with violin and guitar. Mrs. Smith, as Matron of Honor, appears in the doorway pausing in the shadows seemingly for an eternity before slowly approaching to take her position opposite us. Slowly Bush moves gracefully toward the doorway, her beauty revealed to the gasps of the people waiting in anticipation. Oh what a sight!

Pausing momentarily in the doorway, her dazzling white dress reflects the sunlight causing me to squint against the bright glare. She carries a small bouquet of yellow and pink flowers in front of her narrow waist. Sweeping wide at the bottom, her dress flows in a long train behind her as she slowly makes her way toward me. From her narrow waist the dress is tightly form fitted upward to the bodice. A very low cut U shaped neck comes just above the center line of her breasts, her modesty barely retained by a lace covering attached inside the dress, her remarkable cleavage still quite evident. This dress accentuates her well endowed figure perfectly. An emerald colored cloth necklace fits tightly around her neck, a small heart shaped pendant in front. A veil attached to the pinnacle of a small hat gives the appearance of a small tent flowing over her face. WOW! What a beauty!

The preacher's words are barely discernible as I marvel at the beauty next to me. I cannot keep my eyes off what the thin lace reveals above her bodice as my passion rises.

Finally the ceremony is over and we run through a gauntlet formed by fifty of the Raiders extending swords in the air. As we pass through the corridor of glistening steel, flowers and rice are showered upon us. The celebration has begun! Hundreds of wine bottles and ale are chilling in a tank of water kept in the shade. Slices of beef are distributed from rotating carcasses over spits and the crowd is a-buzz. Coming from inside the house, my new bride is ten yards beyond the verandah walls and Quantrill, Todd and Gregg inside the wall facing her. Contentedly approaching the trio of friends, I survey the blissful scene.

"What a piece of ass that will be!" Quantrill tips his glass toward Bush.

Gregg smiles as he and the others look admiringly at my bride.

"I think I'll send Bill on a mission and crawl under the covers with that for a few nights." The Colonel continues. Todd laughs and slaps Quantrill on the back, then notices me behind them, the smile melting away rapidly. Quantrill turns in time to receive my punch.

"You son-of-a-bitch!" I growl through clenched teeth as I leap upon him. "I'll kill you!" I snarl as Todd and Gregg pull my hand from his throat and pull me away. The headache, ringing and buzzing is joined by a crackling, popping sound as if bacon frying in a pan. The combined noise is so great the words I scream are not discernible. The words bounce around inside my head echoing as if in a tight canyon. I see Bush's lips move and her terrified look. I hear nothing, but feel growling in my throat.

Quantrill stands up, straightens his tie, a shocked expression on his face as he and Todd stare at me. "I'll have you in front of a firing squad for assaulting your commanding officer." Quantrill squeaks as he rubs his throat. "Todd, take him in to custody."

William Gregg speaks up. "Colonel, please reconsider, not only is Bill and his company, all of which are here, an important part of our mission, but don't you think you might have been out of line with your comments about his new bride? Why don't you let it slide and I'm sure all will be forgiven and forgotten."

Quantrill looks at Gregg, lowers his eyes, and extends a hand to me. "My apologies Bill. I was out of line."

I look at the extended hand and slap it away.

"Why you." Quantrill began but Todd takes him by the arm, leading him away. Quantrill reluctantly follows. William Gregg looks at the pair as they leave, gives me an apologetic shrug and joins them.

Archie bumps into Gregg as he runs to the verandah, his wild eyes challenging the men that aroused my ire, and at the same time seeking instructions from me. I motion for him to come to my side. For several minutes we watch most of the raiders depart. Turning to Archie I say. "Tell our men they are no longer part of Quantrills' Raiders but now belong to Bloody Bills' Band. We will not follow that son-of-a-bitch any longer."

"WHHOOOOEEEEE!!!!!" He yells excitedly running from one member of the new band to another as the revelry begins anew.

Late that afternoon Bush and I are in a carriage driven by Reuben Ruiz, top Vaquero. Surrounded by revelers on horseback or in carriages, we ride in great spirits toward the river. After an hour we crest a rise near the river beyond which a stone cabin has been erected. The Vaqueros have been busy. The cabin, situated on a bend in the river, allows the morning sun to shine in the front door. Facing downstream the cabin is nearly covered in shadows from the late afternoon sun. A small but beautiful cabin, a wisp of smoke escaping from the chimney, awaits us. Olidio Guzman steps happily from within the cabin as we approach.

I do not understand their language, but the wishes the joyous Vaqueros express to us are understandable in any language. Olidio's brother, Aurelio says something and I turn to Olidio for interpretation.

"He say... you… carry... her" Olidio's English is not very good but he points to Bush and continues.

"He say... you carry her... in... there." he points at the cabin, giving me a big smile.

Homer clarifies what is meant. "He says you should carry your new bride across the threshold." Adding with a big grin. "...and we'll leave you love birds alone."

Mrs. Smith jumps from her carriage, approaches her daughter, a tear in her eye and gives her a kiss before stepping aside for me to assist my bride from our carriage.

Still coursing with adrenaline and anger from the encounter with Quantrill a few hours earlier, the buzzing not totally subsided, the moment I await with great anticipation is nearly at hand. "My lady?" My stomach churns with passion and desire as I reach up to assist her. She looks into my eyes with a warm smile, places her hand in mine, rises from her seat and steps gracefully to the ground. No sooner do her feet touch the ground than I sweep her up in my arms to the cheers of the Vaqueros and members of my Raiders. Oblivious to the revelers remarks and cheers, I make my way to the doorway without removing my eyes from Bush's. She has a contented look as she clings to me. Using my peripheral vision, I turn and crouch slightly to bring my bride head first into our honeymoon accommodations.

"Ah! Amigo! You... too tall!" Olidio exclaims as I close the door with my foot not bothering to acknowledge him.

The smile fades from Bush's face as she peers deeply into my eyes. Leaning forward, she kisses me softly, the sparkle in her eye replaced with a longing, she presses her lips against mine in a passionate kiss as I lower her feet gently to the floor.

"Oh Bill!" She sighs softly. "I've loved you for so long." She moans into my neck.

The cheering and shouts continue outside as Bush backs away, smiling sweetly at me as she glances toward the outside. Going to the window, she looks outside briefly before closing the curtains forcefully bringing a huge cheer from the assembly.

The Vaqueros break into a wedding song as they leave, the sounds of their song diminishing as they ride slowly away. Finally we are alone.

My breath comes in short gasps as blood pulses wildly in my veins, I have waited too long for this; I will not be denied. Bush faces me standing between the bed and the window. A cozy fire crackles in the fireplace providing warmth and an eerie glow to the cabin. I am barely aware of a table and two chairs at my back, inspecting the cabin will come later. She looks at me, a sweet smile on her lips, waiting for me to direct her. I take off my coat and began to quickly shed my tie and shirt. She reaches behind her to unbutton her dress but I stop her. "Let me!" I breathe heavily, voice cracking with passion. She looks at me and slowly lets her hands ease forward. She stares awkwardly, shyly, as I shed the remainder of my garments.

Trembling nervously I step quickly to her, reaching behind her to unbutton her wedding gown. I have waited so long for this! "Damn!" I can't undue the stays on her dress, but am not about to let that slow me down from taking her body, I've waited too long. Violently ripping the gown off amidst growing protests, my passion is not about to be denied as I roughly consummate our marriage.

My breathing comes in bursts as my body rests heavily on her. Lifting my body from hers, I roll slowly to the side. She tries to get up but I grab her arm and pull her against me. With her back toward me, she rests her head on her hands and says nothing. We lay there for several minutes until my breathing returns to normal. When I release her arm she gets up quickly and goes to the valise her mother packed for her. With her back to me, the flickering glow of the fireplace casts exotic shadows on her form. Bending forward at the waist toward the valise, her breasts sway freely from side to side. Looking at that exceptional body stirs animal urgings in me again. She holds a blouse to the light of the fireplace as I hasten out of the bed toward her.

Her eyes widen as she tries to pull away, bumping into a chair as she pleads. "No Bill." she pulls the blouse to her body trying to hide herself, whimpering. "No Bill, you hurt me Bill, please.

You're too rough." She began to cry softly and tries to hang onto the blouse as I rip it away. "Please Bill. I don't like what you made me do. I thought... oh no, please! No! No! NO! STAY AWAY!" she screams.

One hard swat across the mouth, and then another, stops her attempts to deny me.

This is not the way I visualized married life. Bush rarely speaks to me preferring the company of her mother who, although cordial, is distant. Even Bush's brothers, boyhood friends of mine, seem uneasy in my presence. I wonder if the only friend I have is Archie... and The Wind of course. That is one thing in my life that never questions nor betrays me, The Wind.

Bush is submissive to me, but passive, turning her face from me as we make love, or to be more precise, have sex. I wonder why the passion in her eyes before we were married is no longer there. Why is she like this? What have I done to offend her? Women! Who can understand them?

My band is restless as Quantrill and Todd left for Missouri in March and now, more than a month later, many are anxious to resume the plunder they enjoyed last Fall. Only a few weeks ago I had intentions of remaining in connubial bliss in Texas, now the camaraderie and excitement of battle are beckoning me. Perhaps my relationship with Bush will be enhanced if I return triumphantly from the war a decorated hero.

"Bill!" Mrs. Smith calls to me as I ride in from the range May 13th, 1864.

"Yes." I say tethering The Wind loosely to a mesquite bush near the verandah.

"Sit with me a minute Bill." the older woman sighs. She looks tired, overworked. I recall how my mother looked haggard and tired before she died, I wonder if Barbara Smith is dying.

"Bill." she begins as we sit on the wooden bench. "Bush wants me to tell you something."

I wait for her to continue.

She smiles wanly at me. "You're going to be a father."

"What!" I say leaping to my feet, walking excitedly around the verandah. "A father? That means... Bush.... Bush... is..."

"Yes silly. Bush is pregnant." she said her smile coming and fading with regularity. She is nervous about something.

I press my hands to my head, allowing the news to penetrate every pore. This is great! "WOW! When?" I grab her hands as I fall to a knee in front of her.

She pulls back startled, then relaxes saying. "November."

"November." rising to my feet I look around. My excitement fades as a thought enters my mind. Why didn't Bush tell me? It's the kind of thing a wife should want to tell her husband. "Barbara? Why didn't Bush tell me?" Mrs. Smith fidgets. She is holding something back. "Where is she Barbara? Where is Bush?"

"She's... ah... not feeling well, you know... morning sickness and all, she'll be alright but..." Mrs. Smith can not hide the lie in her eyes.

"Where is she?" I ask softly yet forcefully. "Where is Jim?" The mother is hiding something about her daughter. She shakes her head and begins to cry.

I back away slowly, anger growing within me as does the buzzing and ringing. I mount The Wind and turn toward the cabin by the river not knowing what draws me there. Bush did not want to return to the cabin after we spent our first month of marriage there, now something tells me to go to the cabin. The breeze presses against my face as The Wind gallops swiftly toward the stone building bathed in late afternoon sunshine, his long black mane stinging my face as we ride. Are his feet touching the ground? They are, but I cannot hear them. I hear only the ringing and buzzing.

My focus is on the door as The Wind slides to a halt and I leap from his back. I hear the crash of the door as it is kicked open and Bush's scream as I burst into the cabin. Jim stands fully clothed by the table but Bush is frantically trying to finish buttoning the front of her dress, eyes are wide with terror and hands shaking as I look at her. Her lips move with no sound, or I can't hear any. The bed is rumpled and only a fool could not ascertain what has been going on.

My brother, I should have known, he has loved her since he first saw her. My gaze falls to the floor a moment before I slowly withdraw my pistol and turn toward Jim. Bush places herself between us screaming, the veins standing out on her throat. What is she saying? Jim displays no fear. Way to go you son-of-a-bitch! You're about to die and now you get brave! I level the barrel at him but Bush is in my line of fire. I pull the hammer back, lowering my Colt at Bushs' face. So what if they both die?

Her eyes widen as she looks at the pistol. "BILL! YOUR BABY! BILL! BILL! YOUR BABY! YOUR BABY! YOUR BABY!" I finally hear her screaming.

I raise the gun a little. "What about the baby?" I ask calmly.

She is breathing heavily but relaxes slightly as she cries. Her reddened eyes study me for a moment. "If you kill us, you will also kill your baby." She moans.

"My baby?" I question with a snicker.

Her mouth drops and eyes widen. "YES! YOUR baby!" She screams emphatically, hands on her hips, leaning toward me.

"And?" I ask, touching the barrel to her forehead.

Fear returns to her eyes as she stands upright. "And he'll never have a chance... to know his father!" She answers.

I look at her over my pistol. She is leaning forward slightly, her hands reaching back toward, but not touching Jim. Somehow she no longer looks desirable; I now have a different attitude toward her. "And what say you Jim?" I ask looking my brother in the eye.

"Fuck you!" He says in control of his emotions.

We stare angrily at each other a few moments, eyes not wavering, Jim seemingly unconcerned about the weapon pointed menacingly at his forehead.

An evil grin spreads across my face. "If I can't take a joke, eh! HA! HA! HA!" I laugh uproariously uncocking the pistol. Returning the gun to my belt, I walk out the door still laughing.

"Archie." I say soon after arriving in the Mineral Creek camp. "I have a job for you."

Eight days into our journey back to Missouri Archie catches up with us. Reaching my side, he answers my unspoken question with a nod, pointing to the hollow of his neck.

Chapter Thirty

"Sergeant Parman? Why aren't patrols from Warrensburg being sent to scout around Holden? Why do we have to come all the way from Lexington? We're thirty miles away! The garrison at Warrensburg is only ten miles from here!" The soldier is asking the question we all have that is not being answered,

"Officers." I grunt. My mind races as we slowly ride over the countryside. Fear is in everyone's heart. We are tense, little idle chatter or laughter accompanying our fifteen man patrol, fearful that at any moment Quantrill's one hundred man band of raiders will swoop out of the woods and overrun our patrol.

Quantrill has the Union army in west central Missouri on edge. He returned to Missouri May 18 and challenged the post commander at Carthage to come out on the plains and fight. Fortunately the commander declined and no shots were fired.

Lamar was not as fortunate as Quantrill attacked the morning of the twentieth, burning and looting much of the town. I don't know how true the story is, but it sure has bolstered pride and courage in many of our troops, of how Sergeant Cavender and nine of his men held off Quantrill for three hours, killing or wounding thirty of the guerrillas.

Still, not knowing exactly where Quantrill is has everyone looking over their shoulder wondering what will happen next. It is rumored there was a rift in the guerrilla forces and they may be operating independently. They are feared, no matter who leads them.

The Union command devised a plan of defense wherein a garrison is set up in the seat of each county. The courthouse, normally constructed of brick or stone, will serve as a fortress against a guerrilla attack. From each garrison, daily patrols are sent out to scout the areas. Their orders are to not engage the enemy, but to inform the garrison commander of the guerrilla location for a larger force to encounter.

My patrol is in its second day away from our garrison at Lexington and will spend one more night in the field before returning tomorrow. It has been more than two weeks since Quantrill destroyed the telegraph lines between Pleasant Hill and Warrensburg and he has not been seen since. The lines are restored and communication is flowing as normal.

The locals are even more concerned than we are, with good reason. General Order Number Eleven banished all known supporters of the guerrillas and those more than a mile from a Union post. The exceptions to the one mile rule are those that are 'friends' of the Union (those that paid the graft) and as loyal citizens, are allowed to remain on their land. Thus these people are identified as enemies of the guerrillas and many have died mercilessly at the hands of the marauding Quantrill and his men.

Many of the people that did remain deserve their fate as they bribed officials and stood to profit immensely from the misfortune of the banished people. I do not feel sorry for them but, as is usually the case, the majority of the people now subjected to the burning and looting of the guerrillas are innocent victims, not idealistically aligned with the North or the South. These people are genuinely concerned with maintaining neutrality but their mere presence in the area, supposedly rid of Southern sympathizers, makes them targets of the guerrillas.

My personal life is in shambles. I'm not sure why I re-upped in November, a moment of weakness I suppose. What else could I have done? With no prospects of marriage and at thirty years old, I guess I am married to the army. It's not so bad, dumb officers but what the hell! I am haunted by the face of the girl that died last year in the Bingham building. Who knows, she might have been the one for me.

This is my second patrol in this area since Quantrill's raid here and we haven't seen anything, thank God! I can't figure out why a patrol isn't sent from nearby Warrensburg. Wait a minute!

There's a patrol, must be from Warrensburg. Why are there two patrol units in the same area?

"Squad halt!" I command. I think it is a patrol; I pull out my field glasses. There are too many of them for a patrol, must be fifty men... don't see a flag... ah... good, they are wearing Union blue uniforms! Good, they see us and have turned toward us. Those lucky guys, I would feel more comfortable out here with fifty men instead of fifteen, but we'd still be outnumbered by Quantrill's one hundred men. Fifteen against one hundred are poor odds. No way! I'd cut and run in a heart beat! I wouldn't stay and fight! I'm no coward, but I'm not stupid either.

HHMMM. What squad are they from, why they don't have a squadron flag and... why are they riding so fast at us? They are yelling! "SHIT! THEY'RE NOT A UNION PATROL!" they're shooting at us! "DEFEND YOURSELF! DRAW YOUR WEAPONS AND FIRE!" I command my small band, but it is too late, we are overwhelmed. Dirty unkempt men clad in Union blue fire point blank at us, my horse one of many bucking violently at the sudden excitement. Unable to maintain my grip, I tumble to the ground. Rolling from side to side to avoid the hooves of the horses, I instinctively pull my hands to my face, my forearm deflecting the leg of an excited horse. A gun is pointed directly at me as a puff of smoke belches from the chamber. I hear the sound of the shot but do not feel anything! Beyond the barrel of the gun, a bearded young man looks at his pistol, apparently surprised he missed me.

The face looks familiar, the eyes, the beard, the hat. It is Bloody Bill Anderson! I AM FACE TO FACE WITH BLOODY BILL ANDERSON! He points the pistol at me again! OH GOD! I AM GOING TO DIE!

I stare at the muzzle of that pistol, the opening seemingly getting larger and larger with each passing second. It does not waver from my eyes. An eternity passes as I await the inevitable explosion that takes my life. Looking past the muzzle, Bill Anderson smiles, yells. "BANG!" and laughs as I flinch. He lifts his revolver, blows on the muzzle and... and... winks at me!

"You better run while you have the chance." He says with a smile.

"Lemme skelp 'im Bill." a small man/boy says.

Bill does not acknowledge him but looks at me and asks. "What's your name?"

My mouth is dry, no words come out as I struggle to speak. Licking my lips, I clear my throat and squeak. "J... J.V.... J.V. Parman."

"Well J... J.V... J.V. Parman... RUN!" His eyes flash as he laughs.

I do just that as do two other men. Isaac Jackson, still on his horse, reaches down and pulls Charlie Horn up behind him. Isaac looks at me knowing his horse cannot carry a third rider. I yell. "GO!" they ride, and I run, as fast as we can as howls of laughter follow us. I do not look back.

At least we know where Quantrill's raiders are, three miles west of Holden Missouri. I run without looking back as Isaac and Charlie fade into the trees some distance ahead of me. Had all but three of us, of my squad, died at the hands of the guerrillas? My first taste of battle, I don't like it!

My legs are heavy, the drills and labor subjected to an army sergeant should have prepared me for this, and I thought I was in good shape. Sneaking a glance backward, I stumble and fall. Bloody Bill and his men are still at the site; I jump up quickly and continue to run. I dare not stop. My lungs burn, a stabbing pain is in my chest, as I fight to draw each breath. My legs get heavier but I dare not stop, although running very slow. Air rasps in my throat as it is pulled into my lungs, how long can I continue this? Where's the town? God, I don't think I can make it! The pain! Can't stop, must... go... on! My head is about to burst!

The pounding of hooves approaching renew my efforts to run, but I can't. Oh God, they're coming after me! Can't... stop... got... to ... go... on! OH GOD! I'M GOING TO DIE! My lungs... are... bursting! I stumble and fall face forward gulping dirt, coughing and gasping violently.

"GET UP!" A voice yells as I lay with my face in the dirt. I'm dead! They've got me!

"GET UP! GET UP!" Someone tugs on my arms. Just shoot me, I can't get up, can't run. My legs are weak and will not respond; my fingers will not grip the person trying to aid me. IT'S A GIRL! She pushes, pulls, and throws me into the back of a wagon bouncing wildly as it careens toward its' destination.

Too weak to support myself, I bounce around the back of the wagon, thrown from side to side, my head bouncing on the board flooring. What a headache! My heart pounds wildly and the pain in my chest increases. No matter how I gasp, not enough air gets into my lungs to relieve the pain. Drawing into a ball eases some of the pain and also gives some protection from the pounding I am taking on the wagon floor.

We stop, excited shouts flood into the wagon from outside as a man peers over the edge of the wagon, "He's alive." he shouts. Geez, did he sound disappointed? I can't dwell on his attitude as people and sounds get farther away; is this dying?

"Welcome back." the voice is sweet as I open my eyes to find its source from under the damp cool cloth on my forehead. "I didn't know if you were going to make it there for a while." she smiles, wiping the cloth across my brow. An Angel? She must be an Angel. She is pretty enough, but do Angels wear Gingham? Do Angels live in a dark room with bars on the windows? BARS! I sit up abruptly. She gently pushes me back onto the cot.

"Stay down! Stay down!" She coo's softly.

"Where am I?" I ask.

"You're in Moody's jail." the 'Angel' smiles, brushing my hair gently back from my forehead.

"JAIL!"

"Shush now! It's just a place to put you until you come back to the living." she said pressing my shoulders back to the cot. She is blond with a hint of freckles on cheeks, which rise and redden beautifully as she smiles. As her full soft lips part in a smile she reveals a front tooth partially covering the next tooth. Well! She can't be an Angel. Angels would surely have perfect teeth, but looking at that face... wow! That tooth is about all that isn't perfect about her. Her blue eyes sparkle as she looks at me before wetting the cloth again and wiping my brow.

" Are you feeling better?" she asks; a sincere tone of concern in her slightly gravelly voice.

"Ye... no!" I lie. If tell her I am feeling better she might go.

"No? What's wrong?" a frown disrupts the smooth skin on her forehead. Seated on the edge of the cot, she looks at me with soft eyes, the ring around the black dot in the center a light bright blue. "Where does it hurt? Your breathing is normal. Shall I call a Doctor, are you injured somewhere?"

My mind races as I seek an appropriate answer. "Here." I point to my chest.

"Your lungs?" she asks, placing her hands on my chest and pressing gently, as she peers intently into my eyes. Leaning closer, her face expresses genuine concern. "Your lungs?" she asks again.

I shake my head.

"What then?"

"My heart." I offer feebly.

"Your heart?" a frightened look comes over her as she pulls back suddenly.

"Yes." I say softly, "I... think you've stolen it." God! I can't believe I said that! J. V., you idiot!

She laughs, lightly pats my chest and quickly rises from the edge of my cot. "Tssk! Oh you!" She laughs softly again, a bright smile on her lips.

Now I've done it! "Don't go! I'm sorry!"

She turns, smiling sweetly at me, her eyes sparkling. "I... ah, I'll be back." There is more in her response than a promise to return.

Ike' and Charlie arrived in town a few minutes after escaping the raiders. Janie Steuvers, my Angel, was aboard her wagon when they came in screaming about the attack, and how I was still out there. Without hesitation she whipped her team into action, dashing out to retrieve me. Why didn't she just unfold her wings and fly out to pick me up. Angels can do that, can't they?

Returning to post in Lexington will be difficult now. Ike and Charlie are mounted awaiting instructions. I am intent on the girl standing beside my horse.

"I... ah... can... would it... ahmmm... would you..." I stammer.

"J. V.! If you are trying to ask if it is alright for you to see me again... it is!" she speaks softly, peering at me with a radiant smile.

I heave a sigh of relief. Not so glib are you, I thought.

"But you can't have it back."

"Wha...?" I start in surprise.

"You can't have it back." She repeats.

I look at her perplexed.

"Your heart." She says softly. "You can't have it back."

"YAHOOOO! LET'S RIDE BOYS!"

Chapter Thirty One

Quantrill was not there that day near Holden. At the same time my patrol was attacked, Quantrill was reported to be attacking the steamboat, Prairie Rose. George Todd has reportedly taken over Quantrills' band of one hundred and 'Bloody Bill', with fifty of his band, has broken away from Quantrill after a rift in Texas. How do they know that stuff? Does somebody ask. "Oh by the way Bloody Bill, are you and Quantrill still friends?" That thought makes me laugh. "Oh hi Bloody. How's it going?" Laughing about Bloody Bill is not easy.

Isaac "Ike" Jackson, Charlie Horn, Anthony "Pee Wee" Haskill and I are assigned to the river boat, West Wind, to provide protection against the raiders. After our harrowing experience near Holden, three of us need an assignment to keep us off patrol for a while. However, four against... a hundred, we... are... protection?

Four iron barricades atop the wheelhouse to crouch behind made me feel better. Each barricade is five feet in length, three feet high and supported to stand on its own. From behind two of these thick iron shields, connected together, we have a 180 degree view of the river.

The tranquility of the river is fantastic! Gently swaying in the currents, the humming of the engines, and warmed by the sun, napping is easy to do. We are supposed to be alert, ever vigilant to the possibility of attack but are only an hour away from the fort at Lexington. The raiders will surely not be this close to the Union troops.

Our cargo of black powder was loaded at Leavenworth for distribution to the garrisons at Lexington, Boonville and Jefferson City. Iron barricades also surround the powder stored on deck protecting it as well as the wheelhouse. The weight of the cargo along with the barricades and the nature of the cargo are such that passengers are not allowed on this trip. The boat rides extremely low in the water and many more of us "protectors", may have caused the boat to sink. Perhaps the officers are not such idiots after all.

This is the life! Ike, Charlie, Pee Wee and I lay on top of the wheel house, enjoying the sun as we doze comfortably. The gentle swaying of the boat, the rhythmic beating of the paddle wheels on each side, the steady drone and vibration of the engines have a soothing, calming effect on us.

A gunshot reverberates across the river disturbing the tranquil setting. We sit up quickly, the bright light of the sun nearly blinding us as our eyes had been closed. Stumbling quickly off the roof of the wheelhouse, we take up position behind the barricades. Rubbing my eyes, I see a solitary figure standing on a rock several yards into the river. He raises his rifle and yells at us to pull in. Ike lowers his rifle and takes aim.

"Wait Ike." my eyes are fixed on the lone figure.

Ike looks at me in surprise. "Do you know who that is?"

I nod.

"Then we gotta kill 'im!" Ike returns his cheek to the stock of his rifle.

"Every one, hold your fire." I whisper loud enough for my three companions to hear, and addressing Ike. "He let us live Ike." I say softly, not taking my eyes from the solitary figure boldly hailing our craft. Standing in the middle of the river, he is an easy target. He is either very brave or very foolish. Ike looks down the barrel of his rifle for several moments before pulling the weapon behind the barricade with a dejected sigh. "Damn J.V.!"

Bloody Bill Anderson hails us again. "You there! Pull in to shore. We will unload your cargo and release you unharmed."

The pilot is whispering loudly to us. "Shoot 'im! Shoot 'im!" In disgust the pilot presses the engine to full speed, a risky maneuver given the shifting nature of the channels of the Missouri river. Crouching behind the barricades inside the wheelhouse, he evidently would rather take his chances on grounding his craft.

"You'll be sorry!" Bill laughs as we pass alongside him barely thirty yards away.

"J. V.? He's an easy target!" Charlie pleads.

I stare at the face of Bloody Bill Anderson, our eyes locking for several seconds. He seems pleased we do not stop for him, sneering at us as we slide by. We shall meet again Bloody Bill. I resist the urge to yell 'bang' at him; we are even Bloody Bill, your life has been spared.

Not two hundred yards downstream gunfire erupts, wood splinters as shot penetrates the wheelhouse. A metallic ping rings out as a ball strikes the barricade. Another shot, another ping. The boat lurches forward as it strikes something in the river, spilling us from behind our barricades. More shots, more pings and the sound of shattering glass as a steady barrage of gunfire strikes the fleeing riverboat. Bullets striking the barricades we scramble behind are especially loud. Pee Wee yells in pain, a shot striking him in the calf as he pulls himself under cover. I look over the side and see the leaves and branches of a tree the raiders felled in the river to stop us. The pilot rammed the tree rather than stop, pushing it aside and now it is a question of how much damage is done to the bow and whether or not we will sink.

If we sink we'll probably drown in the swift current, but should one of those bullets ignite the powder we are dead for sure! GEEZ! There must be a hundred of them pouring lead in on us. But

Bill does not have a hundred men! HOLY SHIT! At least he didn't have! When will it stop?

The firing slows and finally a single shot echoes across the river behind us. We are beyond them, have not blown up and hopefully not sinking.

"Ike! Charlie! You OK?" I ask, looking at Pee Wee's contorted face. "How you doin' Pee Wee?" I cautiously move to his side.

"I'm OK Sarge." he says through gritted teeth.

"Sure you are." I agree. Pee Wee is a nickname earned because of his stature but no one questions his heart or fighting spirit.

As it turns out, we were fortunate. The next day the Wilby Long is hailed, presumably by Bloody Bill, just west of Sibley. They too decline to stop and are fired on by the raiders. This time the raiders board the vessel, kill the pilot and guards before purposely running the boat aground to unload the cargo. The wreck of the Wilby Long effectively blocks the channel halting river traffic. I'd rather take my chances on the ground than stuck in the middle of a river on a boat.

Major Robert "Bobby" Cox confronts me about the events on the West Wind.

"It's personal Major."

"Personal hell! You're in the army Sergeant! You don't HAVE a personal life!"

"Yessir."

"You had him in your sights? And you let him go?"

"Sir. I told you about Holden, he had his pistol only a couple of feet from my face. He let me live."

"Not relevant Sergeant!" the Major yells. "This is war! Bloody Bill Anderson is ravaging the countryside killing innocent citizens, and you… you let him go?"

"Yes sir." I reply meekly.

The Major is storming around his office visibly upset over my actions on the river. He stares at the blank wall, his back to me.

"Sir? I felt it was justice. He could have killed me..."

"Perhaps he should have! Perhaps I should!" The Major turns abruptly. "Justice?"

"Yes sir." I said quietly. "But if he had killed me, he would still be out there killing others. My dying would not have changed that."

The Major sighs.

"Sir. Let him be my responsibility. Let me lead my squad after him to... kill or capture him."

"YOU? You… are going to capture Bloody Bill Anderson?" the Major laughs and looks spitefully at me. "Yes, you... you WILL capture... Bloody... Bill... Anderson?" Fire shoots from his eyes as he steps close to me. Suddenly his eyes soften. "Yes Sergeant. YOU will capture Bloody Bill Anderson. YOU will be assigned to every detail sent after him. YOU will have no reprieve from duty until he is... or you are… dead! Hell! I still should shoot you myself!" He angrily shouts at me.

"Yes sir."

"Do you understand your orders Sergeant?"
"Yes sir!"
"Then get the hell out of here!"

The post at Lexington is buzzing with the news that Bloody Bill sent a letter to the editor reprinted in the July 1, edition. The editor had written scathing denunciations of Quantrills' tactics and especially critical of William Anderson. The editor likens Bloody Bill to a crazed rabid dog and urges the citizens of Lexington and surrounding areas to take up arms and kill the guerrillas on sight. Bloody Bill replied:

Mr. Editor:

In reading your paper, I see you urge the policy of the citizens taking up arms to defend their persons and property. You are only asking them to sign their death warrants. Do you not know that you have some of Missouri's proudest, best, and noblest sons to cope with? Listen to me fellow citizens; do not obey this order. Do not take up arms if you value your lives and property. It is not in my power to save your lives if you do. If you proclaim to be in arms against the guerrillas, I will kill you. I will hunt you down like wolves and murder you. You cannot escape. Your arms will be no protection for you. We have been in the field three years and are armed with two to four pistols and Sharps rifles. I have chosen guerrilla warfare to revenge myself for wrongs that I could not honorably avenge otherwise. I have killed many. I am a guerrilla. I have tried to teach the people of Missouri that I am your friend, but if you think I am wrong, then it is your duty to fight. Take up arms against me and you are federals. Your doctrine is an absurdity and I will kill you for being a fool. Beware men, before you make this fearful leap. Join me and live. Oppose me and die.

W. Anderson

"Ya gotta give 'im credit for having sand!" comments Herb Grove.

Sand? Guts? Fortitude? I have no doubt about the courage of Bill Anderson. One look into those cold eyes convinced me he fears nothing.

The eyes. I recall the photographer a year ago showing fear after looking into those eyes. What is his name? Carlson! I heard he was found with a large hole in his neck below his Adam's apple, propped up on his studio chair as if posing for a picture. His death was attributed to Bloody Bill and cited as an example of the random nature of the guerrilla leaders killing. I don't believe it is a random killing. Retribution, that's what it is. Bills' sisters died in the Bingham building crash and arrested on information provided by Arden Carlson. I knew that, and perhaps Bill did too.

Bill Anderson was reported in the vicinity of Sibley, north of the river in Ray County. Lt. Ray Mack leads a force of fifty men in pursuit and of course I am assigned to the Lieutenant for this patrol.

The column stops in Wellington. A scouting party reported Bloody Bill and three hundred guerrillas are three miles northwest of town. Lt. Mack quickly dispatches a rider to Lexington for reinforcements. Three hundred! Wow, his forces are growing rapidly.

As we pass through town toward the river crossing, I see two familiar figures. A giant of a man following a smaller man with one hand, mount horses to leave as my squad passes. Surely these are the same men encountered at the wreckage of the Bingham building a year ago, the same men so attentive on the welfare of the Anderson girls. What a coincidence to see them again... is it a coincidence?

"Lt. Mack sir." I call out.

"Yes Sergeant."

"Sir. We are assuming a position to the East of Bill Anderson's' reported position to await reinforcements are we not?"

"That is correct Sergeant."

I pause for a moment unsure of how to proceed.

The Lieutenant looks at me. "Sergeant?"

"Sir, the information you received about the where-a-bouts of the raiders. Did that come from a man with one hand accompanied by a very large man?"

Eyeing me carefully for a moment, Lt. Mack turns in his saddle and yells, "Sergeant Conyers!"

The command is passed verbally through the ranks and soon a horseman breaks ranks to ride to our side.

"Yes sir."

"Sergeant Conyers, the information you received about the location of the guerrillas, where did it come from?" The Lieutenant asked.

"It came from a couple of townsfolk." Sergeant Conyers responds.

"Do you know them to be a reliable source Sergeant?"

"Well sir, I don't know them personally but... they seemed innocent enough. They seemed to know what they were talking about."

Lieutenant Mack looks at me as he addresses Sergeant Conyers. "Describe them for me."

"Two men sir, one very big didn't say much, as a matter of fact the smaller man did all the talking. Oh! He only had one hand... the smaller man!"

"What do you make of that Sergeant Parman?"

I ponder the possibility of coincidence but fill in Lt. Mack on the details of when I saw these two before.

"And you suspect they have given us false information?" He asks as I finish.

"I don't know sir."

The Lieutenant holds up his hand halting the column. He sits up in his saddle, his eyes scanning the wooded hills in front of us. I too search for a sign of... anything.

"Sergeant?" the Lieutenant began pensively. "If they are members of the guerrillas would they direct us into an ambush? Of course they would." He answers his own question.

Adjusting himself in the saddle, his eyes search the wooded area for a sign. "If they wish to lead us into an ambush what would be the best way, to tell us to go to the Northwest directly into the guerrilla's strength? But we turned Northeast... to join reinforcements... away from where they said the guerrillas are camped."

He talks aloud to himself and turns toward me. "Did they anticipate we would not go in the direction they pointed us, and the camp is in fact to the Northeast? If it is..." He pauses, again surveying the woods in front of us. "Sergeant, we could be riding into a trap."

We crossed the Missouri River a half mile behind us and proceeded due North on the flat river bottom. The hilly wooded area two hundred yards in front has a natural dividing line meandering through the thick woods. This opening is wide enough for four horses to walk abreast, a perfect location for an ambush. Lt. Mack studies the hills and wooded area for several seconds before he speaks to no one in particular. "If I were a guerrilla, that's where I'd be." The Lieutenant directs our column east, away from the thick woods in front of us.

The wisdom of that maneuver is quickly evident as guerrillas burst from the woods, firing and screaming. Our horses, startled by the charging guerrillas, break into a run urged on by equally startled and frightened Union troopers. Our primary goal is gaining the safety of the Union garrison at Lexington, approximately five miles away, across the river. Dust and dirt fly into my face from the horses ahead as we race for the river near Lexington. Turning my head to shield my face from flying debris, I watch Herb Grove fall from his horse. He must have been shot as Herb is too good a horseman to have fallen from the saddle. Other horses and riders stumble over the fallen comrade.

The shouts and shots cannot be heard anymore as the pounding hooves drown out all other sound. I am fortunate to be in front of the column as those at the rear are more vulnerable to be picked off by pursuing raiders.

Union soldiers cross the Missouri River west of Lexington, still a mile away but a welcome sight. Our racing horses are near exhaustion as they are reined in at the head of the reinforcement column. We turn to face our adversary and are surprised to discover we are not followed; the enemy is not in sight.

Lt. Mack feverishly explains to Colonel McFerran and Major Cox, how we were in imminent danger, attacked by three hundred guerrillas. Our combined forces of over two hundred proceed with caution toward the ambush location.

I am summoned to the front by the Lieutenant who rides behind Colonel McFerran and Major Cox. "Sergeant Parman!" the Colonel addresses me as we approach the scene of the attack. "Lt. Mack tells me this patrol owes its' lives to your perceptive nature." he smiles.

I look at Lt. Mack, and Major Cox, both of whom are smiling at me. Shrugging my shoulders, I am unsure how to respond.

"AH! And modest as well Major, Lieutenant, very good!" the Colonel laughs, obviously pleased. "Sergeant! You are being recommended for a medal commemorating your courage and service to your comrades. Well done son!"

Son. Somehow it does not seem offensive as it was when 'beast' Strachan called me son.

A medal? He's going to give me a medal? I'm a hero?

We find bodies of seven of our patrol, five of which had clothing stripped from them. Uniforms for the guerrillas, we surmise. Three of the dead soldiers are bloodied about the head where their hair has been ripped from their heads. I'd never seen anyone that had been scalped. I heard that this is a common practice of Bloody Bills' band of guerrillas.

All is quiet as we carefully enter the wooded area avoided earlier. Evidence in the woods indicates the guerrillas were waiting for us. Although unable to ascertain an exact count, the number of guerrillas is considerably less than three hundred.

Turning west from the wooded area, we come upon a farm and find a woman filling in a grave. Kathy Nelson is mourning the loss of her husband as she gently places dirt on top of the body. Wiping dirt and tear stained cheeks; she recounts the events of the guerrillas visit to their farm a few hours earlier. Jim Nelson was tending his animals as riders clad in blue approached, thinking they were Union soldiers, Mr. Nelson professed his allegiance to the Union and was shot where he stood.

My heart sinks as I look at the new widow. The responsibility for her lonely life lay in my hands. Only the demise of Bloody Bill Anderson can prevent further agony.

The Colonel assigns a pair of men to finish the burial detail and, in questioning the woman, finds the strength of the raiders is at best fifty men. I feel foolish for having run from a force inferior to our own. Will I still get my medal?

Chapter Thirty Two

DAMN! I am hungry! How long have I been here? The rocks at this vantage point west of the Missouri River are very comfortable as is the warmth of the sun. The sun is setting and there is a slight chill in the September air. Reliving my life of the past couple of years was not a pleasant experience. Although the valley is nearing total darkness, very little time had passed recalling my recent experiences. The lone rider is not much closer, but he will soon be here. If my body did not crave food, I would stay here all night instead of returning to my band of cut throats.

Cut throats! That term is especially appropriate for Archie; he delights in cutting the throats of his victims before scalping them. His bridle is adorned with the scalp of thirty-three men at last count, yet even Archie waits for me to kill first, or my permission to kill. Why do they do that? Why do I have to think for them?

I look for the rider but cannot make him out in the gathering darkness of the valley below. I see the bottom portion of the sun cut off by the horizon in the west and briefly enjoy the reddish hue of the clouds above it. A half hour before dark

I surmise and make my way toward camp a couple hundred yards from my ridge. I dread returning to them, longing for solitude.

"Rider comin' Bill!" a sentry calls to me as I pass a few yards from his position.

"I saw."

"Rider down there Bill." another sentry calls a few minutes later as I approach his vantage point outside camp. I look back toward the dark valley. Silhouetted against the darkening sky behind, the trees on the opposite side are barely visible. To the west the sun is but a small reflection against the sky above it. I marvel at the color of the sky, at its' gold, pink, orange, blue, yellow and a multitude of colors created by the dwindling daylight. God it's beautiful!

"Yeah, I saw him." I acknowledge.

"Should I let 'im into camp?"

Briefly I visualize the alternative. "Yeah! Let 'im in.

He is a man in his late thirties by his facial features although the white hair indicates a man of greater years. Smiling broadly, he rides toward our campfire, eyes sparkling under the flat circular brim of his hat. A long black coat extends beyond his knees as he swings a leg over his horse to dismount. The dirty white starched collar gives his profession away. He is a preacher.

"Good evening kind sirs!" he began with enthusiasm. "Praise the Lord it is good to see friendly faces. I was worried I might run into George Todd, Bill Anderson, or another of the gang of guerrillas." He prattles as he unties a book bag and loosens the belly strap of his saddle.

Archie looks at me as do many of the others seated about the fire, and starts to open his mouth. I motion for them to be silent. As we wear Union uniforms, he has mistaken us for Union troops.

"May I join you?" he asks in a thick foreign brogue walking directly to the fire, hands extended checking its' warmth; he already has.

"Of course... father?" I respond from my position twenty feet away. Comfortably lying against my saddle, I have no desire to stand to greet him.

He turns to me with a smile, my response having identified the leader of the 'troop'. "Thank you, but it's Pastor, not father. Pastor Karl Wittenberg, Lutheran minister on my way to establish a parish in Independence, Missouri." he said extending a hand.

Taking his hand without standing I ask. "Lutheran?"

"Yes, a Protestant sect established in St. Louis Mr...?"

I ignore his question. "Never heard of 'em."

"Ah, yes! Well, we recently immigrated from Germany, well, oof, nearly thirty years ago now. There are many of us along the river between here and St. Louis. Most of the Germans are Lutheran, your affiliation sir?"

A talkative jovial type, his mouth turns easily into a smile, lighting up a large heart shaped face.

Affiliation? "Don't rightly know." I reply slowly.

He looks at the fire, considering his next words. "You have coffee?"

I motion for John Ramsey to pour the preacher a cup.

"Thank you." the preacher says to John as he accepts the cup and sits on the ground near me. "Any Germans in your squad Captain… ahmm...?" He asks noting the rank on my shoulder.

"Not that I am aware of. It's not the sort of question we ask our recruits before they join."

"No! HO! HO! I suppose not!" He laughs, his shoulders rising and falling rapidly in laughter. "So! What detachment are you with Captain...?"

Inquisitive sort this preacher. "The Fourth Missouri out of… Jefferson City." I lie, declining to give him my name.

The preacher's brow furls for an instant as he sips his coffee. "I just came through Jeff City, stayed a few days, I don't recall a Fourth Missouri Cavalry being there?"

"We are relocating from Boonville to Jefferson City."

Nodding, he silently sips his coffee. The partisans are quiet, eyes on the preacher.

"You gonna be on the trail of the guerrillas Captain..."

"Yep! Where they go we'll go." I remark and Archie burst out laughing. I motion for him to be silent.

The preacher studies the short stubby Archie. The commandeered uniform fits him loosely across the shoulders with sleeves rolled up two inches to accommodate Archie's stubby arms. His clothes do not fit him and he has vowed to kill someone his size so he can be properly attired. Many of the uniforms are incomplete and do not fit the men. Perhaps the preacher won't notice.

"You... ah... will be going north of the river?"

I nod.

"There is a report Captain, that... the Fourth Missouri was being disbanded after being overwhelmed by Bloody Bill Anderson on the 28th of August." The preacher is tentative now.

"We've had three weeks to reform." I counter after a short pause.

That seems to relax him, as the preacher nods. "Well! Is it true that Anderson is in Carroll County?"

I shake my head and reply sarcastically. "I don't think so." Archie's sudden laughter stops as I swing sharply toward him and order. "Archie! Get some wood for the fire."

"Aw Bill." he pouts.

"Archie? Bill?" the preacher asks, now suspecting to whom he is speaking.

I stare into his eyes for the expected fear. For a fleeting instant it is there. I know he feels a cold chill down his spine as the confident smile is no longer in evidence.

He reaches for a thick hard covered book beside him, opening it to the middle. Turning his back to the fire for better lighting, his eyes dart over the page before looking at me. "This from the book of Job, the twenty seventh chapter: 'As God liveth, who hath taken away my judgment; and the Almighty, who hath vexed my soul; all the while my breath is in me and the spirit of God is in my nostrils; my lips shall not speak wickedness, nor my tongue utter deceit'." His voice is low, loud enough for me to hear, and a few others that are close, but his reading seems more for his own benefit. He does not project the reading as if for ours.

"Mr. Anderson." He said addressing me with an even voice, his face serious, now certain of my identity. "There is a message for you on every page of Gods' word." He turns about a half inch of pages scanning the page quickly. He looks at me and began reading in a firm voice. "From Jeremiah, chapter six; 'Thus saith the Lord: Stand ye in the ways and see, and ask for the old paths, where is the good way, and walk therein, and ye shall find rest for your souls'." He closes the book. "God is saying to you through the words on these pages, to turn toward the path of the Lord, to turn from your path of unrighteousness, away from your destruction, away from your evil ways."

The men behind the preacher look at me and slowly move to a different location.

The preacher opens his book again, this time near the back. He smiles brightly as his eyes hurriedly scan the page. "Perfect! Listen to this! It is amazing how God directs my gaze to the appropriate passage. Here in Mark, chapter two, Christ is seated at the table of a tax... of a sinner, and those watching think it is terrible for him to associate with, or speak to sinners and Christ says, listen to this; 'They that are whole have no need of the physician, but they that are sick, I came not to call the righteous, but sinners to repentance.' You see, Christ says there is time for you, he has sent me here tonight to show you the error of your ways, to enlighten you to the ways of the Lord! He wants you to set aside your sinful ways and walk in the ways of righteousness."

John Ramsey motions for Thomas Fulton to find a different place to sit other than behind the preacher.

He turns the pages again, this time seeking a particular passage. He smiles looking up at me. "Let me read Romans, chapter six where the Apostle Paul says; 'What shall we say then? Shall we continue in sin that grace may abound? God forbid. How shall we who are dead to sin, live any longer therein? Know ye not, that so many of us as were baptized into Jesus Christ were baptized into his death? Therefore we are buried with him by baptism into death..."

As he continues to read in a clear strong voice, the men are puzzled by his bravado. I wonder if any of them are listening to the words this preacher is reading. What sense does it make? I wince as a sharp pain shoots behind my eye. Pressure from my right hand against the temple provides some relief. When will he shut up?

"... I speak after the manner of men because of the infinity of your flesh; for as ye have yielded your members servant to uncleanness and to iniquity unto iniquity; even so now yield your members servant to righteousness unto holiness. For when ye were the servants of sin, ye were free from righteousness. What fruit had ye in those things whereof ye are now ashamed? For the end of those things is death. But now being made free from sin and become servants to God ye have your fruit unto holiness and the end of everlasting life. For the wages of sin is death but the gift of God is eternal life through Jesus Christ our Lord'." He closed his book and looked at me, "You see! You must turn from your sinful ways and repent."

"Well preacher. That is interesting, but we're not perfect like you so we can't expect much forgiveness for..."

"Oh but I'm not perfect!" he interrupts. "I'm a sinner too! But God forgives me as I confess my sins to him, as long as I am heartily sorry for them and believe in our Lord Jesus Christ!"

"You're a sinner?" I ask.

"Yes!" he said with an enthusiastic laugh that covers a clicking sound in my hand. "And God forgives me all my sins. And I will live forever with Him in Paradise."

"Paradise." I snort. "Tell me. What was that part about wages?"

His smile enlarges as he relaxes. "You mean; the wages of sin is death but..."

"Collect your wages preacher." His eyes widen in fear as my forty four Colt roars in my hand.

Chapter Thirty Three

The wooden bench is hard and Congressman James S. Rollins wonders why these seats can't be padded to make riding a stagecoach more comfortable. Making it even more uncomfortable is the necessity for the three passengers to alternate foot and leg positions to avoid bumping knees. The distance between benches does not allow one to stretch the legs out.

As he boarded the coach in Columbia the congressman took a seat opposite the female passenger who, having boarded earlier, chose to ride in the direction of travel. She is settled into the corner of the bench seat, leaning against the window to her left casting a sorrowful gaze outside, a position she maintains for all but a few minutes of the next two hours. The third occupant, who proudly professes to being a "Jayhawker", pauses briefly as he enters, looks at the female, the elderly male (me), and chose the seat opposite me next to the pretty girl. Attempts by this third occupant to engage her in friendly conversation are ignored, and I feel no urge to engage in idle banter.

She is quite thin and her plain dress hangs limply on her as she sits quietly on the bench. She is fairly tall for a female, and surely not much more than a hundred pounds. Her complexion is light, she must be an indoor person. Only the rich or genteel have the luxury of remaining indoors for any length of time. The poor, including the women, have to labor in the sun and their rough sunburned skin gives their position in life away. But this girls' clothing is not that of the genteel. The dress of simple fabric is probably handed down from a big sister or friend.

Dark brown hair cascades over her shoulders curling nicely at the bottom. Thin dark eyebrows are carefully colored. She is going to meet someone, I think as I nonchalantly study her. A suitor? Her parents? The thought of who she may be meeting occupies several minutes of the boring journey.

The 'Jayhawker' identifies himself as Dan Raymond, a thirty two year old Kansas farmer turned merchant that came to Lawrence, Kansas from the Mississippi town of Quincy, Illinois the fall of 1852. He is a vain man carefully holding his hat in his hand instead of damaging his wavy black hair. Dark eyebrows emphasize his dark wide set eyes. A strong dimpled chin accentuates his good looks, although his thin mustache does give him a sinister look. Confidence bordering on arrogance exudes from this Kansan. I don't know him, but I don't like him.

As the coach strikes a large bump Dan 'accidentally' bumps the young lady and once again attempts to engage her in conversation with an, "OOPS! Sorry. What a bumpy road." She chooses to ignore him with only a perfunctory glance downward, keeping her attention riveted outside the cabin of the coach. I wonder how many women ignored the advances of so handsome a man.

Finally, after an hour of having his advances ignored, Dan turns his attention to me. I learn, from his vantage point, how the nation would not be embroiled in a civil war if not for those 'dirty rotten scoundrels' crossing from Missouri to Kansas in March of 1855. "In spite of a population of only three thousand in Kansas, sixty three hundred people cast their votes for pro-slavery issues." he rails.

I suppress the urge to point out that incident is but one of numerous issues and incidents, nationally and locally, built up over a number of years until secession occurred. I have to admire his fortitude as he continues to rail against 'Missourians' when it should be obvious his traveling companions are in all likelihood, 'Missourians'. Traveling from Columbia to Centralia Missouri, is it not likely the passengers of this coach would be from Missouri? No, it's not fortitude but arrogance.

He raves on about the injustices created by the people of Missouri. I try to think of ways to silence him, a statement that will put him in his place and grant his fellow passengers relief. I am noted as an orator and pride myself on my ability to debate issues; however, opting to use the young ladies method, I choose to ignore him. Dan is well into his opinionated diatribe and it no longer matters if anyone is listening. I consider ways to silence the opinionated braggart, but my tendency to be polite renders me silent.

Soon after he began berating the people of Missouri, I identify myself as a farmer from Moberly which I was before entering politics many years ago. I am surprised at my own silence as I rarely pass up an opportunity to campaign for votes. Had these two been typical Missouri passengers they might recognize the name of Jim Rollins as a congressman who unsuccessfully ran for governor of Missouri in 1848. Perhaps if I had introduced myself as James S. Rollins, as I was better known as, or if I said, 'I am Congressman Rollins' the recognition would have been there, but I am weary of political bickering and my career in congress is coming to an end. I am content to accept a new role, 'Jim Rollins, farmer'.

General Sterling Price entered southeast Missouri September 19th, intent on capturing the state capital at Jefferson City. Unlike some of my fellow legislators, I am not particularly brave and discreetly decided this is a good time to confer with constituents in my part of the state. The guerrilla bands of Anderson and Todd have been reported near Carrollton, thus now seems a good time to skirt their positions.

A curious thing happens as Dan continues his lecture on the evils of Missourians. As he began recounting the dastardly deeds of William Clarke Quantrill and his band, the woman at the window snaps upright looking at the Jayhawkers face. Anger appears briefly in her eyes before softening. He doesn't notice her glare at him, continuing his tale of unprovoked, senseless bloodshed by the Missouri guerrillas. This point I tend to agree with, except his attributing the attack to 'Missourians'. Quantrill is not a Missourian and sane men have disassociated themselves from him and his actions.

Without lowering her eyes, she looks at me with a questioning stare. Smiling slightly, I roll my eyes gently to indicate I too am annoyed by his constant banter. At that her tension wanes and she returns her gaze out the window. He is obnoxious yes, but her look was more than one of annoyance.

I long for the ride to end. This two hour ride seems longer than any of my numerous rides from Columbia to Centralia. Dan mentions he is to catch the noon train to Macon, making connections on an eastbound for Hannibal. Realizing it will be impossible to avoid him, I admit that I too will be on the noon train.

The young woman at the window stiffens as she looks out each side of the coach. Excitedly craning her neck to catch a glimpse of... what, her suitor? I recognize landmarks that tell me we are almost at our destination. Dan stops his insipid chatter, leans toward the window and begins preparations for arrival.

Centralia has grown rapidly since the railroad from St. Louis to Macon erected a depot three years ago. The permanent population is in excess of three hundred people with travelers arriving by horse, the daily coach from Columbia, or the train. I'll be glad when the spur to Columbia is complete and this uncomfortable ride eliminated.

The train makes a run from St. Louis to Macon twice a week with stops at St. Charles, O'Fallon, Mexico, Centralia and Moberly before its' three PM arrival in Macon. It then retraces its' path to St. Louis the following day. Four train arrivals per week and a daily coach to and from Columbia guarantees excitement in this small bustling burg. Today however, the town is strangely quiet. Even the driver's call of 'Whoa' to the team is subdued.

As the coach comes to a halt, the young woman leaps from her position, pushes Dan aside, flings open the door and jumps from the coach. Nearly falling as she lands, she catches herself and limps toward a band of men standing in front of the coach station. She limps severely, almost dragging her right leg behind her, as she hurries to the tallest of six men. She throws her arms around his waist, buries her head in his chest and cries.

Only the tall muscular man acknowledges her, although his eyes never leave the stage hands and passengers. Did he say 'Kay' to her, or was it OK, as he put his arm around her shoulders?

All the men hold revolvers at their sides. No one says anything. Dressed in Union blue, their unbuttoned tunics not fitting properly, they do not cut a military figure.

Dan and I descend slowly from the coach as the drivers stare at the men. Normal activity in town is absent, it is strangely quiet, horse, wagon team and foot traffic is non existent. Townspeople are not in sight, what I see are several clumps of men in alleys, atop buildings and other vantage points, each brandishing weapons. This is what the drivers saw as they drove into town, two to five men per group scattered about the town. A quick estimate tells me there are as many as fifty men in control of the tiny burg of Centralia this day.

"Kay, are you alright?" The big man asks the young woman. She looks at him through tear stained eyes, points at Dan and said. "Jayhawker!"

All six of the men look at Kay in astonishment. "Jayhawker?" The big man asks. She nods.

At that the big man, and a younger man, step forward raising their right arms, and simultaneously place a bullet into the face of our obnoxious coach mate. Dan had not spoken since we entered Centralia and as the two bullets explode into his face and out the back of his head, the only sound I hear is the tremendous explosion of pistols a few feet from me. I shoot pistols, and have been around others fired at close range, but these explosions reverberate loudly upon my senses. The lead balls almost decapitate the man standing at my shoulder.

Fear grips me immediately and I am suddenly cold. This is September 27, 1864, the day I die. I lose control of my bladder, warm urine running down my leg. He is looking at me, this big man that suddenly seems even bigger. "Nice shootin' Jesse." His voice booms out,

"Thanks Bill!" The younger man replies. Did he say, Bill? Am I face to face with Bloody Bill Anderson? I dare not look, but surely they can see I wet myself. The expression of the younger mans' face is one of delight. He smiles at Bloody Bill Anderson.

Fear grips me realizing I am confronted with the notorious guerrilla that has been perpetrating murderous acts throughout Missouri. He has for months been the topic of discussion on the pro union state legislature floor. How to stop the raids of Todd, and especially Anderson, led to many a late night debate. Over sixty thousand soldiers are in pursuit of less than a thousand guerrillas, a constant state of embarrassment for the military.

Bill returns his gaze to me. My knees weaken as he peers into my eyes. Turning slightly, he reaches behind him, Kay limps forward and he drapes his arm over her shoulders. He cocks his pistol and points it at me. My heart is pounding, ears ringing, as I look at the young girl holding my life in her hands. "No." she says softly, looking into my eyes. "He's a farmer." The younger man, Jesse, lowers his pistol. She looks at Dan Raymond briefly before returning her gaze to me. She spared me and she wants me to know it.

Bill's gun hand drops to his side, his eyes soften as he turns toward Kay. "How ya been sis? It's so good to see you again... finally." giving her a squeeze. Together they walk into the coach office with Bill supporting his sister.

I am safe! Although five of the men remain in menacing positions, one motioning for the drivers to pick up the body, I sense I will not be harmed... for now. Dropping my chin to my chest I lean forward slightly, relieved to see the dark color of my pant leg does not clearly reveal my source of embarrassment.

Chapter Thirty Four

They came in quietly before dawn, before the townspeople awoke, slowly leading their horses careful not to arouse the people of Centralia. Dispersing through the town, they are intent on sparing as many lives as possible, not the lives of the people of Centralia, they care not a whit about them; the lives they wish to spare are their own. They expect to do battle and relish the thought of the excitement and adrenaline flow a dangerous encounter brings. Riding into an awakened town allowed for the possibility this battle hardened group of partisans could be overwhelmed by the near ten to one advantage the townspeople have over them, although they are highly confident of their ability to overcome long odds.

The debacle at Fayette is still fresh in the partisan's minds and makes them more cautious. Fayette was prepared and the partisans encountered their heaviest losses of the campaign as troops fired behind four block houses constructed from railroad ties stacked neatly atop each other. With ten troopers behind each block house to load and fire, the partisans faced a withering barrage. No, Fayette taught them prudence more than any other encounter. There will be more battles later and to risk the loss of manpower is not prudent.

Lamps are lit by awakening townspeople startled by the forced entry of two to three armed intruders. Those offering resistance are quickly beaten into submission or, with a quick thrust of a knife, quieted forever.

Things happen quickly now, screams and shouts arouse many in the sleeping populace. Confusion and shouts of; "What's going on? Who are you?" are typical reactions as they awake. Any man brandishing a weapon as he emerges from his home is shot immediately. Within minutes the population of Centralia Missouri is taken over by a band of thirty seven partisan rangers under Bill Anderson.

The emerging dawn of September 27, 1864 finds a somber and sobbing group of people herded in bedclothes across dusty streets into the three hotels of Centralia. Resistance is no longer uppermost in their minds, only existence. Several women, who moments earlier were peacefully sleeping next to husbands, now are widows. Some of the children rubbing sleep from their eyes; are fatherless.

"Where's the mayor?" yells one of the intruders from the center of the street. His question echoed by other intruders around the people. "Where's the mayor?"

A short portly man made smaller by his subdued status as he shuffles toward the hotel stops. Having been identified by glances from constituents, he timidly raises his hand. "You the mayor?" the intruder asks, running to the portly man in the middle of the street. The mayors' lip quivers as he grudgingly admits his identity.

"Mayor!" the tall bearded raider continues loudly for all to hear. "Control your people. Tell them not to resist, the more you resist the more people will be hurt. Keep your people quiet, keep them together in the hotels and you, and they, will not be harmed. Can you do that?" The mayor nods as he motions for people to huddle together.

"Very good mayor! Where's the sheriff?" the raider calls out again.

A strong muscular middle-aged man a few yards from the mayor raises his hand. A raider near the Sheriff stepped up and put a bullet in the back of his head. The sheriff slumps to the ground amidst screams of terror. Shots ring out and men that began to run also are felled.

"Whoa! Hold it! Stop!" the raiders yell as they hold the crowd in place, quieting the shuddering group.

"Mayor. Mayor." exclaims the first raider, a tall handsome long haired man of twenty five in a condescending tone. "I thought you said you can control these people?"

"But... but..." the mayor stammers pointing at the lifeless body of his close friend the sheriff.

"Him?" the partisan said pointing his pistol at the sheriff lying in an enlarging pool of blood. "Is it not his job to protect the people of this town? Your sheriff is..." he pauses, looking down at the body and with a snort, smiles and continues. "WAS, reputed to be very good at his job. Well, we couldn't take a chance that he might lead your people to resist now could we." he says sarcastically. "Come now Mr. Mayor." he said smiling and, putting his arm around the mayors' shoulder, allowing his pistol to dangle below the chin of the portly man. "Lead your people into the hotel like a good little mayor." he laughs uproariously. A smallish blond boy cackles with glee jumping up and down as he laughs, other raiders laughing as well as they nudge the group forward.

The screaming subsides as they huddle together in the hotel lobbies, the crying however continues. One young woman had been married but a few months before her husbands breathing was interrupted by a large knife thrust into his windpipe. Her thoughts are on him and the lost promise of a bright future. They came from St. Louis, where his father is a respected storekeeper, right after they were married. He learned the business and received financial aid from his father, enabling him to open a store in the growing community of Centralia. The business flourished despite competition from two similar stores in operation. His personable manner and her natural beauty made a visit to their store enjoyable to the male and female portion of Centralia's citizenry. Now he is dead and she can't control her sobbing. Grief, fear, apprehension and the uncertainty of her future keep her in a constant state of agitation. As she thought of her husband, of the menacing marauders about her, the unknown, uncertain and lonely future, she cries.

Finally a nearby marauder heard enough of her crying and says in exasperation. "Shut... up! I said... shut... up!" he yells again a few seconds later. She screams, continuing to sob huddled against the stairwell in the lobby of the hotel.

"Shut... up! Shut up! SHUT UP!" he screams jumping toward her, menacingly raising the butt of his rifle above her. That brings more hysterical screams as she pulls herself into a fetal position against the wall, her long hair and hands hiding, protecting her face.

The marauder pauses, the rifle poised to strike; looks to his left and motions for one of his comrades to approach. Relaxing his menacing position, he hands his rifle to the comrade. Grabbing a fistful of her long hair, he pulls her to a standing position and, with the back of his left hand, strikes her across the face.

Her beauty strikes him, just before she does. She is a tall woman, nearly as tall as he is. He had not seen a woman this tall. Women are small and frail, aren't they? Not this one, she is tall, and… not frail! He holds her auburn hair tightly in his hand, as she sobs and flails weakly at him. Her blows do not inflict harm as they are blows of frustration as she continues to sob and softly strike him.

Taking in her beauty, he surveys the woman in front of him. Not muscular, still she appears to have a physical strength not common to women. Her shoulders are quite broad for a female, making her store bought nightgown fit snugly over her shoulders and over her... oh my, yes! This is a BIG woman! The pullover night gown is a three button affair whose opening extends below the bust line. The top button is undone and the remaining two pull the fabric taut across her breasts.

With his fingers enmeshed in her hair he pulls her shoulders back stretching the gown even tighter across those breasts. What a magnificent form! His eyes reluctantly return to her face. Even with her face contorted and eyes red from crying, this is a woman of exceptional beauty.

She cries out again as he pushes her toward the stairs. She stumbles on the first step and he helps her maintain her balance by pulling back on her hair. This brings a yelp of pain from her as she obediently takes the second then third step still sobbing, eyes half closed. With her sixth step she reaches the landing and is guided to her right up the steps. She looks ahead at the hotel rooms above, suddenly aware of their destination. Terror grips her and she screams. "NO!" shaking her head held fast in his right hand. She turns against him pushing off the steps with all her might, hitting and kicking at him as hard as she can. They fall backward against the rail on the landing and the people in the lobby hear the loud exhale as his breath is forced from him.

They also hear the click of hammers cocked on pistols and rifles aimed at them. Men drop their heads in their hands. The women look terror struck at the young woman and her attacker, to their husbands, other men, seeking but not finding a rescuer. The women, realizing the futility of the situation, also drop their heads into their hands to cry silently.

This beautiful woman surprises him with the strength of her attack. When he pulled her from the floor, her blows against his chest were no more than nuisance blows. The realization of what lay ahead causes her to summon all her strength in desperation. He does not lose his grip on her hair although her attack, and his subsequent loss of breath, almost causes him to lose consciousness. As they roll to the floor of the landing, he manages to avoid the thrusts of her knees, deflecting them with the side of his legs. Some of her blows are stopped by his left arm but many strike his face. He feels a trickle of blood from his nose.

As his breath and strength return, she loses the advantage gained at her first charge. Jerking her head back with her hair, he rolls on top of her and sits on her upper thighs. This silences her legs but she continues to scream and flail against him with her fists. For a few moments he sits on her legs, right hand tightly enmeshed in her hair, left arm fending off her blows as he regains his strength.

Gathering his feet under him he stands up quickly, snatching her upright by the hair, and slams her face into the wall of the landing. Like a demon possessed she pushes hard with her hands against the wall, then with her feet. The marauder is caught off balance, his back to the steps. The force of her push catapults them down the six steps to the lobby floor. He does not lose his grip on her hair as they land hard and grapple on the floor. Rolling about the floor, she thrusts her knee toward his groin and with her fists, strikes him in the face. Her screams intermingle with angry guttural, growling sounds. He twists and turns as they roll about, dodging and deflecting her knee thrusts, preventing them from reaching their target. Struggling to his feet, he again yanks her to her feet. The blows from her fists are no longer of frustration but of fury and desperation, and they hurt. His lip begins to swell as she rains blow after blow on him. He forgets about the desire that welled up inside him at the first sight of her. His thought of enjoying her considerable charms with little resistance is not possible. Anger, determination and combativeness replace desire. This is no longer a beautiful desirable woman, but a worthy adversary struggling against him, one to be conquered.

Drawing back his left hand, he strikes her in the stomach with all his might. Her fury continues unabated and he punches there again, then in the face. With his right hand entangled in her hair at the back of her head, he drives her face into his onrushing left fist several times until she goes on the defensive to stop his blows.

He turns her away with his left hand as his right maintains its powerful grip on her thick hair. Grasping the collar of her gown at the back of her neck, he pulls hard. Buttons pop and fabric rips as the gown slams into her throat. Simultaneously lifting and pushing, he runs her into the steps and she falls hard on them. Her body takes the full extent of the blow against the steps, and again when his body slams into hers.

Quickly he pulls her up, forcing her up the six steps, smashing her into the wall. She raises her legs to push against the wall. Thrusting his left hand under her left knee he tries to pin her leg against her chin, but her leg is too strong for him. She thrust out and up, legs now pointing toward the ceiling. Her weight is too much and he drops her head first to the landing floor. Both of his hands now find a grip on her hair as he roughly pulls her to her feet and throws a knee into her face.

He drops her and pulls the top of her gown over her shoulders effectively pinning her arms to her sides. Grasping her gown behind her with his right hand he pulls and twists it to pinch her arms above the elbows, clamping them to her sides. With his left hand he grabs her hair and roughly turns her toward the stairs, breasts revealed to the delight of enthralled partisans. Sweat laces her body as the battle has drawn on for several minutes. He too is drenched with sweat, hands wet with his sweat and hers. Both are breathing heavily, gasping for air.

Again he pushes her hard against the steps and falls on top of her. Picking her up again by the hair, he lifts her up two steps. As her feet touch the steps she turns against him and pushes hard. He loses his grip in her sweaty hair and she is temporarily free from him. As they fall on the landing he is able to get between her and the steps, blocking her escape. The combatants stand facing each other, breathing heavily and sweating profusely. She is no longer screaming, terror replaced by rage. She growls and her torn gown slips to the floor. This is no time for modesty, she is ready to fight.

David Pool is in no mood to admire her naked form; she has made him mad and is an adversary to conquer. A quick feint to his left produces the reaction he hoped for. At his first move, she moves in the opposite direction hoping to sidestep him and run to freedom. Anticipating her move, he changes direction and thrusts his right shoulder into her midsection. He grabs her legs behind her thighs and lifts, driving her up and back into the steps. Landing on her back, the weight of his shoulder drives the air from her lungs. Stunned, she lies wide eyed gasping for breath, mouthing words she is unable to speak. Slowly he stands up and watches her struggle to breathe. She can't fend off his right hand that once again entwines in her hair. Defenseless, she is dragged to her feet and draped over his shoulder. Placing his left arm over the back of her knees, he grasps her left hand in his right. He has finally subdued his prize.

With renewed terror in her eyes, she lifts her head, looking at the townspeople silently watching her battle. Unable to gather the breath to say the words she mouths. "Help me!" to the crowd. "Please!"

A woman cries softly. "Nooo! Nooo!" her husband sobs with her.

As the conquering partisan slowly ascends the stairs, she began to wriggle feebly, fighting to regain her breath. At the top of the stairs she whispers hoarsely what she mouthed seconds ago. "Please!"

He kicks in the first door at the top of the stairs. The townspeople hear the squeaking protest of bed springs as she is flung unceremoniously onto the bed. Her muffled screams of protest increase in volume as her breathing returns to normal. Also heard is the interruption of her screams by the sickening sound of fists slamming into her face. She no longer screams but her whimpers filter down the steps. Suddenly she screams. "No! No! NO! GET AWAY FROM ME! HELP!" her screams stop as his fists strike her repeatedly. When the sound of his blows upon her stop, the huddled mass below hear the muffled sound of her voice change as she addresses her attacker directly. Softly she pleads. "Don't. Please don't. Nooo. Please don't" her pleas continue with changing inflection as he thrusts his body onto and into her. "Sto... op! Unnnh! Get... off! Get..." she pleads to no avail. Her pleas stop. Only the sound of the squeaking bed drifts down to the people.

The vision of what is happening tears into the hearts of the townspeople. The innkeeper has the initial thought that the walls are too thin and do not adequately mute the sounds from within, then realizes. "The bastard didn't have the decency to close the door!"

After a few minutes the marauder appears at the door buckling his belt. Swaggering and smiling, he looks at his comrades and says, "Next?" then laughs. "Socrates." he calls to a giant of a man. "Get up here and give her what for."

The one armed man reaches too late for the giants' sleeve and calls after him. "Get back here! Remember Bills' orders!"

His eyes flashing wildly, the giant looks at the room at the top of the stairs and clumsily charges up the steps two or three at a time. Reaching the man at the top, Socrates hands him his rifle and handgun. Smiling largely, the big man rushes into the room. For a few seconds all that is heard are the muffled pleas of the woman inside. Slowly Socrates comes into view, backing out of the room. He stands in the doorway momentarily before turning to David Pool saying. "Lookee what you done! She's... she's... she's... hurt!"

David peers into the room, at Socrates, shrugs his shoulders and begins a slow descent down the steps. Socrates backs out of the room and turns to follow David Pool.

A tall man strides into the hotel lobby, three men closely following behind. All four are clean shaven and hair cropped short, in sharp contrast to the unkempt dirty look of other partisans in the lobby.

Chapter Thirty Five

It feels good to be clean again. Trying to remember the exact time and place of my last bath, haircut and shave is difficult indeed. I can't recall having a haircut or shave since we left Texas and that was... God, almost five months ago! Washing in the streams does not produce the clean feel and smell a bath does. I could languish in the bath all day but, as usual, there is little time for things like that.

Archie splashes and laughs in the large tub as I get my shave and haircut under the protective eye of Creth Creek and Ike Berry awaiting their turn in the tub.

When the four of us finish cleaning up, we seek other partisans to give them the opportunity to bathe as well. We head for the Sneed Hotel as Bo and Socrates were headed that way earlier.

"We found the barber." I began. "Now you men can..." the silence and look in the eyes of the partisans guarding the townspeople tells me something is amiss. Approximately forty of the townsfolk are huddled tightly in the center of the lobby, strangely silent, some softly crying. The partisan rangers have guilty looks on their faces.

Two men guard the back door, guns at the ready. They look away as I seek their eyes. Bo is alone at the front door and also looks down. David Pool, with Socrates two steps behind him, is stopped halfway down the steps, a small trickle of blood coming from his nose. Socrates looks frightened.

Slowly moving toward the stairway, my eyes remain fixed on David. Socrates falls to the steps behind him, sliding tightly against the wall, trying to hide his face with his hands. "I di'nt do nothin!" he cries repeatedly.

Reaching the landing, I look at the scene on the floor of the hotel as my men nervously look away. Returning my gaze to the two men on the stairway, I slowly make my way up the stairs. David stands in the center of the steps, a rifle in his left hand and a pistol in his right. I slide by David Pool on the inside of the steps. I hear the whimpering Socrates slumped against the wall mumbling. "I di'nt do nothin'!" What is it he 'didn't' do?

Pool runs down the steps and out the door.

The door to the room at the top of the steps is open and I peer down the hall to my right. My eyes are almost adjusted from the bright morning sunshine to the dark of the hotel. A window at the end of the hall provides dim light through the curtains. There is no movement and the doors to the five rooms at the end of the hall are closed. Only a couple of lamps are lit below, one on each side of the large lobby.

A slight movement from the open room catches my eye and I ease my way toward the door. The naked form of a young woman lies quietly on the bed. I see the slight rise and fall of her chest as she lay unmoving, her battered face turned to the ceiling. She is alive.

Now I understand the silence in the hotel, even the ten to fifteen or so young children below, strangely silent. To visualize what happened here is not difficult. Moving to the rail overlooking the lobby, I gaze into the eyes of the people, their faces turned toward me. My eyes fall on a middle aged woman and point to her. "You!" and crook my finger motioning for her to come up the stairs.

"Me!" she gasps in astonishment and began to shake her head and shrink in terror. "NO!"

"Bring her to me." I command the man to her left.

She looks at the man whose arms tightly held her for the past several minutes. With quivering lips she looks into his eyes to see terror rivaling her own. He lowers his eyes.

The couple slowly ascends the steps, the wife looking only at her husband, her gaze questioning, pleading with him to save her from the fate that surely lay ahead. Why did the tall man choose her? She is not pretty, rather plain actually, overweight and getting old, why her? Why won't her husband look at her? Is he planning some brazen assault on this man they are approaching? He has never been a particularly brave man, but is a hero, if only in her eyes. He seems much smaller as they reach the top of the steps, and stop in front of this fearsome man that commanded them at gunpoint to come. She quivers and trembles mightily, peering at her husband who looks at the floor and gently nudges her toward the tall man.

"Would you take care of her?" I say softly, taking her hand from her husband. I point toward the room as the matronly lady looks at me in shocked surprise. She gasps as she looks at the bloodied and broken form lying motionless on the bed. Crying out in relief for her own safety and in dismay for the damage done to her friend, she hurries to the water pitcher on the dresser.

The woman on the bed groans as she tries to get up.

"Oh! Oh!" the older woman cries, gently returning the young woman to the bed. "Easy Lynn. Take it easy girl. That's it, lie back sweetheart, you'll be OK. Just relax honey." The older woman soothingly reassures the young woman.

The soothing tones of the feminine voice quiet Lynn who was preparing to do battle with her next assailant. She lies back as the tension drains from her and tries to open her eyes to see her comforter. Both of Lynns' eyes are blackened and closed by repeated blows from the fists of her rapist. Her nose is broken and splattered against her cheek. Numerous gashes are bleeding above her eyes, cheeks, forehead and chin. Several teeth are dislodged and her lips, a swollen bloody pulp.

Unable to open her eyes or speak, Lynn sighs and passes out from the pain.

As soon as the older woman is sure Lynn is still breathing, she rises from the bed walks to the door and yells sternly. "Rose! Ann! Get up here! NOW!"

Two middle aged women rise to their feet, hesitate a moment looking at me. I glance at the scene in the bedroom and nod for them to come. They hurry up the steps barely glancing at me as they enter the small room. They also pay no heed to the man slumped at the doorway crying.

He feels shame, in fear he was delivering his wife to another man for… whatever suited that man. How can he look at her again? Does she know? Maybe she doesn't know the fear in his heart. He looks in the room where the three women scurry about their task of cleaning up and fixing up as best they can, the young Lynn Thompson.

"Margaret?" he says dolefully rising to his feet. "Margaret?" Margaret pauses briefly from her work to glare at him. She knows.

Socrates sits two steps below the top, feet on the step below. With knees pressed to his chin, arms folded across his knees, he no longer is crying, he is hiding. I stop on the step below him, touch his shoulder and say softly. "Socrates?"

"I'm sorry! I'm sorry!" he blubbers grabbing my hand. He is so used to the teasing of far wiser men that, although innocent, he feels he will be held responsible.

"I know. It's okay, it's okay Socrates, nobody's mad at you." I say trying to reassure him. "Why don't you go to the barber shop and get cleaned up."

"Okay Billy? Okay Billy?" he asks looking at me excitedly. He smiles as I nod. "Okay Billy! Okay!" and noisily bounds down the stairs forgetting to ask where the barber shop is. Socrates burst through the door and is in the middle of the street before realizing he does not know where to go.

"Bo." I call out to the man turning to guide Socrates toward his destination. Bo watches Socrates stop, then turns toward me.

From the top of the stairs I note the three women busily working on restoring their neighbor. Descending the steps I motion to the three men that accompanied me from the barber shop. "Take the men to the rooms upstairs and lock them in." Without looking away from the room above I add, "And don't bother the women in that room. Give them whatever they need. Take the other ladies to their homes; they will prepare breakfast for us." I look around the room making eye contact with each of the women to assure them they will not be troubled. "Archie. Make sure no one else here gets hurt. Chivalry is not dead."

"Yes Bill."

Turning to the unkempt men guarding the townspeople I say. "Paul. Frank. Get cleaned up."

"Yeah Bill?" Bo says as I approach him.

Without warning, I strike him. Bo falls backward from the unexpected blow. "That's for not stopping him." I said, angrily pointing at him as I leave the hotel.

In the street Socrates looks back and forth wondering where to go. I am sorry for having struck Bo. His loyalty is not in question; he is not responsible for what David Pool did. Perhaps it is because I value Bo's judgment that he disappointed me so. Taking Socrates' sleeve I lead him to the barber shop, Bo falls in a few steps behind us. As I stop at the door to the barber shop I look at Bo, no anger in our eyes only understanding. No words are necessary, or spoken.

Kay looks great to me. She was in the Jefferson City Hospital for over a year and although her hip and right leg will be forever damaged, she can walk. She recounted the agony endured during the trek from Kansas City to the hospital in Jefferson City and near death those first few weeks at the hospital. Mary Hodges stayed with her several weeks before Frank returned, taking his wife and daughters to Kentucky. Frank sorrowfully told Kay of her sister's fate the day the Hodges left.

Kay lay in her hospital bed, ribs, arms, legs broken and one side of her hip crushed. The healing process was a long and arduous one. Alone and heartbroken she thought of her father living as a cripple, as she now must. Did he also feel useless, a burden to everyone? Did he wish he had died of his wounds? Did he cry himself to sleep?

As a ward of the hospital, her true identity remained unknown even to the hospital. During the many months of rehabilitation, Kay read accounts of her brothers' guerrilla activities which did not portray the tender, loving brother she knew and loved. These are sensationalized lies they print.

Bill was unaware of her fate until receiving a message from her five weeks ago. A meeting in Centralia is arranged where they can spend a few hours together. After the reunion Kay will board the train to St. Louis, on her way to join the Hodges in Central City, Kentucky.

The time seems to fly; we have so much to talk about.

Chapter Thirty Six

Creth Creek leans in the station house door. "West bound comin' Bill."

"Westbound?"

"Yessir, West bound." he repeated.

"I thought the train was to be eastbound today!" I say exasperated. "Kay?"

"I know Billy, it's OK. I'll be alright for a couple of days until the eastbound comes." she said smiling as she pats my hand.

I look at her before nodding my assent. Gently squeezing her hand, I leave her in the station.

"Creth!" I yell at the man outside the coach station. "Take..." I look around to see who is available. "Frank and Jesse... to the train station. When the train stops board the engine and keep it from leaving. Archie! Take half the men and get ready to board the train! Stay out of sight until the train stops. Be ready for troops being transported!" The adrenaline flows again but the buzzing and popping also return. Whenever I become excited the headaches and strange sounds intensify. The magnitude also increases but so does my tolerance of the noise. It now signals something exciting will happen, and God I love the excitement!

The train is in sight but still a distance away when Creth, Frank, Jesse and I enter the depot. Ike Berry is keeping an eye on the station master. Ike knows Morse code therefore he keeps the station master from sounding an alarm.

"Anything coming over the wire?" I ask.

Ike shakes his head. "Been quiet."

As I look out the window at the approaching train, men scurry about finding barrels, boxes, wagons and other items to hide behind. Main Street of town is fifty yards south of the tracks and men take places inside facing buildings from where they will rush the stopped train.

"How many troops are on board?" I ask the station master. He shakes his head. "I asked, how many?" I shout impatiently at him.

Shrinking in fear his voice trembles as he replies, "There's been no indication of troops aboard sir!"

The train is a hundred yards away when I direct the station master to take the step out to meet the train. He silently obeys.

The train clangs and chugs up to the station landing, steam escaping in a loud hiss as it creaks to a halt. Creth and Frank run from the station and jump into the engine compartment, putting a pistol under the chin of the Engineer and Boilerman. Jesse waits at the step of the engine compartment and looks up and down the landing. Gunfire erupts as Archie and his men rush the train, burst into the three passenger cars, and squelch any thought of rebellion from the passengers.

"LOOKEE HERE WHAT WE GOT!" Archie yells from the second coach. "TROOPERS!"

I step from the station house onto the landing in front of the second car. "Hold them there a minute Archie, send everyone else out." One by one the passengers tentatively step from the train and are directed to place their valuables in a pile on the landing. Once satisfied the passengers are relieved of weapons and valuables, I order the soldiers out.

A handful of partisans are left to guard the townspeople, the remainder on the landing have guns at the ready.

Union troopers slowly disembark and are ordered to remain near the train. Twenty five troopers clump together when Archie sounds the all clear from the train.

"Take off your clothes." I direct the troopers. They look at each other and glance at the women in the assembly that were aboard the train. The ladies obligingly turn their backs allowing the soldiers to retain their modesty. "Boots too!" I order. The pile grows as the Union men disrobe silently, now standing in various stages of undress. Several do not have underdrawers and are left stark naked, self consciously trying to cover themselves.

The engineer stumbles from the engine compartment, blood streaming down the side of his head. "HE AINT GOIN NOWHERE!" Creth calls out explaining. "He was grabbin' fo' the throttle!"

Archie cocked his pistol and ran toward the engineer.

"Wait Archie!" I yell. Archie looks at me, pistol poised above the engineers' head. I look at the engineer wondering if we may need him. I motion Archie to my side.

The nights and mornings of late September have been quite cool but the noon day sun has warmed the air so the undressed troopers are not uncomfortable, temperature wise that is. They are trying to maintain their dignity in the presence of the ladies, the naked men crouching on the landing bent over to hide private parts from view.

"Bill" Bo said quietly. "The ladies ask permission to go into the train station so as not to have to look upon the troopers in their state of undress."

I glance at the five women standing near the station house and the fifteen or so male passengers with them. It appears they all are uncomfortable looking at the squirming soldiers. "Take them all into the Station; it will be easier to watch them in there, assign two men. Check for a rear door." As the passengers are herded into the station house, my attention reverts to the troopers. Derisive laughter rains down on them as they stand, crouch, and in any way possible try to hide their nakedness. They are a comical group and the humor is not lost on the raiders. I make them stand.

One by one I pass in front of them peering into their eyes as much as they will allow; most of the soldiers turn away, trying not to look at me. "Is there an officer in this group?" I ask. No one replies. "No officer... or... no comment?" Still no reply. I go to the pile of clothing and move them around with the toe of my boot, no gold or silver bars on any of the collars. Turning back to the Union troopers I ask. "Any non commissioned officers?"

Heads turn as the men glance around nervously. Even if I hadn't seen the stripes of a sergeant, that look gave it away. There is a non commissioned officer among them, I wonder if anyone will confess to being the leader of these troopers. After several moments pause, a tall muscular man steps forward.

Archie quickly moves toward him raising his pistol at the troopers head.

"Archie! Stop!" This is curious! This man stands before me trembling in faded red underwear scared out of his wits, yet he stepped forward. Walking slowly toward the sergeant I study him carefully. He is my age, or perhaps in his late twenties, clean shaven, probably having shaved prior to boarding in St. Louis, St. Charles or wherever. He is tall as I only have to look down slightly at him, to see his wide set eyes, twitching nervously. He gives the impression of strength, of a presence, thus it is easy to understand why he is the leader, a leadership being severely tested. His body trembles and his lips quiver as he draws his breath sharply through his mouth. He is scared to death! This is fun!

"Why did you step forward Sergeant?" I ask; eager to satisfy my curiosity.

He shakes, eyes darting back and forth rapidly, mouth hanging open. Finally he speaks, voice cracking with emotion. "You… are going to… kill the squad leader… and… and it wouldn't be fair for someone to… to die for me. I can't let you kill my men in order to… kill their leader." He said his voice but a whisper. "It's me."

I look into his eyes hardly able to believe what I heard. The eyes reveal a man gripped with fear, yet he stepped forward. I wonder if I would step forward, or if any of my men would; believing they will die if they do. Impressive!

"Let me make sure I heard you right." I say loudly, turning toward the assembled partisans. "You stepped forward... because you... believe... we will kill you? You stepped forward… because... you… do not want your men to die... in your place? Is that what you are telling me?" Trembling violently, his knees buckle slightly as the sergeant fights to remain standing. He nods unevenly.

Dramatizing the event as much as possible, I make an approving face toward my men, walking slowly along the board landing. Shuffling about in a circle, my head hung as if in deep thought, I push the brim of my hat up with my pistol, dramatically scratching my forehead with the barrel. Smiling at the partisan rangers I turn to face the sergeant, as I stand in front of him. The smile on my face does not reassure him as I place my wrists on his shoulders, my gun loosely dangling in my right hand, my nose nearly touching his.

"I am truly impressed by your bravery sergeant. What is your name?"

His reply is a barely audible whisper. "Thomas Goodman sir.

"What is it?"

Clearing his throat he repeats a little louder. "Thomas Goodman."

"You forgot the 'sir'!"

"Sir!" He quickly adds.

I walk down the landing close to the other Union troopers. They look toward their leader, gratitude and admiration clearly etched on their faces. "And who else do we have here Sergeant? Never mind." I quickly wave my hand. "I don't want to know their names. Where are you headed?" When he doesn't answer, I spin toward him.

"On furlough sir!" He responds feebly. "We are going to various stops along the way. Thirty days at home... with our families, sir."

"Going home are you?"

"Yes sir."

"While the fighting continues?" I ask sarcastically.

He hangs his head. The members of his troop cast furtive glances at me but none will look me in the eye.

"Been chasin' guerrillas Sergeant?" I ask continuing to walk the line of Union troopers. He does not answer. Reaching the end of the line of soldiers, I turn to look at the sergeant. He still has not replied. Slowly I return, stopping a few feet in front of him. "Sergeant?"

He looks down not wanting to face me.

I push his head up with my pistol under his chin and say in a condescending tone. "Sergeant? Have you been chasin' guerillas?"

"Yes sir." He said softly.

"Yes sir! You HAVE been chasing guerrillas?"

He nods, turning his eyes away from me again.

"OOOOHHHH! Shame on you Sergeant!" I moan sarcastically and began a melodramatic walk along the station landing. "Did you... catch any?" He doesn't answer. I stop and turn toward him. He is looking at me now, after a moments hesitation he nods dejectedly hanging his head.

"And what did you do with them? Did you... kill them?" Reluctantly he nods. "Sergeant. Sergeant." I say in a condescending tone returning to face him. "Was that nice?"

My tone more serious, I place my wrists on his shoulders again. "How many?" He shrugs. "Alot of them?" He shakes his head. He is not trembling as violently and I know my 'game' with him is nearly finished. "But more than one?" He nods, looking into my eyes. "Have you been chasin' Bloody Bill Anderson?" He looks away and nods. I tap his head lightly with my weapon. "Here I am, lookee here."

Straightening out my wrist, I raise the Colt forty four, his eyes dart toward my pistol, I cock the weapon. He flinches as it clicks and begins to tremble and moan again. With my left hand I grasp a handful of hair and pull his head back slightly. Deliberately I place the gun under his chin. He is scared again; it thrills me to have power over him. The adrenaline surges.

"Are you ready to die Sergeant?" I ask him softly. He whimpers as he closes his eyes, shaking violently. "You won't." As I level the pistol at an adjacent soldier, and squeeze the trigger.

Screams from the station and groans from the soldiers accompany the slumping soldier whose blood flows from the spot on his forehead where the ball entered. 'My' sergeants' knees give way and he collapses to the landing.

"Whoa! Ha! Ha! Stand up there! Stand up Sergeant!" I laugh as I help him to his feet. Holding him steady, I smile and whisper to him. "Fuck 'em if they can't take a joke." Still laughing, I grab the sergeant by the arm and walk him from the landing. "Archie! Muster them out!" I command and within seconds the deafening roar of pistol and rifle fire fills the air.

I watch as Archie and several others delightedly kill the soldiers. David Pool jumps on the back of one soldier as if astride a horse. Placing his pistol behind the soldiers' ear, Pool pulls the trigger causing his "mount" to slump face forward into the wooden planks of the station landing, never to move again.

"EEEEEYYYAYAAAAHHH!" Pools' scream is matched by Archie's delighted giggle as Archie pulls his knife across the throat of another soldier. The shooting and screaming last but a few seconds and the Union soldiers lay on and under the platform, the bodies of those that tried to run a few yards away.

As the firing stops, I turn the Union sergeant toward the dead soldiers on the landing. "Sergeant Thomas Goodman, that... is for Palmyra."

He is shaking and sobbing uncontrollably, tears streaming down his cheeks. Helping him on a horse I tie his feet together under the horse. "I like you Sergeant. It took guts to come forward believing you were going to die. Well, I want you to live." Raising my hand to slap the horse on the rear, I pause and say. "By the way Sergeant, I'd head west from here if I were you. Do not go south." and slap the horse on the rump, sending them on their way.

I mount The Wind and command. "Gather all the uniforms and valuables. Burn the train and the station!"

Amidst howls and laughter, coal oil is dumped into the cars and lit. The throttle of the engine tied down, it chugs out of town. The tied down whistle soon depletes the steam from the boiler causing the train to slow to a halt a couple hundred yards out of town.

The partisans gather uniforms, and whatever booty they can carry, before heading south to join the two hundred plus guerrillas under

George Todd and John Thrailkill, waiting at Rudy Singletons.

The shooting stopped; I seek a way out of the attic. "Thank God! They're finally gone!" Trembling, my heart pounding and, although fit for a sixty two year old portly congressman, I'm not a young man anymore. This type of excitement is too much, never before have I feared for my life as I did this morning.

Bloody Bill Anderson! What an appropriate name! His eyes are his most compelling feature, cold and penetrating, seemingly able to lift the inner most thoughts from your soul. Those eyes are also unfeeling and indicate a willingness to kill at the slightest provocation, therefore I was only being careful not to provoke him or his band, and endanger more citizens. "Who are you trying to kid James S. Rollins? You were terrified and only trying to save your own ass! Fine leader of men you are!" I berate myself aloud. "SHIT!"

The attic of the Sneed Hotel is my safe haven for nearly two hours while Anderson and his men wreaked havoc upon the citizens of Centralia. It is hot and muggy, but once positioned by the rectangular window facing the depot, I do my best not to move. The slightest sound may reveal my position and... yes... I am scared. Some public servant!

I had a clear view over the train to the depot as the attic of the hotel is nearly twenty feet in the air.

Only a small portion of the landing is obscured by train cars. My horror intensifies as I watch the raiders mercilessly murder the unarmed and undressed soldiers. Worse yet is the manner in which the soldiers are killed. This is not war; it is a game for the guerillas! Laughter accompanies the shooting, cutting, slashing and pure butchery... they are actually having fun! They enjoy the killing! It is killing for thrill, and they laugh and whoop it up as innocent young men are mounted as horses, their throats cut, or shot in the back of the head; or in the back as they try to escape. One of the guerillas laughs uproariously as he steps from one dead soldier to another without touching the wooden train platform. They are animals led by, Bloody... Bloody... Bloody Bill Anderson!

To be certain they are gone, I wait several minutes before making my way out of the attic. I did not reveal my identity upon arriving in town, having sought a safe haven at the first opportunity. It probably will not be in my interest to do so now. For the first time in my life I seek a back row, a role of obscurity.

Cautiously, townspeople come out of hiding places. The guerrillas rode south out of Centralia thus a watchful eye in that direction is kept by all. The people stand in a state of shock, alternately looking south in the direction the guerrillas took and to the depot platform where the bodies lie. Several passengers from the train come out of the station house and search for signs of life among the bodies strewn about the landing. There is none.

Black smoke lifts skyward from the burning train stopped a few hundred yards out of town.

"Aren't you James Rollins, the Congressman?" A man asks after I appear in front of the Sneed Hotel. I cannot hide any longer; they soon will know how I cowered in fear, not offering leadership.

He continues softly. "Yeah! It is you. It's a good thing they didn't see you sir! They'd a killed you for sure, you being an important congressman and all. Yes sir, they'd a killed ya' for sure." The shock produced by the day evident on the faces of others now approaching, he gently squeezes my hand.

"Congressman Rollins." He announces quietly to his neighbors as if introducing a friend. They too express relief at my not being killed. They do not ask, nor do I offer an explanation of how I managed to avoid detection.

The citizens of Centralia stand glassy eyed, arms hanging limply at their sides, mouths slightly open, horrified at the sight on the landing and of the morning's proceedings. Did this really happen?

Chapter Thirty Seven

"Major Johnson! Major Johnson!" I yell. "Smoke rising from the southwest!" It is visible to the column of one hundred fifty eight men of the thirty ninth infantry mounted in Paris, Missouri to give chase to Bloody Bill Anderson, George Todd, John Thrailkill and the rest of the guerrillas. We are mostly farmers that take exception to the treatment Quantrill and his band of guerrillas have been meeting out among farm folk. The Union army was glad to assign us the task of chasing them. The latest information has Bloody Bill, George Todd and John Thrailkill in the vicinity. Many of our troop saddled plow horses, which are considerably larger and slower than the normal riding horse. My mount was also unhitched from a plow and I am fortunate to be a sergeant and ride near the Major.

We proceed cautiously; sending out three pair of riders on major compass points in hopes of coming upon the guerrillas' camp. There it is hoped, we will surprise the marauders and overrun them before they get organized. Major Johnson is frustrated having to lead a bunch of poorly trained but dedicated farmers into a skirmish.

Each pair of scouts departs the main column for one hour before returning. The main body proceeds south southeast in the general direction of Mexico, Missouri. We are in cautious pursuit of Bloody Bill Anderson reported outside Paris on the 26th, heading in the direction of Mexico.

Major A.V.E. Johnson is an infantry commander that does not sit a horse well, although that may be said of many of the men. Walking beside his horse, the Major squints in the direction I indicate. The sun is directly over the column of smoke, checking my pocket watch I note it is twenty minutes past two O'clock in the afternoon.

"What's over there Sargent Wilson?" the Major asks.

Turning in my saddle, I pan the countryside before replying. "I believe that's Centralia sir. The smoke appears to be coming from Centralia."

"Captain Theis! Mount the men!" the Major commands.

"Major! The remaining scouting parties sir. Shall we not wait for them?" the Captain asks.

Major Johnson sighs, looks at the smoke for a moment before rescinding the order to mount.

Nearly a half hour passes before the last pair of scouts are sighted returning to the main body. "Now Captain?" the Major asks sarcastically as he swings up on his horse.

For almost an hour we ride at a rapid pace toward the smoke. The populace of Centralia is loading bodies onto wagons as we ride in. Quietly the Major is filled in on the mornings' debauchery; his face red with anger as the gory details of the horrifying story unfolds.

"Captain Theis!" he bellows. "Divide the troop in half; assist these folks in the clean up and burial detail. I'll take the other half, overtake those murderers and make them pay for their actions today!"

"Sir." Captain Theis begins cautiously. "There's been a report of over two hundred guerrillas in the area sir. Should we not wait for reinforcements or at least take the entire column?"

The Major looks at his subordinate in exasperation. "Captain, do not EVER question my decisions? Thirty to forty guerrillas were involved here; you heard that as well as I did. I am confident the eighty men I have can handle those few that perpetrated this heinous carnage! And!" he continues sarcastically. "Should this small band of guerrillas happen to overcome our superior force, surely you will display your incredible leadership skills and vanquish them." angrily he turns his horse. "Follow your orders Captain!"

I assume my position close to the Major as we take our weary horses and gallop out of Centralia. Not a mile out of town we sight ten riders lazily walking their horses. The Major gleefully orders the charge and we whip our horses into a hard gallop. The ten riders turn south with our troop of eighty men in hot pursuit. The band of thirty to forty raiders must have split up and we are about to rid Missouri of ten of those murdering guerrillas.

We are gaining on them but have not been able to close within one hundred yards. Riding through sparse tree cover it is easy to keep them in sight, although the hard ride over rolling hills is taking its' toll on our horses already nearly spent and breathing heavily. It is a question of which group of horses will give out first, the guerrillas or ours, and ours ran hard for an hour before reaching Centralia. We have to catch them soon as our horses cannot keep this pace for long. My horse is already trying to slow down when the guerrillas disappear over a rise, he won't last much longer.

Cresting the rise, I know we'll stop now. My blood goes cold at the sight in front of us. The ten riders are absorbed into a dismounted force of more than two hundred armed men. We've been drawn into a trap.

Our horses stumble from fatigue as we rein in one hundred yards from the guerrillas. Assessing the situation the Major knows our horses will not carry us out in a hasty retreat. As an infantryman the Major is more accustomed to attacking from the ground rather than horseback.

"Dismount!" the Major orders. Calmly he peers down the hill at the line of guerrillas. Withdrawing his Enfield rifle from its' scabbard, he orders. "Every fifth man, gather the horses, bring them to the rear, out of the firing line." The Major is making a stand, barking commands. "Sergeant

Carter! Sergeant Wilson! Sergeant Lee! Form the men in two firing lines, here and here!" The men take positions along the down side of the hill. The horses are herded into a circle breathing heavily, fifty yards behind our troop, too tired to run, some stumble nearly falling from exhaustion.

It is strangely quiet as both sides evaluate the other. We are outnumbered by nearly three to one but the Major seems confident as he strides behind the firing lines encouraging the men.

Suddenly, screams and whoops of the guerrillas, the thundering sound of horses hooves pounding against the ground, a line of guerrillas are bounding toward us. "OH SHIT! HERE THEY COME!" I exclaim to no one in particular. The first volley from our lines explodes in the late afternoon. Furiously trying to reload the single shot Enflelds, our men are ridden into and over by the charging guerrillas firing repeating pistols point blank at my comrades. Our horses suddenly find the energy to run, dispersing as the marauders ride into us. I should have remained mounted.

The burning sensation of a mini ball entering my side doubles me over just before being ridden into by a raider. As I fall, a flying hoof strikes a glancing blow on my head causing my vision to darken and sound to diminish. Through darkening eyesight, I see guerrillas riding among and after fleeing soldiers, unmercifully shooting them. Major Johnson stands bravely firing his pistol until he is felled by several shots. My vision fades, is this death? Darkness covers me, for a moment I hear the continuous popping of revolvers before I am engulfed by silence.

The pain in my side burns furiously as I open my eyes. Struggling to sit upright, my head feels as if it is about to burst. God, what a headache! Two men move among the bodies twenty yards down the hill.

"Hey!" I call out weakly. One of the men looks my way and motions for his mate to follow. The other man limped, but the first ran to my side.

"You OK? OOOOOHHH, you've got a nasty bump on your head... ah let's see if we can stop that bleeding," he opened my shirt revealing the bloodied side where the mini ball struck. "I think the ball went far enough to the side that this is not a mortal wound. You're lucky!" he said feebly smiling at me.

"How many...?" I began, looking about.

"Are dead?" he says completing my question. He looked down the hill at the many bodies strewn about before looking back at me. "Just the three of us survived."

"So far!" the third man said defiantly, limping to our side. "We haven't finished looking yet!"

Hank, looks at the ground with a defeated look. "It's been nearly an hour."

"I DON'T CARE!" Wayne shouts. "I will keep looking!" He hobbles up the hill dragging a bandaged left leg behind him as Hank sadly watches.

Hank sighs and looks at me. "It'll be dark soon; you think you can walk back to town?"

"I'll try." I reach toward Hank to pull myself upright. The pain is great but I can make it with some assistance.

"Lean on me." Hank says. The pain in my head nearly causes me to faint; reaching to the side of my head I feel the dried blood from the wound and a very large bump. I am determined to stand and struggle on to Centralia and drape an arm over Hank's shoulder.

Hank suddenly stops. "What's wrong Wayne?"

Wayne is on the crest of the hill, facing north, not speaking nor moving. With a few steps, Hank and I reach the top of the rise and see what has Wayne transfixed. A mile to the north the horde of guerrillas is galloping toward us. We are wounded; three men out of a troop of eighty, surely even these vicious marauders will spare us, perhaps even tend to our wounds.

We are unable to move as a few guerrillas break ranks, galloping at us. The chilling sound of rebel yells, make my blood run cold. Rooted to the spot on top of the rise, the other two are in the same emotional state I am, intense fear? Oh yes! Trepidation, most surely! Relief, absolutely not!

The lead rider levels his pistol at me. I see the smoke before feeling the impact of the shot in my chest and my breath being expelled. I see the ground rush up to me as I fall. I bounce once on the ground before slipping painlessly into the onrushing light.

Chapter Thirty Eight

I've got to give John Thrailkill credit, his strategy is working perfectly. He said a small band of raiders sent toward Centralia will lure the Union troops into an ambush at Singletons' farm. Sure enough, the ten riders are hotly pursued by eighty Union soldiers riding into our trap.

Archie said to me as the Union soldiers stop after cresting of the hill. "We's gotta mount up!

"Wait Archie!" I stare at the soldiers dismounting on the rise. They merely stand beside their horses. The horses are then withdrawn as the soldiers form two lines. Commands are bellowed, but at over one hundred yards, we cannot distinguish the words.

"My God!" John Koger says in a voice that carries up and down our lines. "THE FOOLS ARE GOING TO FIGHT US ON FOOT!" he adds quieter. "God help 'em."

George Todd yells. "Let's ride!" Emitting whoops and rebel yells, we mount and surge toward the soldiers. Only a few seconds are required to cover the distance between combatants. Smoke belches from their weapons as they fire. Frank Shepherds head explodes as the mini ball smashes into his face spilling blood and brains onto Frank James alongside me.

They can't kill me, I smile. I let the reins drop to the saddle horn, guiding The Wind with my knees and heels. Each hand holds a Colt forty four, firing nearly straight down as The Wind leaps over columns of scattering, screaming soldiers. I do not know if my simultaneous shots have found their mark as I turn The Wind in pursuit of deserting soldiers. Archie is laughing gleefully, shooting one after another of the fleeing soldiers. Partisan's ride down the hill pursuing soldiers trying desperately to escape, they do not. In a few minutes, there is no movement among the bodies strewn over the hillside. I am amazed at how little resistance they offered. That was easy.

John Thrailkill asks, "How many'd we lose?" then seeing Archie scalping one of the dead, turns to me. "Bill!"

He's too soft, smart but soft. "Archie." I shake my head as he looks at me.

"Aw Bill!" he whines holding up the head of another soldier. I form the word 'no' and he reluctantly lets the head drop, a frown replacing the perpetual grin.

In addition to Frank Shepherd, Richard Kinney one of Todd's men also died, most disconcerting however, is that Hank Williams, one of my men, also was killed. Still, only losing three men in comparison to eighty Union men is not bad.

George Todd commands. "Mount up! The rest of the troop is still in Centralia! Let's go!" and leads us on a slow gallop toward the town we conquered this morning.

We remain out of sight along the tree line of a small meandering creek as we return to Centralia. The partisans ride screaming and yelling into Centralia, seeking to kill all Union soldiers encountered. A band of twenty mount and escape west, chased by a like sized band of partisans including Frank, Jesse, Bo, Socrates, Archie and I. The chase ends, without catching them, near Sturgeon before returning to Centralia as Todd's partisans are leaving, headed toward the Singleton farm, the site of the battle a couple of hours ago.

We are a mile away when three figures are spotted on the knoll. Archie lets out a whoop and charges toward them, followed by Frank, Jesse, Bo, Socrates, myself and a few others spoiling for more fight.

I've got to hand it to Jesse, he is one hell of a shot from the back of a horse. Two of the men are felled by Jesse and the third, trying to limp down the hill, is fallen on by little Arch Clement. Blood soon drains out of a sizable hole in the Union man's throat. Another scalp is on the bridle of my smallish companions' horse. Pulling a stout red silken thread from my pouch, I call out. "How many Archie!" and hold up my knotted string. He grins at me, as I began to count. He retrieves his purple colored thread and began to count, restarting twice. Finished with my count I smile, counting with him until he concludes.

"...forty two, forty three and forty four. I gots forty four Bill!" he exclaims with glee holding up his thread.

I motion to the man on the ground. "Forty five Archie."

He looks down. "Oh yeah!" and ties another knot in the cord, then looks inquisitively at me.

"I have forty four."

"YES!" he exclaims and triumphantly thrust his fist in the air.

Chapter Thirty Nine

The end result of the war in the Eastern campaign becomes more evident as time passes, fighting strength, strategy, and will, no longer are the main factors in battles. The army better able to move munitions and food to the troops fares much better. More than three years of battling has depleted the South of many of its' fighting aged men and, more importantly, its ability to grow and distribute food for the troops. The industrialized strength of the North is overcoming the South.

Here in Missouri, the guerrillas are fighting amongst themselves. Todd and Thrailkill separate from Anderson, reputedly over the Centralia massacre three weeks ago. Anderson raided Danville, one hundred thirty miles east of Lexington, and heading further east, was last reported at High Hill. Thank God! At least that maniac is directing his madness away from the people of Lexington.

Todd and Thrailkill joined General Jo Shelby and are moving toward Independence. If we are lucky, the Jayhawkers under Generals Blunt and Jennison will annihilate, and in turn be annihilated by, General Price and his more able General,

Shelby. The Jayhawkers bear a large portion of the responsibility for the way the war degenerated in Missouri. They felt justified in stealing property and killing the property owner if he objected early in the conflict, but how is that justifiable?

Many of Missouri's citizens became "bushwhackers" in self-defense against the Jayhawkers, however in the past several months the attitude of the citizenry has changed completely, helped by the insanely brutal tactics of Anderson. No longer does the general populace romanticize or consider the partisans heroes.

The atrocities committed at Centralia turn most of those remaining neutral into Union supporters. Citizens no longer aid the partisans as they had, information concerning the movement and whereabouts of the guerrillas is reported as never before. Several companies of one hundred men are tracking Bloody Bill. It is only a matter of time until he is found and a showdown occurs between the forces.

I write a letter asking Janie Stuevers to marry me barely a week after returning to Lexington from my meeting with Bloody Bill, and the more pleasant meeting with my blond beauty. After sending the letter, I lose my nerve and wish I could retrieve it. It is foolish of me to think that so beautiful a woman will agree to marry a man who cannot determine which direction he wishes his future to take. Major Cox assures me that once the war is over, discharges from the service will be granted. I decide that if Janie will agree, we'll return to Warsaw, Illinois and start a farm next to my brothers. Should the expected happen... and she declines… well, army life isn't so bad.

Imagine my joy when her brother Chip arrives at the post to deliver in person the acceptance I only hoped for. The fifteen year old Chip traveled over dangerous territory, against the wishes of his parents, to report the joy felt by his beloved sister.

"Major Cox sir!" I said snapping to attention in front of his desk.

"Yes Sergeant Parman?" he said looking up.

"Request permission to escort the civilian Chip Steuvers, and ensure his safe return to his family in Holden Missouri sir."

The Major looks past me to the boy standing slightly behind me. "What's he doing here Sergeant?" A short explanation brings a quick smile from the Major which fades as he looks at me. "Request denied." and returns to his paperwork.

"Sir, allowing this boy to cross open country alone could endanger his life. I ask the Major to reconsider, sir."

He looks at the boy, folds his hands together resting his elbows on the desk. Turning to me, "I cannot spare a company of soldiers to escort a boy foolish enough to cross the countryside alone. He is lucky Anderson didn't catch him."

"Sir, a squad is all I ask."

"No Sergeant! That is almost certain death as Bloody Bill is too strong to venture a squad of but twenty men. The boy can stay here Sergeant."

"Sir, his family..." I began.

"No Sergeant!"

"Sir! Request a weeks leave sir!"

The Major leans back in his chair. "Sergeant I am not interested in losing..." He pauses, peering into my eyes. Rising from the chair, he looks at Chip and I in succession. He is quiet for several moments. "You know you may not live to return." he utters softly.

"I have a very good reason to live sir." I respond.

He pauses for several more seconds looking at the boy. Finally he walks to the wall calendar. "By the end of the day, Thursday, October twenty five, you are to return to duty Sergeant. Three days Sergeant, what you do with your leave is your business, but I urge you to exercise caution."

"Yes sir! Thank you, sir!"

The trip to Holden is covered easily in one day, leaving a day to meet Mr. Dennis Steuvers and his wife Deborah, and to renew my acquaintance with Janie.

She radiantly joins her mother in making wedding plans with a date to be set when peace is restored to Missouri. Now more than ever I wish to find Bloody Bill.

I leave Janie as late as I dare the twenty fourth, in order to return Thursday afternoon. Traveling in darkness is not a good idea as it is easy to get lost.

There are stars, but no moon, and I have to make my way slowly, still, the additional time spent with Janie is worth it.

About six hours after dark, there is an eerie glow in the distance, a campfire. My cautious nature takes over, tethering my horse about a hundred yards from the glowing fire; I creep up on it through the prairie grass. Shapes of men sitting and lying about the fire and the soft murmur of voices are heard. Crawling closer, I reach a point about twenty yards from the nearest man, when one of the men nearer the fire rises and begins to walk toward me. Has he seen me, or heard me? I was very quiet and did not stir the prairie grasses as I approached, but this huge man is walking directly at me. Should I run? No, they will see me, and none of the other men gives any indication they heard or saw me.

"Where ya goin' Socrates?" a man rises from his prone position yelling at the giant.

The big man stops a few feet from me and yells. "I gotta go!"

"What?"

"I gotta go!" the big man reiterated.

I hear the sound of splashing water as this man relieves himself just out of reach of my position. He finishes his business and turns toward the camp.

Aw jeez. Water or... just ran onto my hand. Slowly, quietly, I wipe my hand on the grass near me.

Socrates? Bo? They are spies for Bloody Bill. I know where the maniac Bloody Bill is, he's too damn close! I must get back to the post and inform the Major where Anderson and his band are located. Most of the efforts to find Bloody Bill have been concentrated above the river

Dawn is nearly breaking before I quietly circumnavigate the camp and ride for the post at Lexington.

"Sergeant Parman reporting sir!" I say bursting in on Major Cox, my face revealing the fatigue of nearly two days without sleep.

My previous nights' experience creates a stir at the post. Major Cox assembles his company, excusing me to get some rest. "Begging the Majors' pardon sir, but I wish to partake in the end of Bloody Bill, sir!"

He looks at me quietly. "Mount your men Sergeant!"

It is nearly dark when we reach the partisan camp south of Odessa, or what had been their camp. Signs indicate they moved in a northwesterly direction several hours earlier. We make camp where the guerrillas were the night before.

Several hours before dawn, we also are moving in a northwesterly direction. The troop is somber, silently contemplating the encounter with the maniac Bloody Bill Anderson, each desiring to be the one that finally rids the world of this menace.

Few words are spoken, resolve written on each face, as they crisply obey orders.

Scouts are sent ahead to ascertain the location of the guerrillas. Two of the four return two hours later reporting the partisans crossed the Missouri River east of Fort Osage. The column moves quickly now, crossing the river before noon. Following the trail west, the remaining scouts return to report Anderson and his men are bivouacked at a farm near Orrick. Two scouts are sent toward the farm to monitor partisan movements.

A narrow road meanders through the woods less than a mile from the farm; Major Cox stops here and surveys the area. He directs Major Grimes and Captain Brown, commanders of the Fifty first and thirty ninth Infantries respectively, into the woods on opposite sides of the road.

Only a few minutes pass until the scouts return with news that the partisans are mounting up to move this way. My breathing comes in nervous gasps as I nudge my horse to the appointed position on the road beside the Major.

"How do you feel about being a decoy Sergeant?" The Major says smiling at me. I look at twenty mounted men in the middle of the road. Each appears as I feel, scared.

The Major placed the majority of the troops in the cover of the woods, his plan now apparent. This is nervous time, get the troops positioned in the woods! Not so much noise! They'll hear 'em and our ambush will not work. Geez! Quiet down!

Surely the noise can be heard for miles as the men thrash about in the woods to tie up horses and find a good vantage point. Finally they are positioned and silence once again descends. We wait.

Where are they? They supposedly were mounting when the scouts returned, what's taking them so long? Did they go the other way? Did they circle us and are coming up behind us? I turn to look. God! Will this ever end?

A rumbling, thunderous sound disturbs our horses. I feel the hairs on the back of my neck begin to rise, they're coming! A large contingent of riders, the guerrillas, is coming over the rise. Oh God! I want to make Bloody Bill feel fear, but there must be a hundred of them, it seems like a thousand pausing at the top of the hill.

They see us! They are not turning around! Compose yourself J. V.!

With a yell, the rebels began to scream and charge toward us.

"HOLD! HOLD YOUR POSITION!" the Major commands over the screaming partisans, some men disobey and run away. My mouth is dry, my knees shaking against my horse. He is also jittery.

"NOW TURN!" the Major orders and we retreat as the guerrilla's fire at us. They are almost entirely into the wooded area tightly compressed between the trees when the infantrymen open fire. Turning our mounts, we fire from the road, charging the partisans. The air is filled with the deafening roar of muskets, rifles, shotguns and pistols. Thick smoke belches from the deadly weapons, filling the air with the sight and smell of gun powder.

As the firing stops and smoke begins to clear, a single rider atop a black horse faces us. Many riders lie in the road, dead or wounded, and still more are escaping to the west. The lone rider sits motionless, looking at men writhing in pain or laying still on the road beside him. The beard is gone and he is forty yards from us, but I recognize him. How many times have I seen those wild eyes, that long hair spilling out under his hat? How many times have I awakened from the nightmare of that sinister stare? It is Bloody Bill Anderson, there is no mistake, I know him well.

How did he escape injury? Three to four hundred rounds were fired at him, and he is... unharmed? He looks at us, eyes wide with a sinister smile, places the reins in his teeth, pulls a pistol for each hand from his belt, lets out a yell and charges.

Chapter Forty

"Good morning Captain Anderson; and how are you this fine morning?" Answering my own question directed at the mirror on the wall, I say with a flare meant for the men seated at the table in the Blythe farm house. "Damn well sir! I can hardly wait for tomorrow." Turning toward the men at the table, "Cause I'm getting' better lookin' every day! Ha! Ha! Ha!" Laughing at my own joke I pull Archie's hat down over his eyes, and playfully slap at him and wrestle him to the ground as we laugh with each other.

"Yes! What a day!" Contentedly lying on my back, I stare at the ceiling as Archie retreats to a seat at the table. Small patches of light shine through the roof and I wonder how much rain seeps through during a storm. It won't take much to repair the roof, a little sod or a board covered with pitch. I wonder why they don't fix the roof? I sit up abruptly as Mrs. Blythe steps angrily around me. "Seventy men won't be too many for breakfast will it?" I say mockingly. "At least your pretty daughters will be able to help you." I say with a smile, placing my arm around the shoulders of thirteen year old Heather Blythe, giving her a 'chuck' under the chin.

There is terror in her eyes, why? I have never harmed a woman? I make sure my men act with chivalry toward the ladies, well... most of the time. Surely they have heard of my reputation, they have no reason to fear me or my men.

"Heather!" Her mother calls sharply, a tinge of urgency in her voice. Heather goes to her mother's side as does nine year old Sabrina. None of the females look at me.

"Come on guys! Let the ladies get on with their baking, outside you rascals!" I direct with a laugh, trying to put the ladies at ease.

W.R. Blythe, and his ten and twelve year old sons, quietly cut off heads and pluck feathers from thirty chickens for our meal. He doesn't seem happy about supplying our day's meal, hell he still has thirty chickens left! We aren't taking them all! The people of Missouri used to willingly prepare meals for us and supply bedding material without being asked. People just aren't friendly anymore.

The primary topic of discussion is the defeat of General Price at Westport Tuesday. Details from the partisan that was there included how George Todd was surveying the battleground near Independence and, standing in the saddle for a better view, inadvertently raised himself into the path of a snipers' mini ball. The ball entered Todd's throat, missing the backbone, but tearing a large hole below the Adam's apple. Blood filled the breathing area and attempts to clear the passage failed. Todd suffered greatly and died hours after being struck.

I look at Archie stroking the nape of his neck, knowing what he is thinking... how many? How many were the men whose lives he ended, thrusting and twisting his knife into that spot in the throat? His sinister smile returns as he notices me watching him. He pulls out the purple thread tied around his waist. There are forty-nine knots in it, I am one behind.

News from the battlegrounds out east isn't good either, but that issue seems so far away. I never did understand what we are fighting for, at least why are we fighting under the guise of the Confederacy? Who cares about the Confederacy?

I watch Mr. Blythe and his sons complete the removal of chicken entrails and wonder if he would accept me as a neighbor after this war is over. What are we going to do after the war is over? He won't look at me, or any of my men. Shoot! He needn't be afraid; we won't hurt him, unless he does something stupid.

Several campfires are utilized to cook the chickens. Mrs. Blythe set out fresh loaves of baked bread and is frying eggs as fast as she can. The men line up using all her plates and anything they find to put the delicious breakfast on, some using boards but most share plates with those that have finished.

We eat our fill and lay back to rest by mid morning. Clouds are forming, obscuring the sunlight that had taken the morning chill away. Men take naps under trees as leaves gently rustle in the tree tops. Now what, where do we go from here? Old Pap is headed toward Arkansas, a beaten man, his command in shambles. He never reached the stature I saw in him at Wilson's' Creek. How different would the Missouri campaigns have been had General Jo Shelby been in charge from the beginning? Who knows? Who cares?

Contemplating our next move, I watch some men playfully wrestle with each other. They still have a lot of energy, shall we continue to fight? Quantrill is gone, I think, we hadn't seen him since he fell in love and left the fighting to Todd. In love, the bastard fell for a whore! The coward did nothing as I roughly fondled her breasts in front of him. I told him I had just come out from under the sheets with her and the son-of-a-bitch wouldn't challenge me. She slapped me, but he did nothing.

With Todd dead, his forces join Thrailkill and retreat with Old Pap toward Arkansas. Both Todd and Thrailkill avoid me and my band since Centralia, and want nothing to do with us. Who is left in Missouri to fight with us? Shit! We don't need help fighting the Union, they hadn't come near us for quite some time, and when they did, we made them sorry.

Still, we probably cannot escape forever the thousands of men in the field intent on killing us. Now may be the time to return to Texas. Texas? Not much in Texas for me, but not much in Missouri ether. Many of the men display a yearning to return to Texas after our stay there last winter. I wonder how Kay is doing in Kentucky? Maybe I'll go there, yeah! Take the men to Texas and backtrack to Kentucky, that's what I'll do!

"What next Bill?" Bo asked as he sat down beside me, Socrates following closely behind as usual.

I look at them thoughtfully for a moment. "Texas." I suddenly feel at ease, as if in saying the word, a weight is lifted from me. The decision made, it seems I have a purpose, something to look forward to... Kay.

Bo smiles and nods, "I'm ready to do some farming."

The horses are readied for the ride south from Orrick. This time of year the Missouri river is pretty low thus crossing east of Sibley should not pose much of a problem. The horses may have to swim a bit, but they have done that many times before.

A glance at the sun between gathering clouds tells me it is past noon. With good speed we should reach the South Grand River by dark. That will be a good place to camp for the night, as we learned long ago river banks afford great natural cover. With the help of the steep banks of many an unnamed stream, we eluded detection right under the noses of Union posts.

The Wind still has dirt caked on his legs from this morning's crossing and I vow to give him a good washing in the South Grand tonight. Me too! "Mount up!" I direct and wait until seventy men settle into their saddles. With Archie, Bo and Socrates in their accustomed places at my side, I tip my hat and thank the Blythe family for their hospitality, and lead the way southeast toward a corridor in the trees surrounding the Blythe farm.

Cresting the hill half a mile from the Blythe house, I am surprised to see twenty Union soldiers across the road in front of us. The fools! Are they going to challenge us? At least this time they had the foresight to remain mounted. Great, one last skirmish before leaving the state, this one should be easy. They'll probably turn tail and run as soon as we charge. Oh boy, this ought to be fun! Looking around me, I began to smile as does Archie. With a whoop, we charge toward the riders a quarter of a mile away.

The fools are not running! They are holding their ground in spite of our vastly superior numbers. Stupid soldiers, just waiting to be massacred.

Now they turn their horses and run. We will overtake them! Forty yards from our adversary, they turn back and the woods erupt with volley after volley. I pull The Wind to an abrupt halt. Bullets whizz about and screams of agony are all around me. The deafening sound seems to continue for an eternity before it suddenly stops.

The Wind stands calmly in the middle of the road, an eerie silence as I look ahead at the soldiers on horseback that remain in the road. Some have run; some were killed, or sought shelter in the woods leaving the... lets's see... eight, yes eight soldiers to face me. The top of the trees are slightly swaying back and forth caused by the freshening breeze as the clouds continue to darken. Below me, Socrates is lying face down over Bo. A mini ball has taken one of Bo's eyes and the other is also filling with blood. There is no sign of a wound on Socrates but there is the stillness of death as neither he nor Bo move. Is Archie or Jesse among those lying on the road? Men are racing toward the Blythe farm, dispersing in all directions. Perhaps Archie is with them. Naw! Archie will never leave me! He's close by and after I break through the soldiers ahead, he'll ride through and together we'll head for Texas.

HA! With all the firing from short range, no one was able to hit me! Don't they know they can't kill me? When are they going to learn... I cannot be killed? One charge through the ranks, shoot those eight soldiers and I'll be free, and then wait for Archie. I'll need two guns to break through. Let's see, hold the reins in my teeth, yeah that's what I'll do! The Wind knows what to do. OK! Ready!

Leaning forward slightly, I squeeze my heels on the underside of The Wind's belly and he lurches into action. Good boy! "EEEYYYAAAHHH!!!!" I scream through clenched teeth. This will be fun!

I see the puffs of smoke from the weapons aimed at me and... do I see the bullets flying past me? They can't kill me! The recoil from my pistols is felt as I alternately fire from the left then the right and watch as two soldiers topple from their horses. I get off three shots with each hand and smoke billows from the guns of the soldiers on the road as I ride, screaming at them. The Wind barely breaks stride as we crash into the soldiers but, two strides past them, The Wind topples forward throwing me several feet in front of him. Landing hard, I roll over and try to push myself up on my right arm, but it was shattered by the fall and will not support my weight. OOOOHHH! Damn, pain! The bone is sticking through the skin in two places above my elbow. Where are my guns?

The Wind screams in pain, his front legs shattered by gunfire. Struggling to rise on broken legs, the pain and terror evident in his eyes, he bellows and flails about unable to control his broken legs.

"OH GOD!" The Wind. My beloved companion. "HELP HIM!" I scream. A soldier steps up and places a pistol to the head of my friend, noisily putting an end to his misery. My friend ceases flailing his legs and slumps to the ground.

My left hand reaches toward The Wind, as he dies I seek a weapon. As I reach for a nearby pistol, a soldier steps on my hand pinning it to the ground. I reach my right hand toward the gun and scream in pain as my right arm flails uselessly at my side.

"NOT SO TOUGH NOW, ARE YOU, YOU SON-OF-A-BITCH!" yells the soldier as he raises a pistol toward my face.

"HOLD IT!" Another yells, pushing the gun skyward before it goes off.

"Thank you Sergeant Parman." A major says calmly. "We'll bring Mr. Anderson to Richmond for public display."

Roughly thrown on a horse, and almost off the other side, I grab the saddle horn with my left arm to keep from falling off. The ride to Richmond is long and painful, as with each step it seems my shattered arm will pull loose from my shoulder. Hmmm! Can it separate from my body and fall off? I try to visualize what is holding it together. I am losing a lot of blood and at times feel like I might faint.

They'll not get the better of me though; as soon as my arm heals I'll bust out of wherever they put me, find Archie and head for Texas. Well shoot, why not go directly to Kentucky? The hell with the rest of the band, it's just me and Archie now anyway. We'll go directly to Kentucky, yes, that's what we'll do... hmmm, where is Archie anyway? I try to look around but pain shoots through me as my right arm moves.

The late afternoon sky turns dark as rain clouds form. A slight chill in the air, and a fresh smell, tells me rain is imminent.

"IS THAT HIM? IS THAT BLOODY BILL ANDERSON?" One of the townsfolk yells as we ride into Richmond, Missouri. People run to take a look; some touch my boots as we ride. I kick at them. "Aagh!" That also hurts my arm! Curiosity seekers! Busybodies! I laugh at the spectacle they make of themselves. Shoot! Why are they so excited that I have been caught? So what?

"Get Sergeant Goodman!" Someone yells.

"String 'im up!" Another exclaims.

"Wait!" Cries yet another.

They stand motionless, staring, their mouths agape. No one speaks as I stare back at them. This is ridiculous! I make faces, stick my tongue out at them and laugh.

"That sombitch is crazy!" One man laughs and points a finger at me.

Crazy! If I could reach my gun I'd show that bastard who is crazy, actually I'd show him who is dead. I laugh; make a face and growl at him.

The crowd parts and a man, vaguely familiar; looks at me with hatred in his eyes. What's with this guy?

"Sergeant?" The Major addresses the man staring at me. "The verdict is yours."

The Sergeant looks at me without acknowledging the Major. Turning toward the officer, he takes his eyes off me for a moment, whispers to the Major who in turn whispers to a nearby soldier. The soldier runs toward the General Store returning in a few minutes with a rope, giving it to the Sergeant.

While staring at me, the Sergeant began to fashion a hangman's noose. Apparently he has practiced for some time, or else making a noose comes naturally for him, as the loops are expertly encircled with barely a glance from the maker.

If he is going to stare at me then I'll return his stare. Many a man has withered under my gaze; he'll probably run as well. Damn, he's not turning to run! Damn, he is good! Who is this guy? He leans toward the Major who pats his shirt pocket and pulls out a short pencil. "Here you are Sergeant Goodman."

Goodman! Goodman? Centralia? That's where I saw him; he's the guy I didn't shoot! Shit! He should be thankful to be alive. He should show some appreciation, I let him live.

Slipping the noose over my head, he tightens it to a point that does not interfere with my breathing.

HA! He thinks he is going to hang me? He thinks he can kill me? Won't he be surprised… they'll all be surprised? I laugh loudly.

Sergeant Goodman leads my horse toward the entrance of town, with a parade of excited townsfolk close behind. Yes, come on people, watch this! Watch and learn that William A. Anderson cannot be killed. The pain in my arm tells me my bones can break, but I cannot be killed. Come on people. Learn what kind of man you are dealing with. "Come on people!" I scream. "Come on!"

On each side of the road entering town are four large pine logs tied together to support a single log stretching across the road. It reminds me of the header Uncle John placed over the entrance to our corral at home. Home, God I long to see home again, oh well! Home now will be in Kentucky, or somewhere else, who cares.

Under the log across the road is a sign proclaiming. 'Richmond, Missouri'. I wonder how they managed to place that log fifteen feet up in the air. God! That must have been heavy! How did they do that?

My horse is led to the center of the road and stopped directly under the sign. Looking upward, the rope chafes my neck. This is uncomfortable. "Get this rope off me." I demand angrily.

Sergeant Goodman looks at me but, without a word, tosses the other end of the rope over the log across the road. The crowd encircles me now, jostling for prime position from which to watch, expecting to see a spectacle. Well they will see a spectacle alright, something they'd never expect, won't they be surprised when they find out they can't kill me.

They look at me curiously as I laugh, my right arm sending a message of pain as my body shakes with laughter. Ignoring the pain, I sneer at the people.

Sergeant Goodman helps me from my horse to a standing position on the back of a wagon. Checking the noose on my neck, he loosens it slightly, turning it to show me he inserted the pencil above the windings to prevent them from being pushed up and loosen the pressure on my neck. "Hold onto the rope." He says quietly, looking at me with hate, relief, resolve and determination in his eyes.

I look at him in surprise as he lifts my left hand, and winds the rope around my wrist once as the slack is taken up by men holding the other end of the rope. Tapping my hand and nodding toward the rope, he indicates I should hold onto the rope. I take a firm grip.

The rumble of thunder is louder and I feel a raindrop on my cheek.

With one last look into my eyes, Sergeant Goodman steps from the wagon. Looking up at me, he steps close to the wagon and, grasping my legs, lifts me clear as the wagon pulls away. Concurrent with the thunder, the Sergeant lowers me gently as the rope tightens around my wrist and hand.

"Show time!" I say loudly, holding the weight of my body with my left hand. The noose has not tightened on my throat at all. HA! I knew they couldn't kill me!

"HA! HA! HA!" They stand expressionless as I laugh at them. How long are they going to keep this up before they realize I can't be killed? Shit, I've been shot at by hundreds of people, some at point blank range, and none have been able to hit me. Surely they don't think a little rope can end my life? They'll stand here a long time waiting for me to die. Sergeant Goodman wants a good show for the people of Richmond, well they're gonna see a great one.

Rain starts to pelt down and there is a chill as rain soaks through my clothing. It is a downpour and I stare through the crystalline raindrops at the unmoving crowd, none leaving to seek shelter, as puddles began to form and lightning flashes nearby. The loud crash of thunder startles many of the townsfolk and they move for the first time, some ladies running for cover.

My hand is getting tired as raindrops splash into my eyes. I must have been weakened by the loss of blood. Perhaps if I just shake my fingers, relax a little, yeah, rest my hand then pick up the rope again.

OH SHIT! That tightened the rope around my neck! Damn! You fool! Grab the rope; I look up, pull, get yourself up so the noose will loosen. My hand is slipping! The rope is wet! Squeeze! Pull! Kick your legs! The rope is not loosening! Shake your head, yes… yes, there… that is a little better. I can breathe better now. Try stretching your neck muscles, maybe that'll loosen it more. A little, but my breathing is still bothered. Hell, my blood vessels must be restricted as well, my ears are ringing louder and pressure is building behind my eyes.

I think of my fathers' blackened face from being hung… no; that will not happen to me.

My hand is getting tired again as several minutes have passed, but I cannot let go of the rope. Must hold on, they'll get tired of watching and waiting for me to die.

GEEZ! The rain is coming down heavily; most of the townspeople have fled for shelter. The rope is slippery; I can feel it slipping in my grasp! Squeeze harder! It's pulling against my neck! Pull! Squeeze! My hand is slipping on the rope!

It's tightening on my neck! Your legs! Kick! On shit, I dropped the rope! I can't... Geez the pressure!!

Kick... reach, get... the rope! Find it! Kick, damn you!

Grab with your left hand! Grab it!

I can't hear anything! The pressure on my neck...!

They can't...

Grab the rope damn you, I'm choking! I reach instinctively with my right hand but with the double breaks, the arm just flops uselessly. The pain in my arm is great, but the pain on my neck...

Pull in air... Damn! I can't breathe!

I can't reach the rope! There, got it, pull, agghh! It's slippery! My hand slips.

Kick! They can't kill me!

They can't... can they?

Oh God, I can't see! Everything is fading, growing dark!

I can't be killed!

I... can't... be...

Bloody Bill Anderson's left hand drops from the rope, his eyes bulging but still ablaze, his face turning a reddish purple as his feet stop twitching. He gently sways in the rain.

Sergeant Goodman watches for several minutes after Bill stops kicking. Rain pelts the few onlookers oblivious of the downpour. Slowly stepping toward the swaying corpse, Thomas Goodman nudges the boot of Bloody Bill Anderson, looks up at him and speaks quietly. "Fuck you if you can't take a joke!"

Bibliography

Bible
King James, Version

"Missouri - The Heart of the Nation"
William E. Parrish
Charles T. Jones Jr.
Lawrence O. Christenson
Forum Press - 1980

"Nation of Nations - A Narrative of the American Republic. Volume 1: to 1877
William E. Gienapp
Christine L. Heyrman
Mark H. Lytle
Michael B. Stoff
McGraw Hill - 1990

CPSIA information can be obtained
at www.ICGtesting.com
Printed in the USA
FFOW04n0337130416
23194FF

9 781495 808951